THE FIRST LOVE

THE FIRST LOVE

Endless
yearning and pain

Arben Nestur Prifti

A Novel

The First Love
Endless yearning and pain

A novel by
Arben Nestur Prifti

Contact: benprifti@yahoo.com

ISBN: 978-0-578-69313-2

Dedicated to the most beautiful girl in my city,
with her everlasting magic.

The first love, who didn't try?
And didn't sing, the pain left behind.

(Verses of the Albanian song "The First Love," sung by Anita Bitri)

Dear reader.

Dear book lover.

This book is the work of my life. I have poured my knowledge, my soul, and my heart in it, always being inspired by the muse of love.

Writing, editing, and publishing a book is like having signed a contract with readers. I have already fulfilled my obligations to this contract, and I am sure you will remain satisfied with my job.

I am going the extra mile giving dozens of books away, trying to reach out to my first readers. Please, bring this novel in life by making it part of your bookshelves.

It is your turn now. Read it. Enjoy it. Be inspired by it and spread the word of your enjoyment.

With love and respect

From the author

Arben Nestur Prifti

1

He took a sheet of paper and, with tears slipping from his weeping eyes, he wrote a title with capital letters, "I Am Weeping for Her." This title came to his mind because this thing was repeatedly happening because of his hidden suffering. He wrote it with beautiful calligraphy on top of the white paper with her portrait always in his mind. Even this act could not stop his tears that were pouring painfully out of his eyes in the same way as last day, last week, last month, and last year. These kinds of weak meltdown moments were happening to him very often in these previous fourteen years. Fourteen years had already gone, and he was still shedding tears, weeping, and crying secretly. Nobody knows that he silently cries and why he cries because nobody has ever seen these tears. He weeps quietly, and it seems like only tears relief him. He always thought that he would go crazy without shedding tears.

"This might be stress or even depression," he always thought in silence. "Oh God, what will happen to me later? Will it worsen? Will something worse happen to me? Will I be able to face this depression all of my life?" Such suffering and such never-ending questions were continually passing in his mind. He had heard a lot of stories about insane people. Every time he cried, he felt relief and believed these tears saved him from the craziness. But..., he was crazy. He was crazy about a girl..., and only he knew this. Nobody else knew that. Those hidden tears kept him safe and have saved him until now.

"What if all of my tears will end one day?" he thought terrified. "I'm getting insane, and the hospital is waiting for me," he continued with

1

these negative thoughts. "Those insane people in psychiatric hospitals are not bad ones. There is a reason for their sickness. Like this of mine. Like me. But I don't want others to know this. If I become insane, I will disclose my secret with my crazy mouth. Oh no, better with tears, for the only reason that nobody learns my crazy suffering," and continued weeping. At the same time, he kept looking at another sheet of paper in his hands, reading and rereading it endlessly. He had already learned by heart the text of that letter. It was her farewell letter that he had received just a few days ago, starting with the words: *"Farewell, Adi. I will leave. I will go far away…, but I don't know where."* With this letter in his hands, he's been crying for some days, thinking to keep it safe as the only souvenir in remembrance of his great love.

That afternoon of the fall of the year 1997, he was home alone. His wife, together with their two children, was out, visiting some relatives of hers. They have been married for thirteen years, making a beautiful couple; happy like all other couples and even happier than them. This couple has never quarreled with each other. They say this is the biggest lie in the world because there is not any couple without any quarrel. But in their case, it was true. Such few couples still exist in this world full of hassles and fights.

His name is Ardian Prela, a professor at the State University of the City of Elbasan in Albania. His wife is a teacher at a primary school in a village near the city. Both are very nice people making a great couple. He is intelligent, wise, and agile while she is beautiful, smart, and quiet. Both are prudent, joyful, and tolerant of each other. Tolerance and understanding were the secrets of their love and family harmony. Their two children—the eight-year-old boy and the six-year-old girl—were like their parents, but reversely. The mother's character, traits, and qualities were mirrored to the son, while the father's characteristics, to the daughter. Their child temperament showed that they had taken the best traits and attributes from their parents' personalities.

This family was very happy—happy at work, happy at home, and content with their parents and relatives. They spent summer holidays every year in his parents' house in the coastline city of Vlorë, by the Ionian Sea, south of Albania. The bitter truth was that he cried in silence so often, and even his wife knew nothing about that. She knew very well that when he was single, he had had a love relationship with a girl, and that he remembered her sometimes in his poems, lyrics, and songs. She even knew that girl by herself, but she didn't know and couldn't imagine that he was crying so often for that girl. She had never been able to discover such a thing during all those years they had spent together. She was very much in love with him, and he, in return, gave her the same love, care, passion, and compassion.

But…, what about these tears? What caused them? Those never-ending tears belonged to a girl. She had set strong, deep roots in his mind and soul, in his heart, blood, and body, in his dreams and his life. They were tears for the first love, the girl and love that had left so much nostalgia, sadness, and longing to him. And he always remembers her through tears for all his life.

*   *   *   *   *

Ardian Prela graduated as a literature teacher from the Pedagogic Institute of Elbasan in July 1980. He had very high scores and was assigned as a part-time professor in that institute immediately after his graduation. To fill the necessary quantity of weekly hours, for a full salary, he was assigned to teach some more literature classes in the evening high school of the city. In this way, he became an institute professor and a high school teacher at the same time. He studied a lot and taught excellently. He was fond of literature and foreign languages, speaking English and Italian. He sang beautifully, and he played the guitar too.

During his first three years of teaching, he became very friendly with his students. He played soccer and sang songs with students on the university campus and dormitories. He often danced with the female students and recited poems or speeches on literature and arts in campus events and leisure activities. Some colleagues started to see as suspicious these innocent acts and engagement in his relationship with students. These colleagues used their suspicion and spread rumors to hide and justify the jealousy for Ardian's quick and undeniable professional success, trying to harm him as much as possible in other directions. They couldn't understand this young man with an expanded horizon and so many hobbies and interests in his life. They suspected in his interest in foreign languages, in his poem reciting, in his songs and his dancing. Above all, they suspected and rumored about his friendship and companionship with female students.

His young age, his excellent way of teaching, his sincerity and correct attitude with everyone, made him win respect and friendship of all his students, boys and girls, very quickly. He became a model for them, and they liked his classes and his thoughts. They liked his friendly behavior, his tolerance, and openness. He never passed the certain boundaries in his talks with girls, and never said anything ambiguous in front of each of them. Girls never saw any suspicious sign in his words and conduct, because girls are very clever and never mistake in distinguishing such things. His open mind was understood from all students who knew him well but could not be understood by those who did not know how to recite a poem, to sing a song, or to dance; those people who saw his foreign languages suspiciously and that have never read any novels or poetry.

Maybe girls fall in love with him. This thing could often be seen in their eyes, in their approach, in the pleasure they showed while discussing or dancing with him, or when they talked to each other about him. But he never thought of falling in love with them. He remained their teacher, their professor, and their friend. He never intended things that some evil-minded colleagues and students thought, suspected, and whispered about him.

During his first three years as a professor, Ardian took and passed three postgraduate exams: English language, philosophy, and literature. After that, he continued further studies for the first level of a scientific degree called "candidate of sciences." He deserved to fall in love with him, and most of the girls thought like this. Love is not a sin, but a feeling that comes from the soul and the bottom of the heart. He was not to blame for girls having a crush on him, but from his part, he never made any fault with his words and actions. He never asked or exploited their adoration and love for him. It was just his good behavior, his openness, and sincerity that brought the girls even more towards him, causing to them sweet dreams, desires, and suffering.

---

* *Albania was under a communist dictatorship from 1945 to 1991. It was isolated from democratic countries and even from the communist bloc countries, considering them as "revisionists."*

2

Everything started on Thursday, September 1, 1983, at the beginning of the fourth school year of him working as a teacher in the evening high school. In that September, among other students, Ardian noticed a girl who drew his attention. "In September, people usually look more beautiful than ever," was his conclusion. Students especially look even more beautiful. This thing might be a result of summer holidays spent on the beaches, mountain hikes, trips, summer work, and other activities that relax and reinvigorate the body and the mind.

Some people in Albania divide the fall season into three parts, calling them the first autumn, the second autumn, and the third autumn, regarding months of fall—September, October, and November. It was just the beginning of the first autumn when he saw that girl for the first time. He was looking in the direction of her desk, and his eyes stopped there for some more seconds. Neither much reasoning nor much time was needed to understand what his eyes were looking at. His intuition—as a man with a high aesthetic level—asked immediately: "Is she really so beautiful? Or is it simply the September fault?" Other students looked wonderful this September, but she shone like a brightening star among them. He started to explain the lesson of the day, but for the first time in his teaching career, he felt difficulties in his speech, uncertainties in his thoughts, and lack of meaning in words and phrases he was articulating. His mouth that had never trembled before started trembling from the presence of a beautiful girl that he suddenly discovered in a classroom desk in front of him.

Her face confused him. "How can such a beautiful portrait or sculpture be done? Where does she take all this brightness from?" he thought. The girl was listening attentively to him and was taking notes on her notebook. He liked her attention too. Ardian continued to feel this kind of emotion during the first days of September, looking forward to the day and the hour of teaching in her classroom. Three weeks, filled with such feelings and emotions, had already gone, and he had not talked to her yet. He learned her name from the class register during the appeal at the beginning of each class period. He read her name carefully, feeling the pleasure given to him just by the pronunciation of her name, followed by her standing up and her answer, "present." He was feeling lucky that she had never missed any of his classes in those first weeks of the school.

Ardian had started the fourth year of teaching students—"the beauty of the beauties," as he often called them—but he had never felt such a feeling that sparked the fiery love for that girl immediately. Everything that was happening to him looked like what happens to the characters of novels and movies. It was just what he had been trying not to allow to happen, keeping these kinds of feelings always away from himself, and he had successfully avoided that until now. He had other interests in his life, such as studying, teaching, and entertaining. He had always kept the reasoning and logic successfully over feelings. But he was twenty-five years old already, and he had resisted long enough till now. Love is like the cosmic ether, as an ideal mix of gas and liquid that comes around the heads of youngsters. "Love found me. Love caught me," he shouted to himself at night. "No…, no…, no…," Ardian challenged himself again and again. "Not with my students," he was repeatedly saying to himself his principle that he had kept and applied well enough until now. But her beautiful, sensual face was already planted in his head and never moved away from his mind.

"All girls are beautiful," a roommate told Ardian very often, teasing him for his indifference toward girls and for his "inability" to exploit the good chances he had with them. But the girl that took his attention that September, was not just a girl. She was a fairy. She was an angel. In front of her would melt not only him, as a twenty-five-year-old man, but even the centuries-old cold icebergs. All the feelings, excitement, the lust, the erotic descriptions he had read in so many novels, novelettes, short stories, poems, and dramas, he had passed with only artistic emotions and pleasure given to him, with such an indifferentism and objective not to be affected as a person, his personal feelings, thoughts, and behavior in his relations with his students.

Every time he saw her during classes, Ardian thought that she was an innocent beauty. Then, another thought went through his mind. "She is guilty. Why is she so beautiful, so silent, and so attentive during classes?"

Many periods of classes had gone, and he hadn't asked Eralda any questions yet to write a grade in the class logbook. Other students had taken their first grades after their engagement from the desk or in front of the classroom. It was Eralda's turn now. Ardian had seen her scores in other school subjects in the class logbook, and she had always scored the maximum grade.

"Eralda Tako," he articulated her name carefully, having a strange feeling that seemed as if it was not him pronouncing her name, but somebody else inside him; it was not him watching her, but the other one inside him. He was like being divided into two separate individuals. The first one was he, the teacher, with his steadfast principles as always. The second one was the other one, "the bad guy," born inside him in that minute, that hour and that day when he saw this attractive girl for the first time, sitting in her desk, in a classroom, on the first day of the school year.

She started answering his question clearly and eloquently. The first individual (the teacher) thought: "she is answering the question very well, even the students of the pedagogical institute don't answer so clearly." The second individual (the "bad guy" inside him that was destroying him for several weeks) thought: "what a sweet voice, what beautiful full lips, scarlet and sensual." Her black eyes radiated their soft shine under the dark scenography of the black and thick eyebrows, long curved eyelashes. Her eyes were gorgeous, not so big, round in their middle part, a little longer, curved and narrowed in their outside corner, taking the beautiful shape of almonds, becoming even more impressive when she smiled.

Her beautiful body looked like a wonderfully carved sculpture, with her white flesh like being shaped from proofing bread dough in its final rise after the fermentation rest period. She was nineteen years old. Ardian had seen her birthday on the logbook page of students' general personal data. Her grown breasts ("the final rise of shaped bread dough," Ardian thought about them) were like an added beauty to her young, curved body, that showed and expressed energy, vigor, and momentum. Her waistline continued down the hips, not so full like the most of other girls, with beautifully arched curved lines towards her thighs and straight legs with calves below the knees in the most beautiful shape. The observation of her body finished to her flat sandals, a little bit old and damaged, but in her feet, they didn't look as such.

Her dress was modest, with a shirt and a skirt not so tight in her body. Inside her clothes, though, you could easily distinguish the arched lines taking the most beautiful shape of a young girl's body, which could be seen better after every small movement of her body. It was just "the bad guy"

---

looking attentively at such things. Her long dark brown hair, combed in such a simple way, showing that she didn't spend too much time in front of the mirror, was like a beautiful crown around her face with a clean, brighten skin. She was a gorgeous brunette with radiating black eyes.

"She is born beautiful, and she does not have any special merits for that," he thought, "but she becomes even more beautiful by her modesty and humbleness, her clothes, her manner, her attention to the classes, and now by the excellent answer she gave for the lesson of the day." As a teacher, he asked her other questions from all the past lessons and chapters. Her answers were quick and precise, and he was pleased by that. But as a young man, he continued staring at her beauties, her eyes, her hair, her face, her breasts, her hips, her thighs, her legs, everything else, and "the bad boy" inside him was delighted as well.

"Very good. Thank you. Sit down!" Two voices of the same man spoke at the same time. While "the teacher part of his mind" wrote her grade to the register, "the other part" scrutinized with the tail of his eyes the girl walking toward her desk. "Oh God…, what an elegant walking, a natural and casual elegance, spontaneous, without any efforts, quiet, without any noise, without any fuss," and both of them gave her the same grade, the maximum, "ten."

Not any other girl could take Ardian's attention during all those September days, neither in the pedagogical institute nor in the evening high school, neither in the street nor the neighborhood, nowhere. For him, no other girls existed in this world. For many days, he tried and tried to avoid this sweet, crazy feeling. "Are you crazy?" He, "the teacher," shouted several times to the other one, "the bad guy" inside him. "Not me, but you are the crazy one," the inner voice of "the bad guy" answered immediately, continuing such endless internal dialog repeatedly for many days, and several times a day.

Ardian could not focus anymore on reading books and studying. On every book's page, he saw her face. It seemed as if lines of her portrait and letters of her name, were written every moment his pen's tip touched the paper. This inner fight was becoming even more difficult and unbearable. Two vital parts of his human being—the reasoning and the feeling—were fighting continuously inside him, inside his mind, his heart, and his soul. Feelings that were oppressed and beaten for so long, this time became more robust, and could not be defeated anymore. The reasoning felt tired by this fight and surrendered in this crucial war. "Yes…, yes…, yes…," feelings cheered victoriously. "Now you can study and love, and you'll enjoy both of them," his heart and his soul whispered to his body and his head.

From the day he took this decision, both his inner individuals united into one again, after the long struggle to challenge his dualism. The second week of October had arrived, and he had not spoken yet to Eralda about his feelings, but he imagined speaking to her several times. In his mind, he proposed her; he promised her, he swore in front of her, he apologized to her, he sang and danced with her, and even he hugged, embraced, and kissed her several times. All these things happened in dreams, not only at night, not only with closed eyes but even at daylight, with open eyes, everywhere, even in the classroom while staying in his desk, and she in hers.

He should not allow this situation to last any longer. He had to do something. He had to take the first step without any delay.

3

One evening, in mid-October, he met her while she was leaving the school and accompanied her, walking and talking together on her way back home. It was late in the evening, and it was darkness. They walked through the main boulevard of the city, among other people under the street's neon lights. Ardian asked her about her parents, her family, and herself. He learned that her father worked as a truck driver, while her mother was a cook in a daycare center. She had an older brother, a sister in seventh grade, and another little brother in the second grade of elementary school.

Seven weeks of school had already gone, and he had never thought of asking any other student or colleague to learn something more about her. He had tried hard to hide, suppress, and challenge the sudden feeling that was born and was growing so fast in him, but this new and beautiful feeling won the struggle, and now that he surrendered to this magical feeling, he wanted to learn everything about her just from her mouth and not from anybody else.

"About the girl you love, you have to ask and believe only her and never others," he thought, and that's why he acted like this with Eralda. That evening he learned a lot of things about her too, while she continued speaking about herself:

"I started the regular high school, and I was an excellent student. I was very good at science, math, and physics. I liked literature and the English language as well. The English language teacher, a very nice lady, treated me like a friend of her, and she taught me in person many times after classes".

"What good luck for me," Ardian spoke in English, almost instinctively, meaning that he could use and practice English with her.

She stayed in silence for a while. They walked some seconds without saying any words. Eralda slowed down her steps a little bit like she wanted to last the time of the talk, and then she continued:

10

THE FIRST LOVE – Endless Yearning and Pain

"I had a very close friend. Her name is Entela. We started spending more and more time with other things, such as clothes, hairstyles, going out with friends in the evenings, and talking endlessly about a lot of things. We spent time in Entela's home watching television, instead of studying. We watched shows on Italian channels ☐ and even Yugoslavian channels too. My father never allowed us to install any antennas for foreign TV channels, having a lot of harsh quarrels with my eldest brother for this reason. Some friends of mine watched foreign TV channels regularly, until early in the morning. On the morrow, they discussed a lot for what they had watched, for foreign movies, actors, actresses, songs, and singers. We thought about ourselves like we were grown up already. We thought we had learned a lot of things from foreign televisions and our 'interesting' discussions. We had learned what to wear, how to comb hairs, how to walk, to talk, to move, and how to dance rock 'n' roll. All these things were significant to us, and nobody wanted to remain behind the others on this 'great knowledge.' The junior year passed very fast, filled with such activities and meaningless discussions. The report card of the year showed some lower grades, and my parents were unhappy about that. Only the English language score was the same. I studied English not only because of my great desire but because I thought this made me look more modern too and brought me nearer to the outside world. I had a lot of congratulations from my friends when I translated for them song lyrics, ads, or words and expressions they had heard or read somewhere. The senior year started, and we thought we were matured enough, and we knew everything. A lot of girls started wearing tight pants, jeans, sneakers, shorter skirts, tight dresses, a lot of new and strange hairstyles, etc., but we had forgotten the classes, the books, the homework, the grades. We could not bear any critique, any advice, and any moralization. We didn't listen to our parents and teachers anymore, rejecting their advice in silence and sometimes in revolt. We started gathering in some friend's houses, having some happy hours by listening to different music, dancing rock 'n' roll, smoking cigarettes, and having some drinks. We couldn't go to every house, but only to some friends that had tape recorders, and had more liberal parents, or 'modern parents', as we called them. Sometimes I slept over to Entela's home and watched TV until early in the morning. Our days looked beautiful and happy to us, though we started feeling more and more tired day after day. We didn't think about school and classes anymore. But few students participated less in our gatherings and our discussions and had better scores in their report cards. Moza and Anila, for example, they are

11

first-year students of the pedagogical institute, and they know you because you teach their classes. The boys in our class were terrific guys, and I had a good friendship with all of them. It was a sincere friendship, and we used to go for strolls together in the boulevard, or the hills around the city. But strangely enough, these boys started to seem younger than us, the girls. So, some girls found friendship and started relationships with other older boys, such as university students or other boys that were waiting in front of the school's gate every day. We, the girls, are very vigilant in watching all these things. We knew all new relations from the first or second day of their start. We knew the preferences our female friends had for their possible boyfriends. Entela and I remained more connected with the boys of our class, and she started spending some more special time with one of them too. One day, as we were leaving the school, one of those guys that stayed every day and all day long at the school gate, stopped in front of me. It was strange and out of the blue sky for me. I had never thought and prepared for such a situation. I had never thought that what was happening with other girls—who received requests, admitted them, and started a relationship so fast—one day would happen to me. And the guy that dared to stop me was hideous and arrogant, with a scary face and ugly, dirty long hair. Why did he mess with me? I don't know. I didn't stop, but stepped aside and walked avoiding him, and hurried toward home. He continued bothering me for several days, but I never stopped to listen to what he was trying to say to me. I always left the school with Entela and her boyfriend, to prevent his attempt to stop and talk to me. One day, he stopped in front of us, joined by another guy. The other guy stopped Entela and her boyfriend forcefully, while this one catches my arm, pulling me aside by force. He started threatening me, saying that he would kill me if I did not accept his proposal, showing me a knife under his belt. I had heard about such behavior used by some thugs and hooligans, but I had never thought that someday it would happen to me too. I wasn't scared of his stupid threats at all, but it came by surprise to me, and I hesitated for some seconds. Then my blood heated immediately, and I punched him in the face. It was just a girlish punch, not a strong one, but it caught him off guard and unprepared for such a response by me. He had no time to react because two men came and kept us apart. I hurried home very worried. I spent all that afternoon closed in my room with a lot of thoughts going through my head. I didn't say anything to my family members. All the students of the school learned about this incident on the morrow, and my friends called me 'brave girl, boxer girl, strong girl,' etc. My elder brother learned about it, as well. He had finished his army conscript service some months before, was unemployed, and had found a bad company with some neighborhood boys. And what I was afraid of happened after three days. My brother and his friends fought with those two guys right in front of the school gate. The guy that harassed me used his knife, injuring one of my brother's friends. They were all detained by the police. My brother spent three days in the police station, and the knife user went to prison. When my brother came back home, he was furious at me, shouted at me, and hit me several times in the face. From his punches, I had a black eye, and I didn't want to go to school like that. I stayed home for three school days until the black color disappeared. My father happened not to be at home those days as it always happens to the truck drivers. The School Principal and some teachers blamed me for both events—for my incident and my brother's fight. The principal had decided to take harsh measures to stop the bad behavior of some students, especially seniors. For this to take effect and give results, they needed some scapegoats and wanted to make an example of us. So, in mid-December, just before the end of the first semester, I was expelled from school with the reasoning, 'incentive of depravity and unexcused absences.' Entela and her boyfriend were expelled, as well. So, it was only three of us, the 'most problematic' ones. The English language teacher tried to protect us, but she was punished too, by being transferred to a remote village school accused of 'liberalism and incentive of depravity among students.' I felt guilty about that, and it hurt me more than my expulsion. In March of the following year, a relative of my father, helped me start working in a new store that had just opened that time. I am still working there".

"Where is this store situated?" He asked immediately.

"It is the school items store on the east end side of the main square. Haven't you seen it yet, teacher?"

"I don't spend any time wandering around. I only have a daily itinerary, from dormitory to the institute, to the library, to the evening high school, and back to dormitory again," Ardian answered, trying to bring some humor to their talk. And she laughed a little bit.

"That's why you are the best teacher. My friends that study in your institute say the same thing about you. They say you are the best professor of the pedagogical institute, and all the students love you."

After a brief silence, she started again:

"When September arrived, I had to start school again, but I didn't want to quit working. I wanted to make my parents happy and proud of myself. I wanted to heal all the harm I had caused them and to help the family with my salary. My brother is still unemployed, and my parents' salaries are small. My father, as a truck driver, spends a lot of money for himself, because most of the time is away from home," she counted all these things about her family, and suddenly stopped.

"Teacher, we arrived at my apartment building. Will you come for a visit to my home?" She smiled and invited him sincerely, like welcoming an old friend of hers.

Ardian stopped and was surprised by her invitation. "How sincerely she told her story? What about this invitation? It was humble, unexpected, and almost naïve. And she said it with a childish sincerity." He did not know what to call this. How could he go to her home like this? He smiled at her, pulled himself together, and extended his right hand toward her:

"No…, no, thank you. Have a good night."

"You too," she answered, and walked in haste toward the entrance of the building.

Ardian stayed put for some seconds, watching her from the back. After some normal slow walking steps, she hurried a little bit and then started running toward the building entrance. Her running reminded him of what he had read somewhere in a book; "when girls run like this, it means that they are happy." "Had she understood anything about my intention?" He asked himself, turning back and walking in an unclear direction. After some minutes of walking, he turned back again, walking toward her apartment building. He looked carefully at all the windows and floors of the building. "Where is she now? Where is she changing her clothes now? Which is her room window?" he asked himself. "Why I didn't ask her for her floor, her apartment number, her balcony, her room window? No, no, it was too early for such questions," he finished this inner dialog and walked back toward the institute's dormitory.

---

* *The communist regime in Albania had banned all the foreign publications, radios, TV channels, and traveling abroad. There was only one state radio, one state TV, few state-controlled newspapers, and state censored books, published by a state publishing house. Listening to foreign radios, watching foreign TV channels, reading foreign publications, were dangerous things. You would become a so-called "internal enemy, collaborating with the external enemy, against the country", - an accusation used so often against a lot of people, followed by harsh punishments.*

4

On the morrow, there were no classes because the evening high school classes took place three times a week, and Eralda went to school on Tuesday, Thursday, and Saturday. Her face, her smile, her voice, and her words, could not go away from Ardian's mind during all the following day, while he was in the pedagogical institute. "How openly, how sincerely, how fluently, and how sweetly she was in telling me all those things and suffering she has gone through in her life," he thought. "How humble she was and how much she has learned from her mistakes," and he felt that perhaps it was the first time for her to tell somebody her story, her life's mistakes, and her lessons learned. She seemed like she was waiting and looking for a chance to tell somebody everything she told him. Maybe she has been lonely, without any good friend, all the time after her expulsion from the regular high school. He had seen that her class' friends loved her, and she helped them often during the lessons and in short and long breaks with their homework and exams. He knew that because he watched her whenever he had such an opportunity, not only in her classroom and during class periods but in the school hallways and schoolyard too. She always looked happy and funny among her school friends, with her beautiful smile that never missed in her lips. And then, she became very serious and attentive during classes. Her scores made her the best one of the evening school, and all other teachers spoke very well about her. But he had heard some suspicious questions as well. "Why she—such an excellent student—was attending the evening high school, instead of going to a regular high school?" The principal knew the reason for sure, but he kept the secret for himself. The admissions office had told him for sure the reason for her expulsion from the regular high school, but he was such a person that liked to let these

15

things as much enigmatic as he could, to exploit such information for his interests when he had the opportunity.

"Did she hide any bad thing to me? Something worse than what she already told me?" Ardian asked himself. "No, no," he answered to himself. "If it were something worse, something more scandalous, or something like sexual immorality, the admission staffers or the principal himself, would tell it to every teacher, warning them to be aware of her." Ardian continued presuming, asking and answering such questions by himself all that night and the following day. "Why did she tell me all those things about herself in the first talk we had?" he asked himself more suspiciously this time. He decided to meet her again that afternoon. He left his room and walked toward the city's main square, toward her store. He arrived there and looked at the Eralda's new store—a bigger one than others, with a distinctive shape and big glass windows, with colorful woodwork under them. The store's counter and showcases, made of translucent plexiglass panels and glass panes, could be seen from outside. "This beautiful new store, quite different from other ones around, seemed like it had been built especially for her," he thought when he saw that. "A special and beautiful new store, for a special and beautiful girl," he thought, while he arrived and entered the store. Eralda was standing behind the counter, wearing a work uniform in a light blue color. She looked like an added beauty to the beautiful glass and plexiglass showcases. They looked at each other. He had not thought how to start the talk, and only said the usual greeting:

"Good evening, Alda," he pronounced her short name, used by her friends to call her.

"Good evening, teacher," she returned the greeting, moving toward a customer that wanted to buy something.

Ardian recalled how difficult it was to find a fountain pen in stores those last years.

"Do you have any fountain pens?" he asked her after she was done with the other buyer.

"No," she gave a terse response, with a small smile on her lips and her eyes, moving away again towards two other shoppers that just entered the store.

When he faced her cold behavior and indifference to him, with her without saying any warm words, without showing any close sign, or any special care for him, he was scared, and a chill wince went through his body. "Is this girl playing games with me?" He thought immediately. "Did she lie to me yesterday?" He had heard about experienced bad girls that know well how to lie a man by playing the good girl, showing a lot of virtue and ethical behavior in certain moments. "Was she playing the good girl with me last night? Has she been playing the good girl all the time since I knew her? How can I think of her so badly now?" He asked himself. For a moment no one was in the store, and Eralda approached him:

"I'm very sorry, and I apologize for what I told you about yesterday. Those things don't belong to you, and I don't know why I spoke so openly in telling you my story. You seemed like a good friend to me, a friend I had been expecting for a long time to share all those teenage behaviors of mine, and all sufferings and troubles I caused to my family and myself. You may forget all my story and disregard everything I told you last night. Everything I told you, is part of my life, filled with my mistakes, my sufferings, my harm, and my lessons learned from them," she finished her speech, without looking at him, but with her eyes looking down all the time.

Her face became enigmatic, naive, and unreadable, but this look made her even more beautiful, more attractive, more interesting, and more intriguing. "No..., she can't play so well and for such a long time. It would be impossible," Ardian answered to himself once more.

"Good night," he said instinctively and stepped back toward the store's door.

"Teacher, I'll try to find a fountain pen for you in the main warehouse," Alda said to him when he arrived at the door.

He already had a fountain pen but let him have another one.

"Okay, thank you. But don't try so hard. I can do without it. See you," Ardian said while exiting the door.

"See you," she answered with her unique sweet voice. Her voice had already taken a right place in Ardian's brain. It became like a beautiful melody, like a song harmony, which you want to listen to again and again.

Ardian left the store and walked to the street thinking of her: "Is she an actress? Is she playing the good girl to me?" The suspicion worm started working again. But no way. Love cannot be ignored and be trounced. "She cannot play like this for one month and a half," Ardian encouraged himself again. "And above all, she didn't know that he had a crush on her. Maybe I need to ask others about her," he thought for a moment, but he threw it away very quickly. "No, no, I can't do that. It would seem like disloyalty that she doesn't deserve".

Walking and thinking about all these things, Ardian arrived at his dormitory room. He was not able to do anything else anymore. He couldn't eat, couldn't speak to anybody else, couldn't watch TV, and couldn't study anymore. He had felt this pressing feeling so often these last days. He felt tired and sleepy, but he couldn't sleep. He tried to close his eyes forcefully and forget everything, but her portrait couldn't go away from his mind, and her sweet voice echoed and re-echoed continuously in his brain. Her last words before he left the store; "I'll look in the main warehouse, teacher," reverberated in his mind. "I'll not bring with me my fountain pen tomorrow when I go to her school," he thought.

* * * * *

Alda, that evening, after Ardian accompanied her to her apartment building, entered home with more joy than other days and by singing a song loudly too. She hugged her mother, as always, and started some house chores immediately and prepared the dinner table. That's what Eralda usually did every evening after returning home from work or school. But tonight, she was doing that with more joy, more love, and more passion. After the dinner, she ironed and made ready the little brother's and sister's clothes for the school. Her father was not going to come back home that night, and Alda, out of the blue, requested to sleep with her mother that night, asking the permission of her sister and brother, because they took turns to sleep with mom every time their daddy was not home. But tonight, Alda wanted to do that as a happy child, the same way she used to do it long ago.

"How so, my little daughter?" Mom asked, caressing Eralda's hair and smiling at other children.

"Just for my pleasure…, without any reason. Since daddy is not coming back home tonight and I just missed those old days," Alda answered, and went away to prepare beds for everybody.

Eralda would never think that the literature teacher had fallen in love with her, but surprisingly, she felt happy that he accompanied her and listened to her during that walk. He reminded her of the English teacher of the regular high school, which she missed so much, and she hadn't seen for one year already. "Some teachers are very good," she thought with her in mind. "They don't bother and don't annoy the students, even when they give negative grades to them, even when students failed their exams and subjects. These good teachers, differently from some others, never yell at the students, never call names to them, and never threaten them with harsh and rude language. Teacher's good behavior reaches out to the students better than their grades, positive or negative ones," she continued with her thoughts about good teachers, with the literature teacher as another example in her mind.

"Have you taken any 'ten' today?" Mom asked, seeing her be so joyous and happy.

"No..., no," she answered twice. "But I have talked with the literature teacher tonight. He is the best teacher in the school. He teaches in the pedagogical institute too. My friends, Moza and Anila, say he is the best professor of the pedagogical institute as well."

"Okay..., this literature teacher..., is a single or a married man?" mom asked her while lying in bed, joking and playing with a suspicious voice.

"He is single," Alda answered immediately, "graduated from the pedagogical institute with excellent scores just three years ago."

As soon as she gave this answer to her mom's question, Alda recalled that he was a single man, indeed. She had always thought about him only as a good teacher, as a good man. Mom's question brought in her mind the other side of the coin. "Yes..., yes. Actually..., he is a young man." Eralda thought in silence, watching this fact from another point of view, by thinking about the reverse of the medal this time. When this thought went through her mind, she became aware and started thinking about him as a young man. "Why did he accompany me?" She asked herself for the first time. "Why he didn't speak almost at all, leaving me to make all the talk? Why did I tell him all those things, all my teenage adventures? Why did I forget that he is just a young man? What will he think of me, after listening to all those terrible things coming out of my mouth? Why did I accept his company? Did my school friends see us walking away from school together? What will they think about us?" And she couldn't sleep anymore that night. She tried everything to stop those thoughts but in vain. She tried all the sleep tricks and positions, rolling herself on the left, on the right, on the back, disturbing her mother. "And why did I choose this night to sleep with mom?!" It was a long sleepless night for Eralda. "He is an excellent teacher and a good young man too," an inner voice started inside her, a little weak first, but becoming more reliable, and going deeper in her mind, igniting the sparks of a new exciting feeling in her mind, her soul and her heart. It was a beautiful, strange feeling she had never experienced before.

On the morrow, when Ardian appeared to her store's door, she decided not to be as friendly and open as she had been last night with him, and that's why she acted like that. As soon as he left, thoughts, suspicions, and assumptions returned to her mind again. "Why did he come here…? He already has a fountain pen! Is this a game of him?! Is he playing with me?! What does he think about me?! No, it's not possible. There are a lot of other beautiful girls for him. But no one thinks or speaks badly of him, though. No…, no. He's not a bad guy," she tried to find the peace of mind, but it didn't last long. "All boys are the same," she recalled what Entela had told her. "All of them think about and want the same thing. They have only one fixation in their mind—sex. They are always in search of an 'easy' and 'available' girl." If Ardian were such a bad guy, he wouldn't deal with me. He could find a lot of other beautiful girls to play. A lot of them would be easy targets and ready to fulfill his desire. But he's not a bad guy. He can't have such immoral thoughts and goals. Has he a crush on me?! Is he really in love with me? Is it possible?! What about all those things I told him? Will they keep him away from me? He is a professor. Is he going to mingle with an evening high school student like me? What if he proposes to me? What will I answer him? No…, no. I'm not for him, and I must keep him away from myself. But he is a nice guy, and it feels so good. I have never had any crush on somebody before. I've been very friendly with boys, but I've never had any crush on any of them. I'm still young for such things, just nineteen years old. Oh, my god! 'Nineteen'—the most beautiful age for a girl to fall in love." She recalled what had read in a novel long ago. "The love age has arrived. Entela fell in love when she was just seventeen. But that love was just an adventure, and he dumped her for another one in just a few months. Entela started another love too, or another adventure better say. What about me? Am I in front of an adventure? Is he a well-hidden sexual predator? Girls have never expressed any such suspicion about him. Did girls see us leaving school together? What did they think about that? What are they going to say about the literature teacher and me tomorrow?" She wondered.

Evil thoughts and good thoughts about Ardian as a teacher and a young man, never ended that night and during all the following day. She didn't read any schoolbooks to study the school lessons but only completed the writing homework. She usually went to school fifteen to twenty minutes before the first period of classes while her school friends were always waiting for her in the schoolyard to take her homework to copy to their notebooks. She explained everything to them for every school subject. Most of the night school students didn't study and didn't complete any homework at all. They attended the school only for a "five," the minimum grade to pass the school year. The only thing they cared about was the number of absences, and that's why they tried hard not to miss any classes, because having a certain amount of unjustified absences, put a danger on them to be expelled from the school and loose that school year. It was enough for them just coming to school and having ethical conduct, and they passed the school year for sure. They could score one or two "four," (as a failing score) in every school subject, followed by one or two "five," (as the lowest passing score), graded by teachers just for mercy, and that was enough because the final score of the subject would be "five," and so they passed the school year. Some of them failed in one or two school subjects, but they had the right to take additional exams on those failed subjects in fall; in so-called "fall exams season," taking place before the start of the new school year. And again, only a "five," given as a mercy to them, was needed to pass the school year. Few students failed the fall exams, forced to attend the same school year again, or abandon the school forever. Eralda always felt sorrow for these students, and that's why she helped them every time they needed her help. She helped them with homework, essays, exams, and even when they were answering the teacher's questions from their desks or in front of the classroom. Some teachers had rebuked her for these actions.

That day, she arrived right in time of the first bell. She was afraid of coming there earlier that day. She thought that her friends would be waiting there ready to ask her about leaving the school accompanied by the literature teacher two days ago. The first class was history. Her friends took her physics and math homework and started immediately copying them in their notebooks. In the short break, after the first class, they just started talking and joking about different things, as always, and nobody asked any of those questions Alda was afraid of. The same thing happened with the other short breaks and the long break as well. She felt well. "I was not right with my fear," she thought. "These friends of mine are excellent. And the literature teacher is a good man too. My fear about him is not right," she tried to put herself at ease and make herself happy while talking and laughing with her friends.

5

Other days passed without any special event. Eralda became more vigilant to understand something from him. Ardian tried very hard not to look at her as often as he would like to. This effort was a weighty burden for him. He made all efforts not to give any sign for her to understand his thought and desire. He only watched her while she was reading or writing on her books and notebooks, and when she was leaving the classroom. When he walked through the desks' aisle, he tried not to approach too much and not to touch her, but he watched her back from the last row of the tables. All her body lines were already reflected in his brain in a full perception. He was able to recognize her body silhouette, her walking, her moves, her speaking, her voice, and her laugh from a long distance.

Eralda, for her part, had already felt the new feeling sparked inside her soul and her heart and tried hard not to show it. She liked him more and more. She only watched him when he was writing on the blackboard, when leaving the classroom or when he was talking with other teachers and students. She became more alert to hear what her friends or other students and teachers of the school were saying about the literature teacher. She avoided every eye contact with him, every smile and greetings. She didn't raise her head when he was teaching in front of the classroom, but she only listened and wrote with her eyes down on the books and notebooks. She was making all this effort with a great struggle inside her. Those sparks of the new feeling were becoming even more robust, and she couldn't get free of that, despite all her attempts.

That Saturday evening of October 29, Eralda was walking down the stairs, alone. Ardian had just entered the school lobby, and when he saw her coming down the stairs, he thought to use this chance by saying something to her. She was alone, and no one else was moving to the school lobby and hallway. But she didn't raise her head to look at him or greet him. Ardian got angry for the moment and didn't know what to say. It was a quick moment, and he had to say something to her while she was passing by his side.

"Why are you walking like that…, like a monument?" He spoke without understanding why he had to say that. Was it the annoyance and angriness about the indifference and the way she didn't mind about him? Or was it just a compliment for her?

Even though Eralda listened well to what he said, she didn't stop but continued walking down the stairs without any answer or reaction to him, with a destructive coldness of hers. What a heavy burden was this act for her. And even she couldn't understand why she had to act like that.

Her odd behavior made Ardian feel angry. The enigma of her became even more mysterious. But an apparent enigmatic girl is always more attractive, though. He thought to "run after and reach her, to curse and yell at her, to bring out his angriness. Oh no…, no. What a bad idea? She does not deserve that. I have to tell how much I love her, how much I'm thinking and dreaming of her, and how much I care about her." He stopped and stayed still in the middle of the stairs, without knowing what to do. "At least there is not anybody else here to see and listen to what happened to me. What about her? What happened to her? Is she angry with me? Has she heard any bad things about me? Has anybody talked to her about me? Am I bothering and annoying her? It's bizarre. There are two people; one of them can't wait to see the other one, and this one, instead, feels annoyed by his presence. Is she continuing her play of the good girl? No…, no. That's impossible," he disagreed to himself again, trying to bring more courage and hope to himself.

For the next seven consecutive days, Ardian went several times to Eralda's store, but there were shoppers in the store every time. He waited until she closed the store, but her elder brother came at that time to escort her back home. He tried to meet her after school too, but she was always accompanied by a girl from her neighborhood. The month of November had just started, but he had not solved this problem yet. The Saturday evening of November 5, he found the courage to do what he had never thought he was capable of. At the end of the class period, he told her:

"Eralda, can you stay a little bit, please?"

The classroom was emptied. "It's strange how other students left the classroom without showing any curiosity at all," he thought. "Maybe, they didn't think about that as something odd, or perhaps they know very well what is happening between us two." Ardian was sitting on his desk, Eralda was standing in front of him, and the classroom door remained open.

"Eralda, I'm very sorry about my conduct at the school stairs, and please forgive me," he started the talk with this apology.

"But..., why did you say that to me?" She asked like a naïve, cute child, and a light smile started in her full lips, forming two beautiful dimples in her cheeks, her cheekbones rose, and her black eyes took the beautiful shape of almonds. "I didn't understand what you meant by that, and my action was just the inertia of walking in the emptiness and silence of the school hallways and stairs, and I don't know where my mind was at that moment," she continued with the smile that made her face look even more beautiful and radiant.

Her smile set Ardian free, inspired him, and made him a poet, giving him the words which he started articulating after that.

"Well..., I called you 'monument' because you deserve it. Monuments and statues are artworks. They don't speak, they don't move, they are just cold bronze, marble or plaster, but their beautifully molded bodies talk very well. Their shape, their dimensions, and their way of standing express a lot. Even though they are silent and cold, we still like them, and they give us aesthetic pleasure..." Ardian stopped for some seconds, feeling reluctant to continue, but then he decided to say it all and to bring to the end what he had started so well. "I want to tell you that's what happens to me too. I feel great pleasure when I see you, and this pleasure is growing day after day. I don't want to play with you. I'm not lying to you. I've seen and known many girls, but what happened to me when I saw you for the first time had never happened to me before..." he remained silenced for an instant. "Do you know how it is?" he continued speaking again, inspired more than ever by her presence and her beautiful face. "It's like this: You are visiting an art exhibition, full of beautiful art pieces, paintings, and sculptures. Walking among hundreds of such artistic creations, you arrive in front of one of them, and observe it, with more attention. You like it more than the other artistic works in that expo. It might be a panoramic painting, a flower vase, a portrait, a mountain, a tree, a sculpture, and whatever, but you stay longer in front of this artwork that you liked the most, observing every square inch of it. You start talking to yourself. You feel surprised and stunned by its mesmerizing beauty. You are filled with the aesthetic pleasure that this painting or sculpture gives you. You continue walking toward other art pieces of the exhibit, but your mind remained there, and you turn your head back toward that one several times. You see other artworks, but none of them attracts your eyes and mind anymore. You reach the end of the exhibit, and you don't go out, but you turn back to the painting or sculpture you liked so much, to watch it again. Finally, you must leave. You go away, but you take its image with you, in your mind, in your perception. You decide to go there again the next day, and you can't wait to watch that art marvel again," Ardian hesitated for an instant, unsure of what to say, then took a deep breath and continued his speech again, looking at her inspiring face:

"That's what happened to me when I saw you for the first time, sitting at your desk. You looked like the most beautiful girl in the world, like the best one, the sweetest one in the 'human big exposition.' The beautiful piece of art you liked the most remains in its exhibition for everybody to watch it and feel the pleasure it gives. Somebody might buy it. He's going to pay a very high price to have it in his house, only for himself. I want the same thing from you. I want you to be mine forever, becoming my pleasure, my inspiration, and my happiness. I could say that you, too, have cost me very much until now. Two months of suffering, inner struggle, troubles, suppression of feelings, sleeplessness, time wasted without studying, and a lot of other consequences," he finished his long speech, and made a deep breath, always looking at her eyes.

Eralda was standing with her eyes down the floor since she understood what he was going to talk about. She was not able to say any words. "He always speaks so beautifully," she thought. "He speaks during class periods for everyone to listen to him. But this time, he was speaking more beautiful than ever and only for her to listen to him. But…, he stopped now, and it is my turn to say something. What could I say…? What does a girl say to the boy after his proposal? Does the girl say that she had been looking forward to this moment? No… That never happens. Does the girl refuse the first time? No…, no, because he goes away and does not return any more. Maybe it would be better not to say anything at all.…" Her soul and her feelings felt suppressed from the first decision of not saying anything at all.

"With this silence, you are raising your price, becoming more expensive for me, and adding my suffering," Ardian tried to bring some humor, interrupting her thoughts.

"Teacher… I'm sorry… I feel worried… I wasn't expecting such a thing… I'll think about it…," Alda spoke with a weak, timorous voice. She tried to raise her eyes to look at him but couldn't do it.

25

"I'm not expecting any final answer tonight. I'm not expecting you to jump and hug me. You can go now, but please, think about me. In this way, we can share my suffering, and you will make it easier for me".

"Good night," she said and left the classroom with a blushful face.

Ardian closed the class door and returned to his desk. He put two elbows on the table and the head between his hands, like trying to relax after fatigue from the prolonged suppression and exhausted nerves. "How did I dare? How did I become so brave?" He thought. "And she will be anxious now. She seemed scared at first, but she faced it very well. How fast those minutes passed? How much respect and good conduct she showed in the end?" He felt relieved from a heavy burden, but he had thrown part of it to her now, waiting to see how she will handle it.

* * * * *

"No…, no. It's impossible." Eralda thought as soon as she left the classroom. "I'm not a worthy girl for his love. I didn't have to stay in the classroom when he asked me such a thing. I had to say "no" to him. But…, how? Who could say that word? Her heart and her mouth could never say it? Will I tell him that I'm taken already, to keep him away from me…?" She thought for a moment, but let it go very quickly. "Why do I need to tell a lie to him? He does not deserve that lie". Her thoughts flew all around but couldn't remove him away from her mind. He had taken his place in her mind, in her heart, and her soul already. But her modesty, humbleness, sincerity, and candor didn't want to accept such a good chance for her. "I'm not worthy of his attention," she repeatedly tried in vain to convince herself. "He stands at a very high level compared to me," she repeated continuously with herself. "Will I be able to make him pleased and happy all the life, with my thoughts and ideas, with my culture and knowledge, with my conduct and my way of thinking, and with my way of handling things? What about him…? Isn't he mistakenly taking this decision to choose me as a friend of his life? Is his decision only based on my appearance? Maybe not, because he told me he has already been thinking about me for more than two months, since the first day of this school year. So, he is seriously into me. Oh…, it feels so good…" She thought again about the new feeling that was born and was growing inside her, becoming stronger and stronger day after day. She tried for the first time to find the true name of this feeling, and it wasn't difficult. It was love.

With all these thoughts crossing her mind, she arrived home and closed herself in her bedroom. She went in front of the mirror and stood there for some minutes, observing her body. For a moment, she closed her eyes and pleased herself with Ardian's portrait painted clearly in her mind. "What did attract him in me?" She asked herself, watching her body and then, one by one, all parts of her body, her face, her hair, her eyes, her lips, her breasts, her waistline, her hips, her thighs, her legs. It's been a long time that she hadn't watched herself like this in front of a mirror. She put her jacket off, and oversaw her body once more, by doing a twirl this time. Her thin waist was followed by a beautifully curved waistline up and down. Then she glanced her breasts. They had grown up fast, making her sweater stay tight over them. She was seeing the movement of her chest and breasts up and down under the respiratory cycle. "They are grown enough," she thought of her breasts. She didn't want them to grow bigger. She spent some more seconds like that, looking at her breast's movement. She, like being enticed by something, took off her sweater and shirt, to watch her tight brassiere like resisting the pressure of breasts from inside and trying to stop them from growing. She touched them and covered both with her hands and. "Please, don't grow anymore," she talked to them again. She felt a kind of pleasure by their appearance and their shape. By the touch of them, she felt their softness, smoothness, and warmth. That reminded her of the old days when she slept over at the Entela's house. They used to sleep together in one bed, and they used to play by touching and squeezing each other's breasts and laughing a lot by these reciprocal actions. At that time, they were just innocent teenagers, when their breasts were growing by magic, and they played with them as children play with their new toys. "Please, stop growing further," she told them again and recalled the days when she understood that they were not toys anymore. As their breasts continued growing, the teenage girls realized very soon that they were not playing with toys, but with their own marvels, with their body's hidden treasures. Eralda, while looking at them at that moment, thought about them as a treasure hidden in the remote island. It was a real treasure so much searched for and wanted by all young men in their "hunt" for girls. Every girl is a "treasure's island," and boys, like pirates, are always in search of the treasure's key that is hidden very deep in every girl's soul; in such a depth where only one boy can reach and find it, and then, the girl will give away this treasure to the lucky boy. "Pirates" were everywhere, in the neighborhood, in streets, in the school, in the workplace, on trains, on buses, but not as wild and wicked as the movies' pirates. They know very well that the treasure they are looking for cannot be taken by force and violently, but softly, with sweet and warm words, with compliments, with reciprocal love.

Girls, from their part, like these pirates' gentle teasing, though they don't show this desire openly. Some of the girls surrender their treasure very quickly, giving the key to the first pirate to requests it. That's what Entela did when she started dating her first boyfriend, and Eralda disagreed with her. After that moment, she didn't sleep with Entela anymore. She didn't want to touch Entela anymore. It seemed as if in between them would lie down him as well, the Entela's boyfriend, her lucky pirate that faced so little resistance and won such a big treasure so easily. Suddenly, Eralda understood what she was doing. "Am I crazy?" she thought and put her clothes on immediately.

Eralda had been focused on her job and school during all that year. She wanted and tried to make her parents happy with her work, her conduct, and the school grades, in return for all worries and troubles she had caused them last year. She wanted to attend the pedagogical institute, studying to become an elementary school teacher, and the good scores in the evening high school would make this thing possible.

Being focused on these essential things in her life, she had almost forgotten about her girlishness and girlie stuff. She had forgotten about songs and movies, singers, actors, and actresses. She didn't waste time with friends or in front of the mirror, dealing with hairstyles and clothes modes. She had forgotten that one day, a man would propose to her. But it's the age itself that can't forget about that. She was nineteen years old now and could not be spared from that. She had the right age and the beauty that everybody could see, though she had forgotten such a thing. She had her ethical conduct, the smartness, the integrity, the courage, and the bravery that only those near her knew.

"What did the teacher appreciate in me?" she thought. "He said he feels a special pleasure when he sees me? I as well, feel a kind of pleasure when I see him, but I tried to hide and push that feeling away. Is this love? Maybe! When you can't wait to see somebody, to meet him, to talk to him, to spend time with him, when you worry about him—isn't that love? Oh..., this might be love. Am I in love now...? Am I into him...? Am I having a crush on him...? Is it happening to me? Oh, God! It's so unexpected, but it feels so good," Eralda thought and felt a kind of longing inside her for the first time. It was a new feeling, new thinking, coming like an impetus just born and spread in her mind, her heart, and her soul. It was something of magic she had never felt before. "If I am in love..., why I don't accept that? Why am I still standing here? What am I waiting for? Let me go out; run, find him, tell him I love him, hug him, kiss him," and with these beautiful thoughts, she tossed herself on the bed. With these sweet feelings coming from his image, she started a nap with a dream as soon as she closed her eyes. She saw a screen with beautiful bright colors, and those two, walking and laughing cheerfully and happily. The street was quiet and empty, clean, and brightened up. The asphalt and sidewalks had been covered with a colorful, big, gigantic, and endless carpet. Where are the other people? Have they gone away to make space for the two of us? Oh, how happy they were...," but a slight crackle of the slowly opening door awakened her. She didn't like that. She felt sorry and sad about the broken dream, but she heard and saw her little brother entering the room, with books and notebooks in his hands, who told her:

"Ada..., Ada... Aren't you going to help me tonight? What's the matter with you? Are you sick?"

She jumped off the bed with a lot of joy and love, and hugged her little brother; squeezing him tight in her arms, kissing him everywhere; on the head, forehead, eyes, cheeks, cuddling and embracing him tight, full of love and affection, sitting on her knees in front of him, and whispering to his ears:

"Oh..., my little brother..., my little heart..., my little soul. How did I forget about you? I love you so much. You are my life. You are my heart. You are my soul. You are the light." She took his books, and they returned to the living room, where she started helping him in doing his homework.

Eralda looked happy and inspired by two loves now—the love for her little brother, and the new love that had just started to her. "This is the happiness," she thought for a moment. "It cannot be searched for and reached directly, but through other things of your life which bring you great pleasure and make you feel happy."

*   *   *   *   *

That evening, Ardian returned to his room as a tired man after heavy work. He took a cigarette from his friend's packet of cigarettes, lit it, and lay down on the bed, smoking with those special moves of lips and fingers of peoples who look clearly that they are not smokers. He usually stayed like this, in that position, every time he had something to think about, or when he brought in his head all kinds of projects for the future. At this moment, he couldn't think of anything at all, or he was thinking, and he was not thinking at the same time. He wanted to think about Eralda, but so many thoughts passed through his head, and so quickly, that he was not able to put them in order, and they disappeared again. Nothing stayed in his head. A lot of thoughts were born in his head, took their shape, and run away very fast, leaving space for other new thoughts, doing the same thing as the previous ones, appearing, and disappearing from his head very fast. Only one clear thing remained there and never went away—her beautiful and attractive portrait. This portrait had positioned clearly and strongly in his brain and was never mixed or confused with other thoughts that run through his mind endlessly. She was posing in his perception, comely, marvelous, seductive. And he had memorized the curve of her just-started smile on her lips, with the dimples on her cheeks, high attractive cheekbones, almond-shaped eyes, dark brown dense forelock falling over the forehead and eyes. Her face could not be detached from his mind. Her smile was the most beautiful thing of her, and Ardian liked it the most. He had painted her smiling face in his brain and kept it there, to relieve his yearning for her.

"This might be love," he thought. "The face of a girl takes roots in your brain and never leaves, staying right there nights and days. The brain is so complicated. It has forgotten all other things it has seen, read, heard, studied, and written until now". Eralda had occupied every cell of his brain—neurons and glial cells. Only she was there—her face, her body, her dress, her voice, her smile, her laughter, her silence, and her movements. So, only these things were now in his memory, nothing else.

"Why does love come with so much vigor? It's like a seabird that flies over the water, flying slowly and softly, playing with the wind. But, as soon as it sees the prey under the water, it tightens its wings and jumps down like lightning. After diving for some seconds under the water, it comes out with the prey in its beak, flaps its wings flying toward its nest. In the same way, like this bird, love flies in the air, looking for its prey, (young boys and girls) and like a lightning, hits their heads, brings them together, makes them like a body, and takes them up there, high very high, where only loved souls and hearts can go. I wanted to survive from this strong bird, but it has already caught both of us and is raising us up in the air, flying toward our love nest. Oh, God, may it not open its beak, for us to fall from this height, because such a thing would hurt us very much".

"Why there aren't any love notifications? There are notices for different things, like meetings, games, shows, movies, and everything else, but not any for falling in love. Let's say: 'In this time and day you will fall in love. Take caution'. But love as well might have a warning or a sign. Oh…, yes. It was a warning when I saw her for the first time. It was a sign. Those cells of my brain that woke up that very moment (as if the brain had kept them on brakes only to be released at that moment) and the sudden excitement of those cells that until that moment I hadn't any idea of their existence, was the warning and the sign. It was the notice itself. It caught me off guard."

"So many songs, lyrics, poems, novels, dramas, and movies are written for love. But, at the same time, there are real-life couples in love more and more than them. It is an elementary statistic—there is love in every two persons. That's why human beings never disappear. Not only humans but every living being".

"Love is the source of life," he recalled an expression.

"Even the death itself forgave the girl that had fallen in love," he recalled Maxim Gorky's tale, "A Girl and Death."

With all these thoughts about love, Ardian fell asleep late that night, without eating anything and without making any preparation for the following day.

6

During all the following week, Ardian and Eralda behaved as if nothing extraordinary had happened between the two. Eralda became timid and had more bashfulness in front of him now. In meanwhile, Ardian was expecting an answer from her. "Maybe she thinks she's still a little girl. Perhaps she does not believe what's happening to her yet. Maybe she is shy and diffident to decide and give an answer," Ardian thought, and he decided to go and meet her at the store. That's what he did in the afternoon, on Sunday, November 13. Oh..., how much happy Eralda became when she saw him entering the store, but she restrained herself by trying not to show that happiness. She answered his greeting in an almost cold way, but it was easy to understand that she was just playing coldness. Ardian knew her well now, and he was able to see the happiness in her face, the desire, the joy and the pleasure in her eyes, things that she tried in vain to hide from him. To conceal these feelings better, she was trying to exploit the presence of shoppers in the store, with whom she spoke staying away from him. In a moment, when no customer was in the store, Ardian said to her:

"Alda, I'll wait for you to the park's main gate, at six o'clock."

"I cannot come," she answered quickly, unconsciously, but she understood at once that it was a wrong answer.

"I'll be waiting for you there, though," he spoke in a decisively way and left the store, smiling at her, like saying, "I know that you'll come."

"Why not?" She thought, as soon as Ardian left the store. "I'll go there," Alda decided, feeling the first emotions for this date. "It will be the first date of my life," she thought happily. The store closing time was at six, and her brother wasn't coming tonight. "I'll go there," she repeated to herself and felt the fervor going through her body and her face. She looked at the clock. It was four. "I'll go there," she wanted to shout. "But..., what will I do there...?" She asked herself. She had been in the park in the daytime, and she had always thought that it would be full darkness in the evening and at night. She had been there with her family and with her school friends as well. Sometimes boys told stories regarding what they had seen in the park during their evening strolls there, making girls laugh. Boys assured girls by showing them the place, the corner, the tree, the bench, where the events they had seen had taken place, and the details of what they had seen. Girls liked such stories and laughed a lot at them. These stories enticed something and seduced them into their dreams. Entela had told her about her adventures at the park when she started dating her first boyfriend.

"Now it's my turn. I'm going to date somebody at the park, at last," she thought surprisingly. "But..., what are we going to do there?" She asked herself again. "What if..., no, no, he is a good man," she tried to reassure herself. "We'll just talk. I'll tell him all. It cannot go on like this. I cannot deny it anymore. Enough is enough. He is suffering too. I must help him. And I have to help myself too." She watched the wall clock time after time, but it looked like it was not working, or its hands were moving too slowly. She approached the clock and listened to its ticktack, to be assured that it was working. It was working well, but this time, her heart's tick-tack was beating faster than the clock's tick-tack; because the winder and the spiral spring of the heart are made of live cells and tissues, muscles, blood, and responding to the human feelings and soul; while the clock's mainspring is just of steel—with its metallic coldness and dry mechanical tick-tacks, without any heart, soul, blood, and feelings.

Eralda became inattentive to the customers and understanding that, she started counting the money twice because she was afraid of counting wrong the first time. Then, she recalled that the store closing time was at six, and after that, she had to account all the money of the day's sale to handover them at the enterprise's cashier. "Why he didn't think about that? Why didn't I tell him? What will I do? Will I close the store earlier? No!" She was correct and disciplined at work. You could see it from a triangle-shaped small red flag hanged on the wall, writing: "The best employee of the month." "But I must be correct at the date too, and above all, this is the first date. If I am late, he's not going to wait longer, and maybe he leaves the date place."

After thinking a little bit about that, Eralda decided to ask her friend, a shopkeeper that worked near there, to take her money to the cashier's office. She counted and prepared the many for handover and, just ten minutes before six o'clock, gave them to her friend, telling her that she needed to return home as soon as possible. She left her friend's store and started walking fast toward the park. A beautiful, magic twilight had just started outside. She hurried up her steps, but her legs wanted to run, her arms wanted to fly, and her heart was beating fast. As she approached the park, she felt sudden shivering through all her body, as if it was cold. Her heart started beating harder, like trying to come out of her chest. She stopped for a moment, taking a deep breath. "What's happening to me?" It looked like her brain was not working anymore, but something else, another unknown force, a new, unclear reflex had just born and had taken the command of her mind and her body, directing her to walk toward the park. To prove it, she tried to stop and turn back, but in vain. Her body and her limbs didn't obey this command, and she understood that at this moment, they were under somebody else's order—love's orders. Love had taken the command and control now. She saw and recognized his silhouette from a distance. He was walking up and down the sidewalk under the only light pole that lighted the main park entrance. First, she felt cold and frightened. Then she felt excited, warm, and happy. Ardian saw her coming and hurried up toward her.

"I knew you would come," he told her, trying to encourage himself and her in this first date of their love.

She didn't answer. She couldn't put the blocked brain into work. She was bewildered and unable to think or speak. She just followed Ardian in silence toward the park entrance. She heard a couple talking and laughing loudly in their own enjoyment while entering the park. The laughter of that girl woke up Eralda. "Why am I acting like this? Get free...," she told herself, but her brain didn't obey her command.

"I invited you here to give me your answer," Ardian started talking slowly, articulating his words carefully.

She wanted to speak, and she attempted to speak, but no words could come out of her mouth. She felt something like a lump in her throat was blocking her speaking. She felt choked up and wanted to cry but couldn't. "What happened to me? Why can't I speak? Why can't I cry?" She asked herself.

This strange behavior of her and this stubborn silence annoyed Ardian first, but he understood and thought about her difficulty in facing such a situation. He tried to reach her arm, but she moved it away as soon as she felt his move and his touch. Her action dazed him. He stopped for a moment and looked at her strangely. "She is playing with me," he thought. "But..., why did she come here? Why did she come?"

34

Eralda continued walking unconsciously, without seeing anything, without knowing where she was going and what she was doing, like a sleepwalker, leaving Ardian behind just where he had stopped. She could continue walking like this. She could walk straight-ahead, always forward, endlessly, and she could pass the park's boundaries without stopping. Ardian hurried his steps and reached her. He caught her, putting his hands around the chest under her breasts, and pulled her tight. But she reacted strongly, getting free of him and continuing walking away. "How is it possible...? What's that...? Is she a girl..., or is she a wild beast instead?" He almost shouted, "You..., wild goat," but he saw that she suddenly stopped and sat down on the nearest bench under the long branches of a willow tree. "Maybe she was tamed now," he thought with higher hopes. He approached her, sat by her left side, and started whispering softly to her ear:

"Alda…, Alda…, Alda. Why do you torment me? Just tell me whether you love me, or you don't."

She didn't answer. She stayed still, with elbows on her knees and the face between her palms, watching down to her feet. Then, Ardian made another attempt. He moved his right hand slowly toward her head, touched her hair, and with a light fondle, reached her neck. Ardian felt the first pleasure of touching her skin, and he didn't feel any reaction from her. He approached her more and whispered again to her ear:

"Alda…, Alda…, Alda, I love you. Do you hear me? I love you." He reached her cheekbone with his closed lips and cheek-kissed her once..., twice... three times. Surprisingly, not any reaction from her. He felt the warmth of her face, the shampoo aroma of her hair, and the pleasant scent coming from her neck and body inside her clothes. He felt the smooth skin of her cheek becoming warmer. Continuing with light kisses, by pecking her cheek, he moved his tight lips down, reaching the right corner of her lips. She liked it..., and raised her head from her palms and, with closed eyes, turned her face toward him. Ardian saw her lips prepared and waiting for the first kiss. He reached them with his open mouth and felt the magic taste of her lips inside his mouth. He felt his mouth filled with her soft, warm, sweet, tasty flesh. He had never felt such a taste and pleasure before. He pulled her tight against himself, and she rounded her hands over his shoulders. They stayed like that for a long time. They kissed and kissed, again and again, exchanging their feelings and silent thoughts, sharing their pleasure and enjoyment, bringing together the love energy that they had kept each one for themselves until now. They kissed endlessly, they cuddled and embraced tirelessly, pulling and squeezing each other firmly against themselves, and never took as much pleasure as wanted, and never felt as much enjoyment as they attempted. They were on fire. It was the love fire, the first love fire, the first kiss fire. Oh, how long was that moment for a short day, and how brief was that moment for a long life? They stopped for a while, looking at each other in their eyes, like two guilty people, with guilty consciousness, but happy and pleased after their very first sin, that looked like a guilty pleasure. They continued watching each other's eyes, feeling another particular joy. It was like eyes were entering each other, exploring and pleasing each other in full silence. After a while, Ardian broke that inspiring silence:

"Oh, no…, no. Love is not just a poem; it's not just a song; it's real life. Love doesn't need any words or music; it just needs two hearts, two souls, two people as sources of love," Ardian spoke being inspired more than ever. They cuddled and kept tight against each other. His hand started almost instinctively moving slowly from her head, fondling her hair, going down to her neck, her shoulders, her chest, and stopped there…, right there where she was more afraid of—near her breasts, "her hidden treasure." He unfastened two top buttons and slid the hand down underneath her shirt. He reached her tightened bra and tried to sneak his fingers inside. He felt more excitement from the touch of that soft, warm mass he discovered there. He attempted to push his fingers deeper under her bra, trying to bring one of those two sleeping birds out of their warm nest.

First, she felt his fingers touching and cooling the skin over her chest, giving her a little shiver. Then, she felt his sneaky fingers sliding softly under her bra, right in between two breasts, searching persistently and occupying more space there. Afterward, she felt his big hand that conquered and squeezed her right boob, trying to bring it out of the bra. That hand, those fingers, their magic touch on her skin, that sly slide of his fingers under her bra in between her breasts, that grasp on her right boob, all these actions together, gave her a new pleasure, a new fire, and total shivering through all over her body. This shiver reminded her what he was looking for and made her understand what he was trying to do right there, with his naughty hand that ignited fire everywhere it touched her body.

"Oh, no…, don't do it…, don't do it," her lips whispered with a low, undecided voice and not strong enough to insist and stop him from doing what he had started to.

"I like them very much," he said, speaking about her breasts, gripping them tightly. "Please, let me have a look at them," he begged her, attempting to unhook her bra, but she stopped him from doing that. He felt some involuntary trembling of his body. "Sexual excitement trembling," he thought. He moved his hand in another direction, looking for something else, sliding it down to the end of her skirt. He started to fold the skirt edge by pulling it up her thighs. Even though it was darkness, he saw the white skin of her legs above her knees, and felt the skin's warmth in his fingers, giving him more excitement, lust, and desire. But her merciless hands unfolded her skirt down to her knees immediately, caught his hand, and stopped him from moving and penetrating further down there.

"No…, stop…, please. Don't do it. Don't do it. Not today," she whispered more loudly and more decisively this time.

He didn't understand why she was trying to stop him from reaching this mutual pleasure, but he decided to obey her will and halted his attempt to go further.

"I'm sorry," he said to her. "I'm very sorry, but I love you so much, and I can't get enough of you. There have been two months and a half waiting for this moment. More than ten weeks of gaining feelings, passion, desire, lust, and love for you, and that's why now I have to explode."

He restarted to kiss her again with more energy and lust, embracing her stronger, squeezing tight her marvelous breasts, and almost biting her lips.

"No like this. Please stop. You bit my lips. It hurts," Eralda complained, pushing him away.

Her sincere pleading and complain, and her sweet voice, made him collect himself and understand that he was going too fast, asking more than he deserves in the first date. "She's right," he thought, "not so much on the first date," and started just fondling her hair.

"I'm sorry, Alda. I apologize. That's love. It's not my fault. Love is like this. I didn't know," he whispered in her ear, fondling her hair gently. He took her head in between his two hands and watched carefully and joyfully the beautiful face that brought him so much trouble since he saw her for the first time. He kissed her hair, her forehead, her eyes, her cheeks, her lips, her neck, her shoulders, and couldn't get enough of her. The fingers of his hands slid softly down her breast, feeling their warmth, their softness, and the flesh between his fingers transformed in a deep pleasure inside him. "Her breasts—the most beautiful part of her body," he thought and wanted to shout: "I like them so much…, I like them so much," being very happy now that he had them on his possession.

37

Eralda didn't speak and didn't move at all. She stayed still, without any action or reaction, surrendering herself, her body, and her soul to him. In the beginning, it was like not having any feelings, any reflexes, any thoughts, without any pleasure and desire. But then, when she felt his lips moving down from her cheek, approaching, reaching and touching her lips corner, suddenly something moved deep inside her body, very deep, right there where her soul was hiding, and he finally found it. His kiss on her lips stimulated and excited her entire body. She just closed her eyes, letting her feelings to go their way, the way filled with pleasure and enjoyment. She liked his grasp. She did the same thing, pressing herself against him, wanting more from him, but couldn't take enough pleasure yet. She felt the warm blood going through her neck up to her face and head. The warmth of the blood spread through all her body. She felt hot, like being next to a fire. She was on fire. "The fire of love," she thought. "The ember of love," she recalled verses of a song. She was burning. Every time she had read and heard such mystic things, she never believed them, but now that she was experiencing it by herself, she understood and accepted that these things happen for real. She was really burning in that magic moment, being transformed into fire and ember of love.

"What sparked this fire? His touch...? His lips...? His kiss...? His hands...?" Eralda asked herself. Oh..., his "bad hand"..., like the hand of a blacksmith that forges and shapes metal to various forms, while moving the metallic hand to blow air and give power to the ember and fire in his furnace. His hand, as well, was doing the same thing when, by touching and grasping her warm, soft breasts, he blew air to the ember and sparked the fire in that hot furnace under her bra, the blaze that was spread immediately in entire her body. "He found my weak point," she thought, when his hand reached, touched and squeezed her breast.

Her breasts experienced for the first time the new pleasure of the touch and the grasp of a man's hand, like a mystic touch that sparks the magic fire. Her breasts had been touched by her hands and Entela hands, but no..., these hands that were squeezing them now, were quite different. When his cold fingers slid under the bra and touched her breast, she felt the first sparks. When his hand started squeezing her breast mercilessly, harming their soft flesh with his nails, she felt the fire burning not only in that part but being spread in all her body, in her heart, in her brain, in her soul, giving her the strange sensation of pain and pleasure at the same time. She liked that very much. But now he was squeezing her breast even harder, and she felt his fingernails hurting her. She tried to stop his hand by pushing it away, but he did it by himself, moving his hand down afterward, right there where she was not expecting to happen. He touched her thighs, which felt his touch immediately and burst into fire. "Oh, my God," she thought, "Now it's a real fire. I'm on fire now, and I can't escape. All my body is burning now."

"No…, please…, don't," she gave a little whimper of protest, while with her hands, like a firefighter, reached and stopped his evil hand from lighting a more dangerous fire in her thighs. "That's enough," she thought, repeating to herself. "That's enough. Otherwise, this fire will burn all of me." When he started kissing her everywhere, she felt another greater pleasure. He was kissing her in every part of her body, without stopping, giving her more and more joy. She wanted to kiss him and tried to do it but gave up under the pleasure he was giving her. She couldn't move under his robust and pleasant grasp. She couldn't get enough of him yet and didn't want this magic moment to end. "How long will these marvelous moments last?" She thought and picked up herself. "How long have we been here?" She asked herself, and pushed Ardian away asking him:

"What time is it?" She raised her voice with fear.

"It's a quarter past seven," he answered, looking at his watch. It was after seven-thirty, but he didn't want to scare Eralda. He understood that she had to go back home. "The family is waiting for her to return home," he thought. They stood up, and he embraced her:

"I'm sorry, Alda. I know you had to be home now. I'm sorry for keeping you so long."

She wanted to tell him what her heart wanted to, but she suppressed this feeling, smiled first, and then laughing told him:

"I'm pleased today. I'm sorry for making you wait so long. I believe you got the answer you were expecting from me today."

"Yes," he answered, embracing her stronger. "It was a clear answer, a little bit long but well-argued and convincible, and I'm delighted with this answer," he spoke like a teacher and laughed in the end. She laughed too. They started walking toward the park exit, embraced with each other.

How unmerciful is the time that passes so fast! They didn't want to separate from each other that night. They walked all the way, embracing and kissing each other, passing through narrow, dark streets of the city's neighborhoods, until they arrived at her apartment building. Near the building entrance, they stopped and started a kiss, a long kiss that seemed like it would never end as if it would last all night long and would bring the dawn of a new sunny day to shine their love. In the end, he stopped the long kiss and looked at his watch.

"It's eight PM," he spoke, mimicking a radio or TV speaker telling the time at the beginning of the evening news edition. "The last kiss lasted thirty minutes. Go and watch it on the 'news at eight PM' now," he mentioned the title of the news edition.

They both laughed but stopped it short because they heard some people approaching. They separated, and she walked toward the building entrance while he toward the main street.

Ardian started walking slowly, but without any apparent reason, he didn't like it. Then, he hurried up his steps a little bit but didn't like it again. After that, he started running and felt the enjoyment of it. He continued running faster, adding the speed, like being in a race, and he was not going to stop until arriving at the race's finish in his room at the institute's dormitory. But his feet took him to the park, instead. He didn't understand how it happened, but he found himself in front of the bench under the willow tree again. He sat down and closed his eyes. He stayed like that for some minutes but felt cold. He stood up and walked toward the back exit of the park. Darkness. Silence. Fear. Nothing moves. No noises. No talks. No laughter. Other couples had already left the park too. They were done for that evening. He and Eralda became the park's newest members this evening, members with full rights. A lot of people come and go in this park every day. A lot of couples like to spend the evenings there. This park knows all the couples in love and all the lovers in the city. It identifies the lovers of the past and the lovers of the present. This park has helped all of them and has contributed to their relations. This park gives them its beauty, its freshness, its shadows, its calm, its darkness, its grass, and its benches so much needed by lovers. That's why they call it "Youth Park." "What about our bench? Why wasn't it taken tonight? Are there enough benches for all couples in the city here, or there might be more? How many couples in love has this bench seen until now? It saw our love today. Maybe it does not belong to any other couple. Or maybe the previous couple had been married last summer, and this bench belongs to us now. Oh yes, it will be ours until we marry, and then another couple will take that, and so on continuously."

"Did I kiss her properly? Is love's kiss like that? Did she like my kiss?" It was the first time for him to kiss a girl, and he continued asking himself: "Who teaches us how to kiss? How do we learn this thing? Is this a natural instinct we are born with? Did she enjoy my kisses? Has she experienced other kisses before mine? How do I dare to ask myself such a question? No..., no. I'm sure it was the first time for her as well. I knew it. I felt it. I understood it was the first time for her too. What a shame when I'll see her at school tomorrow. What will I say to her? Will she call me a teacher or boyfriend? Was I hurried in this love? Maybe she is still too young for love. Is she going to change her mind someday? Why did she accept me? Just because I am her teacher?! No..., no. She loves me. You can see it in her eyes that speak the love language so clearly and so beautifully. With how much pleasure she embraced me. One cannot embrace somebody like that if he/she doesn't love her/him and if it doesn't give or take pleasure in return."

Eralda, walking up the stairs to her apartment, massaged her lips, like being afraid that they had changed their shape by his kisses and bites that might have left marks on them. She shook her breasts and moved the bra, trying to put them in their right position. She fixed her shirt, her skirt, her jacket, and after all these, knocked on the door. Her little brother opened the door.

"Ada..., Ada..., Ada...," he shouted full of childish joy for his sister's arrival.

Eralda embraced and kissed the little brother several times, and entered quickly to her bedroom, standing in front of the mirror. She observed her face, her hair, her lips, where, strangely enough, didn't see any marks, or any visible changes. She bit her lips with her teeth and wiped them with her fingers. "Nothing has happened to them even after those wild kisses and bites of him. What an excellent characteristic of lips," she thought. "They don't show the consequences of the love actions on them. That's why they are so soft, wet, and red." She looked at her breasts to be sure that they were positioned right, shook them with hands up and down once more, and walked toward the living room.

"Mam, I'm sorry. I'm late because we had a school friend's birthday party, and I forgot to tell you about that," she told her mother and sat down in a chair near the table, where her little brother was waiting with his books and notebooks for her to check his preparation for the following school day. She started checking his homework, and this thing helped her to avoid the problematic situation created after she lied to her mother.

41

"Was the literature teacher at that birthday party?" Her mother asked, teasing her, as she always did with her daughter, watching her young body flourishing in her most beautiful age.

"No..., no. He wasn't." Eralda answered very quickly, like being prepared for this question, continuing to deal with her brother's homework, trying to avoid the embarrassment caused by her mother's attention, whose eyes couldn't mistake in such cases.

Eralda knew her mother's habit very well. She joked with Eralda by teasing her very often. Her mother understood her daughter's age, her young age, and her beauty, her feelings, thoughts, and desires. She had been there herself. She had been a beautiful, agile girl as well, and when she was in the Eralda's age, she fell in love with "the chauffeur," as she called him often. The mother was forty-two years old now, with four children, but Eralda, even now, could see her beautiful traits as a young mother. "These chauffeurs always find beautiful girls," Eralda teased her mother time after time. "That happens because they travel a lot with their trucks, they see a lot of girls, and they choose and take the most beautiful one," mother explained every time without hiding her pleasure and happiness. "Watch out for yourself, because someday, one of these chauffeurs will find you as well," her mother had told several times to Eralda. "Not any chauffeurs can see me because I don't stay on the street, and I don't take any bus or any truck," Eralda answered. "No need to take any truck, any bus, any car, or any taxi. I had never taken any of them too, but my chauffeur found me." Eralda recalled these funny dialogues with her mam, thinking about him, the chauffeur of her heart, which already has found and has taken her, starting together their exciting love trip.

7

So, that evening, right in the middle of November, the "contract" of their love was signed, with the wish of two hearts; "May this love lasts forever." After that evening of the first date, Ardian borrowed a guitar from a student of the institute's dormitory and started playing it, singing songs of his high school time, which he hadn't sung for a long time. It had passed a long time without playing the guitar, and now he was feeling a kind of longing for it. Since all the songs sang under the company of a guitar were love songs, this musical instrument is called "love's instrument." Most of the songs that Ardian knew and used to sing with a guitar had the names of girls in their lyrics. Every song that had the name of a girl was dedicated to a girl with that name. There were some songs with the same girl name belonging to different ones. Lyrics of these songs had inside them everything; love, happy love and painful breaks, joy, tears, and bitterness tears. You could find in these songs every kind of feelings, worries, and troubles that may accompany a love, including longing, sorrow, sadness, jealousy, hate, curse, tears, betrayal, repentance, remorse, apology, desire, lust, dreams, mercy, compassion, cogitation, regret, good luck, bad luck, etc. These songs are often called "street songs" because singers and orchestras have never sung them in state radio or television, but only ordinary people and friends sing these songs in their gatherings, though they were beautiful songs and full of feelings. One song—one love story, and these songs are always love stories of the anonym authors themselves, dedicated to their love.

Ardian couldn't do anything else during all those days. He only thought about Eralda, about the first date, and for the future of their love. He thought of writing a song for this love. He wrote and rewrote the lyrics, keeping it simple, like all love songs are. He dedicated the song to the beautiful first moments he experienced when she arrived in the park, for their first date. He titled the song, *"It's called love."*

43

I expected, I waited, and you came.
With a carefully hidden longing, you came.
I couldn't keep the joy and expressed it in words.
You didn't speak at all, but your yearning eyes said it all.

It's her longing, I thought for a moment.
It's her yearning that brought her to me.
I thought and found the golden word.
It's called love. It's called love.

I don't understand why you hide that from me.
While I see it all in your eyes.
It's in you, in me, in us.
It's called love. It's called love,

Don't try in vain to hide that from me.
While I see it all in your eyes.
It's in you, in me, in us.
Clean, beautiful, sweet love.

He left the song without the girl's name because he couldn't write any other name but hers, and he didn't want to do that. He tried a little bit more for the melody by spending more time on it. He recalled a couple of tunes he had composed time ago with an accordion, and he thought to use them. He spent two days in trying to combine lyrics and melody, and the song took its completed content. He sang that new song several times, preparing to sing it in the future dates with Eralda. This new song became part of his repertoire, together with other songs he knew. But this song was very special to him; it was his song, his lyrics, his melody, born by the inspiration of his love, a song that only he knew and only he sang. These are always beautiful songs, especially when they are sung with full passion by their authors.

He went to her store on Tuesday morning, the best time without customers, and asked her for a second date that evening after school. Despite the great desire, they couldn't date every day. Eralda told him that she couldn't be late at home and so that she had to leave two last periods of classes for their date. Eralda seemed to him more and more beautiful that evening in the school, and he couldn't wait to compliment. His love and longing for her became greater and greater. Eralda, for her part, had started looking after herself more than before, for her look, her clothes, her body, her hair, etc. That evening she had combed her hair in a casual ponytail hairstyle with bangs. It was a magnificent hairstyle, providing an alluring, fascinating, charming, seductive, super-sexy, carefree outlook of hers. Her casual forelock, covering her forehead, lying above the eyebrow and her radiating eyes, made her look more beautiful than ever. She looked like a movie star. "In reality," he thought, "we like a movie character, a girl, a young lady, a beautiful actress or singer. But there are plenty of other pretty girls around us in real life as well. There are attractive girls everywhere, in every town, in every city, in every neighborhood, and every school. Maybe we need to build a statue honoring all these girls—the monument of the 'Unknown Beautiful Girl.' This girl in front of me is humble but gorgeous," and Eralda seemed to him more beautiful than all actresses and singers of the screen. Why does it look like this? Maybe because she was his girl now; she was near him, and he could touch her, embrace her, cuddle her; she gave up herself to him, and he enjoys her love.

They arrived at the park. Ardian pulled her against himself, embraced her vigorously, feeling that she was his love, his girl, his movie star, his actress, his singer, his inspiration, his muse. She was warm and full of girly scent and fervor. He relaxed and enjoyed himself while thinking that she belonged to him now. It was mid-November, but the weather was still warm, without any rain or cold winds, and this lovely weather was perfect for all couples in love that wanted to stay outside until late evening.

"Do you know why the weather is still warm even now, near the end of the fall?" Eralda asked him for a moment. "And they say that winter will be warmer this year too," she continued.

"No…. how come?" Ardian asked after thinking some seconds.

"That's because I haven't bought a new winter coat yet," she laughed, answering his question.

"I'll give you a big coat…," he said, covering her with his arms and his body, keeping her tight against his body, like a big warm coat.

"Under this coat, so big and so warm, I'll never be cold," she spoke joyously, happily, and playfully, giggling under his arms and his chest.

He kissed and kissed her restlessly. Her soft, full lips were grown in such a shape like being created just to be kissed. "Like red flower petals, like red roses," poets say. But her lips were more than that. They were soft, alive, full of life, sweet, tasty, wet, warm, scarlet, and healthy. He couldn't get enough of her lips and couldn't pull away from them. Their taste and aroma never ended. "Why do we like so much the girls' lips? Perhaps, not all of them have such nice lips? But Alda has marvelous lips. Though, I have only tried hers, not any other. But one can see them with his eyes. Look what a shape; what a smile, what a color, what sensuality. Not all girls have such lips." But the beauty of Alda's lips was not only that. They were so good, not only for kissing. From those lips, from that mouth, came out a sweet voice, warm and candid love words, showing the sweetness of her soul and her heart. From those lips came out wise words, her knowledge, and the light of her mind. Those lips showed her noble and gentle silence of a girl with a solid, boyish character. When her lips were silent, when they weren't moving, when they came together—like a bud of a red rose, blossoming under the morning dew and the light of first rays of the rising sun—they were waiting for his kiss. And he kissed them repeatedly, like he wanted to pull them apart from her face, to bite and swallow them inside him. But, after that, he remembered that they were her lips, her flesh, and pulled away in sorrow. Then, he touched her lips fondling them with his fingers and felt their warmth, their softness, their wet, that left their mark on his fingers and his palm, giving him the same tempting pleasure. She smiled and put her head over his chest, where she felt his heart beatings, assuring herself that his heart was only beating for her.

Their love was like a new game they had just discovered by surprise in their mind, in their heart, in their soul. It was a beautiful game, candid and playful, almost childish, and that's why they didn't want to stop this game and the pleasure it brought. They became like children forgotten after their play. Children that never felt tired and never wanted to end the game, forgetting everything else that exists outside of their game. Those two, all the time, thought and couldn't wait for the day and time of the next date; for that mesmeric moment when they would start to play their fascinating love game; their happy, relaxing, and entertaining love game.

"How come this game is so beautiful?" Ardian asked, whispering in her ears.

"Because it is the hearts' game…, feelings' game…, love's game…," she answered with sweet whispering, articulating slowly, separately, and carefully her words.

He sang songs with a low voice in her ears. He knew a lot of songs, and he sang very well. She selected the most beautiful song, and he sang that again for her. He decided not to tell her about his new song, because he wanted to sing and surprise her during another date.

46

8

There are two important days for Albanians in late November. November 28 is the National Day, the day when Albania proclaimed independence from the Ottoman Empire in 1912. November 29 is the Liberation Day; the day when Albania was liberated from Nazi occupation in the Second World War in 1944. On the eve of these two festive days, the seniors of the evening high school organized a dancing party, where all the teachers and the principal were invited. The literature teacher, Ardian Prela, never missed such parties in the pedagogical institute or the evening high school because he liked dancing, and he was looking forward to participating in this party. He was the first teacher to arrive at the venue of the party, where he started talking joyfully with the students he found there.

The joyful atmosphere of the dancing party hall, the sounds of the electric guitar, and the drums' rhythms brought pleasure, joy, and happiness for all the party participants. Ardian was experiencing another pleasure, given by her eyes, her face, her hair, her body, her moves, her smiles, and her signs. They were sitting across from each other, looking to each other very often. They danced together to the very first dance at the party. It was Eralda that walked toward Ardian and invited him to the dance, trying to keep and show the teacher-student approach. In every such dancing parties, teachers sit and wait for a student to ask them to dance. Male teachers might have their preferences for the girls they would like to dance with, but they cannot express such a thing because others would misunderstand it, and that's why they usually sit and wait to be invited by girls to dance. Even when the party moderator announces, "It's the gentlemen's turn" (meaning that it's the male's turn to invite the girls for dancing), male teachers don't move from their chairs. This kind of passive waiting destroys their possible preferences; because a girl that they would never have invited to dance

47

comes and asks them to dance, and he is obliged to rise and dance with her, against his will. In such a case, that poor teacher keeps watching the girl he would like to dance with, while she is dancing, laughing, and talking joyfully to somebody else.

Ardian had broken this kind of approach in his teacher-student relationship. A lot of girls wanted to dance with him because he was very friendly with all of them and he was a terrific dancer too. As soon as the music started, and the party moderator declared that it was the "Ladies' turn"—as it always happens in the first dance—Eralda hurried up to be the first one to reach Ardian before other girls. She stopped in front of him and, with her beautiful smile, invited him to dance. He stood up, followed her to the dancing floor, where he passed his right hand around her waist, caught her right hand with his left hand, and started dancing following the music rhythm. It was the first dancing party for that school year, and it was the first time for them to dance together. He was once in a dancing party with the institute's students, earlier that month, but he spent there only a few minutes because his mind was not there. Other people might assume: "He's only thinking about his studies, and his mind is at books," but only he knew where his mind was. His mind was always at the girl he was dancing with—his lady, his student, his beautiful girl, his dream, his love, his Alda.

"I had never thought that the girl I would love would be called Eralda," he was the first one to speak during the dance.

"What kind of names had you thought?" She asked to push the talk further.

"Hmmm…, Mahmude…, Xhemile…, Ofeli…, Desdemonda…, Parashqevi…, etc.," he answered with a mixture of names, laughing and trying to find distinct female names.

"You have had a very advanced taste," Eralda said.

"But now I brought all of them together, forming only one name…."

"Which one…?" She asked immediately, not waiting for him to say it, and the beautiful smile started on her lips, eyes, and face, expecting for his predictable answer.

"Eralda…, Eralda…, Eralda," he repeated her full name three times, squeezing her hand and waist lightly and carefully, trying not to be seen by others.

Continuing dancing, they almost forgot about the others around them, and it seemed like only those two were dancing on the floor. They started approaching each other even more, rubbing their bodies by touching each other's legs, thighs, and knees. But one touch was more special for Ardian—the moment when her breasts and his chest brushed seemed to bring more pleasure and excitement to him.

"I would like to dance all dances with you tonight," he said, moving his eyes and head, showing others around them.

"The same for me," Eralda answered, squeezing his hand affectionately, with a smile on her lips and with her eyes full of love, desire, and fire.

For a while, they continued dancing in silence. Eralda danced beautifully, without too many movements and keeping her body straight. Her elegance could be seen and felt during the dance also. Ardian was a good dancer as well, and he liked rotations. He knew that most of the girls wanted to revolve during the dance, and he was able to fulfill this desire of theirs better than any other dancing partner. He usually rotates them very fast for several minutes. Some girls feel dizzy and give up very soon, shouting "enough..., stop please." "Your head is full," he says to these girls, while to those that resist longer, he says: "Your head is empty." Girls laugh and never misunderstand him.

Now he was looking at Eralda. Her forehead reached up to his mouth. Her grown breasts were touching his chest more often. He tried to take these things away from his mind, and for this reason, he asked her:

"Shall we revolve?"

"Yes," she answered at once like she had been waiting for this demand. Ardian pulled her a little bit against his body, and they started revolving. He was seduced by the squeeze of her breast on his chest. And he was allured by the friction of her thighs in his legs. After a while, he whispered in her ears:

"Come on..., come on. Faster..., faster. How do you feel? Don't you feel like you are flying, yet? As if we both are flying? Here we are, a little bit more speed and we'll take off. Come on...! Speed up...! Faster...."

"Please stop! I'm feeling dizzy," she said with a begging voice.

He stopped revolving in that direction for a moment and started rotating in reverse direction to prevent further dizziness.

"Your head is full," he told her, squeezing her hand and her waist once more.

Her eyes, full of light and joy, expressed only pleasure and happiness. The music stopped.

"Oh..., what a short dance," Eralda complained.

"Thank you," Ardian told her, and they separated, each one walking in different directions, toward their chairs.

Ardian danced two more dances with two other girls. He danced and talked with them with no desire and no pleasure, trying not to show his dislike. While dancing with other girls, his eyes were always in search of Eralda's eyes, and those eyes in love found very quickly each other, from every part of the dancing hall, because she was doing the same thing, searching his eyes in every moment. Those eyes were searching for their love, and they spoke the love language beautifully. He saw that she wasn't talking and wasn't smiling at all with the student she was dancing with. Ardian, being in control of the dance, moved toward and approached Eralda. Her longing eyes became more eager by his approach. He kept looking at her body, her gorgeous legs with curved calves like "a beer bottle," he remembered such an expression heard in the street. Her hips were not too wide, coming up in a beautiful curved line from her thighs to the waist, and then, the grown breast made her waist look thinner and sexier. She had dressed her daily clothes, a skirt, a shirt, and her short jacket, with red and black rectangles, which had placed in the back of her chair. The style of her black flared skirt, combined with a tight pink shirt, a little bit open over her big breast, made her alluring body lines more visible, being curved in such an ideal shape that every artist would like to have as a model for photos, paintings, and sculptures.

"How beautiful, how elegant, and how humble she is at the same time. Behind that humbleness, the greatness of her beauty hides. If all girls were so beautiful and so unpretentious at the same time, no one would try to misbehave with them, not even those bad boys of streets that spend all their time insulting and jeering at those frivolous and prettified girls. No one would dare to approach, touch, and harm this 'natural beauty.' She is marvelous. She is astonishing. Mother nature has given her such a beauty, and no need for her to do anything else—just keeping her beauty as clean as it is, adding to it the beauty of her mind, soul, and heart. And Eralda has accomplished this very well." Ardian was immersed in such thoughts about Eralda and had forgotten about the girl he was dancing with.

"People must have everything beautiful," he spoke unintentionally while watching toward Eralda. Then he turned his head toward the girl he was dancing with. He understood instantly that she had heard what he had said, and that's why he continued speaking to her now:

"Oh, yes, everything beautiful; the face and the soul, the dress and the mind," and he saw her listening to him full of attention.

That girl thought he was complimenting her, and in response, she mobilized and reactivated all her body parts, while Ardian laughed inside himself and continued:

"I mean..., a real beauty..., a natural beauty; without any makeup, earrings, necklaces, bracelets, or other useless accessories."

The girl took what Ardian said as a joke, and spoke with a wry delicacy:

"Why are you kidding, teacher? All the girls wear such things nowadays. All girls want and try everything to become more beautiful. Aren't you going to allow your wife to wear makeup and accessories to look beautiful?"

"I have seen a lot of beautiful girls without any makeup, and a lot of nice women with very little makeup and very few accessories."

"They are just silly, and they know nothing about life," she answered with her competent conclusion.

"That would be an artificial beauty," Ardian told her. "Prefabricated beauty...," he continued. "But I would rather prefer natural beauty. I mean girls and women with the beauties nature has given them, in addition to the beauty of their mind and soul," he finished, recalling an expression of a wise old man, a neighbor of him in Vlorë: "the woman's dress—the real stress."

With this discussion with his dancing girl, the third dance of the party ended. In the fourth dance, he invited Eralda. He stood up as soon as the music started, approached her and said:

"Eralda, I came to return the invitation. Would you like to dance with me?"

She smiled slightly, showing her acceptance of his invitation, and stood up filled with happiness.

Eralda's girlfriends that were sitting next to her heard the teacher's words and smiled at him, without misunderstanding him at all. They two started dancing without talking to each other. Ardian enjoyed watching her and feeling her presence and her body's particular aroma; a girly, sweet scent that seems to invite you for more because you smell it, you taste it, you need more of it, and you never get enough of it. Above all, he enjoyed her "spontaneous" magic touch, her elegant movement, the brightness of her face's skin and her eyes, the color and shape of her sensual lips, and..., oh..., god..., the repetitive, magic touch of her legs and her breasts.

Eralda as well enjoyed his presence. She was pleased by the way he looked at her and by the grasp and squeeze of his hands. Feeling and thinking about these things, she couldn't speak any words. She only stayed silent and pleased herself with her great love. They danced like that, in silence, all the time, just feeling the pleasure of being next to each other. Near the end of that dance, he asked her:

"Do you want to watch and listen to me playing the guitar and singing some songs?"

"Yes, of course. You have told me that you play the guitar, and I can't wait to watch and to listen to you for the first time tonight."

The dance ended, and they separated from each other. Eralda sat down on her chair while Ardian walked toward the orchestra and took the place of the guitarist, who admitted Ardian's request, with his will and the pleasure to dance with girls while Ardian would be playing the guitar. Ardian practiced his fingers a little bit with the guitar strings, while the students continued with other routines of the party program, with poetry, monologs, and humor from the students that mimicked interesting gestures and particular expressions of their teachers. Ardian started playing some chords. The drum and keyboard followed him. All the students ran toward each other to form the dancing couples and started dancing. Ardian looked at Alda and saw her staying put on the chair, refusing a dancing request by a friend of her class. From the actions and the movement of her hands, she looked like explaining to her friend that she didn't feel well and had some headaches. She didn't want to dance with anybody else, but Ardian. She stayed sitting in her chair to watch him playing the guitar and singing songs. Ardian kept rhythmic music for some minutes and then started the accords and the melody of a slow waltz. The dancing couples started swaying their bodies, moving their shoulders and hands, stepping by the musical rhythm of the dance. Ardian made a sign to a student near him to bring the microphone and keep it near his mouth, and then he started singing a song titled *"Entela."*

I'll take the guitar and will sing.
This grief of mine, I don't forget.
Every day that comes, it increases.
My heart is breaking into pieces.

Where are you now that I'm calling out?
Maybe strolling the streets full of laughter?
Have you changed and forgotten about me?
Or with somebody else, you are in love.

THE FIRST LOVE – Endless Yearning and Pain

Oh, Entela. Oh, Entela.
Why do you hide your love for me?
Oh, Entela. Entela, you.
Why is it so great, my love for you?

Even though we were young and shy.
We only had love in our eyes.
And couldn't wait for the sun to rise.
To see each other and smile.

But the jealousy separated us.
Our little hearts were broken in pieces.
Where are you now that I'm calling out?
Maybe strolling the streets full of laughter?
Have you changed and forgotten about me?
Or with somebody else, you are in love.

Oh, Entela. Oh, Entela.
Why do you hide your love for me?
Oh, Entela. Entela, you.
Why is it so great, my love for you?

Ardian repeated this song twice. The author of this song, like all other such love songs, was anonymous, and Ardian had learned this song during the high school years, in his city, where he used to sing and play the guitar with his friends on the beach. Listening to this song, Eralda was thinking of some similarities with their relationship. She felt delighted and fully satisfied, watching her boyfriend's performance, by playing the guitar and singing so well, and she wondered: "What's this man? How is it possible? He is an excellent teacher, an outstanding professor, a splendid scholar, and a perfect singer, guitarist, and dancer at the same time. He is good in English and Italian languages, in chess, and in soccer as well. He is a serious teacher, but at the same time, he gets along very well with all students, who in return, love and respect him so much", and she immersed herself in deep thoughts about him. "Ardian is not such a good-looking person for girls to crush on him at first sight. It's his behavior, his relations with students, his intelligence, his knowledge, his way of teaching, and his way of speaking, which make him look a handsome man. To a girl that looks at him for the

53

first time, somewhere in the street or neighborhood, bus, train, he will not give any impressions or attraction from his body or face, or the way of walking and the dress. From this point of view, he is just an ordinary man, and he would never have had girls' heads turned. But, on the other side, a girl that has the opportunity to know him in person; as a friend, a peer, a teacher, or professor, recognizing his thoughts, his capabilities, his conduct, his wisdom, his agility, would fall in love with him. I'm sure that all female students feel such hidden suffering for him. All of them would like to be lucky enough to have such a boyfriend, or fiancé, or husband. Furthermore, he is still single, a fact that makes girls more interested in him. I fell in love with him, not at first sight, not in the first period of classes, but later on, when he entered in my heart as the best teacher, and then, as the best man, and now, as a good-looking man, almost the most handsome man I've seen".

Ardian finished playing the waltz and started playing some new chords with another rhythm. He waited some moments for the drums and keyboard to enter his rhythm and then started singing his song: "It's called love." Alda could understand the lyrics of this song, knowing what this song was about. He had sung this song for her, at their bench, some days ago, but now, with a guitar, keyboard, and drum, it sounded quite different and more beautiful. The song introduction itself was something special, like a quiet melody in its start, with low and slow notes, but you feel the preparation, like a warning for the burst that will come with the first lyrics, and then finalized in the song refrain. His voice made the entire song sound beautiful, especially when he sang the song's refrain for the second time at the end of the song, culminating like in a finale of a symphony, making the song more exciting and emotional, especially to Eralda.

Ardian was excited even more from the electric guitar and from Eralda that was watching him performing. He forgot about the venue where he was singing and the audience he was singing for. It looked like he was singing in another world, and he sang two English rock songs and an Italian song, singing and playing loudly, bringing more enthusiasm to the dancing hall. But they were foreign countries' songs, which you could never sing in such parties, in such an audience, in the presence of all the teachers and the school principal as well. When the dance and the Ardian's performance ended, all the students clapped their hands and burst in loud and long ovations for him, congratulating him as an excellent guitarist and singer. Eralda joined the ovations, cheering for him the same as other students, but with more heart and more love for him. "I am the subject and the motive of his song. A song was just sung for me. He has not put my name in this song because he cannot say my name openly. But he has it in his heart and does not want others to know it," she thought while clapping her hands, being more pleased and happier than ever.

She didn't want to stay there anymore. She didn't want to dance with anybody else anymore and couldn't dance with Ardian because such a thing would bring suspicions to other students and teachers. A devious thought sparked in her head. "I'll go out of here, and he will follow me. No need to stay here anymore." She made a sign to Ardian, who had just sat in his chair. He didn't understand her sign at first instance, but when he saw her walking toward the door and leaving the dancing hall, he understood what her sign meant. "How clever and wily the girls in love become?" he thought. "Love makes them cleverer and cunning at the same time. Love changes those it touches," he had read somewhere. "When in love, you become another person, because love transforms you forever," Ardian added in his mind. He stayed sitting some more minutes in his chair, before leaving the dancing hall.

Eralda was waiting for him in a corner without much light across the street from the school gate. He saw her and hurried up toward her. She didn't refrain herself, but jumped up in his neck, giving him a firm hug.

"Oh…, oh…, oh…, hold on…, hold on…. We are in the middle of the street here," Ardian told her.

"You were wonderful tonight," she exploded. "You are an excellent singer, an outstanding guitarist, and you sang better than the band's singer. Thank you for the song. It was marvelous. What about the students' ovations? It was amazing," Eralda spoke with great enthusiasm.

"Oh, Alda…, stop…, please. We don't need such things now," he said, pulling her a little further into a darker corner, next to a concrete fence, where they started a long, passionate kiss.

It felt better than anything else in this world. The two lovers were at the top of the world, and nothing else existed around them. After that long kiss, they walked through the narrow streets between the buildings and houses of the neighborhood, holding each other's hands, singing, and laughing loudly. They sometimes stopped for long kisses before running, singing, and laughing again and again, without knowing where they were going. Where else…? They only understood it when they saw the first line of the trees of the park. Their love has directed them toward that destination. They saw each other in their eyes, laughed once more, and walked toward the only witness of their love, the witness of their first kiss, toward the bench under the willow, whose branches and leaves covered it, creating a quiet, dark, hidden place so much needed for lovers.

The deep silence of the park darkness was sometimes broken by joyful noises, gaiety, cheerful voices, and small laughter of other couples, and sometimes by complaints, refusal, or arguments. They two didn't lose any more time, and embraced each other, pushing and pulling hard against each other, squeezing each other, exchanging the endless lust of their great love. They laughed, and their voices joined the other couples' noise spread in the park; in their hidden corners, in benches, on the grass or against trees' trunks, giving life to the quiet park occupied by darkness. Ardian started light kisses all over her face before reaching her plump lips that seemed prepared and like awaiting the battle with his lips and tongue. As soon as he arrived there, he opened his mouth to engulf her lips in one bite. He sucked her lips as hard as he could, like trying to swallow them up, along with her active, tasty, energetic tongue. After that, he pulled back like feeling sorrow and pleading guilty for damage caused to her lips. He touched them with his fingers, like trying to verify the harm. Her lips were still there, not harmed at all, but always soft, wet, fragile, warm, full of fervor and fire, enticing and waiting for other kisses, and he didn't show any repentance but jumped again on them with more lust, and pleasure. Then, he retreated from the battle, verified her lips with his fingers, feeling sorry and pleaded guilty again, but he couldn't wait long and attacked her lips again and again, without any remorse, as a recidivist in his misdoing. Endless, continuous kisses, in their love nest, covered by the willow's branches and leaves.

It was warm weather and a splendid evening. It looked like September weather, and as if the winter was far away or not coming at all that year. The sky was full of stars with the beautiful shape of a half-moon. Everything was and looked like being arranged by hand by somebody. As the writers and artists would like to describe it in their artworks—as a background for love moments. But, in those moments, they were not thinking about the sky, the moon, and stars. Every love is like a clear sky of happiness with its own star—the man, and with its own moon—the girl. Every love has the heat of its own fire, not caring about the cold winter. Love doesn't care about the weather because it has its own atmosphere filled with light, sun, joy, pleasure, and happiness.

Both were very happy that evening. Ardian sang for her some other songs, that kind of songs that only evoke love, speak love, search love, and entice love. Eralda recited some love quotes, love verses, and lyrics of the kind that middle and high school students write in their pocket notebooks and diaries. Ardian knew by heart such stuff more than her. Eralda invited him in a contest by taking turns in reciting love quotes. She was doing well for some minutes, being very fast with a lot of quotes one after another, but then more slowly, with more difficulty in remembering them, until her repertoire was over. After that, it was only him saying a lot of love quotes taken from poems, novels, and song lyrics. He recited dozens of love quotes; first from Shakespeare works, continuing with quotes from "Rubaiyat" of Omar Khayyam, from "Bustan" and "Gulistan" of Saadi Shirazi, and then from "Eugene Onegin" of Alexander Pushkin, from "The Decameron" of Giovanni Boccaccio, from "Bel Ami" of Guy de Maupassant, from "Anna Karenina" of Leo Tolstoy, from Sergey Yesenin's famous lyrics, and the best Albanian poets.

"All writers and poets of this world have invoked love and have written about it with a lot of talent," he said.

She was full of pleasure, joy, and happiness until that moment, but then, a bad feeling occupied her while listening to him and seeing him having all that knowledge. "I'm not worthy of him. I don't deserve him. He knows a lot of things. He has great knowledge. He speaks beautifully." And she asked him like a desperate child:

"What about me? When will I learn all these things that you know?"

"Oh, my sweet, little heart…," he answered, understanding her concern. "You will attend the pedagogical institute, and you will learn a lot of things there, and become a good teacher, I mean a beautiful teacher. Disregard all that stuff we just mentioned in our contest, because this kind of stuff is not important. You will become an excellent teacher, a beautiful, happy wife, and I will always be there for you."

She understood that he was trying to make her feel better. "Oh…, he is such a good person," she thought, and pushed herself a little more against him, putting her head on his shoulders. That's what he wanted that moment, and he conquered her, pulling her tight against his body. He thought for a moment about her softest body parts, her breasts that were pushed flat and squeezed against his chest, waiting for them to burst by the pressure. But that was not happening, and despite that, it was she now pulling him against herself as well, feeling the love's pleasure for him like trying to convince herself that she didn't have to break free or go away from his grasp. "We are in love," she thought. "That's important, and love has not any need for great schooling, it only needs nice hearts and souls, and a clear mind as well." She felt that she was crazy in love with him thinking that this love was becoming "like a disease that she liked very much and from which she didn't want to recover," Eralda remembered an expression read in a book. And here it is; the germ, the microbe, the bacteria, the virus of her disease, staying in front of her, and she wasn't afraid of it. She was just watching, hugging, embracing, and kissing him, full of lust and fire.

"I wish these moments never end," she whispered in his ear.

He laughed.

"I wish the same, and that's what all lovers say," he answered. "People don't live only for making love, but for a lot of other important things in life as well," he added.

"But…, among all these other things, love is the best one, the most beautiful one, the sweetest one, the most desirable one, especially for you, males," she teased him joyfully and playfully.

"Why is it only for us and not for you girls as well?" Ardian asked her with the same joyful tone and continued more seriously: "That's why people marry; to keep love alive, not simply as a pleasure, even though this is what they feel more. But love is the source of life, and this is a necessity. It is called reproduction of the biological species."

"How many people are making love in a minute?" Eralda asked suddenly, thinking about statistics that speak of different things happening in a year, in a month, in a day, an hour, a minute, like the number of births, accidents, deaths, homicides, etc.

"Millions of people," Ardian answered without thinking longer. "But in the evening and at night, the number goes higher. Behind every home window and on every bench, there is a couple in love," he added.

"But I think that this number remains constant, it does not differ, because in every given moment of the day, in the half of the globe is daylight, and in the other half is night," she continued her reasoning as if they were discussing a serious question.

"In this way, the making love's statistic goes up or down in different areas of the planet, following the earth rotation around itself and respective sunrise and sunset in those areas," he followed her seriousness because he liked her reasoning and logic very much.

"How many couples in love are there in this park now?" Eralda asked, immersing herself more in-depth in her serious analysis.

"Only one," Ardian answered immediately as being prepared for this question. "I don't care for other couples," he said and kissed her like trying to make her close her mouth that became a little bit talkative by the happiness she was experiencing in those moments.

"It might be true," she said when he left her mouth free. "Maybe it is only us remaining here now. All other couples have gone because I'm not hearing any noise coming from them."

Ardian looked at his watch. It was too late already.

"You're right. It's a little bit late. Let's go now." They stood up, came out of the willow's branches and leaves, and walked toward the park exit slowly as if they didn't want to leave.

They passed by the school, where everything was silent. Then, they walked through a shorter route and arrived at Eralda's apartment building. There, next to the building entrance, a long kiss was always happening as sorrow for their separation.

9

Students and teachers, in general, didn't see either Eralda or Ardian leaving the dancing hall. But one of them, Neta—the adorned skull—the girl that danced with Ardian the third dance, saw them departing, and felt terrible, she felt a twinge of envy and became jealous and covetous about Eralda's good luck. Her evilness and her well-experienced mind in such things had been suspicious that something was going on between Eralda and literature teacher. She had observed all their actions and interactions during that evening. She watched Eralda hurrying toward Ardian, the very first dance, and their amiable actions during that dance. She recalled Ardian's words on "natural and artificial beauty," while she was dancing with him. She watched Ardian taking Eralda for their second dance, and then she watched Eralda that didn't dance with anybody else, while Ardian was singing and playing the guitar. And the last significative thing, she watched them two leaving the venue one after the other. "So, they are in a relationship and left the dancing party to meet each other outside to make love," was the first thought to cross her wicked mind. Neta knew Eralda and the beauties of her body but didn't consider her as a contender or rival because Eralda didn't make any effort to show her body's beauty and didn't wear any makeup on her face. Neta envied the grace and humility of Eralda, her cleverness, her candor toward other class friends, and their respect for Eralda in return. Neta didn't have any personal rancor or malice against Eralda, because it was Eralda that never misbehave with friends. Neta had asked her several times to help with homework, and Eralda had helped her willingly as she did with all other friends. But now, when she watched those two leaving the hall, she felt something terrible, just a lousy feeling without any reason, without any meaning, something like old revenge, waiting a long time for such an opportunity for retaliation. Her brain, her mind, her heart, dismissed and disregarded all Eralda's ethical conduct and virtues, and she thought of her as an immoral girl, bad girl, wicked one, dishonest, sly, deceitful, etc. And why all that bad feelings about Eralda? Just because she felt jealous about Eralda's good luck in love and her opportunity to have such a good man.

"Why does he like her? What does attract him to her?" Neta asked herself while recalling Ardian's words when she was dancing with him: "Natural beauty, artificial beauty, prefabricated beauty. It means that he loves Eralda's natural beauty," she thought, knowing very well Eralda's strong point. Neta from her part had told Eralda a couple of times that if she looked after herself a little bit more; by wearing makeup or some modern hairstyle, clothes, and accessories to beautify herself, she would look better and become a stunning girl. But Eralda, as always, just laughed at such discussions. She had suffered once from such useless and meaningless lures and dangerous conduct for young girls. She didn't deny that girls and women must take care of themselves, their hair, face, body, clothes, etc., but to a specific limit, because then it becomes just a waste of time, money, and nerves. That's what Eralda thought every time she saw girls and women that had spent a lot of money and time on these things. She evaluated the virtues, the morality, and the character of a girl and had already understood what was more important in a girl's life; what brings the real and meaningful happiness for a soon-to-be woman. Eralda felt more comfortable like this, without showing herself, without trying to be seen, without exposing herself, and without trying to turn heads, especially boys and men's heads, as perpetual hunters of primped up girls.

As soon as Neta discovered and assumed that a relationship between Eralda and literature teacher existed, and after the bad feelings of envy and jealousy, a strong need for revenge crossed her mind, and she couldn't find relief and peace of mind without destroying this love and these two lovers. And that's why, the following dance, she invited the school principal to dance. The principal was in his early fifties, without any intellect, but dogmatic, categorical, self-confident, arrogant, and behaved like a strong man in carrying out his duties.

"Comrade Principal…," Neta told him as soon as they started dancing, "Eralda Tako just left the dancing hall."

"And so, what? There is nothing wrong with that," the principal answered calmly, but in his mind, as an experienced, evil person that likes to investigate the others' life and privacy, he understood that she had something exciting and valuable to tell, and he couldn't wait to learn that.

61

"There is nothing wrong, indeed," Neta continued, "but the literature teacher left immediately after her as well."

"What is that...? Do those two have any special relationship?" the principal asked, pushing her for more explanations.

"Here we are," he thought about those two. "That girl is suspicious, enigmatic, and with contradictions within herself. She is the best student at our school but was expelled from the regular morning school for bad behavior and moral depravity. What about the literature teacher...? A good teacher, a good institute professor, a splendid scholar, with a splendid future ahead! Now I'll show him what he deserves and how worthy he is," the principal was thinking sarcastically while listening to her answer.

"They have been in a relationship since the start of the school. All the students know that, and everybody speaks about them," she lied, trying to become more believable for the principal, being insatiable and unstoppable in her primitive revenge. She thought that after this service of her, the principal would help her by advising some teachers in whose subjects she risked failure to revise and improve her grades, and so she would pass the school year.

"Really...? Why haven't you informed me before?" the principal continued. "You have to come to my office tomorrow to tell me everything. Bring another friend with you, somebody that knows about this issue too."

But then, suddenly, something else crossed the principal's mind, regarding the girl he was dancing with, trying to exploit this girl's confidentiality and take something more from her. With this devilish reason in his head, he asked her:

"What about you? How are you doing with your grades?" He already knew very well that she was failing in most of the school subjects, but he had to start with such a question to end up where he wanted to.

"Not so good comrade principal," she answered, telling what he was expecting to hear from her.

"Do you know that I can help you?" He asked, squeezing her hand, groping her waist, and pulling her a little bit more toward himself, touching her breast and legs.

"Yes, I do," she answered, looking down like a shy girl but understanding what the principal meant with his help, and what he wanted from her in return.

"Come to my office after the party, where we can talk longer about the subjects you risk failure and teachers I can discuss with," he tried to convince her, and he was sure that she knew what he was speaking about, and what he wanted from her in exchange for his help.

"Yes…, comrade principal. I'll come," she gave a short answer, speaking slowly, with her eyes down the floor, playing still the shy and good girl, but feeling happy for what she had already achieved during this dance with the principal. "I just killed two birds with one stone," she thought about the revenge against two innocent lovers and passing the school year. "Or…, maybe…, three birds," she conceived again, including the start of a useful love affair with the school principal.

School principal thought that he was right with his suspicions about the literature teacher. "That man is not a good one. I knew that. He is amoral. He is a womanizer. He has had several love affairs with his female students, for sure". That's what another teacher had told him last year, a female teacher that wanted the principal's help in becoming a member of the communist party, and he helped her, as he always helped such females in need. With the assistance of the principal's friends in the Communist Party Committee of the County, she became a communist party member very soon, before being assigned to a higher job position.

"He is a cunning and insidious man. He's like a covered smoldering ember," that teacher had told him, but they were not able to find any facts or evidence to prove it. But strangely enough, and to his surprise, when he had asked the communist party comrades of the pedagogical institute, they had told him great words about Ardian and his conduct with students. "You have to raise the vigilance," he had told them. "I think you have weakened the class warfare," he had warned them, using such a big, political proclamation to pass his suspicion to them. But now, at last, he had caught him. He had facts now. He had witnesses and would act fast and firmly against the moral depravity of his school. He started to think about how to work and made the plan he would follow. "First, he would call the girl—'the splendid student,' into his office to investigate her," he thought. The principal was well known for the fear he spread to the teachers and students. Threats were his best weapon in confronting problematic students and teachers. Under his threats, students surrender and admit every wrongdoing they or their friends have done, and teachers become silent and never complain about his conduct or speak and act against him. He always threatens teachers with transfer to the county's remote villages—and there is not any more significant threat than that for a teacher. He threatens the students with school year failure or expulsion from the school—and there is not any greater threat than that for a student.

With girls, things were easier for the principal because they were always scared of him. But with some boys, he had found some difficulties last year. He remembered what had happened in the previous year with such a male student that was a kind of thug but just needed an evening high school diploma to keep his job in a state plant. He had listened calmly to the principal's threats, mimicking a scary face ironically, but when the principal had finished his threats, the student had used the same weapon against him—threats. "You are threatening me, but I don't care about your threats. You can expel me from the school, but what comes after that? Do you have any idea, comrade principal? Have you ever thought about my good friends and our retaliation? Do you know that I can smash all your apartment windows? Do you know how many strong, brave friends I have, and that they can give you a good thrashing, to remember all your life? What do you think now? Will we start this battle..., or better not?" All of a sudden, he, the fearful principal, the terrible one, the wild one, evaporated, smiled at him, rubbed his shoulders, appeased the situation, made a smooth talk, and helped him to pass the school year. From that day, the principal tried to avoid the confrontation with such bad temper students, but he continued his frightening tactics with shy students, the obedient ones, by threatening them even after minimal and not relevant mistakes, trying in this way to keep alive his strong and scary authoritarian leadership to have everything under his control.

"With this one, it will be easy," he thought about Eralda. "She is a girl. She is a nasty girl indeed, and he, as a school principal, couldn't allow such immoral conduct in his school".

Eralda, with joy and happiness in her soul, entered the school gate on the morrow and greeted her class friends in schoolyard joyfully and smiling as always, but her friends seemed reserved, reticent, and distant. Among those was standing Neta as well, the personification of the jealousy itself, with heavy makeup, more than other days. Eralda didn't like this cold attitude of her friends. "They have seen Ardian and me leaving the dancing party last night," she thought. "But why Bardha didn't tell me anything when she came to my store today in the morning?" She thought about her desk friend, whom she had said something about her relationship with Ardian. "What's wrong here? Let them know it now. It will happen someday," she tried to stay calm and justify herself, but she admitted to herself that it would be a difficult situation.

Neta had just told them for the exit of Eralda and the literature teacher from the dancing party, but no one had supported her attempt to cause trouble to Eralda. Some girls opposed her strongly, telling her not to bring such things in their discussion because she was a girl herself. And what a girl? Twenty-six years old, three or four times engaged and separated in eight years. No one agreed to join her in reporting to the principal's office and inform him of Eralda and literature teacher. "Eralda is not like you," one of the girls told her, "and she is the best of all of us." "Even the most beautiful one," another girl added, trying to raise Neta's killing jealousy because they understood the main reason behind her words and actions.

As soon as Eralda arrived, Neta left the group, like going to the restroom, and went to the principal's office alone.

"All girls are speaking about them and their love affair but are afraid of coming here because the literature teacher and his friends can give them negative grades after that," Neta told the principal. "And for the same reason, I would not like you to tell him that I informed you, comrade principal," she added in the end.

"Okay, don't worry," the principal told her. "You can go now. I know how to make them open their mouth and tell everything by themselves."

No one told Eralda for the argument they had with Neta before her arrival, and for Neta's attempt to inform the principal of what had happened. A few minutes after the first period had started, the student on duty in the school's lobby, knocked on the classroom door, and told the class:

"The school principal wants Eralda Tako to report to his office."

All the students understood what had happened, and turned their heads toward Neta's desk, with angry looks on her, the jealousy itself, the witch, the whore. She raised her shoulders and shook her head slightly, meaning that it wasn't her to blame.

The principal had thought in advance how to start his investigative questions to be successful, starting from those little things he knew. He planned to begin with straightforward questions, to take her off guard, and make her speak and admit the forbidden relationship.

"Why did you leave the dancing party last night?" He asked Eralda, with the tone and face of an investigator that knows everything but is just making routine questions as part of a protocol and formal procedures of an investigation.

"I had some headache and could not bear the noise," she answered calmly.

"Where did you go afterward?" The principal continued, with the same tone and body position of an interrogator that is sure that the defendant will go through the path he has prepared for him, to continue with other questions prepared in advance.

"For respect and courtesy, I will answer this question," Eralda said. "I went back home, but I know that as soon as I leave the school door, I'm not your subordinate, and I don't report to you where I go and what I do. And above all, yesterday was not a school day, comrade principal," she reminded him, "it was a dancing party, and I was not in the school last night, but I was in a dancing party, with my friends," she stressed the last words.

Her unflappable answer infuriated the principal and made him go wild. He became angry and started shouting the way such people do when they don't have any facts, evidence, or convincible sense, but just by yelling, try to replace the lack of logic.

"Listen to me, you…, nasty girl. You are a student of my school, and I don't allow such moral depravity here. That's why the communist party has assigned me here. I have a reason why I ask you where you went and what you did, because all the school knows that, and all the students are speaking about that," he yelled at her, moving from his desk toward her, pointing his finger at her face, thinking that in this way, she will be forced to tell everything.

"It's not true. My friends have not said anything," Eralda thought. She decided to stay calm in front of this wild animal that was almost biting her.

"You are my superior only at school and during school hours. I have other superiors at work and during working hours. And then, I have my parents at home. But outside the school and outside the workplace, I am the boss of myself," Eralda raised the voice, stressing the last words.

"Shut your mouth up! You bitch, made love with the literature teacher last night," the principal exceeded all the possible ethical and moral limits. "You try to deny it in vain, but I don't allow such immorality in my school. I cannot allow fornicating to happen here. That's why I was assigned here. I work and fight for a clean youth," the principal continued with a higher voice, fist hitting on his desk and pointing his finger at her face again. In a frenzy of rage, he spoke on behalf of the communist party, which had assigned him to that high job position.

"These things, even when they are true, are not asked even by the police officers and prosecutors, but you, comrade principal, exceeded them. What you said is not true, and it is not your duty to protect the girls' dignity, honor, and morality. It's not your business," Eralda told him.

"I will inform your parents about that," the principal said, without waiting for Eralda to finish her sentence.

This time, he had shot on target. The principal had touched Eralda in that part of her life that she protected as being a holy thing. She had decided not to bring any troubles to her parents. Hearing the principal saying that, she almost lost her calmness and patience. She felt the knot of tears in her throat, but her strong character and bravery saved her from his trap. She decided to answer him with the same weapon as his—the threat.

"You are going to tell my parents something untrue because they know very well what time I returned home last night."

"I will verify with them," the principal said.

"Yes…, yes. You will verify that, but if what you say is proved to be untrue, my brother will retaliate against you because he cannot allow such rumors, spread by you, for his sister. He is going to smash all the glass of your apartment windows. He has some close friends that are masters of that work," Eralda used the same threat as the story of the principal with that guy because she knew that the principal was afraid of and didn't like to deal with such vandals and hooligans.

"Get out of here! Nasty bitch! Family of thugs! Degenerated family! You must be sent to the internment. All of you!" The principal screamed at her and continued his usual speech filled with the communist party spirit, called by them as "partyism." "You deserve the internment. Together with the splendid professor…, the brilliant scholar…, the great scientist! All of you have to be interned in the most remote village." Eralda heard his last words while leaving in a hurry the office door of that insane principal, who continued to spew out gall loudly, but she couldn't hear his words anymore.

Eralda entered the classroom and sat at her desk. Even though she tried hard to stay calm and unflappable in front of the principal, as soon as she left his office, she felt the heavyweight of the intense stress with its consequences already becoming unbearable; tired nerves, headache, and the knot in her throat ready to burst into tears. "What a pity that it happened like this. Who has told on us to the principal? What about Ardian? Are they going to punish him?" She remembered the last words of the crazy principal, and she felt sorrier and sadder for what could happen to Ardian than any kind of consequences that she could suffer. She sat in her desk, and despite her attempt to stay calm, her face and her eyes showed her significant suffering, and the knot of tears in her throat became bigger and bigger, ready to burst into crying.

After the bell, in the short break, a harsh debate started in the classroom.

"Alda, she told the principal on you," a girl told her, finger-pointing toward Neta.

"Neta has decided to guard the dignity and honor of other girls, because she has already wrecked hers," Bardha, the Eralda's desk friend, continued the debate because she couldn't restrain herself while seeing her desk friend suffering so much because of Neta, the real bitch of the class.

Neta said some vulgar words from her curses vocabulary and rushed toward Bardha, but two boys stopped her before reaching there, and kept them away from each other, because, Bardha as well, angry with Neta, ran toward her.

"I only told you, not the principal," Neta said, trying to lie. "Somebody else might have told him on you."

"I saw you, Neta leaving the principal's office before the first period started," a male student said to her because he had seen Neta exiting the principal's office.

Eralda didn't speak and was touched very much while listening to all friends who tried to protect her. This kind of act of her friends affected her even more, and as a result, she couldn't hold her tears. She placed her head between two hands, with both elbows on the desk, and let her tears burst out. Students didn't ask and didn't bother her, but they continued to support her, standing by her side, protecting her, and giving her more courage. All of them knew what a good girl Eralda was, how much she had helped them, and they all loved her very much. They thought that even if there is something real from these rumors, from their heart, they wished Eralda the best of luck. All girls of the class would like to have such good luck, but in this case, they accepted in silence that Eralda deserved such love more than everyone else.

"The principal has to watch and guard his wife, and not us," a girl spoke loudly.

"Don't mention his wife because she is just doing the duty of the party," another one mocked.

"What about the principal's daughter...?" Another student asked loudly, keeping the words longer. He was the student that was "the thug" of the class, but always ready to act as a good protector of his class friends. "She is just sixteen years old but seems to join the bad company very soon. She belongs to the young, irresistible generation," he continued, making everybody laugh loudly.

"You are watching her," a girl teased him.

"No..., no. She is watching me," he answered. "But I'm afraid of her father. Let me finish school first, and then I'll see what can be done."

"She likes you because you wear clothes coming from abroad," another boy continued the funny discussion.

"At the end of school, I'll have a motorcycle, too," he added, full of happiness.

"Oh..., come on. The principal will have a son in law with a motorcycle," someone cheered from the end of the classroom, making everybody cheer and laugh loudly.

"No son in law, because I don't have any intention to marry her," he answered as if everything said there was happening for real.

This joyful atmosphere, the respect, and protection that her class' friends showed her, brought some relief for Eralda's soul, and she was almost ready to open her mouth and reveal the secret of her heart. She was thinking for a moment to stand up and tell everybody: "Yes, it's true. I love the literature teacher, and he loves me too. We are very much in love, and we are going to marry each other someday," but she refrained herself, understanding that it was dangerous, and she didn't have to admit and tell such a thing, especially in this situation.

Neta, exploiting the noise and mess created there, left the classroom. While going down the stairs, she saw Ardian entering the school door, and heard the student on duty telling him:

"Teacher, the principal wants you to report to his office."

This short time was enough for Neta, and her dirty mind, to think and apply new tactics to make Ardian enter her trap. She approached him and, while passing by him, whispered very fast:

"Teacher, Eralda told everything you did last night after leaving the party," and she went away in a hurry, with her head down.

"What has happened? How is it possible? What is going on? Why has Eralda spoken?" Ardian started asking himself. "Why did this girl tell me that? She looked like she was waiting for me in the hallway to tell me such a thing. Why did she whisper in that way and went away so quickly and so strangely? Her eyes, her face, her moves, and the way she whispered, were bizarre and devilish, like a fox in cartoons. Her eyes and her face showed only intrigue and devilishness. What about the principal? Is he calling me for the same reason?" Ardian had learned some psychology from what he had read, regarding the evil characters and their description in novels, movies, dramas, and Shakespearian tragedies. "This girl looked and acted the same way as them," he thought. "She approached me like a shadow, like a ghost, like a witch, like a snake that spills its venom and goes away. She did the same thing, and she is watching the victim from a distance now, waiting for the effect of her poison. She wishes the destruction of her victim, the death of her victim, to celebrate her victory, with a lot of joy, satisfaction, and happiness, gained after her successful revenge."

Unfortunately, in this life, there are a lot of such evil people that only think about how to harm others, how to cause pain on them, by framing other people, fabricating and spreading rumors, intrigues, slurs, threats, etc. The world and humanity would be quieter, more pristine, and happier without this kind of evil people among us.

10

Ardian knew very well that the school principal liked such things and such cases to investigate like he was trying to stop the "moral depravity, decadence and degeneracy," in his school. "Oh, my God! What am I forced to listen to? How can I listen to him now?" While in his mind, Ardian imagined a snowman, placed in an office, with the written sign on the desk: "The School Principal." The real moral decadence and degeneration of society is nepotism and cronyism that assigned him to this job position and protected this snowman from melting. He had been just a woodworker years ago, meaning a "working class" man. Then, his friends and relatives, working in the Communist Party high offices, helped him to enroll and attended the School of Marxism-Leninism Studies, "Vladimir Ilyich Lenin," in Tirana, so-called the Higher School of the Party. That school's diploma gave him the right to teach in the high school education system the subjects: The Marxism-Leninism Theory, and The History of the Albanian Communist Party.

After some years of working as a teacher, they appointed him as the principal of the evening high school, "to improve the problematic situation of the evening high school, justifying the trust the Communist Party had in him." Some rumors said that his successful career came thanks to the beauty and "dexterity" of his wife that worked as a clerk in the County's Party Committee offices, but Ardian didn't want to believe such things. And the principal accomplished very well the job he was appointed. He defended the Party's principles by always showing a high vigilance against everything that was against the Party's directives. For his excellent work, he was commended from the County's Education Department and the County Party leaders. In this way, he convinced himself that he was born to become a leader, and his snow never melted. Even though a snowman, he had under his control real people, actual humans, with flesh, soul, heart, and above all, with the real brain, not like his snow-made brain, a product of the Higher School of the Party, a highly politicized and ideologized institution.

Ardian knocked on the principal's office door and waited for some seconds to hear his voice from inside; "come in." After that, he opened the door and used all the human courtesy in front of "the snowman."

"Good evening, comrade Principal," Ardian greeted him while saying to himself: "Call the pig, Uncle," remembering the famous Albanian adage.

"Do you have classes to teach this period?" The principal asked immediately, with his eyes down on the desk, without answering Ardian's greeting.

"Yes," Ardian answered his question. "And that's why I don't want to be late."

"We don't need to teach classes in the face of those other ugly things that are happening in our school," the principal started his speech and attack. "What were those street songs you sang last night? What…? Love…! Girls…! What…?" The principal said these words in a scornfully derisive way. "What about those songs in English...? British…! American…! Italian…! Capitalism...! Bourgeoisie…! Degeneration…!" The principal continued his partyism-filled speech. "What do you want to bring here...? E…? The capitalist ideology and culture…? You want to bring Americans…, Brits…, and Italians here? Did the communist party send you to school for these things? These things are you going to teach students today?"

"Comrade Principal, those were just songs. I repeat, just songs. Lyrics and music. They were not ideological principles," Ardian answered, trying to interrupt his annoying expressions.

"Have you ever heard those songs on our radio station and our television channel? Or…, you are listening to foreign radio stations? Or…, you are watching foreign television channels?" The principal spoke more seriously, giving his speech the political and ideological direction, with a threatening voice at the same time.

"People make so many songs that need more tapes than radio and television studios can take in," Ardian answered with irony.

"What you sang last night, were not songs, but decadence and foreign ideology influence against all the Party and Great Leader's directives, and they aim to stupefy and spoil the mind of our splendid youth."

"But don't forget that I was not teaching in a classroom. We were at a party, and I think that the Education Department and the Party Committee have other more serious things to deal with than some songs sung in an entertaining dancing party," Ardian tried to explain it to a snowman.

"That's what you say? Do you really think that these things are not crucial for the Party? And you have passed the postgraduate exam of the Marxism-Leninism philosophy with the maximum grade? What about the "class warfare" on the ideologic front, in education, in culture. Where is it? Where are the principles of the Communist Party and the guidance of our Great Leader? I will send an official letter to the Tirana University's Philosophy Department and ask them to cancel your exam certificate because you have passed this exam just for theory and you are not applying your knowledge in practice. What about foreign languages…? That's why you have learned them…? To bring here the foreign ideology. Where are the beautiful Albanian folk songs? Where is our rich folklore? And you are a literature teacher. And you are graduated with maximum grades. With excellent scores. You…, the splendid student…, the great scholar…, with a bright future…" The snowman continued with his foolish expressions, trying to be ironic with Ardian's achievements. And Ardian had to listen to him calmly and with respect until the end.

"Okay. That's what we'll do comrade principal. I will bring you the songs' lyrics, and you do whatever you want with them," Ardian told him in a moment of a brief pause of his revolutionary monolog because he didn't want to hear such foolishness anymore.

"Write them down correctly, as you sang them because I remember most of them very well."

"I agree. May I go now, because I'm late for class," Ardian asked permission to leave, turning toward the door.

"No…, no. Wait! Where are you going? I've not finished yet. All the school is buzzing for you. What have you done last night? Why did you leave in the middle of the party? Where did you go? With whom did you go?" The principal threw these questions in preparation for the other accusation. He waited (like an experienced interrogator), for the effect, reaction and consequences of such a surprise attack on his victim.

The smart people use a better cunning when they need it, not like the foolish, wily principal. From this point of view, cunning might be a product of cleverness. The brighter you are, the smarter and more sophisticated your cunning is. And vice versa; less clever you are more foolish your cunning is.

Suddenly, Ardian recalled Neta's words in the hallway; "Alda told everything." But he knew very well Alda's strong character and smartness, and that's why he reached very quickly the conclusion that the principal and Neta are parts and instruments of this intrigue. But now he was being accused like never before. It was the first time for him to be in such a situation. What does he have to do? What does he have to say to this dangerous and threatening principal? Will he tell him that he loved Eralda and he would marry her? He was ready to say it loudly and to everybody, but not now, not to this kind of the principal who would call this clean and sincere love of theirs as "depravity, immorality, degeneration," to punish him for such things, and to raise for himself the flag of being vigilant against every sign of foreign decadent and hostile ideology. These kinds of people treat other people's feelings like a medieval inquisition. For them, every friendship, companionship, and love are just depravity, immorality, and degeneration. For them, youngsters are just like work tools, without a brain, without feelings, without a soul. Ardian had not to admit the existence of this love right now, in this kind of dangerous situation, because he would be named a heretic, and his head would be cut in a guillotine, or he would be burned at the stake. They would transfer him to the most remote village in the county, or even worst, he could be called "enemy of the Party, enemy of the people, enemy of the working class," and would be sent to prison or internment, very far away, right there where the human being is not treated like a human anymore. In this situation, telling the truth had not any value anymore. Instead, the lie, the feelings' suppression, the retreat must be used in protection from the attack of these devils and wild beasts.

"I think I'm not in the police station offices here," Ardian answered, trying to stay calm.

"But you are in the Party's offices. You are in the school principal's office, and it is the principal's responsibility to protect the morality of the teachers and students and not to allow depravity and immorality to take place in the school."

"The principal might have some more important responsibilities, more pedagogic and organizational ones," Ardian answered ironically. "And regarding the individual morale, every girl, and every boy will look after and care about his own morality and dignity, as their own responsibility and not as the school principal's responsibility."

"You, lad, are a skilled orator, but the Party has nominated us here to educate a clean and healthy youth, without any slag and bourgeois remnant like those of yours," the principal started using words and expressions he had learned by heart from the Great Leader's speeches and books. His head was full of phrases and quotations from the textbooks of the Party's School that were the core of his knowledge. It was all he knew and all he had read in addition to the Party's newspaper. All the people that worked in the Communist Party's offices or had Party job positions, so-called Party cadres, did the same thing, they only repeated such phrases and quotes. Every time Ardian listened to those people, using quotes for everything, it reminded him of the Chinese dazibaos, using their Great Leader's citations on everything. Despite that, the quotes the principal had learned remained just quotes, without the ability to connect this kind of knowledge with the related issues under discussion, so they became just empty quotations. These political citations served just like candies to treat the audience that was listening. Sometimes some quotes were used as the "sword of Damocles" for those who didn't obey the Party principles and guidance and were not staying in the Party's lines. So, they had to be punished harshly. The citations of the Great Leader were used in these cases to convince them and the public that they deserved the consequences of the harsh punishment for them. In this way, the school principal and all the Party officials became sectarians and dogmatics without a brain, as their party wanted them to be. The superiors of the education department and the county communist party committee congratulated the principal as a champion and a warrior of the class warfare, as a man of principles, and commended him for his high vigilance.

"Comrade Principal, I left the dancing party and not the classroom," Ardian said, without listening to the quotes the principal was repeating with a dramatic voice, full of zeal and passion, almost passing in ecstasy.

"Really…?" The principal spoke with an ironic voice. "But why did you leave with her…, the splendid student…, Eralda Tako?" The principal stressed his voice sarcastically in saying "splendid," and while mentioning her name.

"I've never thought about the thing you are thinking about. I left the dancing party alone, and I went back directly to my room in the pedagogical institute's dormitory," Ardian spoke with contained anger, being forced to answer such questions, like being in the police station or to the prosecutor's office.

"No…, no. It's not only me thinking about that thing, but all students and teachers that saw both of you leaving the school one after the other. All of them are speaking about your ugly, immoral behavior because they know very well where you have gone and what you have done after leaving the dancing party. Nothing can be out of the vigilant eyes of the Party." The principal continued politicizing the issue with assumptions that always served as criteria of the truth for him.

"Comrade Principal, I want to think that you know very well the female students of our school that might have problems with their conduct and their morality," Ardian asked him cunningly, waiting for the principal to come in his path.

"Yes…, surely I know. I know everything that happens at my school. That's why the Party has appointed me here," the principal answered proudly, saying what Ardian was waiting for.

"What about the behavior and morality of the girl that supplies you with such untrue stories?" Ardian asked him immediately after his answer. "Do you know well her morality? The girl you listen to, with so much zeal, is the most immoral one. Her lies, rumors, and intrigues are part of her immorality, and spreading such dangerous rumors, is the worst immorality of people like her, because in this way they threaten and put in danger the lives of innocent people, and sometimes the best ones, by shaming them in public without any guilt. An amoral girl like the hooker you listen to, cannot be the protector of other people's honor, and she is leading you to a blind alley by including you in her immoral slurs and intrigues.

"Comrade teacher, you are in my office, and it's me asking you questions here, and not the other way around," the principal interrupted Ardian.

"I, as well, have the right to ask you questions, comrade principal. You are trying to humiliate and demean the personality of a teacher and the best student in the school. And you are doing that only based on what is said by a whore, a bitch, known as such by all the school staff and students," Ardian spoke loudly, more annoyed and infuriated than ever.

These words had an instant effect on the principal, reminding him of his own love affair that he had just started with the "whore and bitch" that the literature teacher had just mentioned. And he retreated a little bit from this fact, and for the other reason that Neta had told him that no other student supports her in what she was saying.

"But…, look! You danced twice with that girl, and everybody understood that there is something between you two," the principal spoke with a lower voice this time, like being gentler and more tolerant.

"What are you saying, comrade principal? Is that why you go to the dancing party...? To count our dances...? I can dance all the dances with just one girl because I like dancing with her. I'm dancing right there, under everybody's watch, not in any hidden way like your informants do their immoralities," Ardian continued attacking at the same point when he understood that there he was having more success, and he continued: "Comrade principal, I'm not going to answer any other question about this issue, because these kind of questions are insulting for me, and violate the morale, the dignity, and the freedom of mine and another innocent and splendid girl. If you continue dealing with this issue, I'll accuse you as a source of such untrue and unethical rumors, in cooperation with that kind of girl that informs you of such things."

The principal understood that he was not lucky in his investigation, either with the literature teacher or with Eralda. They both didn't admit anything, and their calm and persistence in their innocence forced him to retreat for the moment, being unsure how to continue his interrogations.

"Okay... go to the class. I will continue this issue by myself," the principal found how to quit for the moment from this unsuccessful interrogation.

Ardian left the principal's office, understanding that the principal remained with empty hands and that Eralda had not admitted anything too. Around twenty-five minutes had already passed to the principal's office, and he entered the classroom where he had to teach that class period. For the twenty remaining minutes, he just sat at his desk and immersed himself in his thoughts, looking toward the window on his right. On the other side of the window was deep darkness, and nothing could be seen. This dark emptiness outside the window and his shadowed portrait reflected from the window's glass, helped him diving even deeper into his thoughts. He didn't communicate with students in the classroom at all. They knew that the teacher had been to the principal's office but didn't see the reason why. When they saw him sad and that he didn't teach anything at all, they understood that it might have been something serious, and started discussing their assumptions with each other, causing more noise in the classroom. Despite their noise, Ardian didn't hear anything and wasn't bothered at all, and it seemed to him like students were very quiet, even quieter than usual. He wasn't thinking about students in the classroom, while many thoughts were crossing his mind.

"Why is it like this?" He thought, asking himself. "To love a girl, you must face all these obstacles, suffering, and intrigues? Why the love of two people become the subject of the discussions amongst other people? Don't they have any other things to discuss between them? Is this a lack of freedom? Why are some people so talkative, intrigant, and why they like plotting? Why do they make the paths of love so complicated? Yes..., yes, very difficult, and sometimes almost impassable roads. What kind of humans are these enemies of love, these killers of love? Everybody is interested in the morality, honor, and dignity of others. Why don't they only look after their own reputation, honesty, and dignity, their love, their worries, and troubles in their life? Only in this way, people would not quarrel and fight with each other anymore, and everybody's life would be better, more beautiful, and happier. But there are always some people out there that only like to watch and spy what others do, and prejudge them for everything, and spread rumors based on their assumptions and sick imaginations. And then..., this thing is called the 'public opinion.' What a beautifully justified name has been given to it? This kind of 'public opinion,' or 'opinion of society,' whatever it's called, is so indifferent to real ruffians, true cads, delinquents, thugs, and the real immoral ones, but, in the same time, it is hitting harshly good people, the obedient ones, that girl and that boy that love for the first time being seriously in love with each other. Is this public opinion the guardian or the killer of society's morality and dignity? Sometimes the immorality of some people takes place openly, in front of everybody's eyes, and does not care at all about the 'opinion of society,' that in return, remains silent. Then, the same public and society becomes harsher and hits harder the honest people, causing them harm, suffering, suppression, sadness, and uncountable difficulties in their life. This is the killing of feelings, the killing of thoughts, the killing of freedom. This is the destruction and the end of human society. This is a victory for bad people, ignorant and immoral people, which place themselves forcefully in the lead of the public opinion. This is a significant loss for the best people of the society, the wiser ones, the real honest ones, people with moral principles. There is something real in all this situation; the more dishonest and immoral people become spokespersons of the public opinion, the more noise, fog, uncertainty will be, and more good people will be victimized by such an occupied public opinion. This lousy thing becomes catastrophic when wrong, ignorant, and corrupt people hold the leadership positions of state institutions, organizations, and enterprises helped by nepotism and cronyism. In this way, the community and society are suffering, because the so-called opinion of society, has become a property of the real immoral and regressive people, the ignorant ones, bad ones, the real enemies of freedom, which stay up there, in higher positions, and, by spreading rumors and intrigues, they rule and keep everything under their control, leading the society and the public opinion in whatever direction they want."

"In this way, the public opinion has been changed, has taken other shape, other ownership, being occupied by those who are supposed to be fought by a real and progressive public opinion. These bad, shameless people have occupied our community and society, and they rule and act freely, by using their advantage to help and protect each other and to attack others by spreading rumors to frame and punish their innocent victims. They couldn't be seen by the public opinion, on top of which they stay, firing against everyone else, against whoever they want, but not against each other. Look how soft the principal himself is with jerks and strong guys, with delinquents and immoral ones, but how strong he fights against others, the obedient ones, the good ones."

It was only the bell signaling the end of the period that interrupted his thoughts. He will have to walk in the school hallways and was not sure how he would face the students' eyes. He thought that it would be tough. All the students left the classroom without waiting for him to go first. When the class remained empty, he spent some more minutes sitting there, alone at his desk, before leaving the classroom, bashfully, shamefully, and scary. But strangely enough, he didn't see anything different from other days in student's greetings, in their eyes and their behavior. All the students and colleagues were greeting him as usual, smiling warmly and with respect. A group of students, like in a chorus, complimented him for his songs and guitar playing. Ardian felt better and approached them, talking about the dancing party and other entertaining things.

Ardian understood that from the part of the students and colleagues, nothing wrong had happened. So, it was only the school principal and Neta, trying to build a storm in a glass of water, even by lying that all the students and teachers knew and were speaking about their secret love affair.

11

Ardian didn't have any more classes for that day. He left the school and wandered around the city for almost two hours before returning to wait for Eralda to finish her last period of class. She tried to hide her sadness, but Ardian could see the desperation easily in her eyes. She smiled to hide her distress, but he understood that it was a superficial, empty smile. He saw that her eyes and her lips didn't smile as always. It was her smiley eyes, taking their beautiful almond shape, which he liked the most from her smiling face, but tonight they were not like that. Her eyes and her face were not fully smiling because her heart was not smiling. He had always seen her happy heart in her smiling eyes and cheerful face, but not tonight. Tonight, her heart had been hurt, her eyes had been harmed, and her smile had been injured.

"I was in the Principal's office the first period," Eralda spoke first. "Neta had spotted us leaving the dancing party one after the other and reported that to the Principal.

"And how did you do with his interrogations?" Ardian asked her with a worried face.

"It was a terrible investigation, a threatening one, and…, a little bit entertaining as well. Does the School Principal deal with such things?"

She was trying to make the situation look more relaxed than it really was, and not to show her shock caused by the argument with the principal.

"Did you tell him anything?" Ardian asked her.

"I told him that I left the party because I had some headache and went directly back home. He threatened me, saying that he is going to inform my parents. But do you want to know what I told him?"

"What did you tell him?" he asked curiously.

THE FIRST LOVE – Endless Yearning and Pain

"I told him that my brother and his friends would smash the glass of all his house windows." They both laughed loudly, forgetting for some moments the dramatic situation they were going through. "This kind of threat is the most frightening one for the principal because it's challenging to find glass for windows nowadays," Eralda continued laughing while speaking.

"These kinds of people deserve such a threatening language, but we are people of good conduct. I was in his office too," Ardian told her when he understood that she didn't know that.

"Really...? What did you tell him?" She asked with a big concern.

"I told him that I'm not obliged to answer such questions," he answered Eralda's worrisome question, but he didn't want and didn't like to reproduce the entire ugly dialogue he had with the principal. "It is a shame for a principal to ask about such very private things."

"It was Neta..., the crow of your third dance," Eralda mimicked her face. "Maybe she wished to leave the party with you," she continued, teasing him with a joking voice.

"Neta showed up in front of me when I entered the school lobby telling me: 'Alda told everything.'"

"Did you believe that?"

"Absolutely not. With the way she approached me, the way she spoke and went away, she seemed like a real viper in action, that just poisoned the victim with its venom, and ran away," he answered, embracing and squeezing her in his arms when he saw that they had already reached the park.

"What will we do now, after what happened tonight," she asked with a low voice, leaning her head on his chest.

"In school, we will behave as always, as if nothing has happened. For everything else, I'll come to talk with you in your store," Ardian suggested.

"Okay..., you have to come and take the fountain pen you ordered some weeks ago," she laughed, teasing him for the lie he had said when he visited her store for the first time.

"But the fountain pen was the game," Ardian imitated the well-known expression of a character from an Albanian movie, and he embraced Eralda, raising her and revolving together around themselves, as the movie characters do in that scene.

"Bravo..., Bepin," she answered, continuing the same dialog of the movie characters, expressing great pleasure, joy, and happiness from being squeezed inside his arms.

They stayed embraced for some minutes; without saying anything being immersed in the love's silence that doesn't accept and doesn't need unnecessary words. Love acts like that, being exchanged to each other silently, softly, without being noticed and heard; but it brings so much pleasure, it transmits thousands of messages between the lovers' bodies and souls and raises them up in limitless new spaces of their happiness, bringing these beautiful moments of their escape from the surrounding world. There are those love moments where it seems like nothing else exists; neither the bench on which you are sitting, nor the tree under which you are staying, nor the grass and the soil where you lie down. Only love that you are touching, trying and tasting, exists in those moments when lovers forget even their own names and they are called just lovers; when they forget their birthdays and that they will die someday; in those moments when lovers don't think and don't care about the drama and tragedy that so-called "opinion of the society" is preparing for them. His naughty hands started groping, fondling, caressing and squeezing through all her body; her head, her hair, her neck, her face, her eyes, her cheeks, her lips, her shoulders, her chest and..., oh my god..., her breasts..., right there, in between her breasts, grown and shaped so beautifully, enticing just love, lust, and pleasure. She trembled when his hand reached and touched her breasts when she felt the cold of his hand and fingers on her warm, smooth skin, and she shivered more when he rubbed their smooth skin and squeezed their soft flesh. His "nasty" hand sparked the fire, and she felt his fingers' nails deeper in their soft tissue, squeezing them so hard, hurting and causing pain; a kind of bittersweet pain, something between pain and pleasure that she had never felt before, something that only the love's lust can bring, making her unable to try stopping him and thinking about and accepting that bittersweet thing as a hidden, guilty pleasure.

"Girls' and women's breasts—the girls' and women's beauty," Ardian thought. They are the very first victim of men's admiration, adoration, love, and lust to gaining gratification. Girls' breasts are the first thing that excites the eyes, the mind, and the feelings of boys; the first thing to enter in their fantasy, in their sweet dreams, the first to be touched and squeezed by boys' hands. And strangely enough, even for girls themselves, their breasts are the first space of their body that they give up to the boys, to the power and rule of masculine hands, as a start of the path that seduces you toward an unstoppable lure, like an endless mystery. That's how it happened to Ardian too. How many times he touched her breasts in his dreams, but now he had them in his possession in real life, he touched them, rubbed them, squeezed them, kissed them, sucks them, bites them, and he gets excited more and more and gets drunk from their aroma, warmth, smoothness, and softness. He kept squeezing them again and again but couldn't get enough of them. He felt pleasure from the smell coming from her body, her breasts, her neck, her shoulders, where he stopped with his kissing mouth a little bit longer and felt like breathing a fresh, clean air with a pleasant scent; and what an aroma, neither perfumes' fragrance nor flowers' smell, but the best aroma on earth, a fresh scent of a girl that enters and fills your lungs up to its most profound smallest spaces, in its tiny sacs called alveoli, taking her perfume mixed with oxygen, and spreading it through the bloodstream to the most remote cells of his body, very deep, in the love's unknown mysterious corners.

When his hands went down and reached her thighs, she woke up from these sweet dreaming moments, as if suddenly woken up from her deep lethargic sleep caused by the loving pleasure of his touch, his kisses, his fondles, and his squeezes. She woke up like after an alarm fire, needing a high level of response to save herself from a danger approaching her, and she must not allow it to happen.

"No..., not there, please," she whispered with a weak imploring voice. "Please..., stop..., not there... please."

She knew and realized that just a little insistence from his part in those heavenly moments, and she would allow him to go further. She would surrender herself to his naughty hands, and it was something that she really wanted to let, but couldn't accept it to happen so fast. That's why she always begged him by whispering in a weak voice, like saying "yes" and "no" at the same time, because she wanted to explore new love experiences and take more pleasure from it, but just by letting him decide for that. And he decided. He retreated in those moments when another man would never retreat. He found the strength to give up by respecting her as a person and her sincere love.

"I will never exceed your desires," he whispered in her ears, without really understanding what her real desire was, and what she really wanted the most in those magical moments. He couldn't understand Eralda's inner thoughts for possible further exploration in their love experience. He retreated, he found pleasure up to where she allowed him. (Later, Eralda would appreciate Ardian for his retreat at the right time.) He was taking great pleasure from kissing her lips and playing with her alluring breasts. He was enjoying them so much but couldn't get enough of them.

"Why is it like this…? Why other people don't let us alone to enjoy our love?" she asked him, putting her head comfortably on his shoulder.

"Nobody is hindering us now," Ardian answered as if he didn't understand what she really meant.

"What about Neta? What's her issue with us?" Alda continued her ingenuous cogitation.

"She is just one of that kind of people that cannot live their own life without talking about others, without prattling, without slandering and smearing others, without snitching on others' life. For this kind of people is easier staying without eating and starving, than staying without doing such things, and without causing harm to other people".

"Perhaps it's just jealousy," Eralda spoke meditating.

"It might be jealousy as well, but I would never think about her," Ardian answered. "This is jealousy with revenge, badly intended jealousy, malicious one, jealousy just for somebody else's good luck, jealousy for somebody else's successes and accomplishments, which the jealous person himself could never achieve. This thing makes some bad people feel bad when they see others having some success, and they just think how to make things difficult for these successful people, with their wish and intention to force them to fail by using every possible bad means."

"All girls love you," she interfered suddenly, without letting him finish his sentence, telling him what she had been thinking so long, waiting for the opportunity to say it as a need for relief. Time after time, when she thought about other girls' love for Ardian, she accepted that such strange feelings and thoughts were just her jealousy, the dislike that others don't have the right to touch and take what she possesses and what is only hers now. Sometimes Eralda thought that perhaps she had taken what would belong to somebody else, but she felt more pleasure and became happier when she realized that the man, whom other girls liked, adored, and loved so much, had chosen her.

"I have not understood such a thing. I think girls just respect me. Maybe you mix up these things; liking is something else and respecting is something else; adoring is something else, and love is something else," he answered modestly, trying to make her feel better, pleasing her and even himself, on such a stressful day for both.

"I am capable of distinguishing all these things, because that's what I felt and experienced myself, going through all those emotions and feelings you just mentioned; passing too fast from respecting you to liking you; from liking you to adoring you; from adoring you to loving you; and from loving you to spending the evening with you…, right here…, on this bench…, under this weeping willow tree," she answered, speaking slowly, dividing and articulating each word carefully, with a particular stress on each of them, and touching with her pointing finger his forehead, his nose, his eyes, his cheekbones, his lips, his chin, every time she repeated the word "you," letting him know what she had gone through.

The words she was saying, and especially the way she was speaking by pointing him with her finger in all the parts of his face, made Ardian feel very happy. What he liked the most about her was her smile and smiling eyes and face, her girlish coquetry and cute giggles, making her lips, her eyes, and her face, with dimples in her cheeks, even more enticing.

"So, based on what you just said, if I had not proposed you, you would have experienced all of those feelings, except the last one," Ardian reached this conclusion, just to tease her further.

"All feelings that other girls are feeling for you now," she answered immediately, as being prepared for such a dialog. "But I would have proposed you by myself then," she added with a flirtatious manner and childish sincerity, like a happy, naïve little girl with an innocent, cute face.

"Would you become jealous if I had proposed another girl instead of you?" he asked, wanting to tease her more and being entertained more with this beautiful little girl.

"Some months before…, no, but now yes, even their watch on you, makes me feel jealous sometimes," she said, approaching his face with her open mouth searching for his lips, and finding them quickly.

When her lips reached and touched his lips, she opened her mouth as if wanting to guzzle them down. She sucked in his lips into her mouth, full of hankering and lust, like trying to gulp this large mouthful down, inside her body, her chest, her heart, and her blood, in a deep place from where they could never leave anymore. He felt the warmth, the wetness, and softness of the inner part of her lips on his lips for the first time. Ardian felt her tongue, pressing, pushing, and sliding between his lips in search of his tongue, and when both tongues found and touched each other, he felt such a new great pleasure he had never felt before. She was kissing him for the first time. She was giving him an extraordinary enjoyment. She was kissing him the way that only girls in love know how to do it while kissing their beloved. It was not a simple kiss. Her heart and her soul were in this kiss. It was a kiss full of feelings, lust, passion, and pleasure. It was that kind of kiss that conquers and rules over you, making you feel another man. Eralda pushed Ardian, making him lie down on the bench jumping on him without interrupting her kiss. She rubbed and squeezed him harder, pulling him against her body, where her full round breasts were compressed and expanded on her chest, like being ready to burst at any given moment. Ardian closed his eyes and didn't act at all. He didn't want to interfere and interrupt her wild moves, letting her free to do whatever she wanted. It was her turn to express her excitement and desire. He was feeling happier just by allowing her to please herself with her acts full of lust and love. It was her turn now, and it all seemed like he was sleeping, and a fairy or an angel was kissing him. This thought reminded him of a fairytale, where a fairy entered at night the bedroom of a highlander and kissed him, with the condition that he must keep this mystery for himself and never tell that to anybody else. But, when the highlander leaked out the secret, the beautiful fairy cut his tongue and made him mute for all his life. This legend came to his mind while he was enjoying his fairytale and the kiss of his fairy delightfully. He wished that this legend of him, this pleasurable sleep, these sweet dreams, and these unique feelings never ended. But there is nothing you can do. Time never stops, and it flows without thinking about us, and without obeying us. Time is merciless.

Eralda was getting up into a frenzy. She pulled him harder and squeezed him like wanting to take more from him, from his body, and she couldn't get enough. He felt the soft bite of her teeth on his lips, chin, neck, shoulders, and chest. She was sucking in and biting him everywhere, groaning and moaning loudly, like being under the control of a mysterious subconscious power. She was experiencing for the first time the pleasant orgasmic flow going through her entire body and the magic of the physically pleasurable bliss. She trembled excessively several times and suddenly stopped and raised her head like waking up after a wet dream in a deep sleep. She looked at his eyes and tried to regain her self-control. "What happened to me? What was that?" Eralda asked herself and leaned her head on his chest, feeling exhausted and guilty for her actions and started crying in silence. He understood that she was crying when he felt the heat of her tears on the skin of his chest. It caught him completely off guard, and he didn't know what to say to her and what to do in this delicate moment. He wiped her tears from her eyes with his fingers. Her tears were warm, very warm.

"Alda, what's the matter?" He asked, whispering near her ear.

She didn't answer and continued sobbing. This thing worried Ardian even more. He had read somewhere that some girls cry while making love, but he didn't think this was the case.

"Alda, what's the matter? Please..., don't cry," he begged her and raised her head with his hand under her chin. "What's the matter? Why are you crying? Tell me." And when he saw her eyes and face in tears, he thought that she looked even more beautiful, like a crying angel statue with dropping tears on her cheeks. He embraced this angel by wrapping his arms around her. Her tears reminded him of a song that he had not sung before for Eralda, which he started singing in a low voice, near her ear, while she was still crying.

Between the hands, she kept her head.
And her tears flowed like runlet.
Weeping has no charm at all.
But her face radiates prettiness.

Then she suddenly raised her head,
Smiling in bitterness, she said:
You told me you've never been a girl,
And that's why you can't understand.

Ardian thought that it was the best thing he could do for her in such touching moments. He felt that she needed to cry, and that's why he didn't try to stop her, but just continued singing other songs for her, fondling her hair. He thought that tears relieved the significant pressure of the events of that day. A human is a human and can endure and resist as much as possible, but, in the end, it explodes and bursts into tears. He thought that with his songs, he could help her a little bit. After some minutes, Eralda felt better.

While listening to him singing exclusively for her; feeling his lips singing and touching her ear, feeling the warm air coming out of his mouth and his lungs and the soft sound of his beautiful melodious voice, she felt better and relaxed and started thinking: "What a good guy he is. What about me? Why am I crying? Why do I make him worry about me? Why am I so stupid?" And she tried to get rid of her foolish thoughts, regarding her worthlessness in front of this wonderful man and splendid professor. These evil thoughts that made her cry made her suspect and fed her uncertainty, giving her the sense of foreboding that this great love of theirs would be temporary and could not last long. The more she loved him, the more uncertain she became, growing the fear of a sudden fall from the dangerous heights where this great love was lifting them.

Ardian didn't speak and didn't ask anything. He finished a song and stopped for some minutes. It was only after this pause that she raised her head.

"I'm sorry," she said very short, wiping her last tears from her face.

Even though he didn't speak and didn't ask her, Ardian kept inside of him the worry her tears and her weeping caused to him. They stood up and started walking toward her home without saying any word all the way, but just holding each other's hands. But they didn't forget the usual, long, silent kiss near the entrance of her apartment building, being done to keep as a pleasant remembrance until the next date. Furthermore, Ardian would be away for three days this time. Their kiss was only interrupted after hearing some approaching steps, and they separated, each one going in his direction.

Ardian, as soon as arrived in the main street, walking toward the institute's dormitory, recalled some complaining verses, written by the Albanian poet Ndoc Gjetja, titled *"The Kiss"*.

So many ugly things,
like quarreling and cursing,
occur openly,
in the middle of the streets.

But, the most human thing,
the greatest one, the most divine,
the kiss,
is still banned.

This painful complaint of the poet seemed more accurate than ever to Ardian, and he felt a kind of joy while thinking that he was going to recite these verses in the upcoming date with Eralda.

12

Two national holidays of November 28 and 29, together with the Sunday before them, made a long weekend with three days off, and Ardian went to spend these holidays with his family to his hometown, Vlorë. Three months had gone without going back home, but he didn't feel this at all. Even now that he had arrived home, he didn't feel cozy and relaxed. His mind was at Eralda, in Elbasan, and he wanted to leave Vlorë as soon as possible. Even though he was pleased, staying home with his parents, sister, and grandmother, his mind was always with Eralda. Sometimes, a careful thought crossed his mind: "Why didn't I bring her over with me, to present her to my family." He was sure that if only two days they had stayed together, they would like and love Eralda the same as he does, not even for two days, but just with the first sight, like him. Despite these kinds of thoughts, he didn't tell them about Eralda. He didn't say either his mother and father or his sister and grandmother. Even though his sister repeated her usual phrase: "My lovely brother…, three years of working as a professor have passed, and you have not found a female student yet, a nice girl as you would want her." Ardian didn't tell her anything about Eralda. His sister's name was Rajmonda (short, Monda), and she was a high school senior. Monda was one year younger than Eralda, and even though she didn't look like Eralda, every time Ardian looked at Monda, she reminded him Eralda; not from the traits or the body size and shape, but from some of her body moves, some girlish coquetries, and some female ways of speaking and acting, that look like being the same for all the girls of this age. There are some similar actions in all of them, regardless of a lot of other personal characteristics that make them look different, like the body size and shape, the color and length of hair, or the color of skin and eyes, etc.

His mother, in the same way as Monda, told him time after time to find a good girl among the female students of the pedagogical institute, and sometimes recommended to him female students from their city, with which she had already written a long list. Ardian and Monda called it the "candidates waiting list." These requests and advice from his mother and sister, made Ardian feel bad. All of his family, and even he, for a very long time, had thought that his potential wife would be a girl with a bachelor's degree, a girl from their city or region, from a well-educated family with fine political biography. "And now, what could he say to them?" He thought all those days. "Would he say that he was in love with a female student of the evening high school...? A shopkeeper...? A girl expelled from the regular high school...?" So..., they, only based on these things, would refuse and deny it immediately and would never admit such a girl to become their daughter in law. It would be a destruction of their family harmony, especially the mother, who would have sickened and gone crazy. "If they could know what a nice girl Eralda was and how humble, clever, and agile she was, they would not refuse her just from the first superficial things about her. But how could they know that? What if he brings her home, as a friend of him? No, it can never happen. What if Monda comes to Elbasan, and meets Eralda and spends time with her, to know her better?" This idea seemed like the best option, more reasonable, and that's what he decided to do.

He wandered in the streets of his city those days, and it seemed to him like in every store he passed by, he would find Eralda inside them. Being caught from the magic of her, he entered many stores with a vague hope to find Eralda there. In every store, he saw similarities in their counters, showcases, and articles, but he couldn't find her; the best one, the most beautiful one, the most loved one, his Eralda. He continued walking the streets but couldn't break free from the magic that she—with her face, her eyes, her smile, her hair, her body, her name, her moves—had created and planted in his mind, and he couldn't stop himself from entering other stores, with the same aim of finding her there. He had the pleasant feeling that, by visiting these stores, at least he could relieve the yearn for Eralda. He couldn't wait until returning to Elbasan and seeing her again. Only to have a glimpse of her in those moments, he would pay a lot, and he would give even more to cuddle, fondle and kiss her as he desired and as she deserved.

Ardian had always been a kind of indifferent guy toward girls and women, but now he was even more uninterested toward them, because in his head he only had Eralda's portrait, and he only thought about her all the time. Girls and women passed by him and in front of him, but he didn't look at them. After returning home, he tried to remember what he had seen in the neighborhood and city streets, and it seemed like there were no girls and women in the city because he hadn't seen any of them during those days. Days in his home passed one after the other, and her magic never left his mind. He, sometimes, almost called his sister, Monda, by Alda's name. He didn't spend a lot of time with his hometown friends when he met them, because he wanted to return home with the idea that Eralda was waiting for him there. He slept in Monda's bedroom, while she slept in the living room couch, and so he was sure that, if he called Eralda's name at night, nobody would be there to listen to him. Oh…, how many beautiful dreams he dreamt about Alda; how many times he met and talked to her, embraced and kissed her, fondled and kept her tight in his arms, and he even slept with her. In his dreams, both entered their bedroom, she was wearing the bride's white dress that made her look more beautiful than ever, and their matrimonial bed was there waiting for them. He helped her to take off her white dress, and she remained with some white, thin, transparent underwear, while he watched her half-naked, stunning, natural curvy body. He was staying with the marvel of his love, excited with lust and desire, but seemed like he didn't know what to do. He tried but couldn't reach and touch her. Sometimes, he lay down with her in bed. Oh…, not with her, but with the magic of her, that he had brought with himself and couldn't get rid of it because he just didn't want to.

It was the last day and the very last moment at the train station, while he was giving the goodbye hugs to his mother and his sister when he told his sister.

"Monda, if you want, come to Elbasan after two weeks, and I can present you a potential candidate as my future wife."

Both, his mother and his sister, looked at each other joyfully, smiled, and laughed on this excellent news, but they didn't have any more time left to ask further questions because the train was about to close the doors and leave the station. That's why Ardian chose this moment to tell them because he didn't want to have any other questions about likely-to-be his wife. He didn't want them to start questions like: "What's her name? Where is she from? Where does she live? What do her parents do? Where are her parents from?" and other such questions. But they were not going to ask additional questions from the moment when he would tell them that she was a student of the evening high school, and she was just a shopkeeper. That would be enough for them to shut their mouth and not ask any more questions about her and her family.

"How tough love itself becomes in this way? You love a girl, and that is not enough, because your parents and family have to like her as well. You must consider their opinion and ask for their permission. You love that girl because you know her very well, while parents couldn't like her just because they have heard some superficial things about her and her family, things that have nothing to do with the real love feeling and with the girl's behavior, respect, wisdom, humbleness, and other such important traits that my Eralda has. The strength of her character makes her be an exceptional one, quite different from other girls. Girls are very talkative in general, but not Eralda, who is very serious, strong, sensible, sincere, and very beautiful." It reminded him of the last evening they spent together. "Why did she cry last time? Did she cry from the stress caused by the debate with the school principal? Did she cry because I would be away for three days? Does she have any suspicion of my love?" He knew that girls in love cry sometimes, but was not sure about the reason; was it just joy tears, stress tears, lust tears, inner suffering tears, pain tears, or tears coming from a kind of anxiety and fear caused by a foreboding that their love is not meant to last longer, as a legitimate uncertainty that all girls usually have.

"I love Eralda, and I'll marry her. But how would the parents react to this fact?" It was so strange that ever since he had known Eralda, and during all the time he had spent with her, he had never thought about his family's reaction to his love and his choice. He only thought about his family's involvement and opinion, the day he left Elbasan by train, going to Vlorë. Because of the joy and happiness her love brought to him, he could never think about such things. He, himself, considered this love as finalized, but now he had to face the parents' attitude. It's not so easy for them to accept such love. They all have been waiting and hoping their son to find a graduate girl from the pedagogical institute or other universities, with a profession like a teacher, a doctor, an economist, a lawyer, etc. His parents couldn't face and accept such an unexpected situation for them. And despite their thoughts and opinion, parents usually are susceptible to others' words and judgments. "What are people going to say?" That's the question that makes them worry so much, and parents use it so often when they are against any thought, act, choice, and decision of their own children, which they don't like. The question: "What are people going to say," stays like a sword over their heads, ready to fall over them. It's like a trap, a lasso, an ambush against the freedom of every individual. This concept is neither written nor expressed anywhere; it's not a law, it's not a rule, but it's even more influential than laws and more active and applicable than all other written laws and regulations. "What are people going to say?" Ardian was repeating in his mind this kind of self-restraint and dependence of our actions by other people's prejudice and opinion. It's an abstract obstacle, an obscure enemy, but more substantial than all real enemies and more impassable than all concrete barriers. He feared that even his love would not pass through this obstacle, and he didn't know what to do about that. Such a hurdle is raised in front of you by all your loving people; parents, grandparents, brothers and sisters, cousins and relatives, but especially by mothers, that in such cases become more egoist for their children. His mother was suffering from this kind of egoism too.

His mother was proud of and bragged about Ardian's achievements everywhere she could, to the work friends, to the neighbors, relatives, in stores, etc.. She was proud of saying that her son had graduated with splendid results; he was appointed as a professor; he is continuing with postgraduate studies; he knows two foreign languages, etc. What about now? What would she say? "What are people going to say?" She would repeat to him when he will tell her that Eralda is a shopkeeper and an evening high school student. "It will be tough for me," he repeated to himself, and he thought for himself like being in between two loves, his parent's love, and Eralda's love. But now he liked more and appreciated more, Eralda's love, which he didn't want to lose. He knew from others' experiences in such cases, when parents didn't agree with their children's choices, decisions, and actions, and as a reaction, parents would hold a grudge against their children for some months or even years, but after some time, they became friendly again. A parent is and remains a parent forever for his children, and a child is and remains a child forever for his parents, and such a relationship lives forever, they can't forsake each other for a long time. It has happened with a lot of families, where parents have not accepted their children's choice and have not allowed them to enter their house. After some more reflection, they forgive and forget what they have said, and accept and return to each other again, with a renewed love. So, the parents' love can be impinged on and harmed a little bit, but it will not disappear, it will recover and return someday. From this point of view, the parents' love is a love that recuperates and comes back, but the girl's love is fragile, that needs to be treated carefully, must not be impinged on and harmed, because unlike the parents, the girl goes away and doesn't come back; she goes somewhere else, she finds somebody else, she finds another warmer nest and does not return to you anymore, and so you lose that girl forever. Ardian didn't want to lose Eralda, and that's why he kept the side of Eralda's love, the side of his passion for Eralda. "Look how happy we are with each other," he thought. "What a wonderful girl she is. I would never find another girl as good as Eralda. Not any other girl would give me as much joy, love, and happiness as Eralda." Ardian reached in a kind of an important conclusion for his love, and he never wanted to lose Eralda.

With all these thoughts coming and going in his mind, Ardian spent the travel time on the train, watching all the time through the train window, and without talking with other passengers near him. He got off the train with the conclusion and the decision he has reached after all this inner talking: "I'll never lose Eralda. She is mine, and she will be mine forever."

* * * * *

Eralda as well passed those holidays full of feelings, full of longing and thoughts. "What is Ardian doing now?" was the question crossing her mind all the time. "How bad it is when your lover is far away, and you know that you can't see him for some days. How much longing and worries bring it for the hearts in love being far apart." There were only three days, and it seemed like three months for Eralda. She was used to seeing him every day, even three or four times a day, at her store. But she had other worries too. "Has he told his parents? Has he told his sister? What will they think about me?" She knew that Ardian loved her full of passion and desire, and she didn't have any doubt about that. "But..., perhaps..., his parents are not going to admit his love. What will happen then? It would be so difficult for me to become the wife of somebody whose family doesn't accept such a thing. I can't become such a wife. I don't want to divide families. But..., maybe they are right. How can a professor marry a shopkeeper that has just an evening high school diploma?" Eralda had had such a worry and had sensed this kind of anguish since the beginning of this relationship. But the love feeling had been stronger and defeated her uncertainty. Now that she was thinking about the possible attitude of his parents toward this love, it made her more fearful. She had this bad thought in the beginning, but love became stronger and won this inner battle. Now it seemed to her as if this obstacle became stronger than ever, and later on, the gap would become wider and deeper, like an impassable abyss that would divide two hearts that loved so much each other and would kill a wonderful love. When she thought about that on the second night of the holidays, she started crying. It was the same reason that made her cry on the last date. She was very much in love with him, but she was very much scared as well. She was terrified of these scary thoughts about the future of this relationship, about a possible separation. "It is an impossible love. It is a banned love. But I'll attend the pedagogical institute and become a teacher," she tried to justify and relieve herself. "That's what Ardian has told me too. We love each other; we understand each other, we are happy with each other, even like this, as we are now, but…, there is a need for something else…, the bachelor's degree. Who invents such prerequisites for love? It seems just like another obstacle brought deliberately with a bad reason; to divide and destroy the hearts in love, to bring more difficulties, more dramas, and more tragedies that usually happen after a lost love."

"I will never lose Ardian. No…, no! Never!" Eralda concluded at the end of all these inner thoughts. How happy she felt with Ardian? Look…, even these days that he was far from her, she was only thinking about him, and only him. "Isn't this love? When you wait for somebody with so much longing, when you worry about him, when you feel dejected just because he's far away for few days and is not next to you, isn't this love? I will love him forever." All those days, she wished and wanted magic to bring him to her store. She was waiting for him—her teacher and her lover—to enter her store every moment. She felt proud of this love, and for this good luck, (to speak with the others' language), and that's why she didn't care about rumors whispered among evening high school students, as her close friend, Bardha, had told her.

But she knew and was conscious, that this kind of rumors would spread very fast in all the city. It always happens like this with such hearsays. People seem to be very eager for such gossip, which spreads with the speed of the wind or better said with the velocity of the garrulous mouths. It looks like they have nothing else in their life to deal with, and just want to eavesdrop and scrutinize somebody else's life and love, interfering and harming them hard.

13

The school principal didn't call either Ardian or Eralda at his office anymore, but he mentioned this case in a meeting with the school's teachers, to raise their attention for being more careful in their relations with students, to not become subjects of the social opinion and make them whisper suspiciously. Ardian had not participated in this meeting, but when the principal had mentioned Ardian's name, a servile teacher, well-known as the principal's yes-man, had said that it was a need to discuss further this issue in another separate meeting, and to punish the literature teacher if everything whispered under voice is proved to be true. Other teachers didn't agree with him but said that they had to do their job, to stop such hearsays. The principal himself was sure that he couldn't have the support of other teachers, and he was conscious that they would defend Ardian, instead. So, he decided to follow another way, declaring in front of them: "That's why I mentioned Ardian's case so that everybody is careful and try to avoid such rumors." It seemed like this issue was closed, and that's why Ardian—after his colleagues told him what the principal had said—didn't discuss this issue with the principal anymore. But the school principal followed another tactic, continuing this issue in a hidden way, behind Ardian's back, as the easiest way to cause harm to other people. He wrote an official information letter to the County's Education Department and to the County's Communist Party Committee that reads as follow:

"The literature teacher of our school, comrade Ardian Prela, who works as a professor in the pedagogical institute as well, has shown signs of the foreign bourgeois-revisionist ideology and acts of immorality by having affairs with female students. He played the guitar during the dancing party organized on the eve of November 28 and 29 festivity days, where he sang some street-thugs songs and even foreign-music songs in English and Italian;

things that have a negative influence on and cause the depravity of our clean youth that is the aim of all our foreign enemies. He has been the subject of rumors for immorality and love affairs with female students, and this happens for the fourth year in a row since he started working in our school. This time, I'm fully convinced, and some students testified that he has a love affair with the female student called Eralda Tako, who has been expelled from the regular high school for the same immoral reasons. I called them into my office in separate meetings, but they didn't admit such a thing, while all students and teachers are indignant from this immoral case, that these days has been the issue of the day, and they are asking to take measures and make an example of both. All students are saying that the literature teacher is immoral, and a womanizer and I propose for him not to teach in our school anymore and this issue to be followed further in Party lines, to investigate his immoral behavior deeply as a well-hidden sexual predator in the pedagogical institute as well."

That was the content of the official information letter, but at the same time, the school principal discussed this issue in person with the head of County's Communist Party Committee, which was a friend of the principal (and a "close friend" of his wife as well), with whose help he first attended the two-year-long Communist Party Higher School in Tirana, then became a teacher, and later on, was promoted as the evening high school principal. The principal was happy when he learned from his wife that the head of County's Communist Party Committee had a niece who graduated in literature from Tirana University, and was trying to nominate her as a literature professor at the Pedagogical Institute of Elbasan. So that his information arrived at the right time, to expel Ardian from his job position in the Pedagogical Institute, and assign the niece in place of him. "We, from our part, will urge the County's Education Department to discuss this flagrant act of this teacher and professor, as soon as possible, because he does not deserve to be in such important educational positions for our youth. We'll follow this issue in the Party line in the Party sections in the pedagogical institute and the County's Education Department." That's what the head of County's Communist Party Committee told the principal; not forgetting to thank and commend him for a high level of vigilance and as an active fighter against all the signs of the foreign bourgeois and revisionist ideology and culture, following the directives of the communist party and the Great Leader.

For the teachers and students of the evening high school, the early December days were just regular school days, without that, "issue of the day," as the school principal wrote in his letter. The students, during the day, worked in different state plants and enterprises, and some of them were unemployed, so they only met each other in the school days, three times a week. Eralda had a close girlfriend in the evening high school, called Bardha, who worked as a shopkeeper in a store near Eralda. Neta, with her continuous effort, became a close friend with another female student those days, and both of them sometimes mentioned the rumor about Eralda and the literature teacher, but the rest of the students were not supportive of them in this gossip. But, as it happens with all rumors, something remained in their minds, and they were becoming very vigilant to distinguish any supportive sign for these rumors, watching the behavior of the literature teacher and Eralda, to use it as a fact for the truth or untruth of these hearsays. Despite their careful observation, they never saw anything suspicious in their behavior in the classroom, in school hallways, or outside the school. So, there were only words by Neta's suspicion that initiated and spread this rumor, and that's why Neta became just a bad girl that caused all these troubles for the literature teacher and the good friend of all of them, Eralda, who never said any bad word about Neta and never quarreled with her about this issue. Even though she was told by her friends about Neta's rumors, Eralda never tried to revenge against her.

Eralda continued preparing for school and doing her homework as always, but now she was trying harder to score maximum grades in all school subjects, making happy not only herself but Ardian as well. During the literature class periods, all the students were trying to distinguish any signs or something significant in Eralda's behavior and Ardian's words and actions, to assure themselves for the existence of a special relationship between the two, but they never saw such a thing. Some of them concluded that nothing was happening between those two, but at the same time, others were thinking that they were excellent players in hiding their love affair. For her part, Eralda tried so hard not to show or express anything suspicious in her face, her eyes, her lips, in her words, actions, and movements, trying to seem like everybody else in the literature class periods. In talks with her school friends, she stayed indifferent whenever they spoke something related to the subject of the literature or about the literature teacher. Ardian as well tried hard not to show any visible sign while teaching in Eralda's classroom, by not walking and not looking toward her desk.

THE FIRST LOVE – Endless Yearning and Pain

Ardian raised her in front of the class when her turn had arrived per "the schedule." (The order in which students were asked questions on the lesson of the day and previous ones. After everybody has gotten the first grade in the respective subject, the same "schedule" would be followed by the teacher to give the second grade to all the students, and so on for the third and fourth grade. When a teacher doesn't obey to this informal "schedule," it is called a "provocation," because students prepare better when his/her turn approaches, adding the possibility for a better grade. In the case of "provocation," students are caught off guard and unprepared, scoring a lower or even a negative grade). Eralda answered his questions very well, but he evaluated her answer with a "nine," without explaining to her why and where she was wrong in her answers. Ardian had not thought about that in advance, and at that moment, he had a kind of dilemma to give her a "ten" or a "nine," and without any apparent reason, at the very last moment, he just articulated; "sit down, 'nine,'" and Eralda walked in silence toward her desk. It sounded like a surprise to some students in the classroom because they thought that she, after her excellent answers, deserved a "ten." They believed that the teacher was in an awkward position for his choice; "nine" or "ten." With "nine," he was trying to avoid any possible suspicion, but sometimes, the attempt to avoid suspicion causes and brings other doubts. "He evaluated her answer with "nine" to prevent the suspicion for their affair," some students would think (among them, Neta and her close friend would whisper such conclusion later on). In this way, thoughts, suspicion, findings, and the interpretation of different things go by the various interests of different people, at different times.

Only one of the class friends knew the truth very well—Bardha. She had seen the literature teacher several times walking around, entering and exiting the Eralda's store, and Eralda didn't hide anything from her. She had told Bardha that they were in love with each other and that they had spent some evenings at the park. Eralda told her even other things, as girls tell each other in such cases. In this way, Bardha became the third person to know about their love. It seems like always the hidden love needs a third person, to whom the girl in love opens her heart and tells her things and asks for her thoughts and her help. Bardha, for her part, kept this secret very well, and she was always the best Eralda's protector in the classroom, in the fight against Neta and her rumors. Bardha liked and supported this love, and this good luck for Eralda, and she wished her the best and encouraged her whenever Eralda expressed any worries about her love's future. When girls tell each other about their love relationship, it serves as an inducement, and they teach and encourage each other in this way. Bardha's feelings excited from what Eralda told her about her love. "A grape sees another grape, and ripens," they say in Albania, meaning that grapes ripen in the presence of others. The same thing happens with girls, and you will have the same result when the girl in love tells the other girl about the excitement and pleasure of love. It only sparks the fire to the other girl, with the desire, needs, and the dream to find her own prince of love. That's why Bardha, in that time, thought more seriously about two or three men that had expressed a kind of interest to her, and she decided to accept one of them, starting her game of love with all accompanying excitements and pleasures. She told her decision to Eralda, and they laughed when Eralda told her: "I wish nobody is going to tell the school principal about that."

That's how it happens with all girls that are close friends with each other. It takes just the first girl to start a love relationship, and her friends will follow her, one after the other. In this way, you will find a group of girls that have started their love and have concluded in marriage at a younger age, compared to other groups that have fallen in love and have been married at an elder age, just because no one of them started earlier this attractive game, to spark the love fire among the others, only by telling them her excitement and pleasure, encouraging them to plunge without any fear and not to wait any longer.

Eralda's brother had just found a job, working the afternoon shift in the steel factory, so that he didn't come to her store in the closing time. In this way, Eralda was free to spend some more time with Ardian, after closing the store. It was December, but the weather was still warmer than usual, without rain and winds. They met and had a pleasant time with each other several times, but it looked like something was missing in their relationship. Ardian was honest, and he knew that Eralda had her right to ask him whether and when he was going to visit her family to ask her parents' blessing. Eralda had thought about that several times, but she never asked Ardian such a thing, because she thought he knew that he had to do this someday. But, when she saw that he was not mentioning his visit to her house even after returning from his home, she worried enough, experiencing her bad moments filled with doubt and uncertainty about this love. Ardian, one evening, when they were sitting on their bench in the park, understood her concern and tried to explain to her:

"Alda, when I was home, I didn't tell my parents about us, because they had some other issues. But I'll tell them when I go back there for the winter break and New Year's Eve holidays."

Eralda stayed silent for some minutes, and then told him:

"You know that I love you, and you act as you think by yourself, but it would be better for both of us to not continue too long in this way. I am a girl, and others have understood our relationship, and badmouths have started to whisper about us. Above all, it would be better because, after that, we can meet openly, without any fear of others, and will spend more time together."

After these words, he gave her a long kiss as a bonus for her sincerity, trust, and love.

"My sister, Monda, will come to Elbasan this Saturday," Ardian told her, after that long kiss, "and I'll present you to her."

"Very good," Eralda expressed her joy. "Why haven't you told me before about that? Let her come for a sleepover to my house," Eralda continued full of enjoyment.

14

Ardian met his sister, Monda, in the train station, on Saturday afternoon. They hugged, and Monda expressed her eagerness immediately.

"Why are you alone? Where is she? I didn't come here for you."

"You are right," he answered, "and I'm very sorry, but she wasn't available tonight, and we are going to meet her tomorrow morning."

"What's her name? What does she look like? Is she beautiful? What year is she studying? Where is she from?" Monda unloaded all her questions, like firing with an automatic weapon.

"You will learn everything tomorrow morning. I'm not going to tell you anything tonight because I'm angry with her. She has gone with a friend of hers without telling me anything at all."

"There is nothing wrong since you are not engaged or married, and she is not obliged to ask your permission. Did she know that I was coming?"

"That's the problem. I didn't tell her in advance because I wanted to make a surprise to her."

The dusk was just starting, and the neon lights of the boulevard turned on at that moment. They two continued walking without speaking for some minutes, joining other people, that were making the traditional evening stroll in the main boulevard of the city. Ardian was walking with his head down, like counting his steps. While Monda was looking at the buildings and stores' windows on both sides of the boulevard. Then she started talking to him about their parents, their grandmother, with their advice for Ardian that he had to think a lot of things before deciding and starting a serious relationship with a girl.

"Good advice," he answered when they approached the Eralda's store and entered the store. Eralda was there, waiting for them, and that's why she hadn't gone to school that evening.

"A student of mine in the evening high school," Ardian presented Eralda to Monda after the usual greetings, "and she is my sister, Monda."

"Welcome to our city," Eralda said, shaking hands with Monda and presenting herself, "Eralda," with her attractive smile on her lips, cheeks, and eyes.

The first impression for Monda was the beauty of this shopkeeper, her gentle, warm voice, the sweet, beautiful smile, her elegant moves, and her manner. "What a charming girl! What a beautiful smile! What elegance! What a nice person!" Monda thought while Ardian continued the talk with Eralda.

"We entered your store because we were passing by, and my sister, like all other girls and women, want to enter every store, without any good reason," he was explaining to Eralda.

"Do you like anything here?" Ardian asked Monda. "Are you going to buy any school articles?"

"I like the shopkeeper," Monda answered, smiling with a girlish coquetry.

They all laughed loudly. Eralda's laughter was the most beautiful one; genuine, sincere, and candid. The entire her face was joyous. Her open mouth with shining white regular teeth, her lips, her eyes, her cheekbones, everything of her was cheerful. Her long curly hair over the shoulders with her casual forelock over her forehead and eyes formed a beautiful garland being added to the beauty of her smiling face.

"Don't touch the shopkeeper. She is not for you," Ardian talked while laughing.

"Why? Is she already sold?" Monda continued with humor. "Or is she only for the store vitrine?" And all three of them laughed loudly again.

"Yes, you are right. She is already sold," Ardian answered immediately.

"Yes..., sure. The good stuff is sold very fast because it sells itself—no need for any ads. I'm feeling sorry, though," Monda continued, expressing her sorrow.

"We are going to the institute dormitory to find a room for Monda there," Ardian interrupted the laughter, stretching out his hand to Eralda.

"Why are you taking her to the dormitory?" Eralda interfered, without extending her hand to Ardian. "Let her come to my house. It's been a long time that I haven't taken a girl to my home for a sleepover, though I like it very much."

"No..., no. How did you become friends so fast?" Ardian played the game, contesting her request.

"Yes..., yes. We girls become friends very fast," Monda spoke joyfully because she liked the idea of having a sleepover to this beautiful girl's home.

"Okay, since you two agree to this idea, I'm not going to argue with you, but I have to go to my room because I have a lot to prepare for Monday morning. Monda," he said to his sister, "I'm leaving you in good, safe hands. Tomorrow morning, at nine, you come together to open the store, and I'll come to take my little sister here," Ardian told them, shaking hands with both of them, and leaving the store.

As soon as he left the store, he heard their laughter again. "Monda is going to like her for sure," he thought happily.

There were no customers in the store, and Monda and Eralda started talking like they knew each other for a long time. Monda was one year younger than Eralda, but they both were "maturante," (as high school seniors are called in Albania, meaning "the mature ones," according to the term used in the high school diploma, called "Certificate of Maturity.") They talked about their schools. Monda understood that Eralda knew a lot about all the school subjects. It was a surprise for Monda because she had another opinion about the evening high school students. Eralda told her that she was attending the evening high school because she wanted to help her parents and support her family. "I would like to attend the pedagogical institute, and I'd like to become an elementary school teacher. Ardian is the best teacher in our school, and my friends in the institute say that he is the best professor there as well. He has an excellent way of teaching. He treats all students very well, and they all love and respect him more than other teachers. Lucky you that have such a brother." Eralda told all these things during their stay in the store.

"What about you?" Eralda asked Monda in a moment. "What do you want to continue your higher studies for?"

"I would like to study for economics, but it seems difficult, because of my grade point average is low. I'm not as good as Ardian is. I'm not like him," she answered, with a sad face and smiling at the same time.

"Try a little bit harder for the rest of this year," Eralda tried to encourage her.

Eralda closed the store, and they went home, where Monda found a warm ambient, not just from the wood fire burning in the stove, but from the welcome, hospitality, generosity, and the good humor she found in her family. They, first, spent some minutes with the little brother, who was an articulate child and became friends with Monda very fast.

"Ada has found a good friend," the little brother spoke, with his way of childish speaking, pointing toward Monda.

Eralda told the parents that Monda was the sister of the literature teacher that had come from Vlorë, to spend the weekend with her brother in Elbasan.

"She arrived at our city this evening, they came to my store by chance, and the teacher wanted to take her to the institute dormitory, but I invited her home instead, and she agreed."

"Very good," said Eralda's mother, and started asking Monda about herself, her family, her parents, and their professions. She didn't forget to ask her even about the food market situation in her city; for articles like meat, eggs, milk, cheese, cooking oil, olive oil, flour, dry beans, rice, coffee, etc., because it was a shortage of such main food articles in stores, becoming a worry for cities' populace and the main subject of discussions among people.

The elder brother didn't take part in their discussions and didn't talk at all, staying aside, shy, reserved, and silent. The sister just finished her shower that time and sat down on a small stool near the stove, drying and combing her hair without engaging in their talk. Monda saw that Eralda's sister, as well, had a beautiful facial physiognomy like Eralda, but she was slimmer and a little taller than Eralda. From their big eyes, full lips, and curly hair, Monda concluded that both sisters had taken from their mother, in whose face one can still see the beautiful characteristics of her girlhood, but for the body height and elegance, they had it from their father.

"Why the teacher himself didn't come?" Eralda's mother asked. This question was without any evil intent for others, but for Eralda, it was a kind of teasing. Her mother had sensed and understood that something was going on between her daughter and the literature teacher. She knew Eralda's sympathy and adoration for him, and, while making that question, she winked at Eralda, like saying to her, "you cannot fool me."

"I invited him too," Eralda answered, like being indifferent to mother intention, "but he said that he had a lot of things to prepare for Monday."

"Yes…, yes. Eralda invited him too," Monda supported her answer.

Their apartment was a simple one; a usual living room with the same furniture and fittings like in all Albanian families—two sofas, a dining table and chairs in the middle, and a sideboard (with cupboards for glasses, cups and porcelain articles, some drawers for table linens, bookshelves, and an open place for the TV set in the middle of it). There is an adjacent small kitchen (called annex) adjoining the living room (with the wood-burning stove in the middle, a sink in the corner, and a cupboard for food and dishes). Eralda's father was lain down on an ottoman next to the stove reading the Communist Party's daily newspaper, "The People's Voice." Everything in that apartment looked neat and clean, showing that a good housewife cared for that. There weren't expensive types of furniture or appliances, but everything was in its place. Some minutes later, her father finished reading the paper, and the sister finished with her hair, and they joined others in the living room, sitting on the sofas and chairs around the dining table. Father had been several times in Monda's city, Vlorë, and started asking her for people and places in her town. While the sister had never been there and asked Monda about summer beaches in the Ionian Sea and for the beautiful Ionian Riviera, that starts from Vlorë, continuing the entire south seaside of Albania, by the Ionian Sea.

"We have never been to a beach, and we don't know to swim." Eralda's sister complained, watching her father.

"You will go there only with your husband when you marry," father responded to her complaint, with loud laughter.

"As my husband did," mother ironized him in response, laughing with her daughters.

"But we have been busy, and we knew nothing about beaches and summer camps in that time," father justified himself.

"Come together with Eralda to spend some days in our house next summer," Monda told the sister. "We'll go together to the beach, where you can learn swimming too," Monda added, and it looked like they knew each other for a long time, and like being old friends already. Monda was liking Eralda, after every minute they were spending together. She liked Eralda very much not only for the beauty she saw from the first contact in the store, but for her wisdom too, for her desire and willpower to study, her high scores at school, her involvement in house works, and the preparation for dinner that she started as soon as they arrived home. "A beautiful and tireless girl," she found out and remembered the wrong opinion that girls and women, in general, whisper with jealousy to each other about the beautiful ones that supposedly are not as good housewives as other ordinary girls and women. "But there must be some exceptions," Monda concluded while noticing skillfulness, elegance, and charm in Eralda's moves while doing housework. In this case, old women would say: "She looks fascinating while doing household chores," (watching the skillful and charming way a girl or a woman moves around the house for cleaning, cooking, washing dishes, making beds or preparing the dinner table.) Monda watched and liked Eralda's body and especially her beautiful round-shaped big breasts, and she was thinking about her: "What a nice girl she is—a beautiful, lovely, genuine girl, and a tireless housewife at the same time."

"Blessed is he who will marry you," Monda told Eralda when she prepared the dinner table and invited everybody there.

All others laughed and obeyed Eralda's order, approaching and sitting around the dining table, following her arrangement.

"She cannot leave her mother," Eralda's mother said, conscious and convinced that Monda's visit to their home has a connection with Eralda's love for the literature teacher.

"What about you? Why did you leave your mother?" father teased his wife.

"Because of you. You hypnotized me with your beautiful truck," wife responded ironically to him.

"Oh…, 'Skoda—a lovely lorry,'" the elder brother spoke sarcastically. He had stayed silent all the evening, but when his mother mentioned his father's truck, he didn't resist, because he was unhappy that his father had been driving a very old "Skoda" for so many years and was not able to take one of the newest trucks called "Saurer."

"You have been working for such a long time there, and couldn't take a new "Saurer," his son expressed openly his preferred truck, that had recently arrived at the State Enterprise of Transportation, where his father was working.

"That's because the new trucks are for young chauffeurs, to lure easily young girls with them. My "Skoda" was a new truck when I needed it, back in our time. Do you remember it?" He asked his wife.

Everybody laughed while Eralda had put everything on the table. She had not forgotten anything, even small details, like napkins, spoons, forks, knives, glasses, and everything else in its place on the table. She also didn't forget to wash the hands of her little brother.

"Ada has told me that we have to wash hands every time before eating food," he spoke childishly, adding the joy of the evening, and making everybody happy.

The dinner was with a simple main course and side dishes, and not excessive, but Monda's mind remained to Eralda, which had prepared everything by herself, without any need to ask her mother or somebody else to help her.

"We will sleep together tonight," Monda told Eralda later, expressing her desire and her pleasure to spend more time with her.

"I told you before that I haven't had a sleepover with another girl for a very long time so that it will be fun," Eralda answered, approving her request.

It was Saturday evening—the day and the moment when everybody in a family takes the weekly shower. It happens just before Sunday; "the prophylactic day," as mother called it because it was the day used for a general cleaning of the house; or "the depot day," as father called it, by the expression used for the day when trucks are driven back in the enterprise's truck-servicing depot for cleaning and maintenance before being dispatched for service again. After six working days of the week, all family members must wash their bodies on Saturday evening, and their clothes will be boiled and hand-washed by mothers or sisters till the late hours of the evening. On Sunday morning, washed clothes will be hung up in ropes to dry outdoors and will be ironed Sunday evening (again by mothers or sisters), and will be ready to be worn again by everybody on Monday morning, to go to school or work.

After the dinner, Eralda went to take a shower, as the only one left. The other sister cleaned the dinner table and started to hand-wash dishes, while the rest of the family continued the talk and humor watching TV for some more minutes. Eralda left the bathroom and continued drying and combing her hair near the stove in the kitchen annex. Mother went to the bathroom, where she started to hand-wash the family's clothes. About ten o'clock, all beds were ready, prepared by the sister. Eralda and Monda would weld the two beds of the "small room," as they called the bedroom of two sisters.

It's a usual willingness and desire that girls like to share their bed with a girlfriend. When they are little girls, this is just a spontaneous will and a childish desire to just play tirelessly with each other under sheets and blankets. When they grow up in their adolescence years (watching and feeling those dramatic, magic changes that have just started and advanced so quickly in their girlish bodies), it seems like they want to sleep together just to play by touching each other in those parts where not any boy has arrived yet, poking and indulging each other, tittering and giggling in-between the warm white linens. It seems like just in this way, girls anticipate and prepare for the second one in their beds—their lover, their fiancé, their husband. Monda had slept with her girlfriends before, and Eralda had slept with Entela a long time ago, so both of them had experienced these joyful childish games, but this time was different because they had just met and known each other, and it would be the first time for them to share the bed, and above all, they were not little girls anymore. Monda thought that Eralda didn't deserve to be touched in those beautiful magic parts of hers because they had to remain untouched, waiting for the one that would merit them. She had to keep and preserve them fresh, intact, virgin, full of feelings, and passion for the man that would deserve her soul and her body.

When they lay in bed, Monda got impressed by observing how clean and white the sheets and pillowcases were. They wore their pajamas and entered under the sheets and blankets quickly to warm each other because the bedroom was colder than the living room. Sheets and pillowcases had a pleasant detergent aroma and a kind of deodorant used for clothes in their wardrobe. But another better scent came from Eralda's body, which enticed Monda to push herself further toward her. They crossed their arms around each other, brought their faces together and their hair mixed, at the same time, their breasts touched and felt each other, and Monda couldn't keep her mouth:

"What a lucky man he who will marry you..., and these...," Monda whispered, touching and shaking Eralda's breasts. They laughed and tightened near each other. After that icebreaker, Monda, as the youngest one, got free of shyness and tickled Eralda in different parts, right there where she knew that the girl's body might be more sensitive, causing some laughter to Eralda and herself.

"You are warm," Eralda told Monda.

"While you are hot," and they both laughed loudly, "I mean, you are gorgeous. You are lovely. Why don't you wear some makeup? It would make you even more beautiful," Monda said to her.

"I have never used any cosmetics," Eralda answered to her advice.

And like that, like two old friends in each other's arms, they fell asleep after being tired of their talk, moves, and jokes. Monda was the first to fell asleep while Eralda stayed awake a little longer, thinking about that day's events. She was feeling happy that she was winning the Monda's heart, his sister's heart. But the problem was that Monda, for her part, knew nothing about their relationship until now. "What will happen when Ardian tells her? Will she be annoyed by this trick?" Eralda continued with her thoughts about things that she would prepare for breakfast until she fell asleep, tightened against Monda's body, with crossed legs and arms to exchange and keep their warmth. The very last seconds before falling asleep, she felt Monda's hands around her chest, wishing to be Ardian's hands.

When Monda awoke in the morning, she found herself alone in bed and saw the daylight outside the window. Eralda had been got up much earlier; she had bought and boiled the milk, had cooked some pita and had placed butter and jam on the table, everything ready for breakfast. When Monda entered the living room, Alda was dressing the little brother caressing, embracing, teasing, and laughing with him.

"Do you see what a good sister I have," he told Monda, with his joyous childish voice.

"Do you see what a good little brother I have," Eralda repeated after him, using the same funny childish voice, and hugging her brother tightly.

They had breakfast together. Father and the elder brother had already left home. "What a good family," Monda thought. She hugged the Eralda's mother, sister, and little brother, and went together with Eralda. Mother invited her to come back for lunch, along with Eralda. Walking toward the store, side by side with Eralda, Monda felt happy and almost proud that she was walking on the city's streets with a beautiful girl, perhaps…, with the most beautiful girl in town.

"How many boys have proposed you until now?" Monda asked Eralda, bringing laughter to both of them.

"Only one," Eralda answered, speaking earnestly and jokingly at the same time.

"They don't dare to talk to you because you are so beautiful. Have you already decided on that one?" Monda continued the same subject.

"We are very much in love with each other, but we have not told our families yet, either he or I," Eralda answered, with a voice that sounded more serious and less joking.

Monda thought that it was a good thing that this beautiful girl was in love with a man, but at the same time, found it to be a bad thing for the fact that this sexy girl had given up so soon, and maybe to the first man that had proposed her. They approached the store and saw Ardian standing in front of it, waiting for them.

"What punctuality," Ardian said. "It is exactly nine o'clock," he added, showing his watch.

"Good morning," both girls greeted at the same time.

"How were your evening and night?" Ardian asked them when Eralda was opening the store door.

"Very good," Monda answered immediately, giving a wink to Eralda, an act that Ardian saw as well.

"Why did you wink at her?" he asked Monda.

"Because we slept together," Monda answered, laughing joyfully.

This answer teased Ardian, and he wanted to say, "I wish it were me," but he couldn't speak in this way in front of his sister, and he just stayed silent, thinking and wishing to have the opportunity to spend a night in bed with Eralda.

"And we had a delicious breakfast as well: pitas, butter, milk, and cherry jam. We have brought two pitas for you too," Monda continued showing Ardian her bag. "I didn't want to take, but Eralda had already prepared them for you," she justified herself.

"Very good, because I miss the home-cooked food," Ardian answered, approving Eralda's action.

"Have you ever asked anybody, and they didn't bring you home-cooked food?" Eralda teased him, with her characteristic beautiful smile on her face, which made her even more attractive. She had brought him some home-cooked food a couple of times because she already knew this desire of him. "I'm spending all of my life with food from dormitory's canteen," he had told Eralda several times.

"Monda and I have other things to do now," Ardian told Eralda, after some minutes. "May we go," he asked Eralda's permission.

"Mom wants Monda back for lunch. You can join us too," Eralda added, shaking their hands.

They left the store and continued walking through the boulevard, eastward toward the park.

"We'll meet her at the park," he told Monda, after some minutes of walking in silence.

"Eralda was very nice…," Monda spoke, thinking still for the great time she had spent with Eralda, while she had almost forgotten the reason for her trip to Elbasan.

"What's her name," she asked suddenly for the girl they were going to meet, remembering why she had come to Elbasan.

"Eralda," Ardian answered her question coldly.

"Wow? Her name is Eralda too?" Monda was surprised by the name.

"Where is she from?" she asked the second question.

"From here. From Elbasan," Ardian answered very short.

Monda understood it at last and was about to shout at him, "You...,
bastard. Why did you cheat me? Why didn't you tell me last night? Wow...?
How did I behave with her? How many teases and foolish questions I have
asked her?" But Monda didn't say any of these and just continued thinking
without saying any word at all. "Eralda will be Ardian's wife? What a nice
girl! What a beautiful girl! What a versatile girl, and what a good housewife at
the same time!"

"You, my brother, have been so brave. How did you dare to propose
such a beautiful girl? What about mom? What is she going to say? She is
expecting the girl to be a student of the pedagogical institute or a college
graduate girl...," Monda told him.

"Eralda is going to attend the pedagogical institute next year," he tried
to encourage her.

"But she is still an evening high school student," Monda answered to
him, like trying to tell him the hurdle their mother would bring.

"That's why I invited you here. I need your help. You will go back
home to tell them what a nice girl your brother has chosen," Ardian told
Monda, putting his hand on her neck. In a meanwhile, they had arrived at
the bench in the park and sat down.

"This is our bench," he told Monda.

"It means that you come here.... What a nice girl she is. I loved her
very much. She is a lovely girl and a perfect housewife. She is beautiful,
clever, and wise too. But..., it will be challenging for me when I return
home," and she stopped for some minutes, with a lot of thoughts in her
mind, and then she started speaking again:

"But..., there are a lot of beautiful female students in the pedagogical
institute," Monda stayed silent for a while before continuing: "Eralda is a
perfect girl, and as it seems, you have already made your mind up."

"Eralda is more beautiful, and cleverer, and braver than any other
pedagogical institute's student," he spoke firmly.

"I saw her, and I believe it...," Monda spoke with a low voice and
thinking for a while. Then she spoke again:

"Why did you cheat me? I feel very embarrassed to return and meet
Eralda again. I don't like what you did to me. Keep it in your mind. I'm not
going to help you at all. I'm not going to defend your choice at home," she
threatened Ardian jokingly.

"But I'll take you for lunch to the restaurant of the tourists' hotel, where
I'll treat you with the most delicious dessert. I'll buy a zuppa inglese for you,

and you will become a good sister that is going to help her brother in need," Ardian told Monda, standing up and pulling her from her hands.

"What a good idea," Monda spoke joyfully. "But we are going to take Eralda with us as well," she added.

"It would be a good thing, but she cannot join us because she is in the working time now," Ardian answered.

"But we'll take a dessert to her, after that," Monda found the solution.

"Yes, of course," he accepted her solution.

They walked through the boulevard again, visited some other stores, and arrived at the tourists' hotel, the highest building in the city center, with its luxury restaurant and café on the ground floor. Monda had to leave before the evening, and they didn't have too much time to spend together. After having lunch there, with a dessert in her hands, they returned to the Eralda's store. Monda approached her, hugged her, and said:

"I am very happy for you two. Even though you tricked me".

"It wasn't me. It was his idea," Eralda answered, laughing and justifying herself by pointing to Ardian.

"Congratulations, and good luck with your school," Monda told her, giving the dessert.

"Thank you. You too," Eralda answered, shaking hands and hugging Monda.

Ardian and Monda walked toward the train station, discussing what to do and what to say to their parents.

"I think it will be tough..., for you and for me," she said while approaching the train platform. "However, don't lose Eralda because she is such a nice and lovely girl, and you cannot find another one like her. We have to try, and we'll try hard, though," Monda encouraged him.

Monda greeted him from the train window again while the train was leaving the station. Ardian stayed there, without moving from the station platform until the train disappeared from his eyes, running among the houses in the city's western periphery.

"A difficult trip. A challenging mission," Ardian said to himself while leaving the train station. The train toot reached his ears from a far distance, sounding like a moving, remote, fading echo, warning and foreboding an impossible mission for him and his love.

15

On the morrow, on Monday afternoon, Ardian received a telephone call notification from the Post Telephone Telecommunications office, called PTT. It was a way of communication, where relatives from different villages, towns, and cities spoke with each other using small telephonic booths installed in the PTT offices. A notification is sent from the sender to the receiver one day in advance, assigning the exact time when the three-minute-long prepaid telephonic communication will take place on the morrow. Ardian received this telephone call notification just one day after Monda's visit in Elbasan and after her arrival with her news in Vlorë. So, he understood at once that the news had embittered his parents, and it became clearer from the sender's name; it was his mother's name instead of the father's name as usual. He had been thinking about his parents' reaction since the moment he saw Monda off at the train station, but this unexpected telephone call notification was a clear sign of his parents' adverse reaction, and that worried him even more than before. "Mom has gone completely crazy," he thought.

The telephone call that took place on Tuesday afternoon was short, harsh, and nervous. It was only his mother speaking from the other side of the telephonic wireline, who didn't ask about his health or other things but entered immediately and directly on the issue.

"You have to stop immediately the affair you have started at the night school," his mother spoke loudly, using and stressing the words "night school" instead of "evening school."

"But we have already decided mom. How can I leave her?"

"Forget about her from this moment. You must leave her now, and you can do this because you are a man, a professor, and thus you deserve much more than a shopkeeper and a night school student."

"She is a very nice girl, mom, and she is going to attend the pedagogical institute too."

"Listen to me, son. You coaxed your sister, but not us, even if fallen from the sky that girl to be, she is not and will never be for us. Such a bride will never step into our home. When you come back home for New Year's Eve holidays, I don't want to hear about this issue anymore. That's what I say. Did you listen well? Was I clear?"

"I can't, mom. We love each other...," but his mother hung up the phone without trying to listen to Ardian's words and explanation, causing him more worries and trouble.

What should he choose between these two loves; mother's love or his girl's love? He knew that his mother was full of prejudices, that she was expecting more from her son, and that she has been dreaming a better chance and fate for him. "They are not able to understand that just Eralda is the best fate for me. She will be a wonderful wife, not just for me, but for them too. What a pity? What a shame, when they humiliate the other person, without knowing her at all. What about me? Why don't they trust me? Do they think that an ordinary girl, or a bad and immoral one, has taken my mind? Why do parents have such a lack of trust in their children? In most cases, they don't agree with their choice, their love, and their decision to choose the friend of their own life? Why is this kind of family obligation so strong? How am I going to face and challenge this family pressure? No..., no! I will never leave Eralda. I will never lose her. I am going to marry her and live our life together, here, in Elbasan, far away from my family. Parents will be attenuated someday, and we'll approach each other again, after some time, when they will understand and be convinced that Eralda is a wonderful girl and she will be a wonderful wife. Look what happened with Monda. She loved Eralda from just one evening she spent with her. Grandma is going to love her very quickly, as well."

During the remaining days of December, Ardian tried hard not to show his worries in front of Eralda. He never told her about the telephone call with his mother and the disapproval of his parents. Despite his attempts to hide these things from her, Eralda's eye understood very well his inner spirit situation. That's how girls in love are. They distinguish what's going on with their lovers just by looking in their eyes. They can read their thoughts, sorrows, sufferings, and worries in their lover's eyes, even though they may be trying to hide these things. Ardian couldn't tell Eralda anything about his parents' objection, and especially his mother's attitude, because he didn't know how to explain it to her. He was afraid of offending her. He already knew very well her strong character and her personality type as a combination of sanguine and phlegmatic temperament that is something rare among girls. He was sure that if he told Eralda about his parents' objection and pressure on him, it would create a dangerous rift in his relationship with her and for the destiny of their love. And after that, Eralda, with her kind of personality, would not try at all to fill and close that rift, but she would go away instead, making the gap between them vaster, like a dangerous abyss, more challenging to pass and to recover afterward. She had what it takes to do it, and she was capable of doing it. She was different from all other girls, and as such, she would never beg him as most of the girls do to their lovers. He remembered her telling him that she would never marry somebody that is undetermined or hesitant for marriage. Thus, there were a lot of reasons for him not to say to her about his family objection to his choice.

During those two remaining weeks, they spoke a lot about Monda's "successful visit," as Ardian called it, and he said Eralda that Monda had liked her very much and was very happy with his choice.

"Your lovely sister was a little bit talkative," Eralda told him, speaking sincerely as always. "But she was agile and brave, with a good soul, like you," she added. "And…, regarding her school results, she wasn't like you at all," Eralda told him.

So, both of them thought and discussed for that kind of bridge between the two and Ardian's parents, that understanding bridge built by Monda's visit to Elbasan.

Eralda, from her part, like a smart girl, had understood that Ardian would have some difficulties in convincing his parents for his choice. It was understandable that his parents would expect him to marry a girl with a college degree, and, from her deep sincerity, she didn't blame his parents for their point of view and their expectation from their son. Eralda had understood the aim of Monda's visit to Elbasan, and she was happy that Ardian was convinced and so sure that Monda would like her brother's future wife. But she was worried while thinking about his parent's possible disapproval. She felt scared when she thought about it. She imagined two opposing forces: Ardian, extending his hand to pull her toward himself, battling against his parents that were pulling Ardian away from her, trying not to allow him to reach her hands. She wished that Ardian reach her hands, seize and pull her toward him, but when she visualized Ardian's parents trying to pull him away from her, making it more difficult for him to reach her, she didn't like it at all, and she stepped back, pulling her hands away from him and going back without him. "No…, no," she shouted, terrified, and waking up from this nightmare. "Why do I think so badly about them?" she tried to give some hope to herself. "Ardian has not told me that his parents don't want this marriage. What about Monda? She was very happy for me, and she is going to say good words about me to her parents, so they are going to trust their son and their daughter. What about Ardian? He doesn't seem so optimistic these days. He seems worried, and he looks like hiding something from me."

The last days of December were passing in this way, filled with love and worries at the same time, but each one kept the concerns inside themselves and didn't show it because they both didn't want to spoil the beautiful moments they spent together. In the meantime, both felt that it was not the same love fire coming out of them, or better say the flame was still there, blazing fiercely inside them, but something hampered it in coming outside as fully as it was inside. Eralda had some difficulties to focus on studying and preparing her homework, and she scored two nines in two school subjects those days, putting in danger the grade point average of the first semester that would end on December 28. Ardian was feeling even worse. He didn't open any book at all those days and didn't make any additional preparation for lectures and classes.

They wrote New Year cards to each other and exchanged them while sitting on their bench in the park, in darkness, where cannot read them. It was the last evening that they were spending together on their bench for that year—the year of their love, the year 1983. Eralda closed her store one hour before the closing time that evening, to spend more time with her lover on this last date before his departure to his city, where he would spend one week for the winter school break and New Year's Eve holidays, in his home with his parents.

"Now, in the wintertime, even though it is a little bit colder, it is better for lovers, because the dusk and following darkness start earlier, before five o'clock," she said to Ardian, with an expressive face.

"And you have to close the store earlier more often, like today," he advised her.

"Oh, poor me. What will I care more about? About my job, or about…?

"About your future husband," Ardian finished Eralda's sentence.

Oh…, what a great pleasure and happiness his words, "your future husband," brought to her. It was not just words, but it was his firm

117

conviction that he would be her husband, and she would be his wife someday. He had never used these words before. This certainty of his kept her hope alive, and she, in return, gave him all her love, with all the strength of her soul, and she loved him more and more and didn't stop herself and her love for him. Only one thing she never allowed him. Something that he wanted from her and had asked her several times, and he had tried to take it forcefully a couple of times, but in vain. Despite the great pleasure and satisfaction that she felt somewhere in that mysterious depth of her body and her soul—places that she only discovered when he kissed, rubbed and squeezed her in every part of her body—and despite the lust's call and the great desire for more while being engulfed in flames of the love's fire, she always found the strength it takes to stop him and herself from further advances of the lust's invitation toward other greater pleasures. She gave him all the parts of her body, except the piece and the magic act of that final step that the lover would earn only in the matrimonial bed. That's what most of the girls do. But few girls don't obey such an unwritten rule. They cannot find the strength to stop themselves and their lover in those moments of maximum pleasure, and they are not to blame for this. They do this just for the sake of their love for somebody, who sometimes might not be loyal till the end, and don't become her future husband, and thus, these girls become victims of themselves, victims of their love for somebody else. The great responsibility falls entirely on girls, while men don't feel such a burden at all.

It takes a lot of strength and courage to face and challenge those culminant moments of love, passion, desire, excitement, and lust because a luring force of the magic of love invites and pull you toward new pleasures, not experienced before; toward a greater satisfaction, the greatest one, the final one, but the logic and reasoning win over the feelings, the passion, desire, excitement and over the lust of the moment, even though they are reasonable and logical too. Girls want to go with dignity and proudly toward the first night in their matrimonial bed, and that's why they become smart and determined in challenging such a delicate and challenging situation in those luring moments. These intelligent girls allow you to go as far as you deserve, and give you as much space as they consider reasonable. They will enable you to seize areas of their body following a logical order, like telling you: "I gave you my lips, my breasts, my thighs, my heart, and my soul, to show that I accept and love you, but I can't allow you more than what you deserve now. You as well, asked me for all these things because, as you say, you love me too, but for the moment, don't ask for more."

"We'll do it only with the permission of our parents, and after having a marriage certificate," Eralda had told him several times, justifying her resistance in those decisive and delicate moments.

Ardian understood and appreciated this approach, sincerity, and maturity of her. He had heard people saying that men must check the girl's virginity before proposing her for marriage, but in his relationship with Eralda, he couldn't ask her such a foolish question. Ardian didn't need such a test. Her conduct, her humbleness, her character, and her love for him were proper proof that he was going to marry a perfect girl. "What if…?" a wicked thought crossed his mind time after time. "What if… she does not allow me because she is afraid of discovering that she is not a virgin. Perhaps she might have made a mistake during the 'teenage adventurous years,' as she called the years in the morning high school. No…, no. It's impossible." He cleared his evil thoughts about her. He knew her for four months already, and she never said or acted in the way of creating such suspicions.

Eralda was terrified every time she thought that he could leave her. Every girl has such suspicion in a relationship with a man, even when everything looks and goes alright. Girls believe that the pain of a possible separation must not be accompanied by the worry of the loss of virginity. Even though girls themselves would like to go further and harvest the culminant pleasure of love in its superior magic level, they still find the strength it takes to stop the man and themselves as well, because they have the right suspicion of a potential separation. And that's an excellent precaution for them. Some girls have not applied this precaution measure and have suffered such a thing. It happens to fail in a relationship, but at least you have not invested everything of yours in this love, at least you are still a virgin, and such a thing would help and make things easier to find and finalize another better love and continue a normal life.

"What about men?" Eralda thought. "Why they don't feel the same responsibility and accountability? I think they might have proof of their virginity too, but girls don't know and cannot see it. Do men have exclusive rights to play with girls and cheat on them one after another?

Their last date before Ardian's trip to Vlorë was gentler and more silent than previous ones, but they stayed together longer, spending most of the time in silent embraces, cuddles, and caresses, with their arms crossed around each other. That evening they felt more worries and uncertainty for the fate of the future of their love. But at the same time, there were some other vigorous moments, with kissing and loving action as a self-critique for evil thoughts and suspicion that were crossing through their heads. Then, Eralda became more melancholic, and some teardrops slid down her cheeks and chin. She was experiencing an awful feeling. "He will go to his family just for a week, and it goes fast, but..., how he would come back. With what results? What will his parents tell him?" She had started to suspect that Ardian himself was not sure for this love, and the mentality of his parents— according to which he had to marry a college graduated girl—was rooted in his mind as well. "Or..., maybe he already feels sated with me and wants to use the parents' disapproval as a 'strong reason' to justify the separation, like some guys do when they want to break up a relationship. And..., maybe that's why he has insisted even more for sexual intercourse, just to take something more before dumping me." His persistence in this direction made Eralda more suspicious. That evening, he was making the same request several times, with such insistence that just added more to Eralda's suspicion. "Maybe he has made his mind up to dump me. Maybe he has already started another relationship with a pedagogical institute female student?" and at this moment, more tears fell from her eyes, and he wiped them softly, with his fingers, saying to her: "I'm sorry, Alda." And in this cozy, intimate moment, Eralda collected herself. "He is a good guy. He doesn't deserve my suspicion and my fear," she thought. "His parents are good ones too, but...?"

That evening they didn't speak, didn't smile and didn't laugh at all. The date of that evening went through a melancholic atmosphere. "Love, Hope, and Despair," might be the caption of that night. Ardian started fearing and suspecting from Eralda's coldness too. The entire walk toward her home passed in silence. The traditional long kiss near her building's entrance was very short, being interrupted without waiting for disturbing steps of other people approaching them, as they always did. They separated by whispering greetings, "see you next week," said with a half voice by both of them. Eralda started walking up the stairs, feeling the knot of tears in her throat. She entered her apartment, went to the bathroom, and started crying, spending some more minutes there, to collect herself before entering the living room.

Ardian walked toward institute dormitory taking with himself great desperation and sadness. He had always envisioned their love, like being two alpinists climbing a high mountain full of joy and happiness. They stop time after time and raise their heads, looking at the mountain summit where the two will climb and arrive together. But..., after they come there, right on the top of the mountain, they don't see any other peak to occupy, and they only see the downward slope waiting for them. Suddenly they feel terrified. After conquering the top of the mountain, they have to start the sharp downhill. They have to go down now because there is not any other higher mountaintop to climb to, to reach, and to occupy it. What a scary situation. What about their love? Did it reach its peak so quickly, and they must go down now? "No..., no..., it's impossible. Love lives and lasts all the marital life," he had heard by older people. When does love reach the highest height, the greatest pleasure, and happiness? It might be like this; like love is walking and climbing in some challenging paths, reaching and occupying lower elevations first, and after that going down and then climbing up again towards higher heights; like an endless ascending, reaching numerous heights, until they die together, taking their love with them on "the other side," without reaching never to the highest mountain peak. "Yes..., it has to be like this," he thought. "It has to happen like this. Let us never reach the highest mountain peak. Let us only see the mountaintop from down up. Let us see the heights we want to reach and walk happily toward it all the time, without reaching there, because if we reach there, after that, we have to start the dangerous downward slope, toward the deep chasm, where we will be violently rolled, and our love will be severely harmed with everlasting consequences for both of us."

He couldn't find peace from all these thoughts that occupied his head. "Did we reach the peak so quick?" he thought again. "What was such a scary coldness of her about? What is this cliff created in front of us, like an abyss appearing in front of the alpinists? Do we need to go down now? Are we going to roll down with a fast speed toward where all this love started, right where we didn't know each other, right where the strong bird of love had not seen and had not lifted us yet? What a terrifying situation? But how can we escape this joint climbing? It's like alpinists abandoning the climbing of a difficult, daring, attractive new path, but they never do that; they never give up. How can we forget all that difficult long way we have passed together, all the heights we have reached together, all that happiness we found and enjoyed together? Why will we retreat and surrender in front of the new heights we have in front of us? Where will all this happiness that we have reached until now, go? Where will it hide? Where will it be forgotten? No..., no. It will never happen. Our love and happiness can never be hidden and can never be forgotten. We, like alpinists, will never give up. Our love is going to live forever, as long as our life." Ardian reached his conclusion.

16

Ardian arrived home around noon, where he found his grandmother and sister.

"We were expecting you to come last evening," the grandmother said to him.

"I told them that you were not going to come yesterday," Monda interfered. "And it was a beautiful evening yesterday, wasn't it, brother? How is Eralda?" she continued with her questions.

"Eralda is very good, and she sends her greetings especially for you and grandma," Ardian tried to win the heart of his grandmother, to have her support later.

"But I don't know her, and she doesn't know me," the grandmother said smartly.

"She knows you very well because I have told her a lot of things about you," Ardian said, to convince her.

"I have spoken to her about you as well," Monda added.

"All grandmothers are alike," Ardian continued his attempt. "Eralda says the same about her grandmother, which lives in a village, in comparing her with you."

"Why don't you show me a photograph of her?" the grandmother asked Ardian.

A photo...? But he didn't have any pictures of her. Eralda had told him that she had very few photographs, and for the last two years, she hadn't taken any photos at all. "I'm not fond of photography, and I'm not so photogenic," she had told him one evening when they had mentioned the photographs. But Ardian had not thought any longer of such a thing. He had her live picture in his eyes, mind, heart, and soul. He didn't need a printed picture because he had a lot of images of her in his mind, like an alive figure, with her voice, her colors, her moves, her body curves. But…, he needed a photograph of her right now to show it to his grandmother and parents. He hadn't thought about that before. If he had one, it would serve him a lot now, to show them how beautiful she is, and they would like her just from the picture.

His mother came back home around one o'clock. After she hugged her son, entered directly on the issue:

"You have started dalliances in the night school," she spoke ironically of his love with Eralda.

"I have just followed your advice, mom," Ardian answered her.

"That relationship was meaningless," his mother said, looking very pleased because she thought that Ardian had followed her last advice she had given to him on that telephone call two weeks ago.

"No, mother…, no," Ardian interrupted her because he understood the misunderstanding of his mother. "I mean the usual, continuous advice you have always given to me. 'Open your eyes, son. Find a good girl. When are you going to bring a bride home?' And here you are. I have found a perfect girl like I want her to be. And I'm sure that you, too, will love her as soon as you know her."

"We have not advised you to find a shopkeeper…, a student from the night school…," she stressed the last two words ironically, and then continued with a softer voice:

"Listen to me, son. There are a lot of good female students in your pedagogical institute, coming from different cities, even from our city, and all of them will become teachers. It's up to you, and you can choose the best one among them because you are a professor. Your relationship with a shopkeeper, a night school female student, is meaningless and shame for your societal level. You are going to lose the respect of all your friends, students, colleagues, and professors. Think of what people are going to say," his mother ended her speech with the excruciating expression that Ardian hated so much—"What are people going to say?"

"Mom, you are right about what you say, and I don't disagree, but that beautiful feeling, something that you had experienced by yourself when you were young, knows by itself when it is born and for which girl it is born, and it does not follow such advice. It is a real feeling, a gut feeling, and it doesn't get wrong because it comes from the heart. Above all, our love is a reciprocal one, being felt equally from both sides. I can find a female institute student, as you say, and I'll try to love her, but I'm not sure that such a beautiful, sweet feeling of love will be born, so that I have to love her only because she is an institute student, and because she will be my future wife, but I would never love her with such a passion, feeling and fire as I love Eralda. And then, it will be the same calculated reason for love from the part of the supposed institute student. She will not have any real love feelings for me too, but she must love me just because I'm a professor, so just for interest, and she would never love me as Eralda does. No need to tell you the story of our love, but you have to now that it is not a dalliance, as you sarcastically just named it, and it is not a love just to live the moment for both of us; it's not a love for interest, but it's a deep love, with foundation, full of passion, such a love that both of us tried to hide, to stop and suppress for a long time, but couldn't stop it, because it was powerful, like your love with dad, that you have proudly told us about so many times. Your parents too didn't accept your love, but your love won, it survived, and time showed that it was a solid marriage".

"Don't try in vain to persuade me with such romantic things," his nervous mother interrupted him. "I will never accept this relationship, and you don't tell me about it anymore. I don't want to hear about it anymore," she continued speaking loudly, standing up and leaving the living room after finishing her words.

A deep silence occupied the room. Grandmother, Monda, and Ardian remained silenced in the living room, trying to find their arguments for this relationship. Ardian understood this thing when he saw grandmother and Monda in their eyes. Grandmother smiled at him, making a face of sorrow and sadness.

"I, as well, have not accepted your parents' love in the beginning. Such a thing happens so often with a lot of mothers. That's because we just thought of her best at that time. Your mother was attending the pedagogical high school to become a teacher, while he that is your father today, was just an ordinary worker, but nobody knows how life will go on and what it will bring for everybody. The same thing is happening to your mother now. She wishes the best of luck for her son and a good life for you and your future family. I have a strong trust in you and your choice, though. Monda has told me a lot of good words about Eralda. She has described her the same as if I had her here, in front of me. And, when a sister likes the girl chosen by her brother, it means the girl must be a very nice one, indeed."

Grandmother's warm words gave some hope to Ardian, and he tried to release himself, but he couldn't face the choking up. He stood up and went to the kitchen sink, like he wanted to drink water, to hide the tears dropping from his eyes, which he wiped with his hands. Monda and grandmother were observing his actions and saw what he was doing, and they watched each other with sorrow for what was happening to Ardian. Monda left the living room and went to her mother in her bedroom.

"Mom, Ardian is weeping, and tears don't lie. He loves her very much, and she loves him too. I told you she is a nice, lovely girl and with maximum grades in high school. She will attend the pedagogical institute and become a teacher too," Monda told her mother, and she felt the tears gathering like a knot in her throat, and burning eyes, before tears started dropping from her eyes.

Ardian's tears touched grandmother, and she understood how much he loved that girl, just by believing in his tears. She decided to discuss this issue with his parents later on but remained afraid that her stubborn daughter would never accept this marriage.

Ardian's father arrived home two hours later. He worked as a mechanic in a cement factory near the city. He was tall and energetic, with his body still maintaining and showing the energy of its young age. He hugged Ardian with his strong arms and hands and then observed him from head to toe. Ardian seemed frail and feeble, with a pale face, and father felt and expressed his sorrow to him:

"Professor…, you are a young lad. Don't surrender your youth so fast. Go and do some physical activity and sports. You don't look well this year. You are going down. I have always told you not to spend all the time on books, inside the room. Go and help the campus workers sometimes, and don't be ashamed of that. Are you playing soccer with your students anymore, or not? Or…, are you afraid of losing your authority by playing soccer with them? Do you do the morning workout, or not? Your arms and hands are becoming softer like ladies' arms and hands. Your face is becoming white and yellow. You are getting weaker. Do you eat food or not?"

"He is suffering from anorexia caused by his dalliances at the night school. That's why he so frail and feeble," his wife interrupted him while preparing the dining table because she couldn't wait to express her fury.

Her husband made an artificial cough and looked reproachfully at his wife. In a meanwhile, Monda had prepared the table, and they sat around it to have lunch together. Father was the last one to join them at the dining table, after changing his clothes and washing his hands. Some minutes passed in silence, and the only sounds were spoons crackles on the china plates. All five of them were staying quiet, seemingly waiting for somebody to start the talk left in half. Father understood this situation and was the first one to break the silence.

"My son, I think you don't need to hurry. Just continue with your studies. You have already passed the postgraduate exams successfully, and this is an excellent start for you. Now it's time to pursue your path of education toward the 'candidate of science' degree. And then, the time to decide for your future wife will arrive by itself. That's because starting a relationship and marriage now brings other problems and spoils your studies. So, try to postpone this kind of trouble for a later time. You can wait for at least two or three more years before starting a serious relationship with a girl and deciding for your future wife sometime before your thirties. That's what happened to me; this girl hindered me from studying," he pointed in the direction of his wife, "otherwise, I would have attended the university." His father tried to bring some humor to the dining table, but he saw that it was a failed attempt. Nobody smiled or laughed. Nobody raised his head. Then he spoke more directly and shorter: "Just try to push and keep this love away from yourself. Continue studying. Do more physical activities and sports. It will be difficult in the beginning, but with time passing, it will go away little by little".

Ardian thought that his father, too, had become an egoist. He was expecting more from his son. Mother was and spoke openly against this love, while father didn't accept this love because he didn't like that his son to forsake studying, or at least, this was just his justification to avoid disapproving his love directly. He had always advised him: "Stay away from girls. Focus on your studies. Time for love will come by itself." This advice from his father had been applied very well by Ardian until four months ago. That's why he completed the undergraduate degree courses and passed three postgraduate exams with excellent results. He had seen many of his friends losing a lot of time dealing with girls. He always felt pity for the way they were spending their time with endless talks and arguments with those girls in front of the main gate of girls' dormitory. Few of the male students were behaving like being "Don Juan" (the legendary, fictional libertine), even though they weren't successful at all in their "girl hunting" just by stalking them. These kinds of students used to mock Ardian by calling him "angler" because he studied very hard and spent a lot of time "fishing" in the institute's library, which was called "the fishpond" by those "smart guys."

These words were name-calling used by those that "were born clever" and didn't need to study at all. From the other side, they were trying with all the means to score a "five," which is the lowest grade sufficient to pass the academic years and graduate, having a college diploma in their pocket. Ardian didn't feel bad leaving aside his books only when he played soccer, playing guitar in his room, or going to the dancing parties. He was correct in dividing his time, following the principle of choosing and applying an excellent ratio between the busy time spent on studying and the free time spent for recreation.

Ardian always thought that the disproportion between the time students spend on studying and the leisure time they spend on recreation is the main reason and the weakness that causes failure in schools. And it happens to most of the children, teenagers, and college students. At such a delicate young age, everybody has the right to enjoy the free, golden years of childhood and youth. But, at the same time, they have to think and work for their future that, strangely enough, arrives faster than perceived, and lasts much longer than the present time of the young age. Spoiling this ratio at a younger age brings negative consequences for everybody in the coming adult years, and this is the crucial contradiction that brings failure to most of the people. Ardian never included in his concept of leisure time things like never-ending empty talks with girls and about girls, and he never spent time bickering and arguing with his friends about petty and trivial matters. This conduct made him look like a lonely guy, even though he liked and respected all his school friends, but sometimes he loved more staying alone, because in this way he had more time to spend with books, in his room or at the institute's library. He used to go to theaters very rarely, just for new movies, and he never went to the soccer stadium of the city. He thought that it was better to play soccer with friends than going to watch how others play soccer in the stadium. He only watched TV in the dormitory's TV room, once or twice a week, when beautiful movies were on.

But now something has changed in his life. The change's name was Eralda. He was spending more time staying and talking with Eralda and thinking about her. It became like a leisure time activity, to which he was devoting a lot of time now. Though this great love was not just a recreational activity; it was transformed into a need for him, bringing great joy and pleasure, and became an obligation too, that now was causing a great worry and concern. Before and after any of entertainment, you can focus on studying or concentrate in other professional things, but now that he was in

127

love with Eralda, with all these worries and uncertainties about parent's acceptance, it couldn't go away from his mind and didn't allow him to do anything else. Love worries and insecurities make you feel stressed and fall in desperation, and so often you feel a useless, meaningless emptiness.

After they had finished lunch, when Monda started moving the dishes away, it was the grandmother that opened the talk again.

"My darling daughter...," she addressed to Ardian's mother, "let us not interfere with Ardian's life and his essential decisions because he is an adult now. He knows better than us what he is doing. It's easy for you when you boast about your son and feel satisfied with his achievement. You feel proud when you say: 'We have a clever son. He studies hard, and he speaks two foreign languages. He has scored splendid grades, and he was assigned as a professor at the pedagogical institute. He continues postgraduate studies, and he will earn the 'candidate of science' degree, etc.' So, you speak proudly about him, and you like to brag. But why you don't believe in him now? Listen to me, my daughter. You are making the same mistake that we, your parents, made with you years ago. Ardian has always listened to your advice, but he already has his right to decide on his own for his life and his future, because he is a clever man, and I don't believe that he can mistake".

It looked like a heated argument, or even strife or a quarrel was about to begin, and they would start quarreling loudly and yelling at each other. But it didn't happen. This family has never had any quarrels. Every time they understood that they were approaching a possible harsh argument among themselves, all of them would retreat immediately from such a situation, like following and obeying an order. The same thing happened there right now. Nobody spoke after grandmother's words, and they all stayed silent and each one thinking on their own. Ardian's mother had to shout, disagreeing with her mother, and she had the words she had to say right in her mouth, but the family's conduct and its unwritten rule, made her stay silent, and she didn't open her mouth, didn't say anything, keeping inside the frustration. "Let us all try to extinguish the fire and not pour gasoline on it," was their father's advice, which they applied in such situations. "The first thought belongs to the horse, the second thought belongs to the horseman," was another expression the father used to de-escalate the case, and all the family members followed his bright advice. That's why this family had never quarreled, either the parents or the children and grandmother. It wasn't because they didn't have any different opinions, but they restrained themselves in such moments when everybody else would shout defending his argument and view. The retreat before a possible quarrel brought the possibility that each one of them to think and analyze his words and actions, and later, the blood and heads would be colder, thoughts more mature, with better-thought decisions and actions. That's why that afternoon nobody spoke after grandmother, but all of them stayed in silence for several minutes before father started another talk related to his work in the factory telling something funny that had happened there. Ardian accepted this retreat too. "I'll discuss it later with dad," he thought. "I'm going to discuss it with him in person."

"We…, I mean your mother and I, have thought about that and have discussed that since the day Monda told us," his father told Ardian later. "That's why your mother and I have the same conclusion and the same advice for you; we don't change it and let us not discuss it before New Year's Eve celebration night. But…, despite our advice, it is you to decide, and after your final decision, tell us."

"But I have already decided it, dad," Ardian said.

"Not this week. You have to think once more about our advice and then, around late January, tell us what you have decided," his father answered.

"Dad, I have been in this relationship for four months already. It's time for us to go to her family and ask for her parents' blessing. I promised her that I was going to solve this issue this week," Ardian spoke with an imploring voice to his father.

His father stayed silent for some minutes.

"But we have just discussed this week the issue, and such an important decision cannot be taken so fast. We, as parents, have our work to do for such an issue. We must inquire and ask others about that girl, about her family, her parents, their place of origin, their political biography, their morality, etc. And it takes time. So that we need at least one or two months, and we can discuss and decide about it late February."

"But I know her very well, dad. Why my word is not enough for you? Why don't you believe me? Will you believe others more than me?"

"There are a lot of prerequisites for marriage, my son. It's not so easy and as simple as you say. Marriage connects two people for all their lives, but it connects two families as well, and that's why we have to look carefully and inquire about that family before deciding for a connection with marriage. During that time, I'll try to discuss this issue with your mother again and convince her that we have to start to inquire about that girl and her family because I cannot decide alone for such family important things. Before making any decision, we need some more information and knowledge about the girl and her family. For example, let me ask you: Do you know anything about the political biography of her family and kinsfolk? If there is something bad in their biography, your marriage with her will bring a lot of problems for you and will hurt your future professional career."

"What about her family political biography?" Ardian asked himself in silence. He had never thought about such an issue, and he knew nothing about her family in this regard. He wasn't happy that a decision couldn't be taken that week, and he was scared when he thought that they would ask and learn that Eralda was expelled from the regular high school. That was enough to put an end to all discussions, considering what they will be told about the reason for her expulsion. Ardian had never thought about his family's inquiries about Eralda's family. "How bad our parents become? They love us so much, and they impede us so much," he thought.

They didn't discuss this issue anymore that week until Ardian left the city at the end of the holidays, on Wednesday, January 4, 1984. He spoke about that with Monda and grandmother, and they both gave him some hope. His mother's aloofness was apparent during all that week, and even during the see off greetings. It was a divisive line between the two already; the love for Eralda, the love that his mother didn't want, and would never accept.

17

That week of holidays seemed longer than ever for Eralda. It was the week that would divide two years from each other, but Eralda, time after time, thought that this week was going to separate those two as well, and this decision was being taken right now in Vlorë, in Ardian's home, by his family. "No…, no," she tried to give some hope to herself. "This week does not divide two years. It brings them together instead, since its days are part of two years, so this week is going to bring the two of us together as well," she changed her reasoning into a more positive way, to convince herself that nothing terrible was happening in his family. In some moments, she was full of hope, trust, and certainty, but in other moments, she was full of fear, suspicion, and uncertainty. In her best moments, she became ready to open herself and tell her mother, but suddenly, she scared and retreated, driving herself to despair. "What if they don't agree with Ardian, and don't accept this marriage?" she thought in those bad moments and fell into deep sadness. This week seemed longer for Eralda because, in her mind, she experienced a lot of different emotions during every day of that week. And she didn't feel the celebration for the New Year's Eve night, which seemed like having less humor and joy than other years; it looked to her like a monotone and boring festivity.

She thought that Ardian was going to decide with his family before the New Year's Eve, and they would come to her family to ask her parents' blessing the first days of the New Year, so they could come the same day with Ardian, who would turn back to Elbasan on January 4. This beautiful thought brought her a lot of joy, made her fly around the apartment, cleaning and singing in the kitchen, living room, bedrooms, bathroom and everywhere, cleaning doors, windows, sinks, furniture, rugs, carpets, and everything else. Several times, she thought about telling her mother why she was doing that, but she didn't do it; and her mother couldn't suspect for anything, because this thorough home cleaning happens every year in this time, when people exchange visits to each other the first days of the New Year, wishing a happy New Year to each other, and they had a lot of such visits. "Let them come. That's important, and if they find her family unprepared for such a visit, it is not important," she thought.

Eralda was waiting for those first days of the New Year anxiously, looking from the apartment's windows several times a day, following trains' arrival times in the city's train station. They didn't come, and this thing caused great desperation and sadness for her. It looked like a terrifying roll from the summit of happiness to the deepest bottom of the sorrow's abyss. She became silent and clumsy in her moves, dizzy and oblivious. Evil thoughts occupied her, only wrong thinkings, without letting any room and time for hopeful views. On the evening of January 3, she decided not to give herself any hope at all, considering it done forever. "His parents have not accepted his choice…, and now we have to separate from each other…," was her final thought. She cried all night long for what was going to happen to her and her first love.

Her strong character and her particular temperament never admitted to forcing others to respect her, to like and accept her without their conviction. Then she started to convince herself that even Ardian himself wasn't showing the same passion and fire as the first weeks of their relationship. "Maybe he too had started to change his mind, becoming undecided, and his parents' mentality has affected him, putting him in a kind of dilemma. He perhaps loves me with all his soul, with all his feelings, but he lacks the courage to break the others' mentality, and he is not brave enough to decide for himself. His rationale is being divided mechanically from his feelings, and he is becoming colder in our love relationship," she thought, feeling sorrow for him, for their love, and their unavoidable separation. She decided to become stronger than him and help him solve his dilemma, making it easier for him by initiating their split-up and being the first one to take the initiative to step back, moving on from him, and this already lost love.

Ardian took the first train from Vlorë and arrived in Elbasan just before noon on January 4. He went directly to her store, while Eralda was waiting with her decision for separation already taken in her mind. They met. She didn't show her decision openly. She still had a faint glimmer of hope deep inside her mind, thinking: "Hope dies last." Ardian entered the store full of joy, smile, and happiness, but while talking with her, he hastened and said something not well-thought, making the biggest mistake of his life just by being fully open and sincere in what he was telling her.

"We talked about it in my family," he said in a moment. "At the end of this month, they will come for a visit to your family, just waiting some more days to convince my mother."

He thought that these words, being said with a maximum sincerity by him, would go smoothly. But not. As much as the first words enjoyed Eralda and made her happy, the same much his last words, "some more days to convince my mother," killed her, and she became silent. He understood his terrible mistake immediately, but it was too late, and the fatal damage had already been done. Those words came out of his mouth and entered like a spear, very deep into her stubborn head, facilitating and contributing to her decision for separation, giving an end to their love relationship.

"Alda," he continued, trying to correct his mistake as soon as possible, "all of them agreed with me, father, grandmother, Monda. Mom was convinced as well. All of them together, in one voice, convinced her, and they will come before the end of the month. I'll call them and tell them to come as soon as possible, somewhere in the middle of the month."

But it was all in vain. Eralda coldness became terrifying. A great affliction had just started in her soul. She felt an emptiness, a tangle, a severe pain in her chest. It was the pain caused by the attempt to pluck her love out of her chest. Something that she was forced to do. She had to uproot this love from the place where it was planted and rooted—from her body, her heart, her soul, and her blood. She imagined the human body in a human anatomy book picture, focusing on the lung's image; starting from larynx and trachea, continuing with primary, secondary, tertiary bronchi, and bronchioles in both lung's lobes, up to alveolar ducts, alveolar sacs, and alveoli, right where the oxygen, together with her love for him, is absorbed into her blood and is spread in all her body's cells, tissues, and into her heart. Like the bronchial tree, the roots of her love for Ardian were rooted and spread deep in her chest. And she must extract them now. Her chest started aching. What a terrifying moment! Those roots were spread out in every cell of her body, and she had to remove them all now. Who...? She...? No..., no. His family. His parents. His mother. Even he that planted the love's seeds inside her, making so deep roots, now looks like he wants to separate. But only the outside part of this deep love, the trunk, might be plucked, while its roots will remain forever right there where they are, and she will feel hurt time after time. Those are the first love's roots. They will never be extracted from there. But..., will these strong roots leave room for another passion, or are they going to remain there forever, keeping that space occupied? Oh..., God. It will be tough.

She decided to find the strength it takes, though. She thought again and again that Ardian loved her, and then, he didn't love her anymore. "His parents have affected him. He didn't dare to tell them about our relationship during the November holidays, or he has told them, but they have not accepted such love since then. The same has happened now, for the New Year's Eve holidays, they have not accepted such a marriage again. But Ardian, too, looks like he has already agreed with his parents' disapproval, but he does not dare to say it to me, and he just wants to drag out and delay for some more days his final decision. I hurried carelessly in this love. Perhaps..., this is the price I must pay because I wanted more than I merit from this life. That bad foreboding of mine came true. What about now? I have to help him because it might be difficult for him, as well. Even for him might not be so easy to separate from me, to pluck roots of my love from his mind, his body, his heart, and his soul. He loved me, indeed, and I don't suspect that. He didn't do it to fool me and play with me, but now he is in a dilemma, and he is suffering. I have to ease his suffering and relieve his pain," she concluded.

* * * * *

The separation—about which Eralda thought, admitted and decided so fast, and with such great courage—had never gone through Ardian's mind. He had never thought that Eralda didn't deserve him. On the contrary, he was sure that she was the kind of girl he was looking for and the worthiest one for him; the right girl with all characteristics and traits he would like in a woman to be chosen as the wife and friend of his life. She was a smart, beautiful girl, with strong willpower, brave, humble, courageous, without those other characteristics that girls have in general; talkative, frivolous, coquette, capricious, primped, panicky, overreacting, and full of drama. He, more than everything else in her, loved her strong character and personality. But he couldn't understand that it was just her strong character and personality, with her stubbornness and strong willingness, that was causing the separation of her from him because she was taking full responsibility for her actions. He had not understood her decision yet, and the idea that their separation had just started, hadn't reached his mind yet. Ardian had decided to marry Eralda even without his parents' acceptance. Even though he looked a little cold, it was just from the troubles and worries that his parents' disapproval caused him. His love for Eralda was as strong as before, and he would never lose her, for whatever reason on earth. He didn't have any dilemmas about that. There were a lot of shoppers in the store, and Ardian left thinking to return there later.

Ardian understood that Eralda felt terrible when he mentioned his mother's disapproval, but he would never think that she had already taken that horrifying decision to make the move that he would never consider. He could never believe that she would take this fatal step for their love. He couldn't understand that his last words hurt her and her sensibility so much. He couldn't think that she had started to suspect in his love's strength, too and that his incapability to decide by himself had made her feel disgusted for him and caused her revulsion. Those words that he said about his mother made Eralda finally to believe that her foreboding, trepidation, and suspicion were already proven to be accurate, based on which, she took this horrifying decision to make such a merciless move for their separation.

"My words hurt her," Ardian thought as soon as he left her store. "But I'll return to her before she closes the store, and I'll talk with her again." With this idea in mind, he stayed in his dormitory room until five o'clock and went back to her store again.

He arrived in front of the store, but it was closed. He waited some minutes there, thinking that Eralda would be somewhere around, in nearby stores, but she didn't show up until five-thirty. He asked the shopkeeper of the nearest store, and she told him that Eralda had not come back after the lunch break. He walked toward her apartment building. He went around the building several times, looking at her apartment windows, on both sides of the building, without knowing what to do. He thought a couple of times to go and knock on her door and tell her parents that he loved Eralda, but it wasn't a convincible decision and looked hasty and premature. "How is it possible?" he asked himself. "She had to have thought that I would come back to the store again. What's the matter? Is she sick?" He climbed the stairs up to the floor of her apartment, peeped e little bit behind the door, but didn't hear any sound from inside. "Has she gone to the hospital?" he thought first, followed by the understanding that she was hurt hard by his words and his indecisiveness.

The winter break for the middle and high schools lasts two weeks, so there were no classes in the evening high school those days, until Thursday, January 12. Eralda didn't open the store for six consecutive days, including

Monday, the weekly day off for her. Ardian went to her apartment building five to six times a day, but he never saw her in her windows or balcony. In addition to his worries, it was freezing and rainy weather all those days, making his situation even more horrible. He went to her store with more hope on Tuesday, but it was closed again. Then he went to the store of Bardha, Eralda's close friend, and asked her about Eralda. She told him that Eralda had some days of sick leave and might start working on the morrow.

18

As soon as Ardian left her store, Eralda felt an unbearable headache around the forehead, including both temples. When she went back home for the lunch break, it seemed like her head would explode by the terrible pain. For a moment, she felt bewildered, unsteady, and dizzy. There was nobody else home. She lay face down on the sofa, spending some minutes like that. When she tried to rise from the couch, because of heavy dizziness, she couldn't stand up and fell on the floor. During the collapse, her head hit the table and the chair near her. She spent several other minutes lying on the floor, powerless and unable to rise. She felt as if her head was inflated by big blood waves filling all her head's blood vessels. She thought she was dying at that moment, and nobody was there to help her, but she liked that. She liked the idea of dying, thinking about her death as the only rescuer for her. She felt sleepy, like seeing a dream, where all the most beautiful moments of her love with Ardian passed in front of her eyes. Ardian was standing there, in front of her, just a few feet away. He was looking at her and the unfortunate situation she was going through, without making any little attempt to approach and help her, because he was scared and hindered by something else behind him. After awakening from this nightmare, Eralda sobbed with convulsive gasps. Then, she tried to rise slowly, but felt the heaviness in the head and couldn't get up. She was afraid that if she would stand up, then she would feel dizzy and collapse again. After some minutes, she tried again, rising more slowly. First, she raised the head, then, after a small pause, the neck, the chest, supporting herself with hands on the floor, and on the sofa near her. She rested some minutes like that, sitting on the floor and leaned back on the couch. She raised the fallen chair and suddenly felt a pain in the back of the head and in the cheekbone near the left eye. She checked with fingers and felt the bulge in the head right where she was hit by the table or chair during the collapse. She continued to get up slowly and sat on the sofa. After spending some more minutes there, she walked toward the bedroom, holding herself to the table first, to the wall, the doors handle, until she arrived there. She stopped at the mirror and saw the part under the left eye, over the cheekbone, that was bruised and already swelling up. The face skin had become yellow like a lemon. The hair was disordered. She recalled that she hadn't eaten anything at all, either for breakfast or lunch. She felt powerless to go to the kitchen and tossed herself onto the bed with another sob of despair.

After a couple of hours, her mother entered the home, saw Eralda in her bedroom, and without knowing what had happened, said to her:

"Alda, what are you doing in the bedroom? Aren't you cold over there? Oh…, but you are very late for work," her mother continued when she saw the clock in the living room.

Eralda didn't answer and didn't move, so her mother went to the bedroom, and found her in that unfortunate situation. She was scared to death when she saw her daughter like that.

"What's the matter with you, Alda?" she asked, being alarmed by her daughter's situation.

"I cannot stand up, mom," Eralda answered with a weak voice. It seemed like her brain couldn't command even the smallest efforts to move her limbs in an attempt to rise because she was too scared after the previous collapse in the living room. She thought that she was already paralyzed since she was unable to move her hands or legs.

"What are you saying, my daughter?" Mom asked her, being scared after Eralda's answer.

"I feel dizzy," Eralda spoke with a little difficulty, without moving from her lying position on the bed and without turning the head toward her mother.

Her mother reached her bed, sat down on the floor next to her, and almost weeping, asked her again:

"What happened to you, my darling? Please let me help you. It's cold here. Let's go to the living room."

Mother held her arms and walked together toward the living room. She helped Eralda to lie on the sofa, putting a pillow under her head and two blankets on her. Mom brought a small electric heater near and sat down on the floor, next to Eralda's head.

"Have you eaten anything for lunch?"

"No," Eralda answered, speaking slowly, with a powerless, weak voice, "I don't feel hungry and can't put anything in the mouth."

Her mother went to the kitchen, prepared orange juice squeezing a couple of fresh oranges, and brought it to Eralda, who swallowed it all with a gulp and a great thirst.

"Bring me another one, please," Eralda said to her mom.

Her mom prepared another orange juice, and this time brought an aspirin too. Eralda felt some relief after that, but, when she recalled the reason for all the suffering and all these terrible consequences, felt horrified and started sobbing, turning the head on the other side. Her mother thought that this cry and those tears could help her relieve her worry, trouble, or anxiety, she might have, and that's why she let her cry, without asking any question to her until Eralda stopped crying. Her mother started worrying more, while thinking that something terrible would have happened to her daughter, causing the situation where she found her and this sobbing of her. "What may have happened to her?" she asked herself all the time that Eralda was crying, without presuming any answer. She asked Eralda as soon as she stopped crying:

"What's the matter, my soul? What's this bruise under your eye? Who has hit you in the face?"

"It's nothing mom. I had lain down on the sofa, and when I stood up, I felt dizzy and fell without being able to stand. While falling, I hit my head on the table and the chair. Then it seemed like I was completely paralyzed and couldn't move my arms and legs at all".

"Why haven't you had anything for lunch?" mom asked her when she found out that the plate left for Eralda's lunch, was still untouched.

"I didn't feel hungry. I couldn't eat," Eralda answered, with a weak voice.

"Would you like something to eat now?" mom asked her, and without waiting for her answer, she rose, moved the chair where she was sitting, bringing it near Eralda's head, and went to the kitchen to prepare something for her. She returned after some minutes and placed on the chair near Eralda toasted bread, milk, butter, cherry jam, all these things that Eralda liked the most, especially for breakfast or for an afternoon snack. Mom prepared a toasted piece of bread, by laying butter and cherry jam on it, and gave it to Eralda, who started eating slowly, in the beginning, chewing slowly, and without much appetite, but after some small bites started eating more normally but still chewing and swallowing slowly. Eralda felt some relief after that. She was released from the fear of a terrible illness, but Ardian came in her mind again.

"I'll go to work," she told her mother, thinking that Ardian would come back to her store that afternoon again.

"I'm not going to let you go anywhere, in this condition you are reduced," her mother answered with a robust and decisive voice. "We'll go for a visit to the neighborhood health clinic when it opens this afternoon at five o'clock," her mother made it clear what she was thinking, and the reason that she couldn't go to work.

Even though she thought, and she wanted to meet Ardian, now that her mother told her that she couldn't go to work, she felt some relief for avoiding meeting with him. "It's better if I don't meet him anymore," such a lousy thought crossed her mind, but it was a significant burden to be accepted, and great pain and suffering for her. These thoughts made her feel bad again. She felt groggy and felt the heatwave of blood going up through the neck blood vessels toward her face and her head. She felt dazed.

"I have fevers," she told her mother.

Mom saw her reddish face and lips, checked her throat out, and put her lips to Eralda's forehead to sense her body temperature.

"Perhaps you have high blood pressure," mom told her and fixed the blankets over her and around her body, telling her to stay like that until five o'clock.

At five o'clock, they went to the doctor of the neighborhood health clinic. The physician measured her blood pressure and found that it was a little bit higher than average. Eralda couldn't tell him what was going on with her, but the doctor understood that she—as a beautiful young girl, and from the way she was answering his questions—might have had love relationship problems. So, he concluded that Eralda might have been stressed or even depressed for a long time, and for that reason, he recommended and referred her for a visit to the psychiatrist of the city's central health clinic. On the morrow morning, they went to the psychiatrist, and Eralda didn't tell the doctor anything about her concerns. But it was easy for the specialist to understand that this girl was going through a difficult time, and was experiencing symptoms of a nervous breakdown, caused after a long period of stress that becomes dangerous if not been adequately dealt with. He prescribed the medication for Eralda and wrote a recommendation for six days of medical leave. The psychiatrist spoke separately to Eralda's mother, telling her that Eralda needs some days of relaxation, that she was hiding and keeping something inside her, but don't ask and don't force her to tell it until she decides to open up and say it by herself to you or somebody else.

After the doctor's words, her mother understood that everything had to do with the literature teacher. She didn't ask Eralda about that and was waiting for Eralda to tell her someday. But Eralda didn't tell her. During those six sick leave days, Eralda tried to get herself busy with all house works to forget Ardian, but it was impossible. She remembered him very often, and she recalled her decision to separate from him and bring an end to this relationship. She thought about him dozens of times during all those days and nights. She tried to get rid of those thoughts just by doing more house chores, but it was still impossible. Even though she tried hard not to think of him and to avoid his portrait from her mind, she couldn't stop that from entering her mind and her head, causing pain in her chest, heart, and soul. After that, she felt lack of desire to do house works or to prepare her school's homework, and she started feeling tired, weak, confused, worthless, sleepless, guilty, sad, desperate, accompanied by a feeling of a permanent emptiness in entire her body and her spiritual being. It was a terrifying situation that only she could face and challenge, but not without some dangerous consequences.

Trying hard to keep away from yourself the man you love, and that loves you; attempting not to love him anymore, and to make him not to love you; making all efforts to forget about him and make him forget about you—it wasn't easy, but she had already decided to do such a thing. She thought that she was going to suffer some weeks or months, but that was better than becoming a wife of somebody that was so hesitant and undecided and to become part of a family that doesn't want you. This last thought comforted her, giving a little bit of solace because that was the reason that pushed her to take such a decision. She recalled again her first hesitation and suspicion in accepting or not this love relationship. "He..., a professor... I..., a shopkeeper, a student at the night school. I was right in my foreboding and uncertainty at that time. But it still is not late, and I'm in time to give an end to this relationship", Eralda thought during all those painful days. She never believed in the wrong way about Ardian, though. "He didn't play with me," she tried to assure herself. "He was very much in love with me. He loved me with all his heart and his soul, but he became hesitant and undecided later, being affected by his parents' disapproval that makes him think differently about this love now. Maybe he feels a kind of regret for this impetuous love and might be more difficult for him to accept

141

this change of mind and tell me about it." Based on the respect and love she had for Ardian, she thought and decided to help him by making this separation easier for him as well, by taking the initiative to start and complete this separation.

Several times during those days, Eralda recalled and passed through her mind the quote that Entela had told her:

"Tis better to have loved and lost
than never to have loved at all." *

"Okay…, but why so… and why me…?" she thought repeatedly about such a situation.

_____

* *From the British poet Alfred, Lord Tennyson's poem, "In Memoriam."*

19

During December, the principal of the evening high school, the chief of the County's Department of Education and the Head of County's Party Committee, continued and applied their plan to expel the literature teacher from the evening high school and from the pedagogical institute as well, to create a vacant job position for the niece of the Head of County's Party Committee. So, in a meeting at the end of December, just before the New Year's Eve, they approved the official decision to transfer the literature professor from the Pedagogical Institute and the evening high school, with the motive: "Signs of the bourgeois and revisionist foreign ideology and for immoral behavior with his female students."

The director of the Pedagogical Institute had great respect for Ardian as a young professor that had advanced more than others in only three years, making him well known as a good scholar and lecturer, but couldn't dare to oppose his superiors in trying to protect Ardian. And above all, his approach became apparent when he learned that it was considered as an ideological and moral issue, and there was guidance from the County's Party Committee to take harsh measures against such behaviors. The dean of faculty and the chief of literature department, from their part, spoke with the institute director about this issue, wanting to protect Ardian. "We have other problematic and incompetent professors in our department and faculty, while Ardian is the best one," they told the director. "He has enriched the scientific work of the literature department, and he promises further accomplishment for the near future. What he has done here for three years and a half, the rest of the department had not done for ten years," they explained to the institute director, continuing:

"Please don't allow them to assign in our faculty other professors like those two last ones. Ardian has not any of those vices that the evening high school principal says. We know him since he was a student, and you, too,

143

know him very well. Things that are being said against him are only slanders and intrigues, used for other reasons, and you must understand that. Ardian has been an excellent student and has become an exceptional professor. There is not any complaint, information, suspicious sign, or even rumors against him in our institute. Let them move him from the evening high school if there is any reason for that, but not from the pedagogical institute. Please, don't allow them to do that. And, regarding the individual that the Party Committee and Education Department are proposing to replace Ardian, let them assign her in a middle school because it would be a disgrace for the institute to admit her as a professor. Aren't you…, comrade director, seeing another 'foreign ideology' coming from the Department of Education and the Party Committee? Don't you understand what is happening these last years? They have transferred from the institute some other professors with birthplace and family origin from different regions and counties, even though they have been outstanding professors, and have replaced them with professors with family origin from our city who aren't as good as the first ones. Don't you see that these last ones are more problematic and incompetent professors in all faculties and departments of the institute, including their immorality and love affairs with female students? That's why we want to protect Ardian, but you too, comrade director, must defend the pedagogical institute and our best professors from such slanders and intrigues used only for narrow individual interests, based on nepotism and cronyism. These actions are destroying the Pedagogical Institute and are against the guidance and speeches of the Great Leader and the decisions of the Central Committee of the Communist Party, regarding the higher education system."

The director of the pedagogical institute promised them that he would try to do something, but he wasn't serious about what he said, and he was not going to make any effort on that issue. That's because he knew very well the function of the Communist Party apparatus that sometimes works like a mill that grinds people following the guidance coming from higher political levels. It happens just because of the interests of some individuals for their political careers. They speak on behalf of the Party, the people, the working class, the country, the fatherland, the socialism, etc., just to justify their rivalry and internal power struggle. But the institute director knew very well that this mechanism didn't spare even its leading players, actors, aides, and authors of this masquerade when their turn arrives. That's why he didn't intend to approach this killing mechanism of that giant machinery—called the Communist Party Committee of the County—in trying to protect the institute and the literature professor, the individual they had decided to grind in their mill this time. If the director acted in this way, he would put himself in great danger of falling inside the gearwheels' teeth of this unstoppable mill that crushes, squashes, and grinds innocent people. He would not do anything at all and would act like all middle-level chiefs do in such cases, by playing with lower-level supervisors when those latter ones—just because of lack of experience and knowledge about the function of this terrible mechanism—dare to complain, object and oppose them sometimes. The institute director was going to tell his subordinates that he had tried hard and had discussed this issue with his superiors, but couldn't find any solution and couldn't reach any results because: "The members of the Communist Party Committee were frustrated and angry with the literature professor's actions, which were against the Communist Party directives and Great Leader guidance being seriously broken by him. And that's why he deserved a harsh punishment."

On Saturday, January 7, the chief of the literature department, called Ardian at his office to discuss this issue with him. When he saw Ardian that looked so weak; with a pale face skin and with that dark color under his eyes, as a sign of an exhausted person, he thought that Ardian knew what the evening high school principal had instigated, and carelessly asked him:

"What's happening in the evening high school?"

"Nothing interesting," Ardian answered. "Their winter break lasts two weeks, and classes start on Thursday, January 12," he continued, like speaking for a usual situation.

The literature department chief was surprised by his calmness, and that's why he entered directly to the issue:

"Hasn't the evening school principal told you anything yet?"

"No," Ardian answered immediately. "What's that about?"

"He has decided to expel you from the evening high school, and you are in danger of moving from the pedagogical institute too. The dean of faculty and I spoke with the institute director, and he promised us that he is going to do something, to keep you here in the institute, because this semester you can have full time here," the chief explained him in haste, trying to calm and help him face this situation. But instead, he saw Ardian tightening his jaws in frustration.

"I would like to close this school year in the evening high school," Ardian said.

"Your place is here, in the pedagogical institute. You have been teaching there temporarily, just to complete the remaining hours for a full salary," the department chief tried again to make Ardian happy.

"Give me more hours here, but don't move me from the evening high school, until the end of this school year," Ardian said to him as if things were depending on his department chief.

The department chief understood that Ardian lost his mind and that he had a relationship in the evening high school, meaning that the school principal was right.

"Ardian, you know very well that these things do not depend on me, but frankly speaking, you are in a dangerous situation, in great danger. It's about so-called 'signs of the bourgeois and revisionist foreign ideology and for immoral behavior, bourgeois ideology and culture, foreign music,' and things like that. You know very well how dangerous these things are, and you risk a lot."

"What a nefarious man," Ardian shouted. "The sneaky principal never called me at his office to speak about that. Something happened at the end of November, but he said that he had closed this issue, and we never discussed it anymore.

"We must pray for these things to stop, but you know that for such things, you can be punished even more. Forget about evening high school. Hopefully, the institute director will arrange things for you to remain here. You continue your studies, and someday you are going to find a wife too," he said, to relieve the situation, and to change the subject of the discussion.

The literature department chief's name was Bashkim, and he was a good man in his forties. He had earned the "candidate of science" scientific degree and had always helped, supported, and inspired Ardian to continue his studies for a scientific degree.

"Come for a visit to my house, because you have not come for the New Year yet, and Alma is keeping your portion of baklava," he said, mentioning his wife. "I have found two more interesting books for your subject of studying," Bashkim added.

Ardian had officially requested by the scientific commission of Tirana University the approval of his scientific studies for the first degree called "Candidate of Science." For this he had chosen a fascinating subject: "The depiction of the dictatorships and military juntas' rule in the Latin America's literature of the twentieth century," but it was not approved yet because some of them said that Ardian was very young and incapable for such a big

146

subject. Ardian had already found all the books he needed to read in Albanian, in English and Italian languages, searching for these books in the city's library in Elbasan and the national library in Tirana. Bashkim helped him in finding all the books he needed. Ardian had started to translate one of them from English to Albanian last summer, but the love relationship he started kept him away from such a work. When Bashkim mentioned the books he had found for Ardian, he didn't show any interest at all on them and didn't express any joy, as he used to do in such cases. Bashkim understood that he was anxious and that he had trouble, so he changed the situation by proposing to skip everything and go for lunch at his home.

"Come with me. Let us go home for lunch right now, because I know that you will not come later, and I don't want to listen to Alma's complaint about that."

They walked toward Bashkim's house without speaking to each other at all. When they approached home, Ardian tried to dismiss Eralda from his mind, to be more relaxed in talking with Bashkim and his wife. Ardian met Alma, and they started the usual talk, telling and asking each other about the New Year's Eve festivities, their families, food, and TV shows. They had lunch together, and after that, Bashkim invited him to play chess. They started the chess game, and Ardian was making a lot of foolish mistakes in moving the chess pieces, showing that his mind was not there. Bashkim didn't bear that anymore, and canceled the game, by collecting the chess pieces, and saying:

"We cannot continue like this, Ardian. Tell me what has happened to you that you are so worried about because it is not a good thing when you keep it inside yourself and suffer like this."

Ardian told them everything, like a need to say it all to a friend and relieve himself from some suffering. In the end, he couldn't keep the choke up anymore, and let the tears drop out from his eyes without any attempt to hide them. They were the first tears of the loss of his first love.

Bashkim and Alma were moved very much by his story and his tears, and they didn't speak for some minutes, just letting him relieve and collect himself.

"I have decided to marry Eralda, even without my parents' approval," Ardian spoke after a long silence. "But something strange has happened to her now. I'm afraid that she has taken a different decision. I'm afraid that she is leaving me now," Ardian explained his real concern in the end, speaking with his eyes in tears.

20

Life in general, with its daily routine activities, seems too monotonous and slow. But, in everyone's life, there are some moments when everything slides impetuously, like an unstoppable snow avalanche, and in front of it, you are powerless and unable to stop these processes. Therefore you have nothing to do; just let the big snowslip—in front of which you look tiny, almost like a Lilliputian—sweep, engorge, and roll you somewhere, deep down in one of the many abysses of life. And after that, if you are still alive, you come out of the snowslip with crippled body and soul, trying again to act as if you are still living your life—if it even might be called "life."

That's what happened to Ardian. The steady impetuous avalanche of the "war against signs of foreign bourgeois and revisionist ideology," swept him, but he was lucky enough to survive and remain alive. The start of the new school semester found Ardian in the most remote village of Elbasan County. In all his past experiences, he had practiced the principle of accepting his life and fate as it would come. Life had come to him with its best sides until that time, and as such, it was easy for him to accept it as it had come. Now that life was offering him its worst side, he still remembered his principle in trying to face and challenge this grave situation, but it was not so easy. The punishment and the transfer in this remote village were easy to be accepted by him, and he made this decision very soon. But the separation from Eralda continued to scoop out his body, mind, and soul like an auger, drilling without stopping, entering deeper, causing so much terrible harm and unbearable pain. "Be happy that this issue ended with only a transfer," his friend, Bashkim, had told him. "You are lucky because the way your issue and your behavior was treated, you would have ended up in prison or internment, where you would suffer, and your family would suffer as well because you would be called an 'enemy of the Party and people,' for all your life."

For these things, Ardian prepared himself and made his mind up very fast by accepting his fate the way it happened, but he couldn't take the unfortunate fate of his love for Eralda and the way it happened. Until January 10, Eralda did not show up in her store, where he went several times during those days, to speak with her once more. On Monday, January 9, Ardian was informed about the decision taken by the County's Communist Party Committee and the Education Department for his expulsion from the Pedagogical Institute and the transfer to a remote village. He didn't care about this assignment because his mind was focused on what was happening with Eralda. When his friends saw him like that, exhausted and destroyed, they thought it was because of his transfer and expulsion from the pedagogical institute, understanding his situation and expressing their regret to him. Ardian started to feel his regrettable appearance, and he realized how bad he looked in his friends' eyes. When he listened to his friends' solace words, he felt relieved, thinking that at least they didn't know and didn't understand that the real cause of this lamentable situation was just a girl— the girl that he loved so much, with a great passion and fire. But now, he understood that he was losing her maybe forever.

Eralda went to work only the last day of the school winter break, while Ardian, on the morrow (the first day of the second school semester), had to report to his new job in the school of the remote village where he was assigned. He entered the store that day with the last hope, but he faced an emotionless attitude from Eralda as if it wasn't her but another girl that he had never known before. She didn't say anything to him, continuing to interact with customers coming in and out of the store.

"Alda…, it's me," Ardian told her in a moment when the store was empty for just a few seconds.

"I see it," she answered coldly, without looking in his eyes, arranging things in a vitrine.

"I want to talk seriously with you," Ardian said to her, but other shoppers entered the store, interrupting him.

He waited some more minutes there to continue his discussion with Eralda, but that day there were a lot of shoppers buying school articles for the new school semester. He saw that even Eralda herself was not thinking about him, and she was running after every customer, as soon as they entered the store, asking them what they were looking for, as the best way in her attempt to avoid him. Ardian left the store without greeting Eralda, thinking to come back again later on. He turned and returned several times that day, but he never found the store without customers.

In the closing time, when Eralda closed the store, he approached her in another tentative to talk with her:

"Eralda, we have to talk, please."

"Please, leave me alone," she answered, running away from him.

Eralda knew nothing about his transfer. Otherwise, she would behave differently. She learned about it on the morrow evening, when she went to school, but it was too late to change her conduct and her decision.

Ardian turned back to his dormitory room, tired and exhausted more than ever, making his luggage ready for the morrow trip.

Thursday, January 12, 1984, Ardian took the bus early in the morning. A small old bus went to the remote village called Red Hill only twice a week— Monday morning to take teachers there and Saturday afternoon to bring them back to Elbasan for the weekend. That's why it is called "the teachers' bus." Some teachers lived in the villages of that area, and this bus takes teachers that live in cities of Elbasan and Cerrik. These teachers taught in four schools of that remote rural area, in villages that constitute the agriculture cooperative of Red Hill. The first thing that impressed Ardian, when he entered the bus and during the entire trip, were the pale faces of those teachers. After he talked with a couple of them, Ardian learned that they had been working in those remote villages' schools for many years. They had been assigned there as young singles, then they had been married, had become with children, and they were still working there, with the worst consequence of being far from their family and children for all weekdays. Take into consideration that Saturdays were working days as well. He started feeling sorrow for those teachers and himself, too, when he thought that he would have the same sad fate as most of them on that bus. "Co-sufferers," he thought. He was going to spend all his life right there, and nobody would help him to return to Elbasan or in a village near the city, from where you could return home every evening. The teachers' bus arrived at the last stop with only five teachers, including Ardian. They jumped off the bus, with a lot of dust over their faces, bodies, clothes, and handbags. He heard the usual greetings villagers and students gave to four teachers after whom Ardian was ambling. They were two ladies and two men, and Ardian was the fifth one. From what Ardian quickly understood, from their way of speaking and behaving with each other, they were two possible future couples. "The best way to spend your youth here," Ardian thought cynically. They arrived in front of a two-floor small building situated near the school.

"Here we arrived at the teachers' palace," one of the teachers said.

They got to the second floor where there were two small rooms, one for two men and one for two ladies. It was the third room near them, full of dirt, with a broken door, mucky walls, and a broken window without glass. This room needed to be prepared for Ardian.

"Here we are," said another teacher. "This is 'the teachers' palace'…, our hotel," he added with a sarcastic voice, making others laugh.

"You see how small these rooms are, and there is not any space to bring in another bed in our room," the other teacher told Ardian. "But we are going to tell the school principal to ask from the administration of the agriculture cooperative to clean and repair the vacant room, and furnish it with a bed, mattress, table, and chairs."

Ardian wanted to laugh and cry at the same time for this epilogue of his trip in this remote village and in this dirty destroyed building, called the "teachers' palace." Its stairs and hallways were full of dirt, dust, and mud from the rains of past days. The walls of the room supposed to be prepared for him were blackened by the smoke of the fires people had burned on the floor, with remaining pieces of unburned wood, ash, and char, being still there in one corner of the room. "Perhaps the night security guards of the agriculture cooperative spend their working time here," Ardian thought. The journey to here and this laugh-and-cry situation that he found in this village, reminded him a poem of a well-known Albanian poet and writer with its famous verses where the poet called the villages' teachers: "The meek ones up to pain, / The humble ones up to greatness." These verses were dedicated to the teachers that commute in such arduous conditions from cities where they live to the villages where they work, including walking long distances under any weather condition. Ardian recalled these verses and paraphrased them differently, with sarcasm and irony in his mind: "The meek ones up to neglect, / The humble ones up to folly." Ardian left his bags to the other male teachers' room and went together with them to the school. The very first impression he had from the village and from the villagers he saw was poverty. He saw and found this poverty everywhere; in peoples' faces, in their old and damaged clothes, in the streets full of mud, dust, and puddles. The trees' branches without any leaves in this wintertime, with their trunks full of dust and dirt, looked like an additional background, like a scenography of this indescribable high poverty.

151

The school was situated in the center of the village. It was a new two-floor building, but the bad quality of construction, the lack of maintenance, and the rainwater leaking from the roof to the walls, deteriorating them so fast, made it look older and ugly. It was an elementary and middle school for students from first to eighth grade. Ardian entered the school building following the teachers from the "teachers' palace." Students were in their classrooms, from where you could hear the characteristic classroom noise. The school principal and teachers that lived in the village were gathered in the teachers' room. A wood fire was burning in a small stove placed in the corner of the room. The first impression Ardian had when he saw other teachers, was their weak, skinny faces, and old clothes, showing the poverty and bad living condition of the village populace. He greeted and shook hands with all teachers in the room after school principal presented him to them. After that, he walked toward the classroom, where he would teach the first period. When he arrived at the classroom door, he saw all the students standing around a stove in the corner after the classroom door, trying to keep the fire going using papers, hay, and straw, producing a lot of smoke that had filled the classroom. They ran away from the stove quickly, hurrying toward their desks like "frightened insects," as soon as they saw teacher to the classroom door. The first thing he distinguished as different from the city's children were boys' heads, with their ugly haircuts, very short haircut done by their parents by using only scissors and not any hair clippers, leaving a lot of dents and nicks, looking like the sheep shearing. Then he saw their old damaged, dirty clothes full of patches, their grimy faces, ears, and necks, the hands' skin damaged by the dirt and cold, and the unwashed, uncombed hair of girls as well.

All elements of the entire situation that he was observing sounded in his mind like a rampant rhapsody of poverty. Ardian recalled Migjeni, the famous Albanian poet and writer that had described such poverty fifty years ago. Migjeni, who worked as a teacher in some remote villages of northern Albania, wrote about what he had discovered all around him; the harsh reality, the appalling level of misery, disease, and poverty. Among other poems, he wrote "Luli, The Little Boy," and "The Poem of Poverty," with its well-known verses: "A morsel that cannot be swallowed is the poverty, / A morsel stuck in your throat, and you by sadness get caught, / When you see pale faces and greenish eyes, / Looking at you like shadows, extending their numb hands…" Ardian thought about the state of the village and about himself being there, like being in the villages and schools where Migjeni had taught, seeing people and children Migjeni had seen fifty years ago, noticing the same level of destitution and misery the poet had observed and written for at that time. After a second thought, Ardian realized that it seemed like a fantasy trip that had taken him back in time. He recalled some books he had read, like: "Gulliver's Travels" by Jonathan Swift and "A Connecticut Yankee in King Arthur's Court" of Mark Twain. And after that, he thought a little bit…, and then murmured to himself two paraphrases of these titles: "Teacher's travel to the kingdom of …" and "A teacher in the villages of the king …." Oh…, no…, no. He couldn't finish this imaginary book titles by putting there the name of the "Great Leader of the Party and the people of Albania." No…, he couldn't even think about such a thing. How did he dare to feel like this? He couldn't go so far. "Let me be happy with this internment because the imprisonment or the death penalty might easily come after that," he thought about his fate and destiny.

After the classes, Ardian turned back to "the teachers' palace," and saw that something was done in his room. They had dyed the room walls with white lime. The window was covered with plastic sheets instead of glass. The broken part of the door, right where the door lock and handles had to be, was covered and reinforced with another flat piece of wood. They had put two fixed staple hasps for a padlock outside the door, and a big bent nail to close the door from inside. Two female students were cleaning and washing the room floor at that moment. Some male students, accompanied by the agriculture cooperative's warehouseman, were bringing some old, half-broken iron and wooden pieces, supposed to be furniture and bed, with which they furnished the room. That first day, Ardian was invited by other residents of "the teachers' palace," to join them for lunch and dinner because it was the day they had come from their homes, and they had brought with them plenty of food. Usually, two female teachers cooked in their room for themselves and two male teachers—their boyfriends—and they had lunches and dinners all together. Sometimes they went to the cooperative's canteen where, like in a military mess hall, you could find only dried beans, rice and tea, and sometimes eggs, milk, natural yogurt, and marmalade.

"Where there is food for four, a fifth one can eat too," one of the teachers told Ardian, inviting him to join them for lunch that first day and two remaining days of this week.

153

"Food is not a big problem," one of the female teachers added, "but the County's Education Department has to assign here another female teacher from Elbasan," she finished.

Big joyful laughter burst from all four of them after her words. These four teachers were graduated from the Elbasan Pedagogical Institute a few years before Ardian had started his studies there, and that's why they didn't know him, but they started telling a lot of funny stories from that time, related to the students and some professors that were still teaching there. They didn't ask Ardian about his transfer because they had already heard something (as it always happens in such cases), and didn't want to bother him with such questions. Ardian liked their companionship with this kind of sincerity, friendship, humor, and their readiness to help him in everything. He understood that the division of their rooms as "female teachers' room" and "male teachers' room" was only for the daytime because, at nighttime, each couple went into their room. In this way, Ardian couldn't spend much time with them and had to stay away from them time after time. On the morrow, he went for breakfast, lunch, and dinner to the cooperative's canteen.

On Saturday afternoon, he took the bus to Elbasan, like all other teachers. The bus arrived in Elbasan a little bit after the dusk. He speeded his steps to go to the Eralda's store, even though he knew that she would be at school at this time. He booked a room in a hotel near the center of the city and then walked toward the evening high school. He found a dark corner next to a building and waited there to see Eralda at the end of every class period. He heard the bell for the end of the third period and saw some students leaving the school from the main gate, but he didn't see Eralda or any other student from her class. He left that dark corner and walked in the city streets, spending half an hour and turned back again there, waiting for the end of the fourth period. He saw all the students from her class but didn't see Eralda. He felt annoyed. Three days had gone easier and faster there, in the remote village. Eralda had crossed several times a day through his mind, but at least, he was far away from her and had something else to deal with, forgetting about her again. But here, in the city, he had come only for her, and couldn't remove her from his mind. He walked toward her apartment building, stopping in front of it, and observing toward her apartment's windows and balcony. He made some rounds around the building without knowing what to do, but just spending some more time right there, feeling a yearning for Eralda and her love. He spent some minutes in front of the building's entrance, right there where their last and longest kiss used to take place at the end of their happy dates. He understood that he was spending time in vain and that he was acting like a fool, like a stupid one, like a crazy one. "Oh, yes…, yes. I'm going crazy because of the separation from her," he concluded. He turned back to the hotel, trying to sleep, but couldn't sleep at all. All kinds of thoughts passed through his mind until his head felt full and tired and couldn't take any more. Then he started crying, and he liked that, and that's why he helped himself crying more and more without stopping. He slept a little bit just before the dawn. He got up at eight o'clock, prepared and went out where he found and entered a restaurant, having breakfast and coffee. He spent some more minutes around the city center, and ten minutes before nine o'clock, he stood in front of Eralda's store, until she showed up, at nine o'clock.

"Good morning Alda," he greeted her, trying hard to seem calm and casual.

"Good morning," she answered, in a cold way, unlocking the store door, without expressing any emotions for his presence.

Eralda opened the door and entered the store, passing behind the counter. Ardian entered the store after her.

"Alda, we are losing each other without any reason," Ardian spoke decisively, after he faced her cold and disdainful attitude, but he didn't take any answer from her.

Eralda took off her jacket and put on the store uniform without saying any word and started moving and arranging things in the vitrines in silence.

"Alda, don't behave like this," he raised the voice. "I'm repeating; we are losing each other without any good reason. You know that I love you with all of my soul, and I know that you love me the same, and I don't understand your strange behavior."

"Let us end this," she spoke with a weak voice, raising her head and watching Ardian in his eyes for the first time, but only for few seconds.

"That's what you have decided?" he asked immediately, speaking loudly.

"No need to blame each other, but we are not fit for each other. A lot of things keep us apart," she answered, turning her back to clean the vitrine.

"Is it so easy for you?" he asked, as soon as she ended her words.

"No…, but I think that this is for the best of both of us," she answered without turning her head.

155

Ardian felt the knot of tears gathering in his throat, and tears were making his eyes wet. In the meanwhile, two women entered the store, and Ardian went out, walking toward the hotel, crying all the way. He entered the hotel room, threw himself on the bed, where he burst in gushing tears.

Eralda, as well, was feeling the same regret for the loss of this love, and that's why she couldn't see Ardian in his eyes. She tried hard not to burst into tears, keeping them inside her, because she had to deal with customers. She had cried every night in her bed, already for two weeks, determined to break this love forever. She never understood where she found the strength for such a decision, but she thought about the separation as the right thing to be done for both of them. She couldn't admit herself to separate a son from his parents just because of her, as it had happened with a lot of other couples when parents and the family of one of them didn't agree with their choice and their marriage. She didn't want this thing to happen to them, with her being the reason for such a thing. She was already convinced that there were a lot of things making them differ a lot from each other, and not to fit each other. She convinced herself that she was right from the beginning with her suspicions and presumptions that she was not worthy of him.

Even now, that she knew about his expulsion from the pedagogical institute and his transfer in a very remote village, she couldn't change her decision as a mercy for him, even though she thought that she was the cause for his transfer.

Ardian spent the rest of the day in bed, without going out and without eating anything at all until Monday morning when he went to the bus station to take the teachers' bus for the remote village.

21

When spring arrived, in March 1984, Ardian started thinking somewhat differently about his love, as a need to find a way to alleviate a little bit of his pain and suffering that the loss of his first love was causing to him. "Perhaps it was an ill-considered, hasty love. Maybe she played with me. Maybe she wasn't so immaculate and chaste as she pretended to be. Perhaps she didn't deserve my love. Look how easy it was for her to forget and run away from me." In this way, by repeating several times a day this suspicion and evil thoughts about her, he began feeling relieved time after time, reaching peace inside himself and becoming more tranquil in his mind and soul. When he started feeding himself with such thoughts about Eralda, he felt for the first time the need to remove from his mind and get rid of "that immoral girl, that had played so beautifully, and that didn't deserve his love. She is nothing but just a shopkeeper, a night school student, being expelled from the regular high school for immoral behavior. Yes, it's true. She is one of those girls that know very well how to conceal her vices and show only the good characteristics of a good, clever girl that knows very well what a man is looking for and what he expects and desires from his girl."

Changes that spring brings to nature made Ardian think to engage in other beautiful things of life, adding other attempts to save himself from the anxiety of the separation from the girl he loved so much. Spring's arrival reminded him to exercise and do sports, to enjoy the beautiful spring nature, to strengthen his body, and fill his daily life with something new to fight the stressful, passive emptiness left behind by the loss of love. He had read that the best natural medicine against apathy, stress, and depression, are sportive and physical activities that keep you in contact with nature, and that's why he started exercising, trying to heal and save himself. Nature and sports perhaps would help him keep the girl that he was thinking so much about away from

157

his mind. He had read that the best way to forget about something is by not thinking about it and not remembering it anymore. But..., how could he do such a thing? How could he be able not to think about and not remember her? This expression was just playing with words because remembrance and forgetting always stay together. You can never forget about something as far as you have good memories of that thing, and above all, when you have such beautiful, love remembrances. And vice versa, if you don't have any good memories, you don't need to try to forget anything.

In this way, with this desire and these attempts, Ardian started the morning physical exercises. The first week, he exercised on the sports ground of the school, consisted of a small sports ground used for soccer, basketball, and volleyball. The second week, he started running in the hills around the village, where new green leaves and trees' blossoms brought more relaxation and joy, helping him have a better mood during the day. It seemed like he felt the results of this activity, bringing the desire to exercise even more, as a goal to fill the time and mind in his attempts to get rid of thoughts and remembrances for the lost love, which could cause sadness, stress, and depression.

Ardian had another kind of hurdle that he felt sometimes, but he tried to disregard it, and he often laughed at himself while thinking about this obstacle. The problem was in the fact that he was transferred to this remote village for immorality and political, ideological reasons. The Communist Party Section of the village had surely done its job as an active limb of that horrific apparatus—the County's Party Committee. They had informed the party members and villagers about this "dangerous individual that had arrived in their village," with whom they had to be very vigilant, to follow the guidance of the Great Leader, and to report everything suspicious about him. They had to observe all his actions and words, and report to the village's Communist Party Section every small suspicion when he could show "signs of the bourgeois, capitalistic, and revisionist's ideology and culture." It was clear for Ardian, and he understood that it had to be like this in the society and the social environment where he lived, and he always thought about it as a situation "to cry and laugh at the same time." When he thought about himself being named as "a very dangerous individual for the society, a revisionist, a servant of the bourgeoisie and capitalism, enemy of the Party, the enemy of the people, enemy of working-class," it looked like he was performing a tragedy and comedy being played in the same stage. These tags were used to name the "domestic enemies," speaking on behalf of the "class warfare." It meant that the overthrown class of wealthy people—representing the interests of the bourgeoisie and capitalism—are always trying to defeat communism and socialism by using all the means. While the working class, considered as "the ruling class," must be vigilant against all attempt of the foreign enemy and their domestic collaborators.

Ardian had studied and had passed school exams about such things taught in the school subjects such as: "The History of the Albanian Communist Party," "The Albanian Modern History," "Dialectical Materialism," "Historical Materialism," and he had passed the postgraduate exam of the "Marxism-Leninism Philosophy" that was the official state ideology. He had scored maximum grades in these school subjects and exams as in all others. Everything was clear to him regarding the class-warfare and numerous successes of the Communist Party led by the Great Leader. They have discovered and destroyed a lot of anti-Party groups, attempts for coups d'état by so-called "putschists,"—groups of domestic enemies as cooperators with the foreign enemies in their effort to overthrow the communist regime. Ardian was aware of the high vigilance implemented through all the populace to discover and report any suspicion. And now..., he was wondering, and couldn't believe that it was his turn to be under the surveillance and have such hostile epithets. For those reasons, he understood the coldness and the distance that his colleagues and villagers kept against him. After being adapted to this situation, he didn't feel bad about it and didn't try to change such a situation. This distance of others made him feel more relaxed, calmer, and even freer, without being involved in their discussions and their daily life difficulties and troubles. He felt more comfortable, and this kind of comfort made him think ironically about himself like a real "micro-bourgeois person," as another epithet used in the process of class warfare and the working-class' vigilance. Though he had never seen or met such a human species called "bourgeois" or "micro-bourgeois," and he didn't know how to perceive such a thing.

For one thing only, he always felt compassion and sadness—the high poverty these people were living in and their false happiness. Ardian himself might be a poor person as well, and it couldn't be different in this country, but the poverty of people that he discovered in this village looked to be more and more extreme than his own misery. Time after time, those living beings that walked around the village and agriculture fields, in his eyes and his perception, didn't look like human beings anymore, but they looked just like miserable living organisms. He was observing this destitution with his eyes and perceived this penury with all his senses. He was experiencing this poverty with his life. He could feel this misery from the unbearable stink in the classrooms and school hallways. It was a stench coming from the sweaty and unwashed children's bodies that couldn't be a human smell at all. Time after time, the nurse of the village's health clinic checked their heads and bellies, discovering lice and nits in their heads, and dangerous skin rashes and scabies in their belly skin. The best way to fight against the head lice and nits was a total haircut for boys—the ugly haircut Ardian noticed the very first day. While for girls, it was fought by using kerosene in their heads after cutting their hair very short, the stench of which Ardian smelled very often among girls. He felt deep sorrow and sadness for those poor, innocent children that were always joyful and bustling. Their ugly haircuts, unwashed faces, hands, and bodies, their old, damaged, dirty clothes with a lot of mends and patches, the old broken and dirty shoes, sandals, slippers or wooden clogs, being cobbled and fixed with copper or aluminum electric wires, their dirty fabric-made school bags hanged in their necks, made him understand the full dimensions of the poverty in villages and feel terrified about that. The mud and sludge of rainy days being spread from the unpaved, muddy streets to the stairs, hallways, and classrooms of the school, complemented the masquerade of this "happy" poverty even more. Ardian never thought and never tried to offend these villagers or to insult these eternally innocent, poor children, and that's why he wanted to include himself and become part of their existence and feel as miserable as them. He was and felt as much wretched and unfortunate as them. Their poverty became like his poverty. All of them together were victims of this political system, this communist regime, this dictatorship. When these new concepts—"victims of the political system, communist regime, dictatorship"—crossed his mind for the first time, he felt a shiver going through his entire body, and he was scared. Yes…, he was frightened, and even terrified by these dangerous thoughts. "Now I became a real domestic enemy, a collaborator of the bourgeoisie and foreign enemies, e servant of the capitalists and revisionists," he thought ironically about himself. "And what can I do now?" he asked himself. "Stay silent, docile, obedient, and don't ever think about such things again," he found the answer very quickly.

These silenced thoughts and analyses about the hopeless situation of the villagers became another element in helping him to keep his mind away from Eralda and decided to restart and focus on something else he had forgotten about. It reminded him of the dissertation for the "candidate of science" scientific degree that he had chosen the previous year, for which he had requested its official approval, already denied. He had chosen the thesis: "The depiction of the dictatorships and military juntas' rule in Latin America's literature of the twentieth century." In selecting this thesis, he was inspired by the so-called "Latin American Boom," a term used for the literature of the period 1960 and 1970 in that continent. Based on a lot of books and authors from these countries ruled by dictatorships and military juntas, he wanted to explore the role of literature, poets, and writers in society, and their service in drawing public attention to those dictatorships and military juntas to bring the need for political change in their countries. Strangely enough, some of such books that spoke against the dictators, totalitarianism, and military juntas in Latin America, were translated and published in Albania too, surviving from the censure of the state apparatus. Ardian realized that this happened because Albanian dictatorship considered itself to be different by calling itself "the dictatorship of the proletariat." He thought that it was not any need for him to go so far for such a study since he discovered that the dictatorship was already installed and was ruling right here, in his country, in Albania. But unlike the Latin American literature that he had in his mind—written by the brave and bold writers that denounced the dictatorships in their countries—the Albanian literature was united with the dictator and dictatorship and served them. Ardian thought that a new actual thesis in Albanian conditions might be titled: "Albanian literature under the dictatorship rule, as a propaganda means in the hands of the dictator." This idea and this will of studying, analyzing, and writing something about this thesis, looked very courageous and very dangerous at the same time, and he tried to disregard this bad idea immediately. Doing such a thing was utterly impossible. After he thought for a second time about this idea, he decided to divide his work into two phases to avoid its risks. In the first phase, he could read, analyze, elaborate, and reach conclusions, but only in his mind, without writing anything on paper. After that, in a second phase, he would write everything kept in his mind. With this idea in his mind, he thought for the first time: "Is this dictatorship going to end someday? Will we live forever under such a dictatorship that had already lasted forty years?" Now he thought of himself as being a real "enemy of the Party and the working class, a dangerous agent working for foreign intelligence agencies, a domestic enemy cooperating with foreign enemies," but he couldn't find how and where his connections with the foreign enemy were. While for Latin America's dictatorships and military juntas, he would read and analyze the works of authors, writers, and poets speaking up against the dictatorships in their countries, in Albanian case, he would reread and analyze the Albanian authors, writers, poets, and their works from another point of view—as a propaganda means of the dictatorship, being masterfully used by the dictator, the "Great Leader." With these conclusions in his mind, he started to describe and put in order his first thoughts about the theory of art, literature, and music, the so-called "socialist realism"—the predominant style in Albania serving to the dictatorship, where the communist party and its members were of the utmost importance and were always to be favorably featured.

When the phrase "Dictatorship in Albania" crossed his mind for the first time, he was scared and caught by surprise, and even bringing more questions at the same time. "What is this? Is the situation we are living, a dictatorship? Is this a 'dictatorship of the proletariat'—as the Communist Party and the Great Leader call it—or is it just a dictatorship ruling over the proletariat? Is this socialism—as they like to call it—or is it just a communist dictatorship? Why haven't I felt and understood such a thing before, but only now?" It seemed like he had made a great discovery. He had just discovered the dictatorship, but he must keep this thing as a secret inside him. He felt about himself like being something else, like a man differing from others, while thinking that others had not understood yet that they were living under a dictatorship. "Or..., perhaps, all the people know this, but they keep this secret inside themselves like I am doing now? Or..., maybe not. I as well, being like all of them, had not understood and didn't know this before. But now that I have made such a great discovery, I have the right to feel different from others?" Even though he was a victim of this dictatorship—like everybody else oppressed and suffering from this dictatorship—after this significant discovery he felt free, completely free, while all the rest of the people are still suppressed and punished to live and suffer during entire their life, being happy under the dictatorship. He was enjoying the freedom of thinking and felt freer than others—even though he was under their surveillance and being watched by their vigilant eyes. This discovery gave him the clearness and the full freedom of thinking, but not the freedom of expression. For him, being free to think differently from others was good enough. "Others are still oppressed and captives because, even in their mind, they have not understood yet that they are living in captivity, under a dictatorship, and they don't realize that the occupation of their mind is the greatest slavery," Ardian concluded after all this meditation.

"The Dictator, 'The Great Leader,' with great mastery, has precisely done this: He has seized, has kept captive, and has enslaved the brain of the people of Albania, and for this act he has used the literature and arts as well, using them in service of his devilish aim," Ardian elaborated deeper his reasoning. Now, after this discovery, he had thrown away from himself the chains of captivity, getting rid of the mental slavery and feeling liberated.

Thinking about this, he recalled the first articles of the new Constitution of the People's Socialist Republic of Albania, which he had learned by heart for a contest that he participated while being a student in the pedagogical institute. The new constitution was approved in December 1976, which changed the name of the Albanian state from "People's Republic of Albania" into "People's Socialist Republic of Albania," by just adding the word "socialist," to reflect the "advancement and achievement in building the socialist society," as the communist leadership liked to justify this change. The first articles of the new constitution go as follow:

Article 1: *Albania is a People's Socialist Republic.*

Article 2: *The People's Socialist Republic of Albania is a state of the dictatorship of the proletariat, which expresses and defends the interests of all the working people.*

Article 3: *The Party of Labor of Albania, the vanguard of the working class, is the sole leading political force of the state and the society.*
In the People's Socialist Republic of Albania, the ruling ideology is Marxism-Leninism, and the entire socialist state and society are built based on its principles.

Article 4: *The People's Socialist Republic of Albania, develops the unceasing revolution, by adhering to the class struggle, and aims at ensuring the final victory of the socialism over the capitalism....*

Article 5: *All the state power, in the People's Socialist Republic of Albania, derives from and belongs to the working people...*

While repeating all these articles of the constitution in his mind, he realized the deceptive way the dictator had chosen to mislead the people by saying that we are building the "dictatorship of the proletariat," disguising in this way that he was just making a personal dictatorship, instead. And everything else after that was just a big lie, just cheating the people of

Albania that followed him with loyalty. And in this deceptive way, this dictator had been successful for forty years already, working and preparing a more extended personal dominion by decimating all possible opponents as "spies, collaborators, and servants of the capitalist countries."

Ardian started analyzing life in the village (and the situation was the same in all rural communities of Albania). In this remote village, they only had tasteless cornbread for most of the year. It was a terrible bread, almost uneatable. It reminded Ardian those women and children from villages near the city asking city residents to buy a loaf of wheat bread for them. At that time, Ardian had not seen this as something significant and never asked himself why that was happening, and he helped them very often, especially children, by buying wheat bread for them. But now that he was watching with his eyes how poor the villagers are, and in what miserable conditions they live, he understood the reason. "To live in such poverty, isn't it a dictatorship? To consume three meals of the day, while working all day long in the crops' fields of the agriculture cooperative, having just cornbread with only sugar and water on it, or tomatoes, salt, and onions, isn't it a dictatorship? When the only food store in the village always has empty shelves, isn't it a dictatorship? The fact that most of the villagers buy their daily bread and basic food items for their families on tick (without paying at the moment, but by writing their name on a list to pay when they get their salary at the end of every month), isn't it a dictatorship?" He thought about those people that had their names on the list of the food store and (thinking positively to help some of them, especially those that owed more), he went to the food store an afternoon, with the decision to pay for them. When Ardian told the shopkeeper what he wanted to do, he looked at him suspiciously, shrugging his shoulders and rolling his eyes, and didn't accept his payment. In those sublime human moments, he forgot that, to the eyes of those villagers, he was nothing else but a dangerous individual, with whom they had to be vigilant, to avoid his provocations, and to report every suspicious word and action of him. That's why the shopkeeper didn't allow him to pay for those poor people. On the morrow of this act, Ardian was called at the central offices of the agriculture cooperative, where the chief of the village's Communist Party Section, and two other people, were waiting for him. All three of them, from their appearance, looked a little bit better-fed than the other villagers; they looked poor but not as weak as the villagers that Ardian wanted to help. Those three, one after the other, told Ardian: "Do not disturb the people. Don't offend the strong character and the proudness of the villagers. Don't jog almost naked in the village's surrounding hills. Follow the guidance of the Party, and read the books of the Great Leader carefully." They told Ardian that "in their village, he would never find any space to plant the seeds of his micro-bourgeois garbage, and the villagers didn't need his insulting help that stinks and seems malicious and suspicious." Also, they told him that "he would never be out of the sight of the vigilant eyes of the Party and the people," and that "the Party had given him the warm helping hand by forgiving him once, instead of sending him to prison or internment for all his life, as he deserved it." They lectured Ardian with a lot of such rubbish, and he listened to them with his head down as a penitent one. He accepted all their remarks and showed a self-critique approach because he knew that it was the best way to make them happy, and he couldn't behave differently in front of them. After their discourse, which lasted more than one hour, Ardian retreated to his room. "Happy, poor, proud people, living under a dictatorship," he found the caption of what had just happened to him. "I don't have to destroy their happiness," he concluded. Then he asked himself again: "Are these people happy for real?" He decided not to jog in the hills of the village with sportswear anymore, but to do just some exercise in the small sports ground of the school.

After that ugly event in the cooperative's central offices, Ardian decided to spend more time rereading the Albanian literature of "socialist realism." He had read almost all the books of Albanian writers and poets belonging to this style, but he wasn't aware of these things that he was considering now. He had studied very well the theory of the "socialist realism" as part of his profession, but now he had to reread those books and analyze them from another point of view. He had read those books that always described the happy life of the people—the optimistic working class and patriotic villagers with their joy and achievement, the vigilance and successes against domestic and foreign enemies, the enthusiasm and the work of the youth in building the socialism, the victory of positive characters over the negative ones in their effort to sabotage and plot against the socialism and the Communist Party, the culminant point of conflicts and the resolution always with the triumph of the positive characters that represented the communist party members and the brave working class. Strangely enough, in all these books and their content, Ardian had not discovered or understood anything wrong with them. But now, he started to read and analyze these books thinking differently about the style, the method, the censorship and auto-censorship, propaganda, political line, political control, and about all other characteristics of this style called with a beautiful name—the socialist realism. Now he was calling it by its real name and function, just the literature under control and in service of the dictatorship. He started thinking differently about some banned books and authors; books of Albanian and foreign authors that were withdrawn from the circulation. He rethought about some plenums of the Central Committee of the Albanian Communist Party that had condemned some writers, singers, painters, artists, compositors, and other professions of the art and culture. They were considered and treated as "enemies of the people" and "servants and carriers of the capitalistic ideology," followed by their harsh punishment with imprisonment, internment, or death penalty. After all this in-depth elaboration in his mind, Ardian clarified the real dimensions of the communist dictatorship and its mechanisms, while the literature that he had read all the life was nothing else but just the exploitation of the "socialist realism" in service of the dictatorship. Literature and arts, with their capability of affecting the readers' mind, have been used with trickery to become one of the most essential mechanisms of this dictatorship, a means of the communist propaganda, and unfortunately, it had accomplished its goals. This kind of literature was not owned by people anymore, but it was owned by the dictator, who used it as he wanted to, and through such censored and auto-censored literature, he reached the aims and goals he wanted to. Those novels, novellas, short stories, poems, songs, folklore, dramas, plays, movies, artworks, that Ardian had read and watched before, which had brought him a lot of aesthetic pleasure and inspiration, looked different now. He was discovering and understanding their falsity and their propagandistic role in service of the dictator and his dictatorship. He found out that the main characteristic of the "socialist realism" style was the glorification of communist values, the "emancipation" of the proletariat, the promotion of communist ideals, and loyalty to the Party, and above all, to the glorifying Great Leader.

"But... What about the authors? Writers, poets, dramaturgs, scenarists, compositors, artists, all artworks' authors—are they to blame about this?" That was a new question coming into his mind. He didn't feel like wanting to blame them, because the authors were nothing else but part of the Albanian people being deceived so cunningly. Like all the people, writers and poets were born and grown up under the dictatorship—poor but happy and enthusiastic—and they loved the Great Leader so much without considering him as a dictator. All their first creative expressions were dedicated to the supreme leader, describing the love and loyalty of the people to him. They always called him: "The Dear Leader of the party and the people of Albania, the Great Leader, the legendary Commandant, our immortal and eternal Leader," and with their works, they educated younger generations with the same unconditional love and veneration for the Great Leader, the same as honoring a saint. For that reason, all peoples' first creative attempts are about the "Dear Leader" and the peoples' love and loyalty toward him.

Ardian was feeling happy by this new realization he was creating in himself, but he was conscious that he had to be careful and protect himself by not writing and not speaking about such dangerous and life-threatening things for him and his family as well.

22

His work of rereading and reanalyzing the Albanian literature of the "socialist realism" from a new point of view, made Ardian remember and think more rarely about Eralda, but it was impossible not to remember her at least several times a day. For some weeks, he didn't go to the city for weekends. Instead, he stayed in the village, spending more time reading books or walking around the hills and the forest, visiting a more expanded area.

But he couldn't resist longer without seeing Eralda, and so that he took the bus one Saturday afternoon to go and spend the weekend in Elbasan. After his arrival, he waited for Eralda near the evening high school. He was staying in a dark corner across the street from the school gate and saw Eralda and her class friends leaving the school at the end of the fourth period. Eralda continued her way back home, walking together with other friends, and Ardian walked after them at a certain distance. He couldn't meet her, because a male friend of her class accompanied her up to her apartment building. While he was following them from a distance, for the first time, he thought with jealousy and evil intention. "She has found another one," was the first jealous thought that went through his mind. He didn't like their way of talking, their slow walking, and the time they spent together by staying some more minutes talking in front of the building entrance. Ardian returned to the hotel room more exhausted than ever. Nex day, in the morning, he strolled toward Eralda's store with less desire to meet her, after watching her accompanied by another boy the night before. He found Eralda in the store talking in a friendly way with another girl. Eralda didn't show any impression when Ardian entered the store. Her eyes and her face didn't express any emotions. With the same indifference and coldness, she answered his greeting, presenting the other girl to him.

168

"This is Entela. This is my ex-literature teacher," she said coldly. Her face and her eyes remained cold and without any expression, even when she mentioned "my ex-literature teacher." She said it with such a dry tone and cold voice as if he hadn't been something more for her, but just an ex-literature teacher. Ardian got upset by her indifference and didn't want to stay any longer there.

"I was passing by and came in just to greet you," he told her and left the store.

He walked toward the hotel, with his head filled with a lot of new evil thoughts about Eralda. When she said the other girl's name, "Entela," Ardian recalled that she was her close friend from the regular high school, about whom Eralda had told him before. As Eralda had told him, Entela had been in love for the first time since the third year of high school. Then, she left him and started the second relationship with a soldier from another city who was a conscript in the barracks near Elbasan. Later on, she had left the second one to marry a man from the capital city, Tirana, whom she had met while vacating on the beach, in Durrës. When Ardian recalled all these love stories of her close friend, Entela, his mind moved directly in the direction of Eralda, thinking that she might be like her friend as well. This thought was reinforced by the fact of seeing Eralda the night before, especially the way of walking and talking with the other guy.

"Maybe it was just a bit of good luck helping me run away from this bad girl, that might be like her close friend, Entela," Ardian thought first, remembering two famous expressions: "Show me who your friends are, and I'll tell you who you are. You are only as good as the company you keep." Ardian spent all day lying on the bed with these evil thoughts going through his mind. He was wondering how he had fallen in love with such a bad girl, and strangely enough, he was determined and ready to marry her without thinking twice. "Perhaps this is why they say, 'Love is blind,'" he remembered the adage in the English language, meaning that, when you love someone, you cannot see any flaws in that person. "Yes…, yes. It was love at first sight, and it was blind," he repeated to himself several times that day.

After having a quiet lunch in a restaurant, he felt sorry for himself and for the evil thoughts that were crossing his mind about Eralda, the girl that he had loved so much, and for whom he was still feeling a strong love. "No…, no. All these bad things I'm thinking about her now cannot be true. Alda cannot be a bad girl," and with this new thought in his mind, he hurried up toward her store again. He entered the store and saw Eralda staying at the end side of the counter, talking with a customer about something he wanted to buy. Ardian didn't greet her and walked toward the other end side of the counter, where he saw some schoolbooks and notebooks. Standing there, he randomly took a notebook in his hands and started leafing through its pages, without any intention. He was enjoying her beautiful calligraphic handwriting without focusing on reading anything on those pages. He reached the last page, and in the inner part of the back cover, he saw a line written on the right side of the bottom of the page. That line drew his attention, and he focused his eyes, where he read: "*I left you, Adi…, I left you.*"

He couldn't believe his eyes, and he didn't understand those words. It seemed like being just a vagary of his mind, already sick and crazy of her. He took another notebook as an attempt to forget about what he read in the first one. He, instinctively, without knowing what was doing, passed all pages quickly to arrive in the last one and checked the inner part of the back cover. The same sentence was written in its bottom right corner, too: "*I left you, Adi…, I left you.*" First, he thought he was looking by mistake at the same notebook, and opened the other one again, kept both open at the last page to ensure himself that the same sentence was written in both of them. Then he took a book, and opened it immediately to the back cover, where, in its bottom right corner, he saw the same sentence, written with the beautiful calligraphy of her handwriting: "*I left you, Adi…, I left you.*" He leafed through another book and discovered the same thing on its last page. It reminded him of a quote, that he had read years ago, and that he had said it to Eralda as well: "I have written your name in all my books and notebooks." While he was thinking this quote, Eralda—that had watched him and had understood what he had discovered in her books and notebooks—was approaching him. Ardian, being inspired by what he had read, forgot their separation and whispered joyfully to her:

"Your name, Alda, is still written in all my books and notebooks."

"And…, you saw and read by yourself what I have written in all my books and notebooks. I have written what is a reality now, and we have to accept that as such. Please, don't come here anymore," Eralda spoke with a low voice without looking at him, picking up her books and notebooks to put them in a drawer under the counter.

"If this is what you really want, I'll not come to bother you anymore," Ardian answered quickly, and left the store immediately, without any greetings. He walked toward the hotel without having any idea what to think about that girl now. Should he believe good things, or should he think bad things about her, after her ultimatum for not bothering her anymore?

Ardian thought that Eralda had written that sentence not with her hand, but with her heart and her soul. It was her heart and her soul that groaned: "*I left you, Adi..., I left you.*" It was her pride and strong character that made her determined in that path: "*I left you, Adi..., I left you.*" It was her love for him, still living deep in her soul, from where it complained: "*I left you, Adi..., I left you.*" It was her final decision to give an end to this love that controlled her willpower: "*I left you, Adi..., I left you.*" Love, heart, soul, character, pride, determination, complaint, decision, willpower—all these words, describing Eralda's feelings and attitude, were passing through Ardian's mind, but they seemed quite empty words, without any meaning, without any connection, without any logic, without any sense, without any reasoning. She was taking the initiative and the enormous burden to leave the guy she was in love with, the man for whom her heart and her soul were still complaining and groaning.

"How could such a thing happen? It looks like something unreal, something that only she could do. I'm not capable of doing such a thing," he thought about what was happening to his love. As soon as he arrived in front of the hotel, he stopped there thinking for few minutes and turned back furiously with the decision to go to her store to tell her that she must not do such a thing since she was still in love with him, and her heart and soul were groaning for her love for him. But he didn't have that chance. Eralda had closed the store and had left.

How could she stay there any longer after the unpleasant ouster from the store she did to Ardian? "What were those words? How did those words come out of my mouth? How was I able to oust the person I love so much, with all my heart, feelings, and soul?" Eralda was thinking about herself as soon as Ardian left the store. She was already transformed into two bodies with two minds and two souls. Her heart and her soul were given forever to only one person and would never be able to accept another one. In her heart and her soul was sitting and had grown deep roots, the love for Ardian. It was her first love and would never leave that place. Another hollow body, another blank mind, and another void soul were making these decisive steps and meaningless actions.

When Ardian returned to the village on Monday morning, he found his room in a real mess, where books and notebooks were spread all over the floor, table, chairs, and bed. His clothes were thrown all over the place, giving the impression that everything had undergone a careful check. He understood what had happened. Somebody from the state secret service had done a thorough inspection, scrutinizing everything, trying to find something compromising and incriminating that might be used for another punishment of him. "So..., I'm still in their plans. I'm still their target. I'm still a person of interest to them. I'm still wanted to be sent to the guillotine," Ardian thought a little bit scared after that. He felt very happy for the critical and smart decision he had taken not to write anything from what he was analyzing in his mind. He had given himself the quality and capability of putting in his mind in a very accurate and precise order all his thoughts, analyses, and conclusions about the dictatorship and "socialist realism." It looked like he was writing everything in his mind in a way that at any moment could all be written in the same accurate order, and this process gave him an inner optimism that he would be free to do that someday.

In contrast to this unique capability, he was not capable of thinking clearly in analyzing and putting in order the conclusions on what was happening with his love. He couldn't find a good reason and couldn't reach a definite conclusion on why Eralda was behaving like that, and he was not able to take his final decision on what he had to do for his part in response to her behavior. "Should I continue to beg her earnestly, or to forget everything, to skip her from my mind, letting it go and move on with my life?" He was eager to entreat her endlessly and tirelessly, even though in this way, he would lose something from his character, his dignity, his pride, and personality. But he was still sure that it was worth it and that it was needed to be done to convince the girl that he always loved so much.

Ardian continued to think about this love the same way as he had felt months ago, forgetting that the situation had changed, and he was not the same person as before. He didn't consider that in other people's eyes, he was another kind of person now. He wasn't the smart professor with a bright future anymore. He wasn't the successful, erudite professor anymore, but he had become just a suspicious individual now. He was somebody transferred to a remote village for political and ideological reasons, becoming an individual without any future. He was like being sent to internment now, and nobody would dare to approach him anymore. The communist regime, parallel with the incarceration used against the "domestic enemies," used more often another form of punishment. It was called internment, but instead of bringing those suspects all together in some internment camps, they and their families were just displaced forcefully from their cities and houses to remote villages and towns, where life would surely be more difficult for them. There, they were employed under challenging jobs and lived in harsh conditions, being always under the surveillance of the state secret service and the vigilance of the ordinary people that would report everything suspicious about their actions. It was something usual that you find interned individuals and families in most of the remote villages and towns where they stayed separated by other inhabitants, being quiet, obedient, and very correct in every task and every job they were given. The locals didn't dare to make company and friendship with them, and youngsters couldn't fall in love or marry youngsters from those families. Ardian had seen a couple of interned families in the remote mountain village of his father, in Vlorë County, but in that time, it hadn't been a big impression on him because it was something quite usual. But now that he recalled members of those families that he had seen in his father's village, Ardian thought about himself that he was almost in the same situation as them—a person in internment in this remote village, placed under the surveillance of the state secret service and the vigilance of the people. The situation in which he found his room helped him to reach this conclusion.

So, he was under the surveillance of the state secret service, "the sharp tip of the sword of the working class," as the Great Leader liked to call this unique and essential mechanism of his tyrannical rule. The dictator used this kind of terminology in his enthusiastic, revolutionary speeches held in front of the cheering crowds and happy people every time he discovered and sent to guillotine "the enemies of the Party and the people" and "the collaborators of the bourgeoisie and capitalistic countries."

After these reflections, and from this new position that he found out for himself, Ardian started to think and reevaluate Eralda's love for him too. He tried to convince himself and be aware that now, as a person in internment and under the surveillance of the state secret service, he had not the right to bother and disturb Eralda anymore. "Perhaps she is thinking in the same way about me now. If this is the real reason for her strange behavior and her estrangement, then…, she is right," Ardian thought from this new point of view he gave to himself. "I must not bother her anymore. I'm just a convicted person now, and I will remain as such for my entire life. Someday, I will become a victim of the state secret service that is in need to fulfill their annual plan of discovering and eliminating 'enemies.' A subsequent imprisonment or death penalty is waiting for me. I will suffer, but no need for her to suffer because of me," he concluded. Ardian loved her so much, and he was conscious that she didn't deserve to endure together with him. He couldn't accept and couldn't cause such unjust suffering to her. That's why he decided not to disturb her anymore. It was a terrifying decision for him, but he had to take such a decision being forced by the situation of living under such a wild, callous, and ruthless dictatorship.

23

The summer holidays arrived, and Ardian went to spend the holidays with his family in Vlorë. From the first days he came there, he started thinking again about Eralda and for the destiny of their love. He had already understood that whatever way he would believe and challenge himself, with good and bad thoughts about Eralda, and whatever decision would take, he would never reach his goal of removing her from his mind. She will remain as the eternal remembrance of his first love, followed by the pain and sadness of its loss. She will remain as the object and the subject of his dreams. Eralda and her love will remain as the ultimate cause of his desperation and tears. He thought that he had lost this love without any reason and without a farewell or closure.

Ardian had been home in April, where he spent the week of the school spring break. He had walked the streets of the city downtown and its periphery, and in silence, he had watched and analyzed the poverty of the city, comparing it with the village's penury. He had seen children and women from villages situated near Vlorë, asking inhabitants of the town to buy a loaf of wheat bread for them, or begging the shopkeepers of the food stores to sell them a bottle of cooking oil, or a kilogram of wheat flour, rice, sugar, cheese, and other necessary food that they couldn't find in their village's food stores. Those children reminded Ardian of his students because they looked very much alike, and he always helped them by buying wheat bread for them. Ardian had walked near all the bread stores of his city, especially in the evening, to help those poor children. It was easier for him in the bread stores because the shopkeeper would sell bread to people just based on their appearance and clothing. That was enough to distinguish city residents from poor peasants with their old dirty clothes, unhealthy and unwashed face skin, and hair. But it was difficult to buy food articles for them in the grocery

175

stores because all essential food articles were sold based on the lists that each grocery store had for the residents of the neighborhood it served. A food rationing for a family was implemented on which basis people could only buy a small portion per month of each article, such as wheat flour, dry beans, sugar, rice, cheese, meat, cooking oil, olive oil, and just a small packet of one hundred grams of coffee beans. So that Ardian couldn't help them with food items, but some women from villages could arrange something by leaving a small tip to the shopkeeper or giving him or her some fruits or eggs from the village.

Ardian found the same situation when he returned to his city for the summer holidays. He got the impression that queues in every food store were made longer, and the food supply lesser. Especially the queues for meat and milk had become longer. People stayed in line starting before midnight, and sometimes they had to fight with each other for their position in the queue. The supply of cheese, eggs, meat, salami, became lesser and lesser and the same thing for every food, that were already rationed in smaller portions for every family in a month. Ardian had a clear understanding of the reason for this food shortage, and he had the right names for this; "poverty and dictatorship," the banned words that could never be said loudly. There had been cases in all cities when people had gone to prison just because of expressing the complaint about the empty food stores, making an example of them, and so that nobody else could dare to speak up about such things. Ardian didn't discuss these things during the school spring break because it was just a week, but now that he had to stay longer with his family, he decided to start this talk with his father.

"Dad, I have forgotten about the love with that girl of the evening high school, and I have forgotten about my unjust transfer in that remote village that might be seen as punishment with internment. I have forgotten about the inspection of the agents of the state secret service in my room, and I will forget a lot of other things, but there is something else that I can never forget. I cannot forget and cannot remove from my mind the poverty and the miserable situation of the villages and the villagers. Their living conditions are the same as Migjeni, our famous poet of poverty, has described it fifty years ago. They are Migjenian villages and villagers indeed. I have discovered there the actuality of Migjeni's poems about the poverty and injustice of that time. And as an irony, we read his poems, we learn them by heart, we recite them, we comment on them, we analyze and discuss his literary works, right there in the classrooms filled with poor starving

children. I teach and explain the Migjeni's "Poem of Poverty," and those innocent skinny children have to learn and recite it by heart, but I'm making a blind eye and cannot speak about the actual poverty and the harsh reality in which those children and their families are living. Most of the children of the school look like Migjeni's "Luli, the Little Boy" and do not differ at all from the Migjeni's descriptions. We criticize and denounce the time and the governance system in which Migjeni lived, wrote, and died, but we don't dare to say anything about our time and our political system we are living in. We, the populace of the cities, are poor, but for the people that live in the villages, it is like a luxury for them to be called needy. They are living in destitution, yes, they live in miserable conditions, and every time I see them, the only thing that comes to my mind is the book of the French writer, Victor Hugo, with a distinctive and significant title, "Les Miserables" (The Miserable Ones), with the principal events taking place in 1832, where the main character, a needy peasant, was imprisoned nineteen years at hard labor for breaking into a bakery, stealing a loaf of bread for his sister's starving child. I cannot forget and cannot take out of my mind the fact that most of the peasants in our country don't have enough money to buy food for their children. They purchase food and bad cornbread "on tick," with their name on the store's list, to pay the owed money with their small salary at the end of the month. And then, the list restarts again month after month. I cannot forget that we, the city residents, buy our food articles with monthly rations, staying in a queue for a long time, but they, the villagers, cannot have such essential food articles at all, not even by portions. I cannot forget your sad faces when you return home empty-handed from the milk store. Even though you have gone to the milk queue at three or four o'clock in the morning, and after staying in line for three or four hours, the milk has finished, and you cannot buy any bottle of milk. You leave the store with the decision to go there one hour earlier in the coming mornings. Finally, I cannot forget and take out of my mind that we…, all of us…, the people of Albania…, all together…, are living in poverty and under a horrifying tyrannical dictatorship, and strangely enough, we all are and have to be happy." Ardian finished his long speech addressed to his father.

His father had listened to entire Ardian's speech with attention and in silence, looking down time after time, without daring to look at his son's eyes.

"My darling son…, I have never thought about these things you are speaking about. We discuss among work peers every day about empty stores, the food shortage, and for the long queues in front of the food stores, with which we are annoyed indeed, but we have never reached as deep and far as you want to go. My son..., these are dangerous things. You might be right in what you just said, but..., please..., one hundred times, please..., for the sake of us, please..., for the sake of the family and our kinsfolk don't speak like this with anybody else. Let's be happy with your transfer to a remote village because even the worst things could have happened. Take away from your mind those thoughts, please...," his father finished by rubbing Ardian's shoulders and arms, just to close such a serious conversation.

It was the first time for Ardian to discuss such things with somebody else, and he chose his father to do that, as the most trusted man for him. He couldn't have such conversation with anybody else, but he felt the need to open himself and talk about that with someone, to share with somebody else the mountain of silent thoughts and analyses gathered in his head. He was sure that every other person who would hear such discussion would denounce and report him to the communist party offices, to the police and the state secret service, followed by a harsh punishment for him, his family, and his relatives.

While staying home, he had more time to think about Eralda, and she came to his mind more often, compared to the time when he was in the village. He recalled the great love he had for her and the great love she as well had shown for him. He recalled all the beautiful moments and happy times they had spent together. He remembered the dates they had had and started asking himself why they had not had sex. If he had had sex with her, it would be better because it wouldn't be so easy for her to leave him if she had lost her virginity to him. Or, maybe, it is a good thing that he hadn't had sex with her because this thing would have forced them to stay together. "Perhaps, it was better that I got rid of her. Maybe Eralda was the same kind of a bad girl like her close friend, Entela," he thought time after time. He recalled the sentence he read in her books and notebooks: "I left you, Adi..., I left you." It was a sentence that expressed groan, complaint, and lament, coming from the bottom of her heart and her soul, and at the same time, those words expressed feelings, love, consolation, responsibility, and the determination of her character. She had taken the burden and responsibility of their separation and was doing that with a strange confidence. He missed her very much and couldn't resist it anymore. He decided to go and see her once more, to try to talk and convince her for the sake of their reciprocal, great love.

178

"I have to go to see my friend Bashkim and ask him to find some books for me," he told his parents, and the next day he arrived at the Eralda's store.

"Alda, I came to ask for your love once more. I'm very much in love with you, and I know you feel the same for me. I'm sure that we are losing each other without any reason," he pleaded her, speaking with entreaty.

"Let us remain just friends," that's all she said. "I have to close the store now because I'm going somewhere," she continued, after some seconds of silence, walking toward the door, with the door's keys in her hands.

Eralda had reached in such a spiritual situation that couldn't endure any more while seeing Ardian coming to her store, begging for her love. He didn't need to beg her. He had her love, but she had already taken a different decision. She loved that man with all of her heart and her soul but was trying hard to keep him away, following her decision. This terrified inner fight tortured her a lot. That's why, when she saw him again entering her store, she couldn't bear anymore and couldn't stay to talk with him anymore, because she was afraid of bursting into tears and cry in front of him. That's why she closed the store and run back home, where she threw herself on her bed and started crying loudly.

Eralda as well thought about Ardian very often. She was feeling very sorry about his expulsion from the Pedagogical Institute, and for his transfer in that remote village. She believed and blamed herself for what happened to him because she was the reason for his actions for which he was punished, but now she couldn't do anything to help and save him from this bad luck. Sometimes she thought that this transfer would keep him far away from her, and therefore they would see each other more rarely. "Out of sight, out of mind," Eralda recalled this famous adage in English. Albanians say: "Away from the eye, away from the heart," sounding more romantic and being used just for people in love and the negative consequence of the absence when they are far from each other. She had wept while telling her mother that the literature teacher had been transferred to a remote village for political and ideological reasons. Her mother thought about her tears as tears for her crush on literature teacher, but she didn't know how far she had gone with her love. She had thought that it was just one-sided love, just Eralda's unexpressed love for her teacher, just a hidden, inner crush of a girl like it happens so often with girls, and she asked her daughter to ensure herself if she was in love with him.

"Yes. I have loved, and I still love him very much. In the meanwhile, he loves me too and keeps begging me continuously for marriage, but I don't want to marry him," Eralda had opened her heart to her mother, at last, but without telling her everything they had done.

"You are right," her mother had been answered. "Think about him like being sent in internment now, and in this way, you can easily keep him far from your mind," she had advised Eralda.

Treating Ardian like this wasn't fair. She knew and was sure that, because of the love she felt for Ardian, she wouldn't care for his transfer or his internment at all, as her mother advised her, but she would go anywhere with him. But she had decided to leave him before his transfer happened, meaning that the reason for her separation was not his transfer, but his family's disapproval of their love. Eralda had been shaken when she heard her mother using the word "internment," but later, she started thinking more often of this new situation of him. Sometimes her reasoning was telling her that a girl has the right to refuse the love of somebody sent in internment in a very remote area, but this approach seemed not honest for real love. Other times, she thought to surrender herself and accept Ardian's repeated requests for marriage, and the reciprocal love they felt for each other deserved it, but later she thought again that her acceptance would cause a lot of trouble for her and her family as well. Eralda remembered what she had felt about Ardian's parents being in their right not to accept her as their son's wife by not allowing their son's love, as a professor's love for a shopkeeper, for a night school student. And now, based on the same reasoning, she thought that her parents and her family as well, had their own right not to admit and not allow their daughter to marry somebody so far away, "somebody in internment," she repeated the words used by her mother. And maybe that's why her mother chose these harsh words, wanting to give Eralda one more reason for her separation. Furthermore, the official "political and ideological" basis used for his transfer was the same reason used so often for the real internment of several people and families.

The way Eralda ousted him from the store, by showing him the door and closing the store, was real devastation for Ardian. He left the store and walked completely shaken toward the train station, where he stayed and spent all the time until the afternoon train arrived. "She is right," he thought, trying to become self-conscious for the reason of her refusal. "Perhaps she has started to think that the love and the marriage with this teacher that works in a remote village, is not worth it anymore. Maybe she considers my transfer as internment, and this fact makes her so strong in her decision and pushes her not to accept any discussion with me anymore. She is on her own right to think like this, and I don't have to bother her anymore." Ardian had to accept this new situation, even though it would be challenging.

Even though she had decided to separate from him, Eralda still felt love for him, somewhere deep inside herself, in the inner part of her body and her soul. She was always connected with this love, and time after time, it looked like she only had a bad dream and as if this bad dream would end very soon, and they would return to their great love again. She liked this kind of inner connection, and it had remained alive being reinvigorated every time Ardian entered the store and repeated his request by telling her: "We are losing each other without any reason." Based on the existence of such an inner love connection, Eralda sometimes thought that they were losing each other without any good reason indeed. And she was just waiting powerlessly that this bad dream to end by itself, and she didn't try at all to wake up, and end this bad dream, like a nightmare that was killing her love.

When she saw Ardian the last time, the confident way he left the store, with the promise that he was not going to disturb her anymore, Eralda feared that this weak thread would break, and this kind of deep inner connection would come to an end and would not exist anymore. She saw Ardian going away convinced and conscious of leaving her alone, and that's why she was shaken a lot. After his leaving, she realized that what was happening in her life was not a dream, and there was not any chance this nightmare to end. It was a reality, a bitter and unbelievable reality. She saw the end of this love, the ending that she had never thought about. She had just thought about the separation, but not about the end of her love, and that's why that day she cried longer than other times when she went back home.

Eralda was not doing well at school during the second semester. She didn't study like before and became like all other students of the evening high school. Teachers were shown mercilessly and didn't forgive her, giving her bad grades. In this way, she gave an end to her desire and hope for continuing studies in the pedagogical institute. But strangely enough, she didn't feel bad about that. After losing her beautiful love, every other loss in her life didn't impress her at all. She had already forgotten about everything else, and nothing was important in her life anymore. She was transformed into a hollow body—without desire, without plans for the future, without hope in her life. She was just waiting for life's waves without the smallest resistance and without any attempt to change the course or stop something terrible from happening to her.

In those moments, when she closed the store just to evict Ardian from there, she was waiting and desiring her death more than ever. She didn't know what to expect from this life anymore. She thought that she was going to die very soon, and death would be the best savior for her. She felt that she had to commit suicide, as the best way to forget everything and leave this nefarious life.

24

In September 1984, with the start of the new school year, a young female teacher arrived in that school, teaching elementary school classes. She was just graduated from the Pedagogical Institute of Elbasan, and Ardian had taught literature in her course; thus, she knew Ardian since she had started the first year as institute's student.

Elsa, the new teacher, despaired very much when she learned about her assignment in this remote village. She was graduated with high results as a teacher of the elementary school for grades one to four, and she was very unhappy with her assignment because they had not considered her excellent grade point average. All her friends were assigned to the schools near the city, while her appointment was the worst one. It happened like this because other students belonged to families with origin from Elbasan or were married in such families and in this way, they were able to find family friends and relatives with good connection to the County's Education Department, the County's Party Committee, or the County's Executive Committee, to help in their first job assignment after graduation, and support them in their career advancement in the future. Elsa's parents, instead, had moved to Elbasan from the county of Korça, and they didn't have any family relatives in Elbasan, remaining without any support and connections so much needed in such cases.

More than ninety percent of the students in the elementary school teachers' branch (EST) were females, and another thing differentiating Elsa from other female students of her course was that all of them were engaged and married during the school years, before graduation and their first assignment as teachers, while she was still single. This was something special that distinguished the female students of the EST branch from the female students of other departments of the pedagogical institute. The acceptance of a man's proposal during the school years was a conscious goal and an objective for the EST female students (EST students were called by others as "the EST-s," a term being used as derision, mockery, and irony most of the time). A theory about their goal for early engagement and marriage explained this phenomenon with the fact that they would not have any more marriage proposals after their assignment in villages' schools. While a funny theory explained this occurrence by saying that most of "the EST-s" were chubby and peppy. Unlike other branches' girls that were more preoccupied with their appearance, the EST's girls accepted the very first proposal addressed to them, starting to taste all pleasures of love. The first engaged girls served like an accelerant for other girls, being urged to do the same thing, and so, month after month and year after year, all of them were already engaged or married before graduation.

At the end of the third year, before the graduation, among the EST's female students, you would find bridegrooms from all the walks of life (students, workers, engineers, teachers, economists, financiers, police officers, army officers, lawyers), while the most beautiful female student would marry a professor of the pedagogical institute. Most of the EST students came from other counties of central Albania and families of the working-class and villagers. As such, they were happy marrying a man in the city of Elbasan and not going back to their small towns and villages. In other branches of the pedagogic institute, most of the girls were from the city and county of Elbasan, and fewer from other provinces. Elsa was from Elbasan, and she always thought that girls from other towns, villages, and counties, by staying together in the institute's dormitory, became more high-spirited, and frenzy, influencing too much to each other in their hurry to accept every marriage proposal addressed to them. Though Elsa envied their zest and easy way of agreeing on a marriage proposal, she had resisted and didn't take any of them so that she was the only female student among "the EST-s" being graduated as a single.

Since the day she learned about her assignment in Red Hill's school, until the first day when she took the teachers' bus to get there, Elsa was very pessimistic, sad, and desperate. But everything changed for her and transformed into a big joy from the moment she saw Ardian, her ex-literature professor, taking the same bus as her in the bus station. Elsa was shy and didn't greet him, but she spent all the travel time wondering whether Ardian was working in the same school as her. When she saw him staying on the bus for the last stop, her joy became happiness. She decided that day, that moment, in that bus, that this wonderful guy, the ex-professor of the pedagogical institute, that had been the institute's bachelor and the dream of every girl, now would become hers. It was her good luck that finally knocked on her door. When a girl accepts and decides with full consciousness for such a thing, there is nothing in the world to stop her, and she would overcome every kind of obstacle. Elsa, the bashful girl that had answered "no" to all proposals, sometimes just because she was too shy to say "yes," now decided to get rid of and throw away her shyness, her timidity, and every kind of reluctance of hers.

Elsa, like all other students of the pedagogical institute, had heard all rumors about the reason for Ardian's expulsion from the Pedagogical Institute and his transfer to a remote village. Rumors said that he was transferred for immorality after a relationship with an evening high school female student, or even worse, with some of them. Other stories said that he was transferred for political and ideological reasons and behaviors that were against the Communist Party and Great Leader's guidance, and even the worst, for hostile acts against the government and the people of Albania. But Elsa, from the first day that saw Ardian working in the same school with her, decided to multiply by zero all these rumors spread about him. She chose not to consider anything of them, either the morality reason or the political and ideological reasons for his transfer. Elsa knew him very well and decided to follow her heart, and she felt right about that. She was not going to consider the danger that his assignment could become everlasting internment in that village since nobody would dare to reassign him back to a city school or in a town near the city. It was a new strange feeling developing and growing inside her so quickly and so actively. She had never experienced this kind of sweet sentiment that was born somewhere deep in the unknown inner part of her soul, her heart, and her body, that until now has been inactive. This new feeling was so great, so sublime, and so alluring, making her feel proud and optimistic, and because of that temptation, all those rumored reasons for his transfer seemed very small and unimportant things to her. She understood and found the name of this new feeling—it was love, and she couldn't say "no" to it for no reason. "This wonderful guy deserves a great love and a stroke of good luck, and I'll give him both of them," was the sublime thought that came into her mind and her decision after that great feeling she was experiencing in the bus. With the clearness and certainty of a grown mature girl, she decided to approach Ardian and try hard to win his mind, his heart, and his love. She was sure that Ardian was worth it, and he deserved her love, and she would be fortunate to marry such a man and make him her husband. From the very first day, she decided to sacrifice everything a young woman needs to sacrifice to win the heart and love of a man. With all these thoughts crossing through her mind, Elsa didn't feel the time spent on the bus. When the bus stopped in the center of the village, Ardian was the first one to get off, and he waited outside the bus for her.

"I think..., I know you," Ardian told her while shaking hands. "I may recall that your name is Elsa..., and I remember that you were the best student of EST. But what surprises me is the fact that I don't see any rings in your fingers," he continued, trying to bring some humor to his first greeting.

She laughed loudly and felt like being in the seventh heaven for everything he said and for the friendly way he greeted her.

"Thank you, professor. I'm pleased that you remember me, my face, and my name," Elsa answered to him, with a big smile and blushing face.

"My name is Ardian, short, Adi," he reminded her of his name, to be called by his name and not as a professor. "And..., enjoy your first assignment! Enjoy this village! And..., I like your rosy cheeks," Ardian tried to relieve her embarrassment and bring joy to her when he saw her blushing cheeks, and because he was sure that she was not happy with her assignment in this remote village.

Ardian was not thinking and was not searching for a new love in his life yet. Eralda was still reigning supreme in his mind and soul. But in that kind of environment, spending days and nights with two other couples in "the teachers' palace," wouldn't be difficult for a third couple to be created, and furthermore, in this case when the girl was self-conscious and determined to do such a thing. One of the couples was already legally married at the city clerk's office during the summer holidays, so they were officially married and could stay in one room as spouses. So that one room would belong to the just married couple now, one for two girls, and one for two men.

"The County Education Department listened to our praying, and that's why they assigned another girl here," the married woman spoke loudly for everybody else to listen, when they arrived at "the teachers' palace," making everybody laughing loudly.

Those two teachers made the official marriage because such a thing became a necessity at that time. The economic crisis, accompanied by the food shortage, and the lack of apartments (that like everything else were state ownership), was at its worst low of all the time. The consequences of these difficulties were the food rationing per family per month, and the living of married couples in the same small apartment with their parents for many years, and sometimes two married couples were staying in the same apartment with their parents. Therefore, new couples used to hurry to make the official marriage as soon as possible, being married just in papers, way before the big wedding party, with a big dinner with the participation of all their families' relatives and friends. In this way, as a new family, they could bring additional food rations and apply for an apartment to the respective state offices. But they still stay and live apart, each one in his or her own family, postponing the real marriage (the wedding party with its rituals, festivities), for some more months or years depending on their age. It happened because of a lack of apartments, and new couples were placed on a waiting list after their application to the state offices.

From the first week of Elsa's arrival, Ardian understood her intention, and he made all the efforts to stay away from her and avoid the opportunity to spend time together. Ardian followed the same daily routine as before, by having meals in the agriculture cooperative's canteen without joining the other teachers who, as always, brought food from their homes every Monday morning. Ardian added to his daily schedule another activity, for his pleasure and to avoid and keep Elsa far from him. He had decided to walk around all that region, from Red Hill to all neighbor villages, to add contacts with nature and to discover nature's beauties of that region. Red Hill was situated right at the southwest end of the County of Elbasan, bordering with the County of Lushnja to the west of Red Hill, and County of Berat in the south. That southwest region of Elbasan County is called Dumre and includes about forty small villages, with its central town called Belësh. Dumre is a beautiful plateau, 300-550 feet above the sea level, with low hills and about eighty karstic lakes, small and big ones.

In autumn, the nature of that area was still beautiful. The first week, Ardian started his walk going through the road connecting with the neighbor village. He had seen this road from the bus, and he liked it because the entire route that connected these two villages passed through a forest. He had seen and learned that two almost parallel roads were going through the woods, one called the summer road (to be used during not rainy days), and the other one called the winter road (to be used during rainy days, the wet and mud season). The winter road was paved with stones and gravel and traveling on it was a terrible experience because of the bus shaking. This road is used to avoid stalling in the mud. The summer road was not paved, and the bus didn't tremble, but a cloud of thick dust was produced behind the bus, entering inside the bus as well. There were no cars or trucks on these roads because the privately-owned cars or trucks didn't exist in Albania. The only vehicles on those roads were the teachers' bus (running there on Mondays and Saturdays during the school season), two small trucks of the agriculture cooperative, the car of the head of the agriculture cooperative, and the agronomist's motorcycle. So Ardian spent the first week by walking every afternoon on these two roads, and other narrow paths through the forest, returning to his room in the evening just before the dusk. He went every week on different routes and destinations, visiting all villages in that area, spending more time in nature. He spent the afternoons of one week walking in the bed of the river Devoll, passing it on foot, going to the other side of the river to visit villages on that side. On Sunday of another week, he went to the villages of the Berat County, up to a town called Stalin City (named after the Soviet Union's dictator, as decided by the Albanian dictator). The old name of this town was Kuçovë, but no one dared to use that name anymore. Ardian found the same poverty in all the villages he visited. He saw and met tired villagers, almost exhausted by working all day long in the agricultural fields, spending a lot of time walking to the workplace and coming back home.

The agriculture cooperatives in Dumre region cultivated wheat, corn, sunflowers, and tobacco plants, but most of the work and product transportation was still done by hand because of the hilly terrain and lack of roads and agriculture machinery.

Ardian usually spent the Saturdays' afternoon and all Sundays staying in his room while the other teachers traveled back to their families in Elbasan. He continued reading books of Albanian authors of socialist realism. He read novels, novellas, short stories, poems, dramas, and folklore, everything influenced by the socialist realism that was sanctioned by the communist state. He analyzed everything in his mind avoiding writing, and he continued this work every weekday afternoon during his long walks and while relaxing in the forest, by a lake or by the river. To help his memory, he started writing down in a notebook the titles of the books, the authors names, main characters, excerpts, paragraphs, and quotations from the books (without any of his comments), with the intention that these parts taken from those books would remind him later what real conclusion he had reached when he had read them. Now and then, he wrote even positive comments and analyses, glorifying the socialist realism style, but in his mind, he meant the

188

opposite of what he had written. It was like a sophisticated way that would help him to rewrite his real conclusions later on.

All this work of rereading and analyzing socialist realism helped Ardian to think and hope that this dictatorship would end someday, and people would have the opportunity to be free and speak openly. It would bring the chance for him to write and speak publicly for his analysis of the socialist realism and dictatorship, and people would finally be free to discover and understand the bitter truth about the tyrannical dictatorship they had been living in and to speak freely against it.

Elsa, for her part, kept making all her efforts to approach Ardian. She was a little bit reluctant and shy by the fact that Ardian was not just an ordinary man, because he had been her ex-professor, and this fact made her shyer and more reserved. Elsa invited him to join her and other teachers for lunch or dinner a couple of times, and after refusals of Ardian, she didn't repeat such invitations anymore. She asked him a couple of times, on Saturdays, before leaving for Elbasan, for what she could buy and bring for him on Monday morning, but Ardian didn't request anything. She understood that he was just trying to keep her away, making her attempts more complicated, and she kept thinking of finding and using other ways and tactics to have more conversation and spend more time with him.

"Since you don't accept my invitations for lunch, let me join you and see what you have in the cooperative's restaurant," she told him one day, after one month of failed efforts to talk longer and spend more time with him.

"Oh..., you are right. I've been rude by not responding to your invitation with a counter invitation after my refusal. Let's go and have lunch together today," Ardian answered amicably, and that made Elsa very happy. She accepted his invitation and accompanied him for lunch that day.

He treated Elsa as his guest, and they had a delicious lunch together. While Ardian was ordering and bringing food on the table, she was thinking about rumors spread about him at the time of his transfer from the pedagogical institute. Elsa, like most of the other students, didn't believe what was being said about him at that time. But now that she saw him every day, watching how humble and gentlemen he was, she thought again that what had happened to him was just an exaggeration of the "revolutionary vigilance," and maybe just a detrimental intrigue to expel him from the institute and create a vacancy for that lady that took his job position; "the magpie," or "the chatterbox," as students nicknamed her from the very first days of her arrival in the pedagogical institute. The fact that the new professor had not been a good student in Tirana State University and her family connections with the high-level apparatchiks of the Communist Party, made every student think and discuss with each other that Ardian's expulsion from the pedagogical institute was just an intrigue, and that's why they hated "the magpie" even more. Students thought that if everything said about him were true, then he would have been sent immediately to prison or internment, but they let him remain and work as a teacher instead. "Ardian is a teacher now, I'm a teacher too, and we are teaching in the same school. So we are colleagues now, good colleagues...," Elsa thought while having lunch with him, watching and listening with admiration and pleasure the man in front of her.

Watching Ardian reminded her of the fact that all the male professors of the pedagogical institute that were single, had found their future wives among their female students, usually the most beautiful ones. It was like an unsaid, silenced contest among female students in trying to win the heart of those bachelor professors. It was only Ardian, the youngest one and the most likable by all female students, who had not done such a thing. So, Elsa was thinking that she was going to give him a chance that he as well marries one of his female students, and she laughed at herself while thinking like this.

The warm months of autumn: September, October, and November, passed very fast, and Ardian became a kind of nature's lover. He learned a lot about geography, topography, and history of Dumre, and about flora and fauna of the region, by visiting and stepping on every site of it. The most beautiful thing he liked was staying and spending time by the numerous lakes of the area, and sometimes deep in the pristine forest, watching birds, rabbits, turtles, hedgehogs, and squirrels. Late November and December became colder and the daytime shorter, and sometimes windy and rainy, so Ardian had no more reasons and excuses to run away and hide from Elsa and other teachers, so he started spending more time staying and talking with them. Usually, when Ardian was leaving his room for some hours every afternoon, was a good thing for other teachers of the "palace," because in this way his room that he shared with the other guy, was available for him and his girlfriend while Ardian was away so that this couple was happy for this thing. What about Elsa? When two couples were having a good time together in their rooms, she had to stay in her room, alone and envious of them, wishing the same luck for herself. When Ardian returned from his expeditions, Elsa's room was always the only place where he could stay for a while until the couple in love "awake from the afternoon nap" and leave his room. In these cases, Elsa and Ardian's situation became funny, and they both felt embarrassed and didn't know what to talk about and what to tell each other. And after that, when Ardian's roommate with his girlfriend returned and found them together in Elsa's room, they always asked them two: "What about you two...? What are you waiting for...? This is your destiny..., and you have to surrender to it now." Both of them felt embarrassed in these moments, and they only answered with silence while Ardian left the room immediately.

To ease a little bit this embarrassment of the time when they were staying together in Elsa's room, Ardian started telling her about everything he had read for Dumre region, and about every site he had visited. Other times, he spoke about books he was reading. And one day, in late December, Elsa dared to tell him that she was going to join him the next spring to enjoy nature together by visiting some of those beautiful sites he was passionately speaking about.

At the end of December, Ardian went home to Vlorë to spend with his family two weeks of winter break and to celebrate the New Year's Eve. During this time, he started thinking of Eralda and her love as lost love, while at the same time, he thought of Elsa as a love waiting for him in the waiting room. He thought a lot about Elsa in those days, and he was sure that she was in love with him, the same way as he was in love with Eralda. Eralda was the first love for him, and he as well might be the first love for Elsa. The famous expression: "Others, we love. Others love us. Others, we marry," passed in Ardian's mind every time he thought about these two women and their love. Both already became part of his life and part of his love experience.

Elsa as well spent those two weeks of winter break at home with her parents. She was the only child of them, and she was the light of their eyes. This holiday season helped them spend more time together and discuss Elsa's future. Her parents, like all parents with daughters at that age, had thought about the marriage of their daughter, and they had two serious requests coming recently from two families that requested Elsa for their sons. They had not discussed this thing with Elsa before, because they were afraid of her refusal and didn't want to disturb her. They couldn't address this issue on Sundays when Elsa was home because they didn't want to spoil the only day of the week they spent together. Her mother had seen how

Elsa, after the very first week of the work in that remote village, returned home happier and more optimistic, making a high contrast with the desperation she had the days before starting her job since she had learned about her assignment. Elsa was showing the same joy and optimism during all four months she had already spent there. Her mother had discussed that strange thing with her husband, and he had the same opinion, but they didn't open this discussion with her because they were just enjoying her optimism, joy, and happiness. Her mother had a kind of intuition, and she sensed that the only reason that can bring such a change might be love but didn't dare to ask Elsa about that. Elsa had told them that there were six teachers from the city working together in that village and that they were having a good time together. She had said to them that one of them was her literature professor in the pedagogical institute that was transferred there for immorality and political-ideological reasons, and that he had been the best professor and a perfect person as well. That was all she had told them, without saying anything about her having a crush on Ardian. Nevertheless, her mother had some suspicion about that, based on the good humor, high optimism, and that kind of happiness of her daughter, that only love can bring to a girl.

Her parents told Elsa about those two requests for a consensual arranged marriage, and especially for one mechanical engineer, whose family hails from old Elbasan families, with a very big kinsfolk in Elbasan, with good connections in city's state institutions and his uncle was working in a high-level position in county's Executive Committee. So, a marriage with him would bring an excellent opportunity and support for her transfer to the city's schools or in a village near the city, from where she could go and come back home every day. Elsa told them that, at least, for this school year, she didn't want to think and discuss her marriage, but just wanted to stay and enjoy her life as a single woman. They didn't address this issue anymore. Elsa was the only child of them, and they had never tried to force her for anything in her life. She had been grown up with a sense of liberty and independence in her thoughts, decisions, and actions.

25

That morning of January 14, 1985—the first day of the second semester of the school year—Ardian had been the first one to get on the teachers' bus, because he had arrived in Elbasan late the previous night, and had spent the remaining hours in the train station, that was near the buses station. When Elsa got on the bus, she saw him sitting alone, and she greeted him and asked if she could sit on the seat next to him.

"Tell me something about Vlorë, because I've never been there," she told him after the first greetings.

Ardian started telling her about the historic city center, the place where the proclamation of independence took place on November 28, 1912, and the first Albanian government was formed. This city center square is called "the flag's square." Then he told her about the beautiful seaside and beautiful beaches in the city and far from it.

"If I come to visit Vlorë, would you accompany me in all these beautiful sites?" She asked him, becoming more valiant and enthusiastic than ever.

"Of course, yes," Ardian answered very quickly in order not to break her joy and optimism that Ardian saw in her eyes and face at that moment. And she looked even more beautiful that day, after two weeks that Ardian had not seen her.

Even though Ardian had thought about Elsa and her obvious crush on him, he was not thinking about a new love in his life. When he saw her smiling and joyful face that day (after the two-week school break that kept them far from each other), and her desire to sit next to him, he understood that she had missed him very much and had been waiting for this day, but he was not able to reply to her with the same optimism. When he saw her determination during the coming days and weeks, he started thinking about her as a perfect girl, and he liked her very much, but couldn't feel anything like being near those beautiful love feelings that he had experienced before with Eralda. His roommate kept telling and reminding Ardian every day: "What are you waiting for? What do you want more? What else do you expect from a girl? She has it all. She is a beautiful blond girl. She is a nice girl, and she is smart, lovely, gorgeous, and above all, she loves you, and she is just waiting for your first move. Don't lose such a good chance that only comes once in your lifetime! Don't lose her. Don't lose your time in vain. You are both in the right age to think and decide about your marriage. And both of you are in the right time and place to start a beautiful love."

All Elsa's actions, her persistence, and her care for him started giving good results. Ardian began to feel something that he couldn't call love yet. At the beginning of February, in one of those afternoons when they were staying together in Elsa's room waiting for two lovers (Elsa's roommate and Ardian's roommate) to leave Ardian's room, she approached him up to a light touch of her leg with his leg. Then he put his hand on her thigh and looked her in her eyes, without saying any words. He felt the warmth of her thigh, while she put her hand over his hand, keeping an intense gaze on his eyes, without saying a word. But her eyes were speaking in that beautiful love language, with that magical stare that only eyes of a girl in love can give. They didn't talk, but their eyes told everything by speaking in their love language, enticing and asking for more from each other. It was the right moment for something more, maybe a caress and a fondle, perhaps a kiss, the first kiss of theirs. But Ardian was not feeling such a desire the same way he used to feel when he touched and wanted to kiss Eralda. And he didn't kiss her, and she didn't dare to kiss him. He pulled his hand away and gave her a smile with an expressive face like regrettably saying: "I'm sorry. I can't." There weren't any kisses, but his hand on her thigh, his melancholic look and the smile he gave her, seemed like hundreds of kisses to Elsa. She had taken the first step, and, in response, she had taken a magic touch and a beautiful, loving smile from him. It was a good start for Elsa, and she felt pleased about that, and she was sure that something more would happen between them.

Ardian thought about this during the coming days, and it seemed like an adventure. There was not love. On the other hand, as a man, he was feeling the vital necessity for a woman too. So, when they had the second opportunity, he kissed her, and she accepted his kiss with pleasure, but it was just a kiss followed by other kisses, without saying anything, without an "I love you." She wanted to say to him: "I love you," several times, before and after every kiss but, she was waiting for him to be the first one to say these essential reassuring words. "He is the man, and he has the right to say it first," she thought. But even without his "I love you," she was delighted and optimistic with this good start and, as she had already decided, she was ready to go even further with her actions in this love, even without waiting for him to say "I love you." The month of March arrived, and they had only exchanged kisses several times, with Ardian being the first one to stop and go away in fear. But the first day of March is the first official day of spring in Albania, and spring brings a lot of nature blossom and human invigoration. It was the first week of March when Elsa locked the room door from inside, and walked toward him, with her determination to get to the end of this adventure. She approached him, unbuttoning her blouse's buttons one by one and slowly always looking at his eyes. He was lured and seduced by her act and her naked breasts and couldn't resist anymore. They both started the most passionate kiss, with him grabbing and squeezing every part of her body, and with her moaning and groaning in pleasure. That day Elsa gave him everything of hers: her body, her soul, and her heart. But above all, that beautiful spring day, she gave him the most essential thing of herself, the most beautiful gift a girl has kept for the man she loves—her virginity, the blood of her body. Ardian saw and understood what had just happened at the end of that vigorous, stormy moment after those incredible magic minutes filled with mutual lust, sex desire, pleasure, and..., with reciprocal silence, without any love words, without an "I love you."

The next morning, Ardian got up earlier than other days, went out and picked some fresh flowers of mimosa from the trees in the schoolyard. He entered her room and gave her that bunch of fresh mimosas whispering in her ear the most magnificent words of this world—"I love you." So, he said it; he was the first one to say those magic words; "I love you." And she got up from her bed like lightning, tossing herself into his arms and answered by repeating endlessly: "I love you too..., I love you too..., I love you too...," with tears in her eyes. They stayed some minutes in the arms of each other in silence, where she wept on his shoulder like discharging a heavyweight from herself, like celebrating a great joy that comes after going through long-time stress and uncertainty. After that big day for both, Ardian picked fresh mimosa flowers for Elsa every morning, till the end of mimosas' blossom season in that love spring of the year 1985.

Ardian understood that he was falling in love with Elsa, but it was not the same as the love he felt for Eralda because it was not as deep as the love for her, not as magical as the love for her, and not as beautiful as it. He was enjoying the pleasure of making love with Elsa every day and several times a day. But the fantastic sexual satisfaction that he was experiencing for the first time in his life was never felt as immense and sublime as the spiritual love he had felt and experienced with Eralda. He was enjoying the physical pleasure of this love very much by unloading his lust and satisfying his sexual appetite, but this love was not adequately feeding his soul, his mind, and his heart which were missing and longing for something else—Eralda, the face and the body of the first love. It reminded him of the expression he had read somewhere: "Love from the belly and up is spiritual love, while love from belly and down is physical love," and he approved it in silence. He was making and enjoying love with Elsa, but his tongue slipped and called her "Alda" dozens of times during the days and nights they were spending together. In the most culminant moments of sex with her, he whispered in her ears, "Alda." In this unconscious way, the two erotic ingredients of the two loves he had experienced were merged into one in his mind. He was bringing together the active spiritual and emotional component of the first love and the great delight of the physical intimacy and sexual activity of the second love.

The process of counting his loves started coming up to the surface quietly. It was the first time that he began counting his loves—the first love…, the second love. It meant that the first love had already ended, and a second love had just started. So…, the first love was done, becoming only a memory of his. The first love…, the first love…, born, shaped, and firmly rooted somewhere in the depth of the soul, hibernates forever in those caves and abysses where unconsciousness lies dormant, and sometimes awakens and comes up to the surface of the mind, making him conscious for its existence by bringing back in his mind the first girl's face, body, and name— Eralda and the magic of hers, the magic of the first love. Unlike the first love, the second one follows the inverse path. The second love (or another possible love after that), is born and shaped in the surface of the human mind (right where the human reasoning and logic interferes with love feelings) and tries to enter the soul's mysterious depth to take her roots there, but it is impossible. This place, this space in an impenetrable depth, is already taken by the first love, leaving no more room for other ones. There is only the first love over there, whose remembrance and echo come up to the open-air very often, making you call the name of the subject and object of your first love. Other loves can come and take place on the surface of the human mind and soul, trying in vain to descent right where the first love has taken roots and is still staying alive. But no other love will be allowed to reach down there where the first one reigns supreme forever.

Every time he called Elsa, "Alda," and every time he whispered in her ear Alda's name, Elsa laughed loudly and encouraged herself and him by repeatedly saying to him: "Yes…, yes. I'm Alda. Come on. Show me how much you loved Alda. Love me the same way as you loved Alda." In those happy and magic moments of mixing the emotional recall of the first love with the physical, girlish body of the second love, he really showed Elsa how much he loved Eralda. And they both experienced the love sex in all its glory in those extraterrestrial moments when sex is full of meaning and emotions, and orgasms make the brain order the release of love hormones that make the sexual passion into love. After some days, when this wild love game with the use of Eralda's name became excessive, Ardian called in his logic and decided not to do it anymore, and for that reason, he spoke seriously with Elsa:

"Elsa…, listen to me. I love you, and only you. I will not mention her name anymore. I will not think of her anymore. Now I'm convinced that it was just an adventure and nothing else. I'm happy that it ended, and I'm pleased that I have you by my side."

And indeed, Ardian didn't mention Eralda's name anymore in the coming days, but unlike him, it was Elsa thinking more often about his ex-girlfriend now. She was delighted with the promise Ardian made to her, but she felt sorry for entering between the two, interfering in that great love, destroying something sublime and divine for Ardian. Elsa was not resisting the temptation to learn more about that girl, and she wanted to give a face to the name Ardian had whispered so many times in her ears in the culminant moments of lovemaking.

"I would like to see this girl called Alda, at least once," Elsa told him the last week of March.

"When you go back home this weekend, go and see her Sunday morning at the school articles store situated in the east side of the city's main square," explained Ardian to her, who looked like he had been waiting for a long time for this interest and request of Elsa.

"The shopkeeper of that store?" she asked again.

"Yes, the girl that works in that store," he answered with a kind of joy and proudness.

"I've been there, and I've seen the beautiful girl, but I'm going to see her differently now."

"Go there, greet her and give her my regards too," Ardian told her with a kind of pleasure and seriousness to ensure Elsa that he was not joking.

Elsa went to Eralda's store with a kind of strange determination, without knowing the real reason and not being able to answer the question, "why do I have to do that," that she asked herself several times before getting there. She could enter the store like all other shoppers just to see the shopkeeper for her curiosity and leave the store without speaking to her, but she had to fulfill Ardian's request to greet Eralda from his part and give her his regards.

"Ardian told me to come here and give you his best regards," Elsa told Eralda in a moment when the store was emptied by other customers after she had spent some minutes in the store watching Eralda's beauty and elegance. Elsa noticed a slight tremble of Eralda's beautiful eyelids and eyelashes, while Eralda asked:

"Who are you? Do I know you?"

"I'm a colleague of Ardian. He has told me a lot of good words about you. He told me that he loved you so much, and he still loves you," Elsa added, just trying to ease a little bit of the tense situation.

Eralda didn't say any words because she didn't know who that girl was. "Is she his colleague or just his new girlfriend that comes here to provoke me?" Eralda asked herself and didn't like the open, straight forwarded way Elsa spoke. She didn't want to talk with this unknown girl because she didn't like that others can learn, judge, and comment about her lost love based on their own assumptions and fantasies.

Elsa left the store with the first thought that she had entered by mistake in between these two lovers. But now it was too late for her; she had gone too far and couldn't retreat. Her love with Ardian was already "signed, sealed and stamped" with the red blood of her virginity. That's why she had hurried to stamp this love with "red ink" as soon as she could. Giving the virginity to the man you love is considered like signing a marriage contract that is more important than the legal one. That's because there are three steps to be taken, or three kinds of deals to be signed, that force you to finalize a marriage: the moral agreement of the couple, "signed" by the loss of girl's virginity; the traditional family agreement, "stamped" by both families and finalized in the wedding party; and the last one, the legal contract of the civil marriage performed, recorded and recognized by a government official. Elsa and Ardian had already signed the first agreement, the moral one, that is not less important than other contracts, and now Elsa was more confident and convinced that their just-started love would conclude someday in a civil marriage.

Elsa, in a bizarre way—perhaps based on her certainty that everything in the relationship of Ardian and Eralda had ended—started feeling a kind of pleasure and pride while thinking that her actual partner, and soon-to-be her husband, had had a love story with this gorgeous and elegant girl; such a love story that everyone would envy. After these thoughts, she started feeling such an envy that very fast was transformed into a kind of jealousy and she felt pity for him and for the fact that he—the best professor of the pedagogical institute, the most adored man by all the female students of the institute—had fallen for a girl of the night school, for an ordinary shopkeeper.

As soon as Elsa left the store, Eralda started thinking of Ardian again. "It looks like he has started a new love. He has found a new girlfriend, and sends her here, to my store, to challenge me. That's why he hasn't come to see me for a long time already. He has started a new love relationship. And he has told her a lot of good words about me..., and he has told her everything..." Eralda recalled Elsa's words, and for the first time, she thought that it was a good thing that she always resisted and never allowed him to have sex with her. That's because there is a real pain for the loss of the love, but it would be another additional bitter pain in case of the loss of virginity, which Eralda considered as a holy thing for a girl, and she would give it only in the matrimonial bed. At first, she felt a kind of relief and solace that at least she had not lost her virginity, and this thing made the separation easier for her. But then, the second thought told her that if she had taken that critical step, it would have been better for her because, in this way, she would have been forced not to separate from him for whatever reason and they two would have been still together, loved, engaged and married already. She became jealous while thinking that what she had not done with Ardian, the other girl has already done. She thought about herself as being a young girl, without any experience and immature in these things. She had suffered a significant loss that was transformed into a big gain for the other girl. She had not been able and didn't know how to keep the victory, leaving it to slide from her hands. "Maintaining the victory is harder than the victory itself," she recalled a movie expression. Now that she learned about his new love, she felt the last threads of hope (being still alive and sheltered somewhere in her soul), started to break off, and she felt the sorrow and the pain of the loss of the first love sounding bitterer and more shocking than ever. The very last string of her hope had just died, and she thought that it was her turn to die after that. "They say, 'Hope dies last,' and it has already died for me. When you lose hope, you have lost everything. What should I do now…? Should I die…? Should I kill myself…? Oh…, no…, no. I have to live, and I will live because our love will live inside us as well, and it will never die." Eralda still felt this strong love without knowing in what part of her body and soul it had sheltered. Their love was living and would live forever right in its own place that only the first love knows where it is. "I have to live for the sake of my fantastic lover, and for the great love we experienced together," Eralda concluded.

Elsa turned back to the village on Monday morning, telling Ardian:

"I met Eralda at her store. I gave her your regards, but she didn't give me any regards for you," she said, and after a brief pause added:

"She is a charming girl."

"Very beautiful, and a strong girl, unlike all other girls," Ardian added immediately after Elsa's words as if he had been waiting for a long time for such a moment to speak about Eralda.

He didn't think that such words could harm and make Elsa feel bad. And she actually felt something but tried hard not to show any sign of that, considering that Ardian was right in his inspiration while speaking about Eralda. Elsa had already decided to multiply everything by zero, including these things that would irritate and make angry every other girl and woman. These things were tiny for her decision to win the great love of this wonderful man. Elsa had reached this goal till now, without being disturbed by his remembrances of his first love and his first girlfriend.

Ardian understood that his words and superlatives about Eralda could harm Elsa, and he hurried to explain and assure her:

"I have promised you that I would not mention her name anymore, and I'm telling you that you are, and you will be the only woman in my life for now and forever. I love you very much, and I owe you very much for all the care and love you give me." Ardian closed his promise extending his arms toward her, and they dived into a deep, quiet, silent, and meditative embrace without any words or movement. But his words and his actions were so heartwarming for Elsa.

After giving this promise to Elsa, he didn't mention Eralda's name during the coming weeks and months and didn't think about her anymore.

The rationale was winning above the feelings, and this was what he had wanted and aimed to achieve. But..., no. It wasn't as easy as it seemed, and it would never happen. The logic would never reach the final victory because nothing in this world would defeat the memory of the first love. Despite all attempts, nothing can reach down there, in the unreachable depth of the human soul and mind, in the human consciousness and subconscious mind, right where the first love has found shelter and refuses to leave, living there forever like a well-stored secret information that waits in silence to be called on-duty time after time, coming out of our soul onto the surface of our mind, as a beautiful, remote remembrance that always fills our hearts with yearning, our eyes with tears, our souls with pain, and our thoughts with love.

26

The spring of love with Elsa was like a golden spring for Ardian. Both of them were very happy and pleased. Elsa filled the Ardian's life with a new passion that arrived at the right time for him, saving him from the pain of the loss of his first love. Elsa, from her part, was thrilled with this first love of hers and didn't try to hide her joy and happiness. The weekends she spent at home with her parents and without Ardian's presence seemed very long to her, and she couldn't wait for the Monday morning to come. She always returned to the village with her heart and mind full of yearning and love for Ardian and with her bags full of special homemade foods cooked especially for Ardian, and she knew what he liked the most. The weekdays passed very fast in the village, spending all the time together without noticing how quickly the days run. They didn't try to hide this love from others' eyes because both were very proud of each other, confident for their love, and sure that this love would end in a happy marriage someday.

The Wednesday of April 10, 1985, started as a typical working day, and it was a beautiful sunny day. And a couple in love like them always wants to make the most from such a beautiful day by escaping somewhere in a hidden place to make love in the open air in this warm spring day. That's what Ardian and Elsa discussed and decided in the long break between classes. They decided to go for a picnic to the best site they had discovered the week before. It was a small grassy space among bushes by a lake among low hills, and it takes about two hours of walk to get there. They finished their classes before two o'clock, went to their rooms, prepared everything to take with them, and arrived there after four o'clock. Elsa had made up her mind and was prepared to spend a long, romantic afternoon, evening, and night making love by the lake, enjoying the splendid sunset, the mysterious twilight, the quiet dusk, the gentle breeze of the evening, and the eerie darkness of the pleasantly cold night, till the light of the dawn and the sunrise of the new day.

Elsa was a very bubbly and vivacious girl, and the love for Ardian made her more vivid and full of vitality. She was an athletic girl from her body, her clothes, and her attitude and had played volleyball and basketball for the high school team, but she was better in and liked more volleyball. She was almost as tall as Ardian. "Altezza—metà bellezza" (Height—half of the beauty), Ardian recalled the famous Italian expression every time he saw Elsa's tall, straight body with long legs. Her dense, short-cropped, blond hair allowed her long neck to be more visible, and her general beauty became more apparent. The most beautiful parts of her body were her long, straight legs, which looked wonderfully sexy, attractive, and seductive from every side and distance you see them. Ardian liked her alluring legs and thighs very much, and he always couldn't wait for the moment to find himself in between them and start the trip of the great pleasure in that "path of happiness" formed in between her legs. He liked her small, round-shaped breasts so much, and never forgot to play and enjoy them. They both were enjoying their sexual life very much, and Elsa, in that regard, was more active than him, always taking the initiative to try different things in their sexual games. In the case of this picnic in this beautiful spring day, she had decided to spend that evening and night making love by the lake, on the grass among bushes. They had already made love everywhere they could: in their beds, on the floor, in the forest, by the river, in the fields with crops, behind the haystacks and straw ricks, against a tree trunk, etc. But tonight, it would be the first time for them spending the entire night together in the open air, like a new game in their lovemaking adventures. Elsa always tried to get as much as she could from this love and seemed like she never could get as much as she wanted and never felt satiated. From the start of this love, Elsa had decided to throw away and forget about every kind of shyness, guilt, and embarrassment in her effort to make this love as beautiful and happy as it could be, by helping herself and Ardian to get the most of their reciprocal sexual pleasure and be satisfied with their love. They were enjoying their love passion in all its physical, spiritual, and magical forms.

With the same desire and lust, they arrived there, and when Ardian saw Elsa laying blankets on the grass, he understood that she was well prepared for this evening. When she expressed her desire to stay and spend the entire night making love right there, he couldn't refuse her request. In front of them was the small oval-shaped lake with the deep, blue color of its water, surrounded by low hills. The afternoon ended with the sun going down, and his fiery, yellow rays were reflecting in the lake's water, creating that kind of spectacular scenery that you often see in artistical photographs and paintings. Under this magical scenery, they only made love; real love; endless love; passionate love; unforgettable love. It was love and sex full of lust and desire. It was spiritual, physical, mystical, and magical at the same time. It was love in all its existential shapes and ways. It was human, terrestrial, and extraterrestrial love. There were magic moments where only they existed in that world, with their bodies and souls melted in one. Nobody else and nothing else existed in that space and time filled with cuddles, fondles, kisses, rubbing, squeezes, lust, love, pleasure, moans, groans, joy, and happiness.

The sun, while going down, looked at them making love and became envious, and didn't want to go further down, under the horizon line. The sun tried to stay a little bit longer, peeking furtively from behind the hills with his fiery eye above the horizon until his yellow rays changed color, becoming orange, red, and violet by the envy and jealousy. The sunlight's infrared rays penetrated through the terrestrial dust of the lower layers of the atmosphere, shedding and doubling the magic reddish-orange light in the air that mirrored in the lake water surface. When the sun fell below the horizon, it gave way to an enchanting twilight with the soft glowing light coming from the sky after the refraction and scattering of the sun's rays from the atmosphere. This magic lighting was blended with the yellow brilliance of thousands of stars whose magical light was doubled from their reflection on the lake water, mirroring another sky cupola full of stars under the lake water.

The lake's quiet water, watching them making love, became more liquid and started to move its waves towards the shore near the couple, like wanting to fondle and refresh the lovers with some soft water waves. When the gentle wash of waves was turned back after being crushed and repelled by the shore, the lake became annoyed and jealous. Hills around the lake tried to raise their heads above the shoulders of each other to have a better view of the couple that was making love. Bushes, trees, their branches, and leaves, were trembling and swinging by the evening sweet breeze trying to bring more fresh air to cool the lovers' hot, naked bodies. Small fishes of the lake started jumping and attempting to come above the water surface, with their curiosity to watch these lovers. All birds stopped their tweets and songs, watching and listening to the pleasing moans and groans, the laughter, the joyful noises, and the mystic silence of lovers that were performing their beautiful song of love with great, mesmerizing pleasure.

"At least, we are free to make love," Ardian repeated several times these words during that evening and night filled with gentle love and wild sex. It was an expression he had started to use every time while lying tired by her side after the culminating moments of sex. Elsa had heard this expression of his several times, without knowing what he truly meant by saying this particular phrase every time after his sexual climax. She considered it just as an expression of the intense pleasure he felt in those reciprocal pleasurable moments, and she felt happier by being able to give him such a great pleasure. That afternoon, that evening, and that night, Elsa got enough of what had wanted from this love with Ardian. For the first time, she felt satiated and fulfilled as a girl in love in her duty of giving and taking deserving love. She wanted his love, and she had won it. She wanted his mind, his soul, and his heart, and she already had them. She wanted his body, and she got a lot from every part of his body. She desired to make as much love as she could with him, and she enjoyed it all that magical evening and night spent together out in the countryside. The site where they spent the night making love was a beautiful romantic site with the most beautiful scenery that enticed and invited them for even more love and sex. And that was what they did all night long, gifting to each other the feelings and pleasure of the most beautiful sex games two youngsters can play endlessly. They did it, and they got it all until they felt fully satiated, extremely pleased, and melted next to each other by exhaustion.

The moon was absent until after midnight. It looked like it was hiding and observing furtively them making love. The sky was clear, without any clouds, so it was a bright sky full of stars, with a magic reflection on the water surface, spreading their light beating the darkness of the night forming two gigantic sky cupolas with bright stars with the couple making love in the middle of those two fascinating worlds. The moon rose at 1:30 AM. It was a first-quarter moon (called by people a half-moon), after completing the first lunar phase called waxing crescent that follows a new moon. First, it showed just a small corner like trying to raise an eye above the hills to spy on them from behind, staying in that position for some minutes. Then it jumped on the top of the hills, continuing its rotation around the earth, joining the stars on the sky, becoming part of the spectacular scenery, and shedding more light around them.

In a moment of pause, they started playing by counting as many stars as they could. Then they started creating different imaginary pictures by joining groups of stars with an imaginary line. Ardian found and explained to her the galaxy of Milky Way, with its appearance as a dim glowing band in the sky where its stars cannot be seen by the naked eye but only by using a telescope. After that, he found and showed Elsa the constellation of stars that form the Ursa Major (also known as the Great she-Bear), and the group of stars that form the Ursa Minor (also known as the Little she-Bear), telling her that an Italian tale speaks of them as being a mother and a child sharing their love. Ardian explained that the star in the tip of the handle of the Little Bear, is the North Star, which has always been the most crucial navigational star in the sky. That's because, from our perspective, it seems like it forever remains in the same location, while all other stars appear to rotate around it. And so, you will see the North Star always in the same northern area, showing you the direction north whenever you look at it at night, and by referring to that, you can easily find three other cardinal directions: south, east, and west. This star is essential in helping sailors to navigate the open sea and oceans in the absence of other orientational points.

That night they slept less than two hours, like two happy, tired children, squeezed against each other after an extended play. They slumbered like that until the dawn's first weak rays appeared above the hilltops behind them, on the east side of the lake. Elsa picked up their stuff and folded the blankets, while Ardian looked for and found the planet Venus in the sky, and started explaining to Elsa:

"Venus (or Venera, as Russians call it), is the second planet from the sun, and it is called the Morning Star too because it appears in the east just before the sunrise. After the moon, it is the brightest natural object in the night sky, and it is named after the Roman goddess of love and beauty," Ardian told her.

Elsa laughed with his detailed explanation about the stars in the sky. She was always surprised by his extensive knowledge in all fields of life. She embraced him once more at the end of his speech, holding him tight against herself and whispering in his ear:

"I love you so much, my Little Bear…, my Venus…, my North Star."

"I love you too…, my Morning Star…, my Venera…, my goddess of love and beauty," he responded to her using the same language and terminology of stars' names.

They left the site marching towards the "teachers' palace," and had some more fun by fighting and stoning the dogs that barked and ran toward them every time they were approaching and passing by village's houses. The only way to keep them at a safe distance was by stoning at them, and that's why, after the first fight with dogs, they picked up a lot of stones, keeping them all the time in their hands, to be used against the dogs all the way back. It was the first time for Elsa to experience such a fight with dogs, and it seemed funny, but sometimes it became frightening, especially when half a dozen of dogs barked at them and attacked running toward them. She yelled, terrified, and tried to protect herself by squeezing and hiding behind Ardian. They arrived at their room after 7 AM and prepared for the new school day.

Thursday, April 11, 1985. It started with a piece of good, bad news. The Great Leader of the Communist Party of Albania had died. The Dear Leader of the people of Albania had died. The tyrannical dictator had died. It was excellent news for Ardian (and maybe for few other people in the country that thought the same as him), but at the same time, it was terrible news for Elsa and for the people of Albania that loved their leader so much. Teachers, students, and villagers were gathered at the schoolyard to listen to the Radio Tirana that was reporting the death of "The Great Leader of the Party and the People of Albania." Everybody in the schoolyard was weeping in grief. Elsa was crying as well. Ardian was staying by her side with his eyes down. For a moment, he embraced Elsa, like comforting and consoling her, and whispered in her ear:

"While we were experiencing the most wonderful and hottest night of our life, making love and enjoying those magic moments by that beautiful lake, just in the most beautiful evening and night of our life, the dictator was languishing and dying in his deathbed."

Elsa couldn't believe her ears. She couldn't believe what she was hearing from his mouth in those bitter moments for all the people. "Did he truly say that? What is wrong with him? How can he say such a thing at this moment? Something bad has to happen to him right now, after saying these terrible words about our Great Leader—our saint." But nothing happened to him. She pushed him away gently and gave him a reproachful look expressing her disappointment for what he had just said. Ardian hadn't spoken with Elsa about his opinion for the dictator and the dictatorship. It was the first time that he mentioned the word "dictator," and Elsa was caught off guard by such a word being said in those moments of deep desperation, sadness, and grief for everybody else. Elsa didn't say a word. After one hour, they walked together toward the teachers building, and Elsa asked him:

"Ardian…, did you really said those words, or I didn't listen well what you said to me? Did those terrible words came out of your mouth?" She grabbed his hand, shooting a severe and disapproving glance at him.

"Elsa…, our 'Dear Leader' was just a dictator. He was a tyrant, and our socialist country is just a dictatorship under his rule. So, you and all other people that weep for him are shedding tears in vain," he answered with the same seriousness and determination as she questioned him.

"No…, please…, don't speak like this"! Elsa raised her voice, squeezing and pulling down his hand. She stopped and held him pulling his hand. "For the sake of our love, please, don't say that anymore. I love you so much, but you scared me when you said that, because it is perilous for you, for me, and our families. I don't want something bad to happen to us," she begged him with her eyes in tears, not for the Great Leader's death this time, but because she cared so much for him and their love.

"You're right. I'm sorry that I spoke like that. I will not repeat it anymore, but I'm not going to speak about such things with anybody else. I only said it to you, because I trust you as myself. I love you, and that's why I don't like it when I see you being so sad and grieving for somebody that doesn't deserve it," Ardian answered with carefully selected words, pulling her between his arms and embracing her tightly.

Ardian was pleased and satisfied with the intense love with Elsa, and he hadn't spoken to her about his ideas, because he didn't want to spoil the happiness they had found and the wonderful time they were spending together, by bringing for discussion such a serious conversation. The dictator's death allowed Ardian to speak with Elsa about his opinion and for his analyses of the socialist realism in Albanian literature and arts, being in service of the dictator and the dictatorship's propaganda. Elsa was unprepared for such a strange discussion. She was surprised by Ardian's dangerous point of view and couldn't accept such a complicated thing. Firstly, she was startled very much with his brave thoughts, listening to him always in silence and by grinding in her mind what was hearing from Ardian's mouth. During those days, she as well started analyzing his point of view on the literature as political and propagandistic literature in service of the dictatorship and not in service of the people. Ardian's thoughts and approach against this "dictatorial system," looked to her more challenging to be swallowed and accepted. The phrase "dictatorial system," surprised her at first, but later, she started to understand and admit that Ardian was right and that they were really living under a dictatorship.

Elsa went back home that Saturday afternoon, where she joined her parents in their grief for the death of the Dear Leader, and she was thinking all the time about what Ardian had told her. The funeral of the Great Leader took place on Monday, April 15, 1985, being watched live on TV by all the people of Albania. Elsa came back on Monday morning in the village, where all the villagers gathered in the village's central square, in front of the cultural center, where two TV sets were installed, and they watched all the funeral activities taking place in Tirana. The Central Committee of the Albanian Communist Party had already elected the Great Leader's successor, and he pledged in the funeral that Albania was going to continue the same path led by the Great Leader, calling it "the path of continuity."

That afternoon after the funeral, Ardian and Elsa made a slow walk toward the forest as a need for serenity under tree shadows for a better reflection in their discussion. During all those days that had passed since Ardian mentioned to her the word "dictator" for the first time, followed by his opinion about "dictatorship," Elsa thought and analyzed a lot, and started changing her mind by thinking that perhaps Ardian was right on what he was saying. They stopped somewhere in the forest, sat down on the grass, and continued their discussion.

"Now I think that you are right, but..., it's complicated for me and for everybody else to start realizing that we were born, grown-up, and educated in a dictatorial system. We have always felt like everything was right in our life: our family, our town, our country, our education, our work, and everywhere. Our life looked very normal to us, to our parents, and grandparents. Three generations have been deceived so easily. We loved our Great Leader, and we are grieving and shedding sincere tears for his death, thinking that he was always right in what he said, and his words have been the guidance for all of us throughout all our life. It seems surreal and unbelievable now. How can it happen?" Elsa finished asking this question to him and herself at the same time.

"It's in human nature not to believe that they have been cheated on for a long time and not to accept the disillusionment and desperation that comes after that. It means that you have trusted something for a long time, thinking that it was the right thing to do, and at some point, someone tries to convince you that it wasn't as correct as it seemed, but it's just gigantic deceit. On the one hand, you want to agree with him, but on the other hand, you still don't want to accept that you have been deceived, abused, and betrayed for everything in your entire life. Besides that, the regime has been successful in deceiving you because it used powerful propaganda, and part of this propaganda has been the literature and all other forms of arts, music, and cinematography. We have been the object of this propaganda from early childhood through the songs about the Great Leader and by watching his portrait hanged on the walls of every house, classroom, and office. Then, most of the children's songs and poems were dedicated to the Dear Leader, to the communist party, and the happy working class. All the education system was led by the "red thread" of the communist ideology becoming the central part of every school subject." Ardian gave some of his arguments and explanations on what had happened with the people of Albania.

"That's why they expelled you from the pedagogical institute and transferred you to this remote village. And that has been for your best because if you were still teaching in the pedagogical institute and if you would speak like this to the students, they would tell on you to the police and you would have ended up in front of the killing squad, punished with death penalty as a dangerous enemy of the Party and the people," Elsa told him, laughingly, but at the same time reminding him that such kind of talk was dangerous, and he had to be careful.

"Without my transfer in this village, our love wouldn't have born, and it was a good thing for you too. And you are lucky," he answered, joking and flattering her.

They spent two remaining months of the school semester (until the school summer holidays), discussing literature, dictatorship, and making love. Enjoying nature and lovemaking, became for them like enjoying freedom, and feel like living as free people. Ardian had interrupted reading books because he wanted to spend all the spare time with Elsa. He felt like he had just discovered a new world, an unknown world that he had not experienced before—the world of love filled with the great pleasure you feel when you have by your side the person you love so much with whom you make passionate love. It made him think that the need and urge for love and sex was the main reason people marry each other, and when they both promise everlasting love to each other by saying the official phrase, "Yes, I do," it means that they swear to fulfill each other's needs for love and sex as well, by sharing the reciprocal pleasure. (He recalled a saying: "Love is the name, sex is the game," that he had read behind the dormitory toilet doors, among other numerous expressions, songs, movie extracts, love quotations, and dirty sexual drawings written and sketched by students in their privacy.) Every time he recalled Eralda and his first love, he thought about it as a "platonic love," that was (as he had read somewhere), a powerful, passionate love without being finalized in a sexual relationship and a marriage. But when Eralda passed through his mind during those weeks, he tried to let it go as soon as possible. He couldn't exchange the real great enjoyment the second love was giving to him, with the abstract, mystic, and magic of the first love that he wanted to consider as a lost love already.

Two weeks before the end of the school year, Ardian brought his parents to Elsa's house to ask her parents for Elsa's hand. Elsa had talked with her parents about her love relationship with Ardian just from early May. At first, they didn't accept her love with a man transferred in that village for political and ideological reasons, and they considered such a love as a second bad thing happening to their daughter after the first bad thing that was her assignment in that remote village. They were forced to accept their daughter's choice only after they realized that Elsa had already made her mind up and that she had done everything with that man, and their acceptance was just a formality to be done. Elsa was the only child they had, and her parents had always desired and wished best of luck to her, but this marriage didn't look like such a thing for them. As a man and as an ex-professor in the pedagogical institute, he might be a right person, but the reason of his transfer in that village and the possibility of another harsher punishment of him—as it happened so often in such cases—made Elsa's parents reluctant in accepting this marriage. Their final answer of acceptance was difficult for them, but they decided to let their daughter go her way. Later on, after they met and talked with Ardian, they understood that their daughter had not mistaken in choosing that man as her future husband.

The new couple had decided to spend that summer in Vlorë, but before going there, they had to fulfill the desire of Elsa's parents, meaning that they had to marry in the civil marriages' office to get their marriage certificate, before going together in Vlorë to spend the summer over there. For that reason, Ardian had to stay some more days in Elbasan after the school year ended, spending some more days with Elsa's parents. They had a one-bedroom apartment, so Elsa's parents let them sleep in their bedroom, in their matrimonial bed, but Ardian didn't want to accept that, with respect for her parents. The parents convinced him by saying that they had to get up early in the morning to buy milk before going to work, while the new couple could sleep as long as they wanted in their bedroom without being disturbed by their morning noise.

"No need for you to get up so early in the morning to buy milk because I have brought a lot of eggs from the village," Elsa said to them. She knew that one of her parents had to go to the milk store's queue as early as four o'clock in the morning, to add chances for getting a bottle of milk before it ended.

"At least you have brought a good thing from that village," her father answered to Elsa when she mentioned the eggs that she had brought every week from the village. It was a habit already that all teachers that worked in villages purchased eggs from their student's families, helping themselves and the villagers with some cash.

"Daddy…, don't forget that I have brought another good thing from that village. Can you guess what it is?" Elsa asked her father, by hugging him and her mother at the same time, with her eyes toward Ardian. They understood what Elsa meant but didn't answer, and they just smiled at her and Ardian. So, Elsa responded to her own question:

"The other good thing that I brought from that remote village is this guy," she said, running toward Ardian and raising his hand like announcing a winner. "So, there are a lot of good things coming from that village," she added with laughter and humor.

Monday morning, just before noon, they left the house and walked toward the marriages' office. They needed to find two people to witness their marriage as an official requirement. They had decided that on their way to the civil marriages' office, to search for anybody they might know and ask them to witness their marriage. They didn't forget to buy a packet of llokume (the original name for Turkish delights), as traditional sweets offered in such an event. They ran into two Elsa's friends of the high school, and they witnessed their civil marriage procedure.

So, on Monday, June 17, 1985, at noon, they said: "Yes, I do." They opened the packet of llokume treating everybody present who wished the new couple an everlasting marriage and a happy life together. Ardian and Elsa signed the official register and took an official marriage certificate becoming a married couple.

They had to do two other things the next day. They applied in the respective state offices for food rations for their new family and for an apartment. They finished these things before noon and returned home for lunch. Then they decided that afternoon to do a walk in the main boulevard, the venue used for such an activity where people walk, see, and greet each other. The evening walk in the main avenue of the city was an expression of the existential human need "to see and to be seen," becoming a vital habit and motivating force for city residents. When they reached the city center, right in the middle of the boulevard, they couldn't avoid the existence of the Eralda's store there. Ardian became silent in those minutes passing by the store. Elsa didn't feel comfortable by his silence, and without understanding the reason, she told him:

"Let's go there to greet Eralda."

This suggestion of hers looked like an unreasonable and meaningless act, but it happened because they were pleased about their marriage and wanted to spread the good news without thinking that their good news was going to put in an awkward position and hurt somebody else, in this case, Eralda.

Ardian hadn't mention Eralda's name for a long time since he gave such a promise to Elsa, but Eralda's face and name had crossed his mind several times, at nights and days, despite his effort to keep her out of his mind and to resist to the remembrance of his first love. Every time that Eralda was displayed in his mind, he was touched and felt very bad and, while thinking about her, he was scared that he could never recover and might become sicker about her in the future. The great love Elsa was giving to him, her excellent care for him, her courage to love him and accept his opinion on the dictatorship, convinced Ardian that Elsa's love for him was a true love, a strong one, and without any interest, and that's why she deserved the same love, care, and respect by him in return. In front of Elsa, he never gave any sign that he was still thinking of his ex-girlfriend and tried very hard not to mention her name anymore.

Elsa had been to Eralda's store some weeks ago, and she had spoken openly with Eralda, telling her about the relationship with Ardian. She had explained to Eralda that she was returned to her store just to correct any misunderstanding from her first visit there. Elsa had told Eralda that she and Ardian were going to be engaged at the end of the school year. "Ardian is a perfect guy, and I can tell you that you are a lucky girl," Eralda had told Elsa during that meeting. "Ardian says that you are the best girl he has ever met, and the most beautiful girl in the city," Elsa had told Eralda. "And now I agree with him," Elsa had spoken sincerely.

Ardian had told Elsa that he hadn't had sex with Eralda, and she believed in his sincerity. This fact made Elsa feel better and didn't mind at all if he was thinking about her, and if he mentioned her name sometimes. Elsa felt good while thinking that even though she had not been the first love for Ardian, she still was the first girl Ardian had had sex with. And now, with her sincere proposal for a visit to Eralda's store, she was doing this act with respect for Ardian, giving him the possibility and the right to see and meet his ex-girlfriend and to remember his first love as a spiritual need for everybody. Elsa was sure that Eralda was still living in his mind, heart, and soul, even though he was trying hard to avoid it, or not to show such a thing in front of her.

"I would never meet her, but since you say this and because we are together, let's go and tell her about our marriage," Ardian answered to Elsa's request.

This time, Eralda behaved as a strong and clever girl, as she really was. She smiled at them as soon as they entered the store, and she shook hands and spoke with Ardian by calling his name, showing joy and a good mood of hers in front of them.

"Congratulations, and a happy life together," Eralda wished them. Her sweet face, the curve of her smile, her beautiful eyes, and those marvelous dimples in her cheeks, touched Ardian very much. It was like a déjà vu for him, and Eralda looked wonderful that night.

"Thank you, and good luck to you too," Ardian and Elsa told Eralda in one voice.

"You are a lovely couple and fit very well to each other," Eralda complimented them without forgetting that beautiful, magic smile that Ardian had missed so much, and he had been yearning for a glimpse of her in a long time.

27

It was the beginning of summer 1985, the first summer after their engagement and official marriage, and they would start their holidays with a visit to Ardian's family in Vlorë. Elsa and her parents thought that they were going to Vlorë to spend some days with Ardian's family and going on the beach, but Ardian had other plans in his head. The night before leaving Elbasan, he told Elsa first, and then to her parents, that they were going to spend all the summer together, exploring the part of the southwestern region of Albania that includes all the Ionian Sea coastline called "South Riviera." Ardian wanted to visit and spend a few days in all the beaches, towns, and villages of that region, from Vlorë to Sarandë. Elsa was flying high since Ardian told her his plan for this beautiful trip, but this proposal caught her parents off guard because they wanted to spend some more time with her daughter. Elsa thought and felt sorry for them remaining alone, without her at home, but she couldn't say "no" to Ardian's excellent plan. It would be like a trip of her dreams, and above all, a summer trip with her amazing husband.

They arrived in Vlorë after experiencing a "fantastic" four-hour travel, changing two crowded trains with dirty cars and broken glass windows. Those broken glass windows were suitable for summer, but they remain like this even for wintertime. Children of the villages and towns where the train went through, practiced the "new sport" of throwing stones at them by hands or slingshots, and it was a dangerous act for people inside the train. They left the train station and walked toward Ardian's home, holding each other's hands and laughing loudly after that travel experience. The first one to open the door and welcome them was Monda, which had been waiting for a long time to see her brother's fiancé. Even though they were already officially married in the civil marriage's office, the couple is still called an "engaged couple." They are called like this for the period starting from the

215

moment when families exchange visits and agree for their marriage, until the day of the wedding party with about one hundred participants, with family members, relatives, and friends. So that Monda, at last, saw her brother's fiancé and expressed great enthusiasm for meeting her. Monda couldn't attend any colleges because her grade point average was less than eight, and so she was staying home and unemployed. Finding a job in that time of crisis was very difficult. The County's Executive Committee assigns the right to attend colleges, and two main prerequisites were the right family political biography and the grade point average of the high school above eight. You would attend whatever college they assigned you to according to the country's needs.

"I'm sorry to tell you that because I'm jobless, and because my brother's fiancé is so nice, I am going to accompany you everywhere and I'll never leave you alone. Or, at least I'll join you on the beach. But I'll give you something in return," she started trading with them.

"What are you going to give us?" Ardian asked her.

"I'm going to give you my bedroom, the most important thing for an engaged couple," she explained with full competence for what they needed most.

They started going to the beach the next day. There are two beaches near the city; the nearest one called the old beach was within walking distance from their house, while the other one, called the new beach, could be reached by bus. The old beach was sandy and shallow, where you have to walk a little bit in water before reaching deeper water to swim, and it was the right place for Elsa to learn and practice swimming. The new beach is with less sand and more gravel, with deeper and clearer water and very good for swimming. The imaginary line that divides these two beaches is the borderline that divides two seas and their coastlines. The Adriatic Sea coastline starts there going north, through Albania, Montenegro, Croatia, and Slovenia coastlines, reaching to Italian cities of Trieste and Venice. The Ionian Sea coastline starts there too, going south through Albanian's South Riviera to Greek coastline and Corfu Island, reaching to the Mediterranean Sea. The Albanian coast of these two seas differs a lot from each other. The Adriatic Sea coastline in its Albanian part is sandy, with a lot of wide beaches, and then becomes rocky, starting from Montenegro till the end, with a lot of beautiful bays, islands, and peninsulas. The Ionian Sea coastline is rocky, with small separate beaches, forming picturesque views of the mountain and sea next to each other.

It was the first time for Elsa to go to the sea and she didn't know how to swim. Ardian and Monda spent a lot of time and effort teaching Elsa how to swim, having a lot of fun with her like it always happens in such cases. They spent two weeks going to the old beach during the day and going for a refreshable evening stroll to the new beach. They spent two other weeks going to the new beach and farther south to a beautiful rocky beach called "the Cold Water," with cold water springs near the beach and under the sea. The water is deep and blue there, with rocks that serve as trampolines to jump and dive into the water.

At the southern end of the "Cold Water" beach, there is a hill with pines, other trees, and bushes. On top of the hill, there was a building called "the house of the leadership," where the Great Leader and his family spent summer holidays. The entire hillside was well fenced with wires and well protected by armed soldiers.

"If you had come here last summer, you would meet him," Ardian told Elsa, pointing with his eyes toward "the house of the leadership" on the top of the hill. "And it would be like meeting the Zeus atop Mount Olympus from where he reigned over the humankind," Ardian spoke with theatrical voice and gestures.

"What a pity. I would have met the highest one among the gods residing there. I know, I'm not lucky," Elsa answered with a false, sad voice.

They were having a great time together, but Elsa missed her parents very much, and she returned home in Elbasan to spend one week with her parents, before starting their trip further south along Ionian Riviera. She arrived home to her parents, but from the first night there, when she lay down on the bed alone, she started missing Ardian, and all the time they had spent together during those four weeks in Vlorë. She missed him more the second day, and even more the third day. Ardian as well missed her very much, starting from the moment he returned home alone after seeing her off to the train station, and he didn't resist more than two days. The third day in the morning, he took the train and arrived in Elbasan, knocked at Elsa's apartment door, that was opened immediately by Elsa, like she had been behind the door all the time waiting for him to come.

"I knew it... I knew it... I knew it very well that you would come," she shouted joyously, embracing him firmly. Without any other word, they kissed and walked toward the bedroom without interrupting their kiss, helped each other to undress without interrupting their kiss, jumped on the bed without interrupting their kiss, and did everything else discharging all their high libido without interrupting their kiss. It was the first time for them to stay separated for more than two days from the day they started their relationship, and they couldn't stay away from each other longer than that.

"I missed you so much. If you hadn't come today, I would come to you tomorrow. But my gut feeling was telling me that you were coming," Elsa told him after that wordless hurricane of love, lust, and sex.

"No..., don't say it! I don't believe you," Ardian answered, kidding with her.

"I'll kill you," she threatened him, squeezing his chin.

"You just did it. And you did it very well. But I'm still alive for you to kill me again," Ardian told her, opening his arms in surrender, being sure that she understood very well what he meant by that.

"At least we are free to make love," they both spoke at the same time laughing loudly, and they restarted the fantastic, magic game of love.

They spent three more days in Elbasan, without leaving home at all. On the fourth day, they traveled back to Vlorë, where they stayed one more day before starting their trip to the South Riviera. Their first stop, where they spent two days, was the town of Orikum, named after the ancient city Oricum. Near this town is situated the naval base called "Pashaliman." It's built right in the southern end of Vlora Bay, a closed bay formed by the Karaburun peninsula on the west with Sazan island in front of the tip of the peninsula like a gatekeeper that controls the entrance to Vlora Bay. They continued their trip in a spectacular, winding, narrow road to the mountain pass called Llogara Pass, in the height of 3,369 feet above sea level. It connects the Dukat Valley and Vlora Bay on the north side with the South Riviera, on the south, and it serves as a picturesque venue overlooking the Ionian coast of the Albanian Riviera. It is part of Llogara National Park, within 2,500 acres with a forest of black pine trees and a complex of wooden mountain cabins used for summer and winter holidays. On the north side of the pass, you see the Vlora Bay, while on the south part of it, you watch the rest of Ionian Riviera. It is a natural balcony on top of the mountain, from where you see beautiful views from all sides, including the higher tops of the mountain range on the east side. They spent two other days in one of those wooden cabins.

The other leg of their trip took them to Dhërmi, one of the most beautiful beaches by the South Riviera, and then to Himarë, Qeparo, Borsh, and Lukova, where most of the hills are terraced to cultivate citrus and olives. They arrived in Saranda, a town with a small harbor in the Bay of

Saranda situated in front of the Greek island, Corfu. The Corfu Channel separates the northeastern edge of Corfu and the coast of Saranda County with the narrowest strait of 1.25 miles. They would like to travel further south to visit the ruins of the ancient city of Butrint, with its Latin name Buthrotum, inhabited since prehistoric time followed by ancient Greeks, and later on by Romans. They wanted to visit the picturesque village of Ksamil (situated near the narrowest strait of the Corfu Channel), from where you can see the Corfu Island and its olive trees plantations less than two miles away. The trip to Ksamil and Butrint needed special permission issued by the police station of Saranda because that area was near the border with Greece, and as such, it has limited access for the public and tourists. Ardian didn't like to apply for such permission in the police station, and they didn't do it, but stayed and spent some more days in Saranda's beaches.

After five days, they took the bus to get to Vlorë, making the back travel in one day, like a summary. At the end of this trip, they decided to spend every summer on long trips in different regions of Albania. Their salaries were enough to cover such expenses because they were living for nine months of the year in the "warm nest of their love," (as Ardian liked to call their room in the "teachers palace"), with very few expenses, saving more money to spend for the summer trips and holidays.

Ardian and Elsa returned to their school in September for the start of the new school year 1985 - 1986. The other couple had married as well so, there were three married couples now, each one in his room, and they got along with each other very well. Ardian started going every other weekend to Elsa's family with her. Elsa and her parents were pleased with the choice of their daughter, but they still didn't like it while thinking that they were going to spend many years, and perhaps all their life, in that remote village. But Elsa and Ardian, for their part, didn't count months and future years because they were enjoying their love relationship very much, and they were delighted with each other. The simple way of life they were living in that village, with maximum contact with nature, their freedom of thinking, their conscience, and knowledge of living under a dictatorship, followed by the magic of their great love, made them enjoy the life in that remote village in their way. All these things gave them a sense of liberty followed by dreams and hopes for a possible demise of this dictatorship, making them always live with the desire for change to come someday.

"The very first day—when I saw you on the teacher's bus, after the worry and sadness for my appointment in this village—I thought that 'God throws you with one hand, and catches you with the other one,' as my grandmother says," Elsa told Ardian one day when they were having a good time together by the river.

"It applies to me too," Ardian added. "God threw me with one hand from the Pedagogical Institute, from the city, and from my first love, and caught me with the other hand, giving me this wonderful love of yours."

He mentioned his first love after a long time because he was still thinking for Eralda time after time, even at that moment. But he understood the mistake he made and stayed silenced for some minutes after that. Elsa stayed quiet, knowing that they both were thinking about the same thing in that moment of silence, and she couldn't find what to say and didn't know how to act to change the discussion. During every beautiful moment of his life, Ardian always thought about Eralda as well. He wished to experience and share such beautiful moments with her too. It seemed inevitable, like something that had to happen generally like this. One can control his conscious mind but is incapable of managing his subconscious mind. Eralda was still there, in his subconscious, and chances were that she would remain there for a long time and maybe forever. Only the first love knows how to stay so quiet, so strong, and so long in the unreachable depths of one's mind and soul, being always ready to come up in surface sometimes.

At the end of the fall and beginning of the winter, when days became shorter and colder, they started spending more time in their room. Ardian restarted his work of reading and analyzing books of Albanian writers and poets from his new point of view related to socialist realism. He explained to Elsa what he was doing, talking about the dangerousness of this work and the risk of another potential inspection of their room by the secret service agents. They were cautious not to speak with others about their secret thoughts for poverty, dictatorship, and socialist realism, not to put their lives in danger. Ardian told her that he needed to write down some of his conclusions, but he knew that it was perilous. Elsa brought the idea that he could write in her notebooks, and she could take these notebooks to her home every Saturday. This idea seemed okay at first, but Ardian didn't agree, because it was still a danger of checking their room during the weekdays or checking her house as well because she already was his wife.

"No, I don't want you to become my accomplice in this dangerous job," he said to her.

"I would do everything for the guy I love," she promised him. "But you haven't told me anything yet about your collaborators, your contacts with other domestic enemies, and your connections with the foreign enemies," she added, laughing with him.

"You are the only collaborator I have. You are the only 'domestic and foreign enemy' I'm connected with. You are the 'enemy of the Party,' 'enemy of the people,' 'enemy of the working class,' 'enemy of the cooperativist peasantry,'" Ardian spoke by pointing at her, "therefore we'll end up in the guillotine of the Communist Party," he concluded.

Ardian told Elsa that he was not going to write anything for some more months, and he would continue with his first method by storing things in order in his mind and writing down positive notes that, in his memory will have a negative meaning. More than eight months had passed since the death of the Great Leader, and Ardian had not seen any signs of change yet. The successor of the Dear Leader was always speaking for continuity and loyalty. It meant that the new communist leader, the Political Bureau, the Central Committee of the Communist Party, all the state institutions, and the people of Albania had to remain loyal to the guidance and legacy of the late Great Leader by continuing in his path.

It was December 1985, and Ardian recalled the day of December 1981 when the prime minister of that time had committed suicide. He had been under the pressure of the Great Leader and the Political Bureau of the Communist Party for the engagement of his son with a girl belonging to a family related to the "overthrown classes," which were eliminated by communists when they took power after the Second World War. He was the last close friend of the dictator that had remained still alive until that time. All other communist friends that participated in the Albanian National Liberation War, led by the Communist Party and the Great Leader, had already been killed by the dictator. Dozens of them were eliminated year after year, being labeled as "putschists," "enemies of the Party and working class," "agents of the foreign intelligence agencies," "collaborators and servants of the foreign capitalistic countries," etc., etc. After the controversial suicide of the Prime Minister, the Great Leader, suddenly, had discovered and called him a "poly agent in service of several foreign intelligence agencies."

"Every time the Great Leader eliminated his close friends," Ardian told Elsa, "we, the people of Albania, believed in his justifications as motives for their execution. Based on his words, we thought that all his close friends of the war have been betraying him. But now it is clear for me that there were not them betraying him, but it was the dictator himself that betrayed and eliminated them all one by one by execution, imprisonment, and internment of them and their families and relatives, to solidify his everlasting rule. So, it was the turn of the prime minister for almost thirty years and Great Leader's close friend for forty years. And don't forget about the interesting fact that all of them had supported the Great Leader in his 'witch hunt' in all previous cases before their own turn came. The prime minister that committed suicide had always been a hardliner who had won a reputation for brutality in persecuting everybody else in search of his successful political career by continually supporting the Great Leader," Ardian concluded his explanation for the dictatorship and the actions of the dictator.

After the New Year's Eve, Ardian bought and installed a small "Illyria" radio in their room to listen to the Radio Tirana, especially the news, hoping to discern any promising sign of change. The spring of 1986 arrived. One year from the death of the Great Leader had already passed, and Ardian hadn't seen any sign of change yet. But then, the first promising weak sign appeared on the horizon. The new communist leader initiated, and the Political Bureau and Central Committee of the Communist Party approved a government decision to help the poor peasants of agrarian cooperatives and the workers of agricultural state farms. According to this decision, the agricultural teams were allowed to use a plot of land to grow vegetables for their own families and they could keep a small drove of cattle, like a dozen of cows, or a more significant number of sheep and goats according to the topographic terrain of the villages. Up to that time, the villagers were not allowed to keep any livestock (only a limited number of chickens), and they didn't have any piece of land for family use. The communist leadership took this decision in a desperate attempt to relieve the food shortage in all villages and cities. Until that moment, everything privately owned (even domestic animals or the land of the peasants), had been considered as something dangerous for the socialism, enforcing the motto of the Great Leader according to which: "The private property gives birth to capitalism every day, every hour, and every minute." And that's why everything in Albania was state ownership, in cities and villages. But the communist leadership was forced to take this different decision to allow small pieces of land and little herds for collective use as a measure to alleviate the food shortage in villages. They didn't intend for any ideological or political change, and the communist leadership was always careful to speak clearly, stressing the need for loyalty and continuity in the Great Leader's trail—in the path of socialism.

28

During the school summer holidays of 1986, Ardian and Elsa spent one month in Vlorë's beaches, then returned and spent one week in Elbasan with Elsa's parents, before starting their trip in the southeast region of Albania, where they spent three more weeks. They spent one week in Pogradec, a picturesque city by the Lake Ohrid, with a maximum depth of 940 feet, making it the deepest lake in Balkans, and it is shared between Albania and Macedonia with cities of Ohrid and Struga on the other side of the lake. Then, they traveled toward Korça, the central town in that region near the border with Greece. Elsa's parents come from a village in Korça county. They spent one week in a hotel in the city and visited Elsa's relatives in villages around the city. The most beautiful villages they visited were Voskopoja and Dardha. Voskopoja once has been a prosperous city and a holy place for the Orthodox Christians culminating in the middle of the 18th century, and you still can find there some important historical objects of that time. After that, they traveled toward Erseka, where they stayed just two days and continued their trip to Përmet for another two-day-long stay. They arrived at the final destination of their journey, Gjirokastër, the birthplace of the Great Leader. They spend three more days there and visited the fortress of the city situated on the top of a hill, overlooking the town and all the valley of the river Drino. In this fortress, the National Folklore Festival is held every five years.

They returned to Elbasan and were very happy with that trip. After spending two weeks in Elbasan, they returned reinvigorated in their village where they had built their warm nest, to start the new school year 1986 - 1987. Their love for each other, their walks around the hills of the village to enjoy the nature, their summer trips in different regions of Albania, seemed like giving them a kind of freedom inside the dictatorship they were living in, making them forget about that dictatorship for some moments. But everywhere they went, they saw poverty and destitution. They saw people and families living in abject poverty in cities, towns, and villages. They saw the adverse conditions of roads, trains, and buses, because of the lack of funding and maintenance. All these circumstances with harsh working and living conditions reminded them always of the tyrannical dictatorship under which the poor people of Albania have been living for more than forty years already.

Ardian wasn't seeing any promising sign of change even after one year and a half from the dictator's death. In November 1986, the ninth Congress of the Communist Party took place. It was the first congress after the dictator's death, and it was called the Congress of Continuity. These congresses take place every five years and are the most important events of the communist party leadership, deciding for the main political and economic developments for the five coming years. So, this last Congress agreed for the "continuity on the Great Leader's path," without any little sign of any change. After that, Ardian became more pessimistic and desperate without any hope for any change to come soon.

"Not any promising sign at all, and it looks like we are going to remain in this village for all the rest of our life," Ardian told Elsa one day.

"Hope dies last," Elsa answered to him without being able to find any other way of encouragement for him and herself.

"La speranza è l'ultima a morire," Ardian repeated in the Italian language the expression that Elsa just said in Albanian, speaking slowly in a low voice with his head down, immersing himself in a pang of deep sadness and hopelessness.

Another day, when they were enjoying the beautiful nature and their love, Ardian was in a good mood, and he told Elsa:

"Let's decide to live here and ask the village council to give us permission to build a house."

Unlike the cities, where apartment buildings were built and owned by the state, houses in villages were built and owned by individuals and were the private property of the villagers.

"I agree with you, but we must deregister ourselves from the city register and become village inhabitants first, and after that, we can apply for a license to build our house here," Elsa explained to him.

"That's okay for me. Let's do it," Ardian answered without thinking any longer.

After some weeks of passionate work, Ardian filled dozens of school notebooks with his analysis, and Elsa placed them inside the suitcases in which she was supposed to put her dowry items. According to the Albanian tradition, girls, as future brides, must prepare and bring a dowry to the marriage consisting of household goods. They have to handcraft and embroider a lot of clothes, bedsheets, pillow covers, blankets, quilts, bedspreads, tablecloths, flouncing, doilies, rugs, and a lot of such stuff, starting years before their marriage, always under their mother's directions and control.

"I'll bring all these notebooks of yours with the suitcases of my dowry, the week before our wedding day," Elsa told Ardian. "But those suitcases are becoming hefty week after week," she added.

"Based on their heavyweight, the movers will think there is gold inside and will steal them," Ardian joked with her.

"Gold, and far better than gold, o Tunxh," Elsa mimicked the words of an Albanian movie character.

Ardian asked Elsa's help to take books from the city's library. He told her to go to his friend Bashkim, who usually helped Ardian to find rare books and banned books of punished authors that were taken out of circulation by the communist regime. Despite the intense fight of the dictatorship and regime's censorship against banned books and authors, those books became more interesting, and passionate readers were giving these books to each other, to their trusted friends, in hiding from the regime.

In the summer of 1988, they spent one month in Vlorë and Elbasan, before starting the trip to the north-east region of Albania, on the border with Macedonia and Kosovo. They began by staying one night in Librazhd—a town just fifteen miles east of Elbasan, by the Shkumbin river. From there, they took a bus early in the morning, traveling toward Peshkopi, going through a mountain dirt road, stopping in several villages, before reaching the final destination, the city of Peshkopi, by the river Black Drin, bordering Dibra e Madhe of Macedonia. Albanians are living on both sides of the border, being separated for already thirty years by ruling political regimes. They spent two more days there before traveling further north toward the city of Kukës, going through another mountain dirt road.

They arrived in Kukës on Thursday, August 11, 1988, about two o'clock. They booked a hotel near the city center and went out to find a restaurant for lunch. They walked through the main city square, entered the restaurant, and ordered the meal. While waiting for their order to come, they both thought that there was a strange situation. The restaurant, city streets, stores, the square, were quiet and almost empty, without people, and it was something unusual. Even the waiter, the cook, and the cleaning woman were more reserved and silent than usual. They looked like acting and talking carefully for not to cause any noise. When the waiter brought their dishes on the table, Ardian asked him:

"Why is it so quiet here? There are no people in the streets, in the central square, in stores, and restaurants."

"Where are you from?" the waiter asked, with a cold voice and face, without answering Ardian's question.

"We are from Elbasan," Elsa answered immediately, waiting for the waiter's answer.

"Aren't you from Tirana?" the waiter asked them and left immediately without answering the Ardian's question.

"Strange," Ardian whispered, and they continued having lunch.

They left the restaurant and walked through the city streets toward the hill with a new park, from where you can see the beautiful view of the big artificial lake formed after the dam of Fierza's Hydroelectric Power Plant was built. The ruins of the old city of Kukës (now covered by the lake water), are right there where two rivers (White Drin, flowing from Kosovo, and Black Drin, flowing from Macedonia and Peshkopi), come and merge into one, forming the river Drin. But now you couldn't see the rivers' beds, because of the Fierza's reservoir that is a long artificial lake going through the river valley. The lake water covered the old city of Kukës, and the New Kukës (where Ardian and Elsa were walking now), was built on a plain by the lake.

After a small stroll, they returned to their hotel, because felt scary from that strange emptiness and silence of the streets and park. Ardian started a talk with the man at the hotel reception desk, speaking about the new city of Kukës, the lake, the new bridge, the mountain, etc. The receptionist spoke slowly and, when Ardian told him that they were coming from Elbasan, he asked the same question the restaurant waiter had asked:

"Aren't you from Tirana?"

"The restaurant waiter made me the same question. How come?" Ardian told him.

"That's because most of the visitors come from the capital city," he tried to assure Ardian. "And last days we have had a lot of them," the receptionist continued after a moment of silence, like thinking whether to continue this talk or not.

"Why? Was there any important event taking place here?" Ardian asked him.

"Yes..., and no."

"What is 'yes,' and what is 'no'?" Ardian insisted on continuing the talk.

"Yesterday..., early in the morning..., they hanged an enemy of the people on gallows erected overnight right there, in the middle of the central square," the receptionist explained to Ardian, speaking with pause intervals between his words.

"Was he a foreign enemy..., or a domestic enemy," Ardian asked seriously, approaching his mouth to his ears.

"A domestic enemy," the man answered. "He was a poet. He had written things against socialism, against the Great Leader, against the communist party," the receptionist raised his voice and seriousness.

"Really...? A poet...? Here in Kukës...?" Ardian asked. "Was he a well-known poet? Was he from Kukës, or they brought him from Tirana?"

"He was from here. He had spent twenty-five years in prison, and he was released on parole and lived in a village, but he broke the conditions of terms of his parole to go and see his dying mother that lived in another village."

"What's the poet's name?" Ardian asked him.

"Havzi Nela," the receptionist answered with a weak voice, continuing: "The enemy is always working and activates his collaborators to speak and act against our country and our Party," the receptionist concluded, with a solemn voice and face.

Ardian said "good night" to the receptionist, pulled Elsa from her hand, and went to their room. It was a grave situation for them. They didn't expect such a thing to happen after some promising signs of change they had seen. Elsa prepared the bed, and lay down on it, waiting for Ardian to join her. Ardian was standing near the window, looking down to the central square where the poet had been hanged the day before and was left there all day long for people to watch. It was a long time that such a thing had not happened. The communist regime had always used the method of the public hanging in gallows erected in cities squares, where the "domestic enemies" were hanged, making examples out of them, showing to the people what is the deserved end "of all enemies of the people." They aim to convince the population that the "foreign enemy" is always working against our country in collaboration with "domestic enemies." Such a deserved end will have whoever dares to act against socialism, the Communist Party, and the Great Leader of the People of Albania.

"A country that kills its poets has killed its own soul, has killed itself," Ardian started speaking with his eyes in tears, watching out of the window on the empty square. "A country that kills its poets has destroyed its own future. This country will never have a prosperous future. A country that kills its poets is writing its calamity with its own hands like Aeschylus wrote his tragedies. An eternal curse, like the "Curse of Macbeth,' will continue to haunt for years, decades, and centuries to come this damned country and its people who kill its own poets. The people of this country will never have a better future." Ardian finished his scary, pathetic speech in front of the window.

Elsa was sitting on the bed's edge and didn't dare to approach him while listening to the harsh language he was speaking. She had never seen and heard him in such a situation, and she was petrified.

"Ardian…, please…, calm down. Come to bed…, please," she begged him.

"No…, I'll go out. I will pick up some flowers in the park to put them right there where they hanged the poet," Ardian said, walking toward the door.

"Please…, don't do it. Please…, for the sake of our love. Please…, don't do it," Elsa moved quickly from the bed, kneeled in front of him, begging, crying, and keeping him from his hands, trying to stop him right behind the room door.

Ardian stopped, raised, and hugged her firmly, keeping her tight for some seconds. Then he took her from her hands to go in front of the window, where he started his aggressive speech again:

"Poets are an eternal, innocent human being. Poets are God's gift to their countries and the entire humanity. Poets are like beautiful, innocent birds that fly free high on the sky. Poets are like the fragile, multicolored flowers under the morning dew. Poets are like the deep, blue, clean ocean's water. Poets are the strong roots and the trunk that make a nation stand up and survive through centuries and millenniums. Poets, with their poetry, lyrics, verses, rhymes, ballads, anthems, and poems, bring love, betterment, and development of the human society the same way as the scientists, with their inventions and innovations, help the economy to advance. This country has killed its own poets by using the same gallows that are used to hang criminals. This country has killed its own poets, meaning that it has already killed its own soul. This country has killed its own intellectuals, meaning that it has already killed its own brain. In this way, this country has already killed its own soul and brain. Poets and intellectuals are the heredities of the magnificent genes of idealism and smartness for a country. For that reason, the people of this damn country—a country without brain..., without soul..., without heart..., without any principles and ideals—will be under a self-inflicted curse for centuries to come. This country and its people will not see any prosperity soon because it has destroyed its own genes of intellect and idealism. This country... these people. This damn country..., these damn people. This land..., and its population that kills poets, will be damned forever." Ardian was screaming, and his body was trembling until he brought out of his mouth the last terrifying words. After that, he turned back, hugged Elsa that was standing behind him, and broke down sobbing on her shoulders.

The next morning, they went out of the hotel and strolled around the city square a couple of times. They stopped in the sidewalk standing there some more minutes in silence to honor the dead poet, watching in the direction of the place where the poet had been hanged. Then they walked toward the small pier of the lake where they took a ferry boat to travel from Kukës to the dam of Fierza Lake. This ferry takes only people and goes through all the length of the lake, making stops in villages on both sides. They arrived at the last stop, near the dam, where they took a bus for a short trip from the top of Fierza's dam to its bottom, where is the end side of the other artificial lake, called Koman Lake, that ends right where the Fierza dam has been built. From there, they took another ferry to get to the Koman Lake's dam, and it was a big ferry carrying passengers, cars, and trucks. Traveling by ferry in those two lakes was supposed to be the best experience of their travel, because it is beautiful sightseeing, watching the high mountains on both sides of the narrow, deep, blue water lakes. It was the trip they had been waiting for a long time, but after the bad news they learned in Kukës about the execution of a poet by public hanging, they couldn't and didn't enjoy it at all. Ardian canceled the visit to Tropoja County with its city Bajram Curri, and the beautiful valley of Valbona river. During all that trip by ferries, they only thought and spoke about a lot of writers and poets, compositors and singers, artists, movie actors, and directors, being killed, imprisoned, and sent to internment and their works were banned, burned, and destroyed by the tyrannical dictatorship. Ardian told Elsa about two poets from Librazhd County, neighboring the Elbasan County, who were teachers and were executed for "agitation and propaganda against the state and the Party," just for some poems that were never published. But it had happened in mid-seventies (fifteen years ago) when the dictator punished and executed a lot of artists and politicians. The Great Leader discovered and eliminated a lot of "putschists" and "enemy groups" acting against him in those years. But such a thing like hanging a poet, happening right now, three years after the dictator's death, was very strange and dangerous at the same time.

"The new communist leader, the successor of the dead dictator, transformed himself into a new dictator from the moment he signed the execution of this innocent poet in Kukës," Ardian told Elsa, speaking in revolt.

In September, they returned to their school and couldn't speak with their colleagues about their trip to Kukës because they didn't want to open a risky discussion about the hanged poet. During their tenure in that village, Ardian and Elsa sometimes went to watch television in a room in the cultural center of the agricultural cooperative. Nobody had a TV set in the village, and the television room is used by villagers to watch news, soccer, movies, and entertaining shows of the state TV. Ardian and Elsa usually went there to spend evenings watching movies from eight-thirty to ten or ten-thirty, before the last edition of the news and the end of the daily television programs aired from six to ten o'clock. Ardian wanted to watch foreign movies to keep alive his English and Italian in the absence of any other contacts and possibilities to practice them. All foreign films were carefully selected by the authorities of state censorship. In November 1988, Ardian watched the Canadian made-for-TV movie "Blades of Courage," where the main character of the film, Lori Laroche (Christianne Hirt), reminded him of Eralda in a lot of things, from her appearance, personality, and determination.

"Lori Laroche looks like Eralda, especially with the ponytail hairstyle and forelock over her eyes," he told Elsa, who was sitting by his side. He spoke with such a childish, naïve sincerity, without thinking that it would hurt Elsa, who, for her part, just stayed silenced.

Ardian was affected too much from Lori Laroche's similarity to Eralda. That night he cried for the first time for his first love and his first girlfriend after a long period. He wept in silence in his bed, next to the other bed where Elsa was sleeping, or maybe she was still awake by his neglect because that night he didn't show a good mood to spend some love moments with her like they usually did every night before sleeping. Eralda remained in his mind for some days, and he was looking forward to going to see and tell her about her resemblance with Lori Laroche. The next Sunday, when he and Elsa went to Elbasan, he said to Elsa that he was going to meet Bashkim, but before going to his house, he stopped at the Eralda's store first.

"I came to tell you that you look very much like Lori Laroche," he told her, speaking full of enthusiasm and passion, as soon as he entered her store and after exchanging their first greetings. Eralda laughed loudly.

"Some friends of mine told me the same thing on the morrow morning after the movie was broadcasted on TV. But I didn't watch it because I like sleeping early," she answered.

They continued joyfully talking for other things as if they hadn't been separated for five years, like being still together or good friends, like nothing had happened between them.

Ardian immediately felt the same deep love and desire for Eralda. In those moments—watching her, talking, and laughing with her—he understood how much he had missed her gorgeousness and beauty; her eyes, smile, lips, breast, thighs, and everything else of hers. He had lost all of her. He had missed a part of him and an essential part of his life. He had missed her love. He stood on the end side of the store's counter, watching her dealing with customers. For a moment, he thought that he was watching a beautiful dream that he didn't want to end. She was there…, he was there…, they both were there. They were still together as if nothing had happened, as if time had stopped and those five years of their separation had not passed. But he opened his eyes…, and the dream ended. It was November 1988; five years after the beautiful November of 1983, five years after their first kiss, five years after their great happiness, five years after the magic autumn of their great love, five years without Eralda and her love. The subconscious power of the first love started working at full steam in his mind, and he realized that his passion and lust for her had returned. All he wanted in those moments was a gentle, loving touch of her lips and her body. "She has taken the half of me, and it's not her fault because I have given her the half of me that will remain with her forever, and I can't recover from the magic of her anymore," Ardian was thinking about his first love while watching her.

That night he wept again in silence while being in the same bed with his wife, Elsa. He was in bed with his second love, thinking, and crying for the first love. He felt the touch of Elsa's body, but in his mind, it was Eralda's face and body. Elsa's physical contact and Eralda's spiritual love were both there, being merged into one in the sick mind of the same man. And then he couldn't resist the magical lure of both his loves. He pulled Elsa tight toward himself, rubbing, squeezing, and kissing her. Then he undressed her and himself and started making crazy sex, shouting several times; "Alda..., Alda..., Alda...," the same way he had done in the first days of their relationship. And after he finished that wild storm of lust and sex, it was Elsa's turn to weep. She didn't say anything to him but wept in silence, staying awake all night long at the edge of the bed.

"Sorry," he said in the morning, hugging her in silence. Both shed tears on the shoulders of each other for some minutes.

29

Four out of five years spent in that village became the best part of Ardian's life, and therefore, he was happy. The freedom of thinking about the dictatorship, the love with Elsa, and the nature enjoyment gave a new meaning to his life and more reasons to live. They didn't have any other engagement over there, just love, nature, and freedom of thinking, followed by hope for more freedom.

Elsa always made fun of him by saying: "At least we are free to enjoy the nature," paraphrasing his usual saying, "At least we are free to make love." These two expressions mentioned two beautiful things—nature and love—that they were experiencing and enjoying very much by living and working in the village. Sometimes she only said "at least," and he understood very well what she meant and what she wanted at that moment—making love in the open air in contact with nature; on the grass, under the trees in the middle of the forest accompanied by birds' songs, in the middle of a field with grown crops, by the lake, by the river, and everywhere making possible the magic merge of love and nature.

"Love and nature are two things that heal the wounds of the body and soul," Elsa told him.

"Love and nature make us stronger and help us recover from life's challenges," Ardian answered her.

"They say that love changes those that it touches," Elsa continued.

"Yes, it's true," Ardian answered. "Love changes you forever. Your body and brain change when you fall in love. Love makes you another person. When you are in love, you are not yourself anymore," Ardian ended his inspiring speech.

"And I think that love makes you a better person," Elsa continued, pulling him against herself.

"Love gives you wings to fly," Ardian said a love quote, and the two lovebirds spread their wings and took flight in their sky of pleasure, joy, and happiness in each other's arms.

Ardian spent the New Year's Eve with Elsa's family. On January 1, 1989, they went for a visit to Bashkim's family—as an Albanian tradition of exchanging visits at the beginning of the year to wish each other, "a happy new year." Bashkim told Ardian that the lady that took Ardian's job position when he was expelled from the Institute was just appointed as the Head of the County's Education Department.

"I'll meet her in her office next week, and I'll ask her to assign you back to the pedagogical institute," Bashkim told him, full of optimism and confidence that it will be done.

"That's impossible," Ardian answered, smiling in a pessimistic and skeptical way.

"There has been guidance from the higher levels of the communist party since last summer, instructing the education departments of the counties that, on a case by case basis, to transfer back in the cities all teachers that have been assigned in remote villages just because of their family's bad political biography. They have already started these returns without much noise," Bashkim explained to him. "So that I'll ask her to help you based in this Party guidance by appointing you in the vacant position created in the institute by her departure."

"It's difficult because a lot of other people will try to take that job position by using their connections in the Party," Ardian spoke, showing his skepticism.

"I'm sure that she will do that because she felt guilty for a long time after replacing you, and she and I became good friends during these years," Bashkim told him. "And that's why I'll ask her to fill the vacancy by assigning you there as soon as possible to avoid others' interferences. You know that she has strong family connections with the highest levels of the communist party in our county," Bashkim continued, explaining to Ardian why he was confident for that to happen.

"A happy New Year to your family," Ardian told him, with a glass of wine that Bashkim's wife had just brought on the table.

"A happy New Year to you and for your return to the pedagogical institute," Bashkim and Alma wished Elsa and Ardian.

Ardian and Elsa couldn't believe that. It seemed beyond reasonable imagination. They went together in the village starting the first week of the

236

new semester and spent every day of the week discussing, wondering, betting, and guessing if it would be done or not, hoping for the best. That weekend Elsa went back home in Elbasan, while Ardian spent all hours of Saturday afternoon and Sunday in bed, without doing anything. On Monday morning, he waited for Elsa at the bus stop in the center of the village, as he always did on Mondays, but this time it was special. Elsa was the first one to get out of the bus with an envelope in her right-hand, yelling joyously and running toward Ardian. He understood that she had brought the good news they had been waiting for. They hugged and kissed, she jumped on him, and he rotated her around full of joy, surprising everybody else. Nobody knew what had happened, because Elsa hadn't told anybody on the bus, keeping her joy inside her to share it in the right moment of meeting Ardian.

"Maybe she has found out that she is pregnant," one of their friends guessed supposing that Elsa had been trying to conceive, but it has been unsuccessful until now.

"What's the reason for all this joy and enthusiasm? Are you pregnant?" another friend approached and asked them.

"Not me, but he. He is pregnant," Elsa answered, leaving everybody with open mouth. "Ardian was assigned back to the pedagogical institute again, and this is the education department's order," Elsa explained to them, showing the envelope she had in her hands.

"And by the way..., she is going to conceive tonight," Ardian told them, embracing Elsa and squeezing her against him. "It's time for a child," he whispered in Elsa's ear, and she approved it, nodding her head.

They had discussed several times the need for a child, but Ardian had always refused to do such a thing. Sometimes he had said that he does not want a child as long as they will be working and living in that remote village. Other times he had repeatedly said that he didn't want to add another victim to this dictatorship. So that's what he thought after this good news of his transfer to the pedagogical institute. It was the right time for a child because both conditions were almost met. What he heard from Bashkim (about the Party guidance to transfer back to the city all teachers with family's bad political biography), was another sign of change. "Small steps, one by one, up to the dictatorship demise," he had thought about this process.

Ardian gave to the principal of the school the County Education Department's letter with the decision for his transfer, and he taught his classes that day as his last day in that school and in that village. They spent their last afternoon and night in that village. It was like a sacred night of their first attempt for Elsa to conceive. On Tuesday, early in the morning, Ardian walked about three hours to get to Belësh, the central town of Dumre region, where he took the bus for Elbasan. On Wednesday morning, Ardian started teaching in the pedagogical institute where most of the professors already knew him. He was in seventh heaven. Even though he missed Elsa from the very first night that he spent alone in the institute's dormitory, and although he was thinking only about her all the coming days (looking forward to her coming back on Saturday afternoon), he couldn't resist the desire of going to Eralda's store to tell her about his return to the pedagogical institute. It was good news for him, and as such, he felt the obligation to share that good news with Eralda too.

"Five years ran so fast," he told Eralda, in a moment during their talk.

"Do you really think so?" Eralda said, looking at his happy face. "Maybe it has not been so fast for everybody else," she added, moving away toward a customer.

Ardian didn't know what to say after her words. What she had just said, sounded like a complaint, like a wail, like a pain. Ardian thought that he was behaving like an egoist. Out of those five years, he had passed four happy, beautiful years in love with Elsa. And what years—the best years of his life. Unlike him, Eralda had remained single, struggling with her loneliness. It was the first time that he thought seriously about this beautiful girl—the most beautiful girl in the city—as a twenty-four-year-old girl and still single. He felt that Eralda has her full rights to love and marry somebody else. Ardian had never thought like this before. But now, after Eralda's reaction that made him think like this, he felt sorrow about her and felt guilty that he was the reason and the cause of this. "Has she been just unlucky in finding another love or is it her stubborn head's decision?" he asked himself without being able to find a reasonable and convincing answer. "Has she been hurt too much by the failure of her first love, or is it just a painful decision to not try another love?" He continued asking himself, but in whatever answer he could assume, he was always finding himself guilty for her situation, and it became a significant burden for him. He left the store without greeting Eralda, while she was dealing with customers, and with a decision to not bother her anymore because he hadn't the right to do it after all the drama he had caused to the life of that beautiful young woman.

He waited for Elsa at the bus station on Saturday afternoon and spent the weekend together in Elsa's parents' house. All the coming weeks and months, passed with him spending the weeknights in the institute's dormitory and Elsa in the village, while the weekend nights were spent together in Elsa's family. Elsa found out very soon that she was pregnant, and it was e great news and e great joy for the couple and for their parents, especially Elsa's mother that had been asking her every week for four years by saying: "What are you waiting for?" In the school spring break, in April 1989 (when Elsa would stay one week without going to the village), they organized a big wedding party, just in time for her baby bump not to be visible. They were so fortunate when in May, the pedagogical institute had a vacant apartment given from the City's Executive Committee, and in that time, Ardian was the only professor in need for shelter, and so the couple became with an apartment of theirs in this challenging time of apartment shortage. Ardian wanted to share this good news with somebody else, while Elsa was in the village. He was walking down the main boulevard going to Elsa's parents to share with them this good news, but something like an instinctive act forced him to walk toward Eralda's store. Ardian understood his mistake only when he entered the store's door and couldn't go back, so he told her that he had just got an apartment, and she just said: "Congratulations and enjoy it."

This new family, including their unborn child in Elsa's tummy, had now their own apartment, which they completed with furniture in the first weekend. They spent the first month of summer holidays in Vlorë, and the rest of the summer holidays in Elbasan, enjoying with each other and with the baby in Elsa's belly. In this time, they started the daily evening strolls in the main boulevard's traditional walk, and sometimes to the park. One evening, while they were walking in the crowded street, a stranger approached them, presenting himself as someone that had had an important job position in the County's Party Committee in the time when they had discussed the punishment for Ardian.

"Based on what you had done and the political-ideological direction that the discussion about you took, you would have been prosecuted. But I protected you, and I helped in deciding for you to be transferred to a remote village. But there you had to be under the surveillance of the Party and secret service agents for one year, to see if you, during that time, would do anything else, any suspicious thing that would be against the principles and directives of the communist party and the Great Leader," he told them.

"Why did you do that?" Elsa asked the stranger.

"Because I asked my daughter, which was a student in the pedagogical institute in that time, and she told me excellent words about him, calling him the best professor of the pedagogical institute," the man answered to Elsa.

"Okay. Thank you very much," Ardian told him. "And you have to know that I have had the most beautiful years of my life over there, where I met my wonderful wife," Ardian continued, pointing at Elsa.

"Wait..., because you don't know everything. My daughter understood that something bad was happening to you, and she left immediately, coming back home with professor Bashkim that night. He begged in tears for mercy for you, saying that you didn't deserve to face prosecution," the man explained, catching them by surprise with this new information.

"It's good to know that there are still good people out there. Thank you. I appreciate it very much," Ardian told him, shaking hands with him.

"They have saved your life. They are your guardian angels assigned by God to protect you," Elsa told Ardian after they separated from that man.

"I have my guardian angels without knowing that. Life is interesting, and it looks like everything in our life happens by chance."

"Everything happens for a reason," Elsa corrected him.

"And it makes people more empathetic and real," Ardian concluded, speaking in a pensive mood, being immersed in deep thoughts about his life.

Ardian hadn't mentioned Eralda anymore, even though every time they walked in the city's center, passing by the Eralda's store, he could watch her store and would think about her. He thought about Eralda several times a day, and he tried hard not to enter her store, based on his decision not to bother her. Every time he was walking with Elsa in the park, he recalled the beautiful dates with Eralda that had taken place in this park and on that bench under the willow tree. But it was only once that he couldn't resist, and he showed Elsa the seat covered by the willow's branches and leaves.

"Do you see that bench under the willow tree?" he asked Elsa.

"Oh, yes. It's a beautiful spot. Let's go there," Elsa answered, without letting him continue, and pulled him toward the bench, which happened to be free at that moment. It was not what Ardian intended to do when he showed Elsa the seat, and he remained silenced and unsure for some minutes after they sat on the bench. But he wanted to be sincere till the end with Elsa.

"I showed you this bench because it has been the place where I had my first date with Eralda, and some other dates later on, for the time we were together," he told Elsa, watching in her eyes, waiting for her reaction.

She smiled slightly, looking at his eyes, without saying anything, but just giving him a hug and whispering in his ear.

"I love you, honey."

"I love you too, darling," Ardian answered, squeezing her stronger and staying like that for a long time, trying hard to keep his choke up in his throat.

He didn't repeat such a mistake anymore, and based on a silent agreement, they both tried to avoid passing by that bench other days by walking through different pathways of the park away from the "famous bench under the willow."

When the new school year started in September 1989, Elsa took the pre-maternity paid leave, waiting to give birth to her child somewhere in the middle of October. After that, she would take the rest of maternity paid leave, altogether nine months, so they were going to spend all the year together, raising their baby. They talked about the baby's name several times without knowing whether it would be a boy or a girl. But they agreed in two names for both cases.

"Do you remember those fresh mimosa flower bouquets I picked for you every morning, starting from the first blossom to the last flowers of the bloom season of those mimosa trees in the schoolyard?" Ardian asked Elsa.

"Sure. How can I forget those wonderful days of our love?" she answered, full of joy.

"Very good. So, I think if the newborn baby is a girl, her name will be Mimosa."

"Oh…, I like it very much. I like the name itself and the reason behind this name," Elsa agreed with a lot of pleasure.

"Please…, be a girl…, a beautiful one, like your mom…, and we'll call you, Mimosa," Ardian spoke to the baby, rubbing Elsa's belly.

"Please…, be a boy…, a smart one, like your dad…, and I'll choose a beautiful name for you," Elsa spoke to the baby, rubbing her belly too.

"Have you thought about it?" he asked Elsa.

"Yes…, of course. All girls think for the names of their future children," she answered, laughing and telling him the secret of all girls waiting to become mothers.

"Okay. Tell me," Ardian requested Elsa's decision.

"I have chosen the name of the scent of another flower," she started answering.

"Another flower? A good idea. I know we both love flowers and nature, and we have a lot of facts to prove that," Ardian urged Elsa to say the name.

"That's why I want to stay with a flower and with a tree. We both love nature, and we have spent a lot of quality time together in nature, enjoying it very much."

"And the winner flower is...," Ardian spoke loudly, starting the winner's pronouncement before Elsa pronouncing it.

"Erblin..., Erblin," Elsa answered, continuing the winner pronouncement. "You know that street that takes you to the new building of the pedagogical institute. There are a lot of fragrant linden trees on both sides of that street; therefore, we call it 'the street of linden trees.' In their blooming season—from early June to late July—the entire road has a pleasant scent coming from the fragrant yellowish blossoms. I used to pass through that street every day, going to and coming back home from the pedagogical institute. From that time, I've thought and decided that I will name my son after the linden flower aroma—Erblin," Elsa said the name that in the Albanian language means the scent of linden flowers.

The great day came, and a healthy, beautiful baby boy was born. Elsa had already won the right to his name. The baby boy was called Erblin. Ardian, thinking for somebody else to share this good news, broke his decision and went to Eralda's store again, while returning home the day Elsa was still in the maternity hospital. He thought to share his joy with Eralda and entered the store, telling her about the newborn baby boy and his name, "Erblin." It was only then—when he pronounced the name "Erblin" to her—that he found out the similarity of his son's name with Eralda's name in two first letters." It was just an unimportant coincidence that he hadn't thought about before, but now that he thought about that, it looked significant to him, thinking that this name would remind him of his first love and his first girlfriend, but this similarity had to remain secret only in his mind.

Starting with Poland, in June 1989, the Communism started falling in all Central and Eastern European communist countries, culminating with the fall of Berlin Wall on November 8, 1989. These significant events, called the "Revolutions of 1989," brought the end of the communist regimes in those countries. This event gave Ardian more hope that something was going to happen in Albania as well. In December 1989, Romania's dictator was killed by the anti-communist revolutionaries. The communism collapsed in all countries of the communist Eastern Bloc, but not yet in Albania.

In the New Year's Eve, Ardian had a lot of good reasons to celebrate for the year leaving behind. He passed through his mind all the year's main events remembering his transfer back to the pedagogical institute, the wedding party, the new apartment, the birth of Erblin, the communism collapse, and the fall of Berlin Wall. And in these last words, Ardian found out the fact that his son's name "Erblin," was almost similar to the word "Berlin," because there were the same letters with just a different positioning of the letter "b" in these two words. He told Elsa about this fact, and she answered by saying to him that he was trying to "find connections among unconnected things," after laughing together for this beautiful coincidence. Ardian wanted to celebrate for all these good things that had happened in his life during that year. For that reason, he bought a guitar, bringing it home as an exciting surprise for Elsa. They invited Ardian's family and Elsa's parents to come and spend together the New Year's Eve dinner in their new apartment. Ardian had sung for Elsa several times in the village and had told her that he played the guitar, and now Elsa was going to listen to him singing and playing the guitar for the first time since they have been together. For ten days, until the New Year's Eve, he played the guitar to exercise and strengthen his fingers and fingertips harmed by the guitar strings in the first days. After this practice, Ardian was in better shape and ready to sing songs and play the guitar during the dinner and the night of festivity. He sang a lot of songs that night, surprising Elsa that was watching and listening to him playing the guitar and singing so well, showing to her this talent that she had not seen before. Ardian was playing the guitar and was singing because he was delighted at the end of this year. He was feeling like coming back from the evil's hell into life's enjoyments. Among other songs, he sang the song that he had written on the occasion of the start of his relationship with Eralda. After he sang that song, Ardian realized that life is not only joy and happiness, and people don't sing only for joyous and happy events, but there are a lot of worries, sorrows, and sadness as well, and people write and sing songs for those sad things too. His first love was and remained such suffering and pain for him, for his heart and his soul.

And he, being filled with such great joy, repeated his mistake. He ran again to Eralda's store to tell her that he had bought a guitar, making her in this way the second person after Elsa with which he wanted to share any good news of his life. He had gone there to tell her every enjoyment of his life—first, about his transfer back to the city, then, about the new apartment, later on, about his son's birth, and finally, for buying the guitar. He didn't tell her about his wedding party because it would be more harmful to Eralda. Every time he went to see Eralda, she seemed more friendly with him. Her behavior gave him more pleasure, and he enjoyed the beautiful Eralda's smile, the beautiful shape of her eyes, and her cheekbones when she smiled, her full lips and those lovely dimples in her cheeks, her sweet voice, and her gorgeous forelock on her forehead. He had still feelings for her, but for now, being a married man to another woman, that was all he deserved—just enjoying her friendship and her angelic appearance. But he was pleased even with that limitation. He was delighted that their friendship remained alive and that she accepted to see him, to shake hands with him, to speak with him, and above all, to smile at him. All those things meant very much for Ardian, but he was capable of understanding what was happening beyond her kindness and beyond her smiling eyes, where he could notice her sadness, and her inner suffering and pain, that even her beautiful forelock couldn't hide.

Eralda, for her part, tried hard to remain friendly, kind, and gentle with Ardian. She expressed her sincere joy openly for Ardian's good luck and for all the good things that were happening in his life. She was happy as well that his life was going in the right direction, after five years of his transfer to that remote village. She thought about her lost love with Ardian, which had happened five years ago. This last year, after his return to the pedagogical institute, he was coming more often to her store. It looked like his presence relit the fire of her love and revived the first love bringing it out to the surface, from the mysterious depth of her soul where the first love was surviving in silence and inactive but still alive, in the way that only the first love can live and endure forever.

Eralda thought of her first love several times, trying to analyze the cause and the consequences of its loss. Looking back in time from the distance of years that have passed is like looking back to a mountain while you are walking away from it. After every mile you walk, you stop and turn your head to watch better the full view of that mountain and all the mountain range. It's the same thing when you think about first love's loss. After every day, every week, every month, and every year that passes, when you turn your mind back to analyze it, you see and feel the full dimensions and the whole shape of your first love and its loss, followed by the unbearable feelings of longing and pain for that great love.

Eralda had not found another convincible love. It seemed like she had decided to punish herself by staying single forever, without love and marriage, just because she had lost the first love because of her rigidity and stubbornness, being incapable of keeping and protecting her marvelous first love. She was missing the first love very much, suffering and feeling its terrible pain caused by the yearning for her lost love, always ending in tears.

30

The fall of communism in Eastern European countries and the execution of Romanian dictator made it clear that communism would fall in Albania as well. The first one to understand and to be frightened by this fact was the Albanian communist leader. Since the "Revolutions of 1989" started, with its inevitable "domino effect," the Albanian communist leader understood his destiny if he didn't take any measures. All he needed was some more time to use it wisely in the interests of the survival of the communist elite. Unfortunately for the future of the people of Albania, he was given plenty of time because, unlike the other communist countries, in Albania, the domestic dissidents against the regime didn't exist. Such dissidence was never created and was inexistent because of the forty-five years of wild communist tyranny that resulted in the execution and elimination of every opponent element and their families, planting fear and terror among the people that could dare to think differently. In the absence of real dissidence and opposition to take the lead of an anti-communist revolution (as it was happening in other communist countries), the Albanian communist dictator acted like an old cunning red fox and took the flag of the transformation toward the democracy "with peaceful means." He engaged the so-called intellectuals by meeting with them, commending and promoting some of them, and by allowing them to write articles in the state-controlled newspapers. These "intellectuals" were members of the communist party and very loyal to the communist elite. Real intellectuals to work on the people and country's interests, didn't exist anymore because they all had been eliminated year after year by the dictatorship. And now the communist "intellectuals" had the permission of the "good dictator" to write and publish "freely" in the state-owned and state-controlled newspapers and speak "freely" on the radio "Voice of America" in the Albanian language service. They were writing and speaking "freely," but not against the dictatorship and the actual communist leader because they were "intellectuals" made by the communist regime to serve the system with loyalty till the end of their life. They were called on duty now to help the Albanian communist elite in this critical time for them. The communist leader was orchestrating their false courage, and they would go as far as the "good dictator" wanted. They would follow his scenario and would execute orders and take actions decided by him. These "intellectuals" in return, didn't forget to thank the "good communist dictator" for allowing the freedom of expression and for his efforts to bring democracy in the country. From June 1989, (when anti-communist revolutions started in other communist countries of Eastern Europe), to December 1990, the "good dictator" had one year and a half of time to orchestrate in detail everything needed to be done, using efficiently the most loyal communists and the state secret service with its agents spread everywhere.

The cunning communist leader had survived successfully from the guillotine of the Great Leader that had eliminated all his old friends. Now he was working again as an old fox to save his head from a potential rebellion. He made a lot of well-calculated moves in advance, by using effectively the state secret service that became an advantageous means at that time. With the help of the secret service agents—as a centralized and well-organized establishment with resources spread all over the country—he spread the news to implement his scenario. First, on July 2, 1990, they spread the rumors for the opening of the gates of foreign embassies in Tirana, by notifying and letting thousands of citizens enter some foreign embassies to be transported abroad later. Second, on December 30, 1990, they spread the news of the open state border, notifying and allowing people to pass freely to Greece. Third, in March 1991, they spread the rumors of the ships in Durrës harbor that were ready to leave, allowing people to board all the ships to sail toward Italy. The sly dictator applied every part of his scenario by using the secret service agents to spread the "good news" very fast in all the country, making people run toward embassies, seaports, and country's border to desert their own country. In this way, he emptied the country from the most potent individuals who would take an active part in the unavoidable anti-communist revolution. It was a very well-orchestrated move to avoid potential demonstrations and firm opposition. These moves served to save the communist elite and their families with the possibility to continue having the political and economic power in the future democracy.

The "good dictator" used the new faces of the communist intellectuals who were recently promoted by him and distinguished for their loyalty to the communist elite. In addition to them, he used the invisible phalanxes of the numerous state secret service agents and members of their families, which were arranged in multiple echelons being ready to be used at the right time and in the right place.

That's what Ardian was thinking about everything happening in Albania at that time. He understood the strategy and the deceiving tactics of the communist dictator and the falsity of this kind of democratic transformation that misled the public. He was not happy at all, and he shared his concerns with Elsa every day.

Some small demonstrations for democracy took place in few cities of Albania in mid-December 1990. Such a display that seemed just like a theatrical gesture took place in Elbasan as well. It was a small group of people demonstrating and going around the main square of the city, surrounded by a lot of passive spectators staying on the sidewalks around the square watching this deceiving theater together with some policemen that didn't react against them at all. Then, the so-called "demonstrators for democracy," moved to other streets of the city and attacked stores, breaking their doors and windows, and looting everything, without being confronted by the police. This situation brought more chaos, fear, and uncertainty for the populace of the city. By logic, a revolution must be violent and destructive to be trusted as such. Therefore, the organizers of these false demonstrations (the communist leadership and the state secret service), made this theatre to be seen as violent and destructive, directing them not against the communist regime, but against stores and innocent people.

Some rioters attacked the Eralda's store, while Eralda tried to stop them, fighting with them in front of her store. She couldn't stop them, and they beat her, broke and looted everything, and set the store on fire. Eralda was taken to the hospital. Ardian, who was walking toward the main square, saw the Eralda's store on fire and hurried toward it. He arrived there and saw the ambulance taking Eralda to the hospital. He went back home and told Elsa about that, asking her to go together to see Eralda in hospital.

"The 'demonstrators for democracy' attacked my store and me because I confronted them. They broke and looted the store and set it on fire, and I ended up here in the hospital," Eralda told them. "The hooligan that eight years ago was sent to prison after the fight with my brother was leading the group of thugs," Eralda explained to them. "I didn't leave the store, and I tried to stop them from breaking and looting my store like they were doing with other nearby stores. The leading thug ran toward me, shouting: 'Our time has come! This is our time.' Police were nowhere to be seen. I couldn't stop them, and I failed in front of their cruelty and brutality. Here I am now, beaten and injured in hospital. But I'm still alive, and thank you for coming to see me," Eralda ended, with a sad smile, with a black eye, bruised and swelled face.

Continuing this theatre, like being "forced" by these "demonstrations for democracy," the communist leader allowed the foundation of the new political parties. With the permit and the hidden contribution of the communist leader and with instructions taken by his office, the first "opposition" party, the Democratic Party of Albania, was founded on December 12, 1990. It was followed by the foundation of other new political parties, starting in this way the new era of "political pluralism" in Albania. It was not a real political pluralism because all leaders of these new political parties were just marionettes of the communist regime and they had the permission of the "good dictator" to speak loudly against the communism, against the communist party, against the dead communist dictator (that had already died six years earlier), without forgetting to thank always the actual communist leader. These poppets played their role very well and deceived the people of Albania that were cheering full of hope and enthusiasm for new "democratic" leaders and the new political parties. Only a few smart people understood this tragic comedy played behind the back of the people of Albania. They said that the mother party, meaning the communist party, gave birth to all those babies, meaning all new political parties. The most successful Albanian writer of the socialist realism, a protégé of the communist regime and the Great Leader, said: "The spring came in winter," comparing the coming democracy with the spring. But a writer that had suffered seventeen years in prison under the dictatorship said: "The baby was born dead," because he recognized the most loyal communists and the "intellectuals" promoted by the "good dictator" being spread everywhere in the leadership and membership of all new political parties. He saw investigators, prosecutors, judges, false witnesses, state secret service agents, along with their friends and family members, and he understood that the "peaceful transition to pluralism and democracy" was masterfully orchestrated by the communist leadership and the cunning "good dictator."

The goal of the communist leadership was to allow a theatrical pluralism for the sake of a transition from communism to democracy, but not to let the overthrown wealthy class coming to power. New faces (representatives of the old communist elite), took the political power in the Albanian "democracy," the "transition" was done peacefully without any blood, and the "good dictator" was given all the merits for this "peaceful transition."

"The truth is that there was no blood because it was not a real anti-communist revolution like in other ex-communist countries. So, it's not a real transition into pluralism and democracy," Ardian told Elsa every time he heard the "intellectuals" speaking about the communist leader's merit for this "peaceful and bloodless transition."

As a result, the first plural election, held on March 31, 1991, was won by the incumbent communist leader and his communist party that had already changed its name to the Socialist Party of Albania as another cosmetic change.

"It is a real tragicomedy," Ardian said to Elsa after this election. "We weren't free to speak during the dictatorship, but now we are completely free to speak, and everybody is speaking, but nobody is listening," he concluded in sadness.

The second pluralistic election took place on March 22, 1992, after one year of the destruction of all existing industries and services of the Albanian economy. The Democratic Party won, but it was led by an authoritarian communist and loyal to the communist elite, promoted by the communist dictator. That's why this party was filled with a lot of other loyal communists and state secret service agents along with their family members and relatives in all Albania territory.

"This kind of democracy is even worse than the communist dictatorship," Ardian told Elsa one day. "It was a real dictatorship, and we knew it as such, but what is happening now is the worst, because it's a false democracy and a new attempt to deceive the people of Albania again. They deceived the people for forty-five years by calling the personal rule of the communist dictator as a 'dictatorship of the proletariat.' While now they are trying to explain to the people the definition of the word 'democracy' (meaning 'the people hold power'). And they are justifying that just with the pluralist elections. From 'the dictatorship of the proletariat,' to 'the people hold power'—new words, the same old tactic for deception. What is happening now is a real threat to the real democracy we desire to build because the new faces elected by the demos (the people) have been preselected by the last communist leader, and his loyal servants spread in all political parties. They say they are building the democracy, but they are just changing faces to be seen as a democracy. So, they are making a 'democratorship' (as people have started to call it by merging into one the words, 'democracy and dictatorship'), and the installment of this new regime will have long-term consequences for decades to come in Albania," Ardian finished in sadness.

The communist leader of the victorious Democratic Party became the Country's President, putting under his control everything and building an authoritarian regime. He followed all the guidance of his communist boss, not to allow the "overthrown bourgeois wealthy classes" to come back to power. He continued cursing the communism just with words by declaring himself as an anti-communist, but he always protected the communist leaders and their families from any potential punishment. He gave the state-owned land of the agricultural cooperatives to its villagers and the land of the state farms to their workers, by using the same motto of the agriculture reform done by communists in 1945: "The land belongs to those who work it." (As soon as communists came to power after the Second World War, they took the land owned by the "bourgeois wealthy classes," and gave it to the poor villagers.) The new "democratic" leader didn't give the land back to whom it belonged before, from whom it was taken forcefully by the communist regime. That's because the legitimate owners had been considered all the time as "overthrown wealthy class," which must not be allowed to rise either politically or economically.

Furthermore, the new president didn't allow the passing of any law to open the files of the communist state secret service, as all other ex-communist countries had already done. He didn't want to pass such a bill because he was cooperating with all members of the state secret service being under the new boss now.

All these things were going through Ardian's mind while he continued teaching in the former pedagogical institute, which already had been transformed into a university as another populist measure taken by the last communist leader to add the number of universities in the country artificially and adding the number of students attending them. He made a lot of young people and families happy by allowing them to attend new universities and being enrolled without the previous reliable criteria for a high grade point average from high school. This act brought down the quality of the students, the quality of teaching itself, and consequently, the quality of the future teachers and professionals.

In the time of these fast, noisy, adverse developments, Ardian followed his way spending more time home and handwriting the final version of his multi-year study: "The Literature and Arts in a Dictatorship," where he analyzed the socialist realism applied in art and literature as a means of the communist propaganda in service of the dictator and dictatorship. He asked the literature department where he worked to approve this thesis for him to earn the scientific degree "doctor of science," but he didn't get any official answer of approval or disapproval for a long time. His close friend, Bashkim (now in the position of the Dean of Faculty), was telling him that the respective official commission was considering it, but some of its members think that it looks a little bit strong analysis, and in addition to that, it is too early to speak and write like that, because all artists, writers, and authors are still alive and we have to be careful to respect them for their contribution, and not to offend them.

The free press of that time had published some articles raising the voice and criticizing the previous censure and the political control over the literature and arts. There were a lot of stories testifying about dozens of artists and writers punished by the communist regime with imprisonment, internment, and capital punishment, accompanied by the ban of their works. The truth about the wild tyranny and its crimes were unfolded in front of the people's eyes, which started to understand the big cheating they had lived in for five decades. Ardian sent parts of his thesis to a newspaper, and they published the first part of it with some corrections, then the second part with more revisions, while the third part was not published at all. Ardian understood that it was a censure used in the interest of certain groups. The old political elite and the old elite of artists and writers of the "socialist realism" were still alive, still active, and above all, yet in power and control of the actual developments. Ardian realized that the old League of Writers and Artists was still there, with the same leadership and doing the same thing— protecting themselves and their works of socialist realism. Thus, he had to keep his prepared thesis for another time. But he was happy while thinking that at least, he was free to think and write without the fear of any punishment. But his failed attempt just proved the inability to publish such things or to approve it officially as a scientific study. He tried to put some hours of the critique and revision of the socialist realism in the literature curriculum, but it was not approved with the same answer, "it is too early for such a thing." Despite that, Ardian started to explain in his lectures his point of view about socialist realism, and students liked it. But the Head of the

Literature Department called him into the office and advised him not to go out of the official curriculum approved by the department and the Dean of Faculty.

Ardian always stayed silent and retreated against all the political movements and fast development of that time. He didn't participate in any political rally and didn't show any interest in membership in new political parties. He received invitations from political parties and from the association of ex-persecuted people to join them, to take part in their events, and to put his name in their lists as a candidate for deputy in parliament. "I only want to be a professor and nothing else," was his answer for them. And he remained an outstanding university professor.

He didn't like it when the new faces of the political leadership, in political rallies and newspapers, were being self-proclaimed as anti-communists and initiators of the change.

"Changes are the merit of time, and this merit doesn't belong to certain people. The change will continue its way, and nobody can prevent it because nobody has the power to stop time. Time for the collapse of communism in Albania had come like in all other communist countries," Ardian thought. "Life is a big stage where people are just small actors of the great director—the time," Ardian recalled several times this expression that he had read somewhere.

In response to all actual developments, Ardian returned to his shell and focused on studying more Italian and English language. He spent some weeks or months studying advanced lessons and reading books in English, and then he spent some more weeks or months studying advanced lessons and reading books in the Italian language, and so on. He played the guitar more often, singing songs for Elsa and their little son. In October 1992, they had a baby girl as a new member of their family, with her name Mimosa, as decided years ago. Ardian was happy with his life and family and sang full of inspiration and happiness. His life was going well, and he had to be satisfied, but something in his heart and soul had remained injured and was groaning time after time. Every time he sang, the songs reminded him of his first love and Eralda. She was still there, in a dark, hidden corner of his mind, his heart, and his soul. He recalled his principle to accept and live life as it comes. It is certainly easy to apply this principle when life comes with all its best sides. But for him, it had been easy too when his life came with all its worst. He had already experienced both life situations separately. But now, he understood that life becomes more challenging to deal with when you feel the consequences of both conditions. How could he deal with life that now was offering him its right and wrong sides at the same time? The right sides of his life were his return to the university, the new apartment, the freedom, the children, and his excellent wife, Elsa—all these things that could be seen and felt by him and others. But the wrong sides of his life were present too; his first love, his spiritual devotion, his broken heart, and his injured soul— things that others couldn't see, couldn't feel, and couldn't know. It was his spiritual life that only he knew and felt strongly. It looked like he was living a double life. On one side was the real-life with his family and work, making him happy, and optimistic. But the other sad side of his life with remembrance of the first love and Eralda made him feel unhappy, depressed, and pessimistic. He still felt the injury caused by the loss of his first love and the pain it had left behind. His happy heart was singing, while his harmed soul was sobbing.

The Eralda's store that was destroyed and burned down in December 1990 was not rebuilt yet. Ardian passed by the store ruins very often, and he felt sorrow that couldn't see Eralda there. He hadn't seen her for a long time. He often made parallelisms in his mind: "A destroyed store and a destroyed dictatorship; a destroyed love and a destroyed soul." The demolition of the dictatorship was a good thing, while the ruins of the store were a bad thing. But the destruction of his first love and his soul were the worst ones to happen in his life and very difficult or quite impossible to be reconstructed or repaired. He missed Eralda very much. Every time he had the opportunity, he walked around her apartment building, being unsure if she was working somewhere or was staying home. He could ask Bardha about Eralda because she was still working in the same store, but it wasn't right for him as a married man, to be still interested in Eralda and ask others about her. But he couldn't resist anymore, and after almost two years without seeing her and without any news about her, he entered Bardha's store and asked her about Eralda. She told him that Eralda was unemployed and was staying home, without going out very often.

In the summer of 1992, he saw some workers and trucks cleaning the ruins of Eralda's store, and for a short time, a new café named "Cafe Democracia," was built there with a lot of tables inside and outside the shop. It was the best site in the city for such a profitable business that mushroomed in that time. When Ardian saw workers there, he was expecting to see Eralda working there someday, but it didn't happen. During the privatization process of the state-owned commercial services at the beginning of the year 1992, all the stores were sold to the shopkeepers that were working in them, and Ardian thought that Eralda might have bought the store and rebuilt it for use. When he didn't see Eralda there, he assumed that she had bought her store from the state and had resold it to somebody else for a good profit.

After three years, in 1995, when he had almost forgotten about her, he ran into her in front of the County's Court House, while walking back home.

"Good afternoon Alda. Long time without seeing you," Ardian greeted her.

"Good afternoon, how are you?" Eralda answered with a cold appearance.

"I'm good," Ardian was pleased with meeting her and became talkative. Without asking other questions, but being inspired by meeting her, he continued:

"Are you coming out of the Court House, from this institution of suffering? Do you know how they call this street?" he asked her.

"No," Eralda answered very short.

"This is called the 'street of sufferings.' That's because right where this street starts, south of the main boulevard, there is the central dental clinic, a lot of pain and suffering there. Then, going up several blocks, on the left, is the primary general health clinic full of sick people that go there to see doctors every day. Walking north, in the next block on the right side, there is the police station, followed by the county's courthouse and the prosecutor's office, with a lot of pain and hardship there too. Two blocks further, on the right side, there is the maternity hospital with real pain and torment there as well. Walking five more blocks, you will arrive at the pedagogical institute campus and dormitories, with a lot of distress and failed exams. At the end of this street, in the legs of the olive hills, there is the general hospital. And if you want to find another place with more suffering and pain, continue walking on the right, arriving at the psychiatric hospital, where you can meet a lot of crazy people. Oh…, no…, sorry. You don't need to go up there to see the crazy ones because such a deranged person is right here, in front of you, speaking such nonsense," Ardian said after he realized that Eralda was not so happy.

"No…, no. You are okay. You made me laugh after a long time without laughing," Eralda answered with a beautiful little smile.

She wasn't happy, not because of meeting with Ardian, but because of her problems with courts, as she explained to Ardian.

"You have seen that my store was not rebuilt since being destroyed by the fire of the 'democratic revolution.' When the process of privatization started, the state enterprise sold my store to somebody else, but according to law, stores must be sold to the shopkeepers that have been operating them. I went to the privatization office, and they told me that the store was sold to the person that had been working there, giving me his name. When I asked the officials to show me the documents of his employment in that store, they didn't answer my request, with their final answer that I could go to the court. But courts are another story now. In these courts, and with these new judges of the democracy, you never find justice nowadays."

"I know," Ardian said, interrupting Eralda. "The courthouses and the prosecutor offices are filled with unqualified, unprofessional, and dishonest judges and prosecutors nominated in these crucial positions of the justice system after attending only a six-month-long course in Plepa, Durrës, and that's why they are called ironically 'the judges of Plepa.' These courses were attended by family members, sons, daughters, nieces, nephews, and relatives of the most loyal communists and state secret service agents, being supported by the communist leader of the ruling Democratic Party. The product of the Plepa course—the new judges and prosecutors— captured all the justice system. In this way, they made the justice to work only for their interests and wealth, and not for the public benefits, and that's why they can't serve true justice, and they can't give justice to you," Ardian spoke with revolt.

"At first, they postponed the date of the first séance several times for almost one year. Then, the court date was postponed several times for the non-presence of the defendant, representatives of the privatization office, and the former state commercial enterprise. After these delays, the judge asked for more official documents, and that's where all the tragedy starts. The respective offices didn't want to serve me any documents. I had to open another court case, which took some more months, for a judge to give an order for the respective offices to give to my attorney the official records and documents needed as evidence of my employment in that store. Those offices answered that they couldn't find any document because they are disappeared and couldn't be found. I'm sure that the personnel that works in those offices have destroyed all possible records that would serve as facts of my employment, issuing false documents to the person that bought my store. In this way, I lost the case in the court of the first level. I cannot go to appeal because, for the same reason, for the lack of documentation, I will lose it too. So, no hope for justice anymore, and my brother is right when he says that in such a situation, we have to kill somebody to solve this terrible injustice for us," Eralda finished, with tears in her eyes.

Ardian couldn't stay with her any longer, and they just said "see you" to each other. Some days later, Ardian inquired and learned that the owner of the "Cafe Democracia" in the central city square, was the son of a former official of the state secret service in Elbasan County. His in-laws as well were in the leadership of the county's Democratic Party branch, which recommended all nominations in all state institutions and enterprises of the county. With such powerful positions and connections, they were able to pull all strings to have under control the economy, the justice, and the needed corruption for themselves, in this kind of regime called democratorship.

In spring 1994, Ardian translated in the Italian language a summary of his thesis about the socialist realism, and he sent it for publication in a scientific magazine of a university in Rome, Italy. The publishers of the scientific magazine found it exciting and published it. Ardian received a letter with their optimistic appreciation for his work, asking Ardian to send them the full study, with the possibility of teaching some classes of the critique of the socialist realism to the literature students of their university. This opportunity gave Ardian new energy and desire, and he worked hard for two months to translate his entire thesis into the Italian language, and he sent it to them. In their answer, they explained Ardian that they had added some classes of the critique of the socialist realism in their curriculum, inviting Ardian to teach these classes, starting from the fall semester of the school year 1995-1996. It was great news and a big joy for Ardian and Elsa. They would have the opportunity to travel together and visit Rome and other famous, antique Italian cities, realizing an old dream of Ardian.

They went to Rome spending there two weeks in October for the fall semester and two other weeks in March for the spring semester. Staying in Rome for two weeks, teaching in an Italian university, and visiting the historical sites of Rome, was a real reinvigoration for Ardian, bringing Elsa over always with him, and enjoying together those beautiful days.

31

Everything was worsening during the first six years of so-called "transition," meaning the transition from a communist state to a democratic one. The communist leader of the Democratic Party was ruling the country as a president with an iron fist, becoming an authoritarian leader with all characteristics of a dictator. Complaining about injustice and the long, painful transition of this time, the poet Bardhyl Londo wrote these famous verses of his poem *"Balance Sheet"*:

The winners—victorious.
The losers—losers in eternity.
If so,
May never come to us, democracy!

The economic situation of the country was deteriorating year after year, and for a lot of people, the only solution was the illegal emigration to neighboring countries, Greece and Italy, using all dangerous means of well-organized human illicit trafficking to reach other countries of Europe, and even Canada and USA. A lot of fraudulent "financial pyramids" that worked like the Ponzi scheme sprang up all over the country in 1996. In the same time, after the problematic elections of May 26, 1996, manipulated and won by the ruling democratic party, the police force and secret service agents were used against the opposition, media, and everybody else that thought differently from the authoritarian leader, who had consolidated his rule with tyrannical methods. The corrupt governance, the poverty, the election's manipulation, and finally, the money lost from a significant part of the population in Ponzi schemes, led to an uprising and rebellion against the new dictatorship, asking the resignation of the prime minister and the return

258

of the lost money. The revolt went out of control and led to state failure at the beginning of the year 1997. The police stations, secret service offices, and military barracks in the entire country were assaulted and looted, and people were armed with all kinds of weapons and ammunition.

March 1997 was the worst situation with armed people firing everywhere. In this time, "Cafe Democracia" was attacked at night with automatic weapons, hand grenades, and explosives. The owner and his brother were killed, and explosions and fire destroyed the store. When Ardian saw the ruins of the store on the morrow, he thought that the authors of this attack might have been Eralda's brothers, as a deserved revenge for the injustice done to their family. But he learned later that it was just a fight between the different rival bands of drug trafficking and other criminal activities.

"At least they are eliminating each other because the incriminated state and the corrupt justice will never do that," Ardian told Elsa that evening, remembering what people usually say in such cases.

"They had named their café, 'Cafe Democracia' because that's what they thought about a prosperous democracy," said Elsa.

"The history of rising and fall of 'Cafe Democracia' is the best symbol of Albanian democracy," Ardian continued.

"Yes, you are right. You find deception, theft, injustice, iniquity, malice, corruption, smuggling, crimes, rival bands, immorality, greed, exploitation for personal profits, and a lot of other bad common things being practiced in both, Cafe Democracia and Albanian democracy," Elsa concluded.

In this situation of the state failure, when everything was out of control, the records office of the University of Elbasan was burned down by the deliberate fire. Ardian learned from media that the same thing had happened to the records office of the Agriculture University of Tirana. Two arsons in two different universities' records offices for the same reason that everybody knew. During this mess of the "democratic" years, a lot of false diplomas and transcripts were issued from these records offices to people that paid for them. Officials that were involved in this vast falsity exploited this opportunity to destroy every evidence and facts of their forgery crimes. A lot of people used false diplomas to be employed in government offices, to become police officers, teachers, customs officers, secret service agents, directors and heads of state institutions, and even deputies in parliament.

A United Nations Multinational Protection Force, called Operation "Alba," was deployed in Albania to solve the state failure situation. It

259

comprised of eight European nations, led by Italy, and served to facilitate a safe and secure environment for new elections organized with the support of the Organization for Security and Cooperation in Europe. The Socialist Party won the elections, a new government was installed in July, and its leader became prime minister. He was one of those devoted communist "intellectuals" handpicked and promoted as a party leader by the "good dictator" that facilitated the "peaceful transition" to democracy.

In September 1997, an employee of the university's front desk gave Ardian a closed envelope with his name as a receiver but without the sender's name. He didn't need the name of the sender because he recognized that handwriting very well. It was Eralda's beautiful calligraphy. He went to his office, opened the envelope in a hurry and read it:

"Farewell Adi.

I will leave. I'll go far away, but I don't know where. I only know that I'm leaving, and I will not come back anymore.

My love for you wasn't a simple one—it was a fire. It's a real fire that still continues to burn in my body, in my soul, in my chest, in my heart, in my blood and, as it looks, this fire will burn to the end all my bones, which have crackled so many times by your gentle squeezes.

Oh, my God, how much I yearn for your squeeze. And I've never allowed anybody else to squeeze me in his arms since then. Your remembrance accompanies me forever, like an unhealed disease, full of suffering and pain, from which I would never desire to recover.

I'm writing this farewell letter, and I'm crying. My tears are dropping on the paper, leaving their marks on it. Let your tears fall over my tears' dots too, even though you are a man, and as such, you don't cry.

I would like to hug you once more before leaving, but I can't. I promise that if we meet someday (like in legends, novels, and movies), I'll be the first one to embrace and kiss you, not like in legends, novels, and movies, but like once upon a time..., when we were together.

You have your own life now, and I don't want to interfere. I have met both of you, and I love and respect both of you. With this letter of mine, I don't want to entice or make you feel despairing, but I just couldn't leave without writing to you.

Yours forever, Ada."

And Ardian couldn't keep his tears but let them shed and drop over her tears' marks on the written paper. He read and reread that letter several times with eyes in tears pouring on his cheeks and falling on the paper. The full story of their love passed through Ardian's mind while weeping endlessly. The story of their love sounded like a novel, and this farewell letter was the epilog of this novel. It was a great love story that had just ended with the first words of her message: *"Farewell Adi. I will leave. I'll go far away, but I don't know where."* So..., she had already gone far away, and he couldn't see her anymore. As long as she had been in the city, he could see her time after time, and this fact kept his first love alive in its hidden place. But she had already gone. His first love had gone far away.

The first love had remained as a feeling of sorrow that asks and needs recovery. Her presence and her friendship relieved a little bit the pain of this affliction. "What about now? What could I do? She's gone. Who knows where? Why wasn't I capable of acting as her love deserved it? Why did I lose this love? Why did I let her go away in this way? Why did I cause to her and myself this pain from which we are suffering forever, and we will never recover?"

Eralda's departure, her farewell letter (which he had already learned by heart), the marks of her tears on that paper, and his own tears made him think and decide to write something for this great love. This love seemed to him like the greatest love of all love stories he had read till now. He reached this conclusion helped by her letter, which was written so beautifully and with a great style. He had to write something about this love because only in this way it would remain alive and never die.

After some days, he began writing on the paper the first lines of his love story, in an attempt to write a short story titled: "I Am Weeping For Her," based on his longing and daily tears since the day he received the farewell letter. He recalled that authors, in general, write their books based on what they have experienced and felt by themselves and what they have observed and heard about others' experiences. Based on the tremendous first love he had experienced, Ardian thought that it would be easier for him to write something about it. He started writing, and the pen looked like sliding on its own on the white papers, adding them quickly day after day. What began as an attempt to write a short story, was becoming a novella. After he had filled dozens of sheets of papers writing the story of his life and love in a speedy way and in a short time, he became aware that he was writing a novel, perhaps his first novel that might be called, "The First Love."

Her farewell letter remained in Ardian's mind like a beautiful poem. Eralda had written that letter with such great mastery and artistry that she couldn't have. That letter had been written by her heart and soul, showing him her great love. Inspired by the words of this letter, Ardian worked some days to write the lyrics of a song practicing the melody with the guitar. He finally completed a song of his own. He understood that this song was written by his heart and soul, being always crazy in love with Eralda—his first love. His mind and body could be able to love for the second time, but his heart and soul had remained actively connected with the first love. The inspiration and muse that wrote the lyrics and melody were coming from the invisible, mysterious depth of his soul, and he gave the final shape to his song titled *"Ada, where are you."*

"I'll go, I'll go, but I don't know where.
I'll leave and never come back here."
These are the words you wrote for me.
In your letter, while going away from me.

"O Ada, o Ada, where are you?
O Ada, why did you go away?"
These are words I shout for you.
Every minute, hour, and day.

"I'll go in a foreign land," you said.
"But I'll keep the love for you alive."
Why do I need these empty words?
Since you left my yearning heart.

O Ada, for you, I weep.
O Ada, for you, I sing.
With you, I am in my dreams.
Embracing each other in tears.

But you'll come back someday.
Without me, how can you stay?
How can you stay there, tell me?
The foreign soil doesn't accept you.
The foreign soil...,
Without love with me.

After some weeks, in a sincere moment, Ardian told Elsa about Eralda's letter and the song he had written being inspired by the words of her message. From Eralda's letter and Ardian's song, Elsa understood that their love had been a genuinely great one. She liked the spiritual and artistic level of Eralda's message and Ardian's song but didn't know what to say and how to act in such a difficult situation for her. These things reminded Eralda again that she had entered in the middle of this great love by mistake, but she could never correct this mistake.

"But…, why did you separate since you loved each other so much?" she dared to ask, being thrilled and touched from Eralda's letter and Ardian's song.

"I don't know," was his short answer.

When he had finished some chapters of his novel, he showed it to Elsa and told her:

"I'm writing something about my first love to reflect and find the answer to your question (and mine as well): 'Why did we separate, while we loved each other so much?' I believe you don't mind," he said, approaching and kissing her on her cheek.

"It is your spiritual life, and you can write whatever you want," she answered with sincerity and love for him.

With the inspiration and muse of those first weeks, Ardian wrote more than one hundred pages, but the inspiration for this work ended one day, and this script remained in a drawer for months and years to come. Suddenly, he couldn't write anymore. He couldn't add anything else to his novel. He didn't know how to end it. He was waiting for something new to happen to him. He was waiting for new inspiration or a mythological muse. He was waiting for an event and an experience to light the fire of inspiration. In a meanwhile, he started reading some new novels, novellas, short stories, and poetry of new authors with a kind of curiosity to compare them with his manuscript, but no one of them looked more beautiful than his book, which was still waiting in his drawers to take the final shape. Even though he was thinking all the time to find the right end for his book, he couldn't find a convincible ending. Sometimes he thought that it was better like this; because in this way, it was only he that had this book, and nobody else; it was only he that knew and kept this love, this suffering, and this pain only for himself, without sharing it with others. With this unfinished manuscript of a novel in his drawers, it looked like his first love was still there with him, and he was still cohabiting with her. He wrote in a sheet of paper some verses of the song "The First Love," sung by Anita Bitri in an Albanian song festival, putting it on the top of his manuscript. Ardian liked that song so much, and he was deeply touched every time he listened to it to the radio. That song looked like being written and sang exclusively for his first love, for the dreams, suffering, and "the pain left behind," as the song goes. He thought that on the very last page of his novel, he would write more lyrical verses from this song that made him weep every time he listened to it.

Months and years were passing fast, and time after time, he lost his mind when most of the girls he saw in the city streets or the university yard looked like Eralda. Every girl that had a little similarity with Eralda looked to him like her, and he wrote a small poem for this impression, titled, "I'm still looking for you."

After the back of every girl,
Full of hope and joy I go.
After the back of every girl,
Your face, I'm looking for.

In the eyes of every girl,
I found you, too.
Cos eyes of every girl,
Preserve love, as you do.

Actually, it happened to him many times when he hurried his steps behind the girls that looked like Eralda, to reach them and verify by seeing their face. He showed Elsa this poem, and she understood that he was burning inside himself from the remembrance and yearning for his first love. Elsa felt better while thinking that Eralda had left the country, and she could be tranquil about it. "Maybe that's the reason she left," Elsa thought time after time. Ardian always looked reasonable and calm in his daily life. Their matrimonial relationship was terrific, and even their sex life was super and was nothing left for any misunderstanding or suspicion. But when Elsa read the Eralda's letter, his novel's manuscript chapters, his poems, and songs about Eralda, she was scared and felt that something dangerous could happen someday. It looked like an explosive, like a powder keg waiting somewhere for somebody to light the detonator. Elsa didn't know that Ardian was crying so often for Eralda and his first love. She didn't see anything abnormal in his daily behavior, but when he showed her his creations, these things scared her enough, but his sincerity and naiveté made her feel better, considering these things as being just his literary creativity.

Ardian went very often to the park, sitting down and spending some minutes alone on the bench under the willow, where the first dates with Eralda had taken place. Most of the seats had been stolen or destroyed, and many trees had been cut down in the park. Their bench and willow had survived only with some damages, and Ardian thought about this fact as a good sign for his first love. Sitting on this bench, covered by the willow's branches and leaves, he wrote another poem, titled "After Every Year That Passes."

The willow was filled with buds.
The buds sprouted into leaves.
The leaves filled the branches.
Under branches, the bench hid.

A hand opened the twigs.
A voice said: "Come in!
Over the old bench,
Were grown, new leaves."

And right there, I sat down.
Like in those evenings with love.
My memory hit the road.
Bringing you back, my love.

What will I say to the willow?
That seems like asking me:
"Where is your girl?
Tell me, where is she?"

The first love always remains the most beautiful one. Loving each other so much and not being finalized in a marriage, it remains a true love, untouched by the everyday routine of the married life, and that's why it remains beautiful in eternity giving the impression that there cannot be any other love like the first one. Love in married life and family is still a perfect love, but not like the first one that remains forever alive in your soul, mind, and heart. In the long road of your short life, you can have a second love and marriage (even a third one), but you will never experience any feelings like the ones you felt in your first love, followed by everlasting nostalgia, suffering, pain, yearning, and tears.

The university where Ardian taught in Rome gave him a scholarship for a master's degree program in "Psychological and Sociological Studies." Ardian had applied for this scholarship with the intention that after earning the master's degree, he would be able to study for a doctorate. At the end of the master's program, he wrote the thesis: "Literature as art, reaching out to the psychology and sociology as social sciences, to complement and serve each other." In this thesis, he analyzes and elaborates the way literature, psychology, and sociology explore the human behavior and mind, individuals, groups, society, social behavior, social order or disorder, changes of individuals and society, etc. Individuals, groups, and society are mutual objects and subjects studied by the sciences of psychology and sociology and depicted in the art of literature. Ardian explains that literature as art reflects the human nature, the social and economic condition, the class stratification, and other same issues that psychology and sociology deal with, so they must find a way to approach and use each other.

Ardian spent the school year 1998-1999 in Rome, attending the master's degree program. Elsa joined him several times by taking unpaid leave and using the school breaks in fall, winter, spring, and summer, leaving their children with her parents. At the end of the year, Ardian's thesis was graded with the maximum grade by all three members of the commission. After the publication of his dissertation in the university's scientific magazine, the respective departments found it very interesting and invited Ardian to elaborate further on his ideas. He did it by reading dozens of books of Italian literature from all times, writing his doctoral dissertation, and cooperating with three Italian professors as his tutors from respective departments of literature, psychology, and sociology. He traveled several times to Rome to teach his lectures on socialist realism, to consult and discuss the doctoral thesis with his tutors, and to take books from the university's library. In spring 2002, he finished and handed in his doctoral dissertation ahead of time. In October of that year, he earned the title, "Doctor of Humanities and Social Sciences."

When Ardian and Elsa were in Rome, they stayed in a neighborhood near the "Olympic Village" built for the Summer Olympic Games of 1960. From there, they could walk to "Ponte Milvio," an old pedestrian bridge over river Tiber, where young and old couples in love, lock their love's padlocks, throwing their keys in the river. Ardian and Elsa did the same thing, placing and locking their padlock the very first time they went there. But Ardian was thinking about Eralda even at that moment, deciding to come back alone another day to lock another padlock for him and Eralda in remembrance of his first love. From there, they could walk toward "Foro Italico," a sports complex (constructed in 1930), consisting of several sports venues, including the "Stadio dei Marmi," decorated with dozens of marvelous marble statues of athletes around it. Next to it, there is the famous "Stadio Olimpico," with a capacity of more than 70,000 seatings, the home stadium of soccer teams "Lazio" and "Roma," and the venue for the "Coppa Italia" final as well.

In the evenings, they used to take the tram to the square "Piazza del Popolo." From there, they strolled through the street "Via del Corso," turning left to the splendid historical fountain, "Fontana di Trevi," and coming back via another antic square, "Piazza di Spagna." In both famous fountains, they tossed their coins for love and luck, like all other numerous tourists do. And there, Ardian thought about Eralda again. While throwing coins in the water, he was thinking about his first love, too, trying to keep it alive forever in his mind.

Exploring the narrow old streets and old buildings nearby Fontana di Trevi, Ardian discovered an alley called "Vicolo Scanderbeg." They walked through this alleyway and arrived at a small square called "Piazza Scanderbeg." Right there, on one side of the square, they discovered the reason for this name. It was an old historical building called "Palazzo Scanderbeg," where the Albanians' national hero, Scanderbeg, had stayed during his trip to Italy in 1465-1466. Ardian became very enthusiastic about this discovery, taking a lot of pictures there. He told Elsa that he knew Scanderbeg had been to Italy in 1458 to help the King of Napoli Ferdinando I, but he had never heard about his trip to Rome. An Italian professor told Ardian about "Piazza Albania," situated in southern Rome, and he and Elsa went together to visit this venue with the statue of Scanderbeg on his horse placed in the middle of the square.

Every time and everywhere he went during his trips to Rome and other Italian cities, in beautiful places he visited and during his happy moments, Ardian always remembered Eralda, wishing to have her near. He had what it takes to read hundreds of books and study hard in his under graduation and graduation studies. He had what it takes to learn two foreign languages and to broaden his horizon. He had what it takes to study and earn a master's degree and a doctorate from an Italian university. He had what it takes to face difficulties in his life, during the dictatorship and the painful transition to democracy. But, strangely enough, he never found what it takes to get that girl out of his mind. He had tried to do such a thing several times, but he was never successful. She always returned stronger in his mind and forever young, beautiful, and alluring in his memory of the ardent love. They say time heals everything, but it wasn't right in Ardian's case. He never recovered from the loss of his first love and from the suffering and pain it left behind. One more reason he didn't want to leave his job at the University of Elbasan, was that he always thought about it as the only place where Eralda can find him if she hopefully returns in the city someday.

In spring 2002, Ardian turned back from Italy with a car that he bought there. It was a used car (like all autos coming in Albania from European developed countries), and it was the first car in his life. The first trip that Ardian and Elsa made with that car was to Red Hill, the remote village where they had spent five beautiful years of their youth, and their great love was born and forged. What they found out on this trip was great devastation and despair. The roads' condition had been worsened because of the lack of maintenance. The forest trees and bushes had been cut down. The lakes were without water. The canals of the irrigation system had been destroyed. Shrubs in the hills surrounding lakes had been burned. The agriculture fields had been left unused and unproductive. Greenhouses had been destroyed everywhere. School buildings and windows had been destroyed, and there were no health clinics in the villages anymore. Most of the populace of rural areas had gone to Greece or Italy. A few new houses had been built here and there with money coming from emigration. The famous teachers' palace, their warm nest for five years, had been occupied by some families, fencing their part of the land around the building. After all this destruction they found during the entire trip to get there, they couldn't stay any longer, but turned back quickly, feeling more devastating than ever. Everything was worse than before. The democracy had not functioned as it meant to, and Ardian started speaking in revolt:

"The worst people of this country, the most devoted communists, the ex-agents of the state secret service, thieves and thugs, the corrupt ones, have taken high-level positions in all political parties, parliament, in the local and central government. All of them together, have created such a situation nowadays where the real thieves shout 'catch the thief;' the secret service agents shout 'catch the spy;' the ex-communists shout 'catch the communist;' the real corrupt people shout 'catch the corrupt ones.' And they support and help each other becoming more trustful and stronger than others. In this way, nobody realizes that individuals who shout the most and louder than others 'catch the thief,' are the real thieves; the individuals who shout 'catch the communists,' are the ex-communist themselves; the individuals who scream in ecstasy 'catch the spy,' are the ex-state secret service spies, and so on. That's why the famous Albanian actor, Mirush Kabashi, says: "This is the time of miscreants," shouting in pain and despair in his most astonishing performance of Plato's 'Apology of Socrates.' They have created such a situation where all those villains have under their control the people—the flock of sheep—who in so-called free elections go to vote again and again for the same ex-communists, ex-spies, corrupt ones, thugs and thieves, without listening and supporting any rare logical voice. The blackguards of this country have already occupied the entire system: political parties, the government, the parliament, and the justice system. They have seized the economic and financial power, the media, and everything else. There is not any more hope in this country, and the only solution left for the people is to run away from this damned country that we call motherland. That's why one-third of the population has already abandoned this accursed country, just like escaping from a war zone." Ardian explained to Elsa the situation in which the people of Albania were living those years.

"The utter devastation we saw everywhere today," Ardian continued some minutes later, "reminds me an Italian saying that goes; 'Quello che non hanno fatto i barbari, lo hanno fatto i Barberini!', (What wasn't done by the barbarians, was done by the Barberini). This satiric phrase means that the ancient Rome was not destroyed by barbarians coming from beyond their borders, but by Romans themselves, year after year, mentioning Pope Urbano VIII Barberini (in the seventeenth century), and members of his family, for the destruction of the ancient buildings, bringing more damages to the city than a barbarian invasion. If I paraphrase this saying, I will say: 'What Albanian people had built under the communist dictatorship, the same Albanian people, destroyed everything under the democratic liberty.' You can see everywhere how they have destroyed everything, month after month and year after year. First, they destroyed all the factories and greenhouses. Then they cut down all trees on the roadsides, trees in the parks and forests. After that, they damaged and destroyed riverbeds, bridges over them, and their protective embankments, using their sand and gravel to build houses, stores, restaurants, hotels, and buildings everywhere they wanted without any permission. Finally, in 1997, they destroyed all the armed forces' barracks, taking most of the weapons and explosives from them. They destroyed all the state functions, the justice, the health system, education system, police, taxes system, financial system, custom service, roads, railway transportation, and everything…, everything…, everything else, making the state nonexistent," Ardian finished being revolted more than ever.

32

"Ah, this white light of the first love is like the light of the morning star that shows up in the sky and brightens the world with light before the sun comes up." This quotation about the first love (taken from the novel "The Dead River" of Albanian writer Jakov Xoxa), was the most beautiful one Ardian had found and learned by heart from the numerous books he had read. Every time he remembered this quote, he thought that the "white light" of his first love brightened his world with light and never faded out. It remained inside him as a white light that sometimes was stronger and sometimes weaker, being sheltered somewhere in the mysterious depths of his soul where he couldn't see and couldn't touch it, but he could feel it. He felt it like a wrench, pain, suffering, wound, and like an unhealed disease—as Eralda had written in her farewell letter. Eralda and her love remained in his perception, in his mind and his soul like a morning star, daylight star, evening star, night star, everlasting star, becoming an orientation star for his life. Ardian had two orientations in his life, like having two experiences in his own life. The first orientation was his visible life, the concrete, real, daily life with all its components; family, wife, children, home, work, friends, relatives, etc. The second orientation was the first love that was an intense spiritual experience. This second life remained abstract, sublime, magic, mysterious, invisible, untouchable, and unchangeable in his mind and his soul.

Ardian had started to go in search of Eralda more often. He went several times to the apartment building where she used to live, looking for any sign of life in her apartment's windows and balcony, from both sides of the building. He went there in the evening, watching for lights, but they were never lit on. But it was not convincible for him, and he climbed the stairs up to her apartment, staying some minutes in front of the door. Sometimes he knocked on that door, waiting in vain for an answer from inside. He asked other tenants: "Where is Alda? Why is nobody living here?" And some of them answered: "Nobody lives there. The apartment is empty. Alda has gone to Greece. All of her family has gone to Greece." In this way, he became well-known by the tenants of the building, and they were telling him the same thing as soon as they saw him in the building entrance, around the building, or in the main street near the building, without waiting for him to ask them. He repeatedly heard from them saying to him: "Don't look for Alda anymore. She's gone to Greece. All the family has gone to Greece." And sometimes some of them told him: "Eralda is married in Greece," like wanting to mock him. "Alda…, Greece…, married…," were the words that regularly echoed in his ears, which he started to repeat continuously within himself, and sometimes loudly while going around the city streets looking for Eralda. He was sick of her love and felt lonely after a long time without seeing her. He went several times to Bardha's store, the close friend of Eralda, asking her about Eralda, and she told him the same thing, that Eralda had gone to Greece, and she had not heard from her since she had left, and she didn't have any contacts with her.

Every day, every week, every month, and every year that passed, he only thought about his first love. He tried hard to find and write some more lines, paragraphs, and pages in his unfinished novel, but he couldn't, and the unfinished manuscript of his book remained sleeping in his drawers for several years. He read and reread the finished chapters many times in search of an idea for a couple of final chapters. A lot of different thoughts were crossing through his head, but they were not convincible enough and didn't work, because even the development of the real love story that was described in that novel, had stalled at some point. He was unable and couldn't find the strength to sit down and write something, despite his numerous thoughts. His novel was not a fiction but a real-life story. It was his own life story, and he didn't know what was going on with the real life of the main character, Eralda, as the crucial part of his story, and he couldn't decide to write something unreal about her. His real-life and the real story of his first love seemed to him more beautiful than any fiction he had read, and he wanted the final chapters to be a description of the real-life as well. He couldn't write anything else without a new great inspiration, without a real-life inspiration, a real-life muse, or perhaps, without the arrival of her, the main character of his life, his love, and his novel, the real inspiration of him—Eralda.

And…, almost like in magic, like in legends, in dreams, in novels, and movies, it happened for real. She, his muse, came. Six years since Eralda's departure had passed, when on Friday, November 14, 2003, Ardian was given a closed envelope from the front desk employee in university.

"At six o'clock, at our bench," was written in the letter inside the envelope.

"Oh, my God! Is this a dream?" he spoke to himself. "No, it cannot be real. It's impossible. It is just another hallucination of mine," he repeated several times the uncertainty to believe what was written in that letter. But the fresh ink and her beautiful handwriting convinced and assured him that it was indeed happening, and that letter had just been drafted by Eralda. It meant that she had come back to the city; she had come back again for him. He didn't know where to pass the time until six o'clock and couldn't stay in one place. It seemed like six o'clock was never coming. He left the university immediately and went to her apartment building, going around it several times. Then he went to the evening high school building, walking through the narrow streets of the neighborhood they used to walk together. After that, he walked toward the place where her store used to be, staying there some minutes. Finally, he went to the park, to their bench, where he found out that a new one had been installed there, replacing the old damaged seat. It looked like a good sign and preparation for her return and their meeting or their date. He didn't go home.

While living those magic moments, he had forgotten about his first life, his first orientation. He forgot that he was a married man, that he had a home, a family, a wife, children. He forgot that he was a professor at university, and everything else relevant from the first life. He was living his second life, his second orientation—his first love, his love for Eralda. His mind was occupied by the magic of her. He thought and felt like he had entered inside his novel, or perhaps he was living the story in real life. His second life and his second orientation had eclipsed everything from his first life and his first orientation. Nothing else was important to him and his life in those moments. It seemed like his first orientation had stopped for some seconds, minutes, or hours, opening the path and allowing him to experience and enjoy his marvelous second life. He sat down on their bench and stayed there for more than two hours, thinking about his first love and passing through his mind all the story of this love. Just twenty minutes before six o'clock, he stood up and came out of the willow's leaves. He positioned himself there, eagerly waiting for her.

Her silhouette appeared in the dim light of the park's main entrance when the dusk was replacing the twilight. "Is it a dream...? Is it a vision...? Is it a hallucination...?" he asked himself several times. "No..., no. It's real.

It's happening. She is coming," he answered himself. Eralda, the woman he had platonically loved entire his life, was coming, was entering the park, walking toward him now. He tried but couldn't move at all from his place, feeling like he didn't believe that what was happening was real. Maybe it was just another dream of his. He was observing her like the woman was a stranger that he didn't know at all. The first thing he realized by looking at her was that she was a beautiful woman, by her body lines and the elegant way she walked. Yes…, yes. The woman that was walking toward him was a wonderful one and, strangely enough, after every step she was taking approaching him, she looked more and more like Eralda. This beautiful woman was not changing her direction but was walking toward him. He remained still, uncertain for what was happening and without being able to move. Then, he made two steps toward her, instinctively, unconsciously, like a somnambulist, and waited passively for the hug of this beautiful woman when she reached him. Her embrace reminded him of Eralda—the woman he was waiting for—and he woke up. It wasn't a dream. It wasn't a vision. It wasn't a hallucination. He looked at her eyes, keeping her head between his hands, like trying to ensure himself that it was right, and then he kissed her lips, almost biting them and squeezing her body against his. Without interrupting their kiss, they entered under the willow's branches and sat on the bench, "their bench," where they continued their long kisses and tight embraces like once upon a time, on the same seat and under the same willow—two silent witnesses of their great love. Hot kisses, embraces, rubbing, squeezes, moves, pleasure, lust, desire, and in the end…, tears…, plenty of tears…, silence, and tears. The tears of both of them were pouring on each other's shoulders. They stayed like that for a long time, without moving and without speaking. Tears were burning their eyes. Tears were burning their cheeks. Tears were burning their shoulders. Tears were burning their souls. Tears were burning their hearts. After a long moment of silence, Eralda was the first one to speak, separating from him and looking at his eyes:

"I've come here to celebrate the twentieth anniversary of our love, our first date, and our first kiss, here on this bench of ours, under this willow tree." That was all she could say before putting her head on his chest to start crying again.

Her words touched Ardian very much. It was the twentieth anniversary of their extraordinary love. Twenty years had already passed from that November 1983, from their first date and their first kiss of their first love.

He always remembered their first dates on this bench, but without their respective days, while she had used this date, this twentieth anniversary, to come back to him at least one more time. Eralda raised her head from his chest and spoke again:

"I had promised you that if we meet someday, I would be the first one to embrace and kiss you, and I did that. So, it's your turn now."

"Oh, God. She is telling me it's my turn. The time for me has come. The time to experience my great first love once more has come." He was embracing and squeezing between his arms the woman he had loved so much for all his life, the woman he adored forever—the forbidden woman—and she was telling him that it was his turn now. "Why am I still staying here? What am I waiting for? Why are we still staying here?" Ardian thought and suddenly stood up, pulling her from her hand toward the park's exit. They took a taxi and went to a quiet motel by the river Shkumbin, along the road to Librazhd. Ardian decided to spend the night in that motel room, and Eralda accepted it without hesitation, like being prepared in advance for such an adventure.

Love and tears. Hugs and weeping. Joy and bitterness. Happiness and meditations. Chat and silence. Laughter and tranquility. Lust and desire. Sex and pleasure. They experienced all these physical and spiritual moods that might serve as captions for that evening, that night, and that morning they spent together in that motel room. It was the night of their life. Endless love and tears. Love for all their life; for the past, the present, and the future. Passion and pleasure that can't be repeated. It's like a chance that only comes once in your life. They spent together that night and the morning of the next day. He had realized his life's dream, at last. Making love with Eralda had been the dream of his entire life. That dream came true in those twenty-four hours they spent together.

A strange desire to die that happy morning—in bed with her—occupied his mind. "Che bella morte! (What a beautiful death!)," he recalled a phrase from a novel he had read in the Italian language, describing two dead lovers on a bed with the words said by the detective that arrived on the scene. But..., "Che bella vita!" (What a beautiful life!), he paraphrased it immediately in his mind. This woman and her love had beautified his life and had given him one more reason to live and enjoy his life. His life had already been fulfilled in both its orientations in this night and day filled with fiery love.

After taking a shower, they spent some time that afternoon on a balcony having lunch, talking, relaxing, and watching the beautiful view of the river Shkumbin and the range of mountains in front of them. The flow and the gurgling water of the river reminded Ardian of the famous quote of Heraclitus: "No man ever steps in the same river twice, for it's not the same river, and he's not the same man." He wanted to tell Eralda this Heraclitus' analogy about the river water and life, but it was not the right moment for such a philosophical talk, and he continued his reasoning on this subject. "It is impossible to step twice into the same water of the river because the river water has flowed toward the its destination—the sea. Our life as well, together with the time that passes, has flowed toward its final destination—death. Life is a flux that always moves, where everything changes, and nothing is permanent. Like the river flow, a lot of things in our life have flown as well. But there is something else inside us that never changes till our death. It is the memory of the first love and the girl that remains in our mind as fresh, young, beautiful, and vital as it was at that time."

Eralda became more silent for some minutes and then broke down into unstoppable sobbing again. Ardian, for his part, looked like he had finished his tears, and stayed watching Eralda crying, without trying to stop her. He thought that she had her right to cry. Her first love had failed and had destroyed her entire life. She had not been able to find another passion, remaining single, without a husband, without her own family, without any children, unlike him, that despite failing in his first love, had found love again and had created his own family. After some minutes, he pulled Eralda by her hands and entered the room. He helped her sit on the bed's edge. He kneeled in front of her, with his arms and head on her lap. Her tears and her angelic face reminded him of a song he had sung years ago for her in one of their dates in the park. He started singing some verses of that song, in silence within himself:

"Between the hands, she kept her head.
And her tears flowed like runlet.
Weeping has no charm at all.
But her face radiates prettiness.

Then she suddenly raised her head,
Smiling in bitterness, she said...,"

Right at that moment—while Ardian was passing through his mind this verse of the song—Eralda raised her head. She watched him right in his eyes

276

and stayed silent for some more seconds. Then, with her eyes in tears and with a low, sad voice, she started singing the same song that he was singing in silence, continuing the same verse where Ardian had arrived by singing it in his mind:

"... You told me you've never been a girl,
And that's why you can't understand."

"I understand you... I understand you very well, Alda. I understand you as I understand myself," Ardian—still kneeling in front of her—responded in tears to the song verse she sang that looked like her real complaint about him.

He realized that they were in the last minutes of their date, and maybe she as well, was feeling and thinking the same thing. They both were feeling the end of this date that they would want never to end. It was a passionate date after so many years of love, longing, suffering, yearning, and pain for both. But now, in these last minutes, they both understood the temporary gratification had come to an end, and they couldn't do anything else to stop the merciless time flow. "Beautiful moments always come to an end," Ardian recalled the right expression for this case, and "It will become just a beautiful memory from now on," he thought.

"I love you, eternally..., Alda...," he whispered in her ear.

"I love you more than myself...," she answered in tears immediately after him.

Eralda told him that she was living a good life in Greece. She was still single, living with her parents and her younger brother, and all of them were working. She had come to Elbasan using a family reason for some documents, but the main reason for her was to see Ardian, whom she had missed so much, and for whom she was still feeling an unforgettable love and great yearning. She wasn't hoping to come again, and she couldn't endure the pain caused by the idea that this would be the last time for her to see him and that she was going to live the rest of her life without meeting Ardian anymore. And this was the reason she wept and wept endlessly in those last hours and minutes of their twenty-four-hour-long magic date.

Ardian turned back home just before the dusk. It seemed like he was turning from a dream into reality. Only when he was approaching his home—walking toward the first orientation of his life—he started to understand what he had done in those last twenty-four hours. But despite that, he didn't feel any remorse or shame for his actions. He had spent twenty-four hours away from his wife and his children, but he wasn't feeling any repentance for this infidelity and adultery yet. He entered the home like he did every day while coming back from work. Elsa, unlike other times, when she usually kissed him every time after opening the door for him, this time didn't move from the sofa in the living room, where she was sitting and staying in silence. Ardian explained very easy and in a simple way about what had happened to him:

"Eralda was in Elbasan. I spent the night in a motel with her. I can't apologize by saying sorry, because I did it with a conscience, and I'm hearing an inner voice telling me that I haven't done any sin, but I'm sure, and I promise you that it will never happen again.

"I understand you…, I understand you very well," Elsa answered with a lot of melancholy and love for him, while some tears dropped from her eyes on her cheeks.

Ardian approached her and wiped her tears with his fingers. He kissed her on the wet cheek and embraced her, squeezing her tight between his arms.

"Pardon me…, please. Elsa, please…, forgive me. Elsa, you never deserve my cheating on you, but I satisfied my longing soul and discharged my yearning heart for her and for my first love, which still lives somewhere in me, and I can't get rid of it, despite my continuous efforts to do such a thing."

"I understand you… I understand you…," Elsa repeated, "Maybe it's just me that mistakenly have interfered in between you two."

"No…, Elsa…, no. Don't say it anymore…, please. You entered my life in the most difficult time for me when I was lonely and desperate more than ever. You saved me and rebuilt my life. You raised me up, and I was reborn with your help. You gave me great love, incredible care, and an extraordinary friend and wife. You gave me a family and two wonderful children. You are everything to me. You are my queen." He kneeled, kissed her hands, and begged her apology with tears in his eyes.

Elsa didn't say any words at all, but her tears, pouring down her cheeks, spoke a lot. She pulled him up into a long, silent, sad hug with tears dripping on each other's shoulders.

Ardian felt exhausted and went to bed, falling asleep immediately. He got up on the morrow just before noon. It was Sunday, and everybody was at home. He entered the living room being nervous and unsure of what was waiting for him in this new day after his adventure. He saw Elsa there doing some house works in the kitchen as usual, and she greeted him, "good morning, darling," as usual. When he saw his breakfast prepared and waiting for him on the table, as usual again, he was surprised and asked himself: "Did it really happened the day before…, or was it just a dream of mine…?" He thought like this because he was not expecting such a usual situation after his behavior on the last day. He couldn't decide what to believe. Elsa greeted and spoke to him, as usual, as nothing wrong had happened. Based on Elsa's behavior, he couldn't understand whether he had just seen a beautiful dream, or Elsa had forgiven him and had forgotten what he had done. "Perhaps…, I've seen the most beautiful dream of my life," Ardian thought and wanted to consider it as being happened for real. "Or maybe…, such a magnificent thing happened in reality," he reconsidered it, realizing that it had been so beautiful and magic and he couldn't believe that such an impossible thing had happened, and he couldn't accept it as being real, but just another dream of his.

He wanted to ask Elsa about that but didn't dare to do it. How could he ask Elsa for such a thing, if it had happened for real? He didn't dare to ask Elsa either that day or the coming days, weeks, and months. He thought and asked himself many times about what had happened that day, but at the same time, he wanted to leave it without any clear answer. He wanted it to be like a blurred line between the dream and reality, just like the first love and its memory remains forever—like a personal legend in the confines of the vision and the fact. This dilemma brought more confusion to his sick mind.

Ardian remained unsure of what had happened. "Was it a reality…? Was it a dream…? Or was it just a vision?" He continued asking these questions to himself time after time. It reminded him of what he had read in an English medical dictionary about the visions, voices, and hallucinations that accompany somebody suffering from schizophrenia. "Did I become a schizophrenic…?" He scared about that. "Did schizophrenia give me all that pleasure and happiness…?" he continued asking himself. "Was it just schizophrenia making me realize the dream of entire my life…? Oh…, God! Am I going crazy…? That's why I haven't wept for a long time. But…, didn't I cry together with her…? Where…? With her…, or with her vision…? I became a schizophrenic now. Though, it doesn't look like a bad thing because only in this way my life's dream come true. No…, no. It was not a vision. It was not a hallucination. It happened for real because it was Alda herself. I met her…. I kissed her…. I embraced her…. I talked with her…. I made love with her…. I slept with her…. I enjoyed her…. I wept together with her…. She was with me…. I was with her…. We were together. And…, in the end…, she went away again, going very far away from me."

"The first love – endless yearning and pain," he wrote in a white sheet of paper and put it on the top of the manuscript like a front cover with the title of his unfinished novel that was still sleeping in a drawer already for six years. He took those papers in his hands and passed them slowly one by one from one hand to the other, sobbing and letting his tears drop over each of them. Because of his tears' drops, many letters and words were transformed into dots and marks of tears and blue ink. The story of his life and love had been written with heart and soul, with ink and tears.

"This is the legend of the first love that continues forever," he wrote in another sheet of paper and placed it at the end of the manuscript, like the last page of it where he had already written the lyrics of his preferred song, *"The First Love."*

No, I don't believe it.
To be easy to deny.
I will never forget.
The first love of mine.

Don't say you don't think of me.
No one will believe it.
Somewhere in your dreams,
I will come, and we'll meet.

The first love,
Who didn't try?
And didn't sing,
The pain left behind.
(Verses of the Albanian song "The First Love," sung by Anita Bitri)

The End

Alexander Papa
Elbasan, 1997 – 2003

33

He thought that the last pages he had just written would be a good ending for his novel—that kind of ending he had thought about and had been waiting for so long. On the very last page of the manuscript, he wrote the lyrics of the song "The First Love," for which he had thought and decided before. At the bottom of the last page, he wrote his real name— Alexander Papa—as the author of the novel and the period he had spent to write this novel; 1997 - 2003. He had written the history of his life and his love. So, it was not fiction. It was his real life and real love. The only fiction in his novel were the names of characters. But he had not changed his children's names, because he wanted to tell the beautiful stories in selecting their names. Furthermore, he used their real-life names as an additional fact connecting the fiction part of this story with his real-life history.

Alexander put all those handwritten papers in a big yellow envelope and gave it to his wife, Teuta, telling her:

"Here, you have the full story of my first love. It looks like a novel, like fiction, but when you read it, you will understand that it is my real life, because only you are the witness of my life and my love in that period of my life the novel speaks about. By the way, having a witness of your life is one more reason why people marry each other and live together. I said 'a novel' because it might be an excellent novel to be published, but I can't do that. This is my first novel. It was my desire and my concern inside me to write and finish it. I don't want to read it, and I don't want to return to this subject anymore. You can read it if you wish. I don't want others to read it and learn about my suffering and pain." Alexander made a long, silent pause here, and after that, he continued:

"And…, above all…, I don't want to cause any problems for…, for Margarita." He mentioned the real-life name of the other main character of

281

his novel, the name of the girl he loved so much during his entire life, the real name of "the most beautiful girl in the city," as he always called her. "You have my permission to publish it, maybe after my death. Writers and artists always become famous after their death," he finished, trying to bring some humor with the last sentence.

Teuta took the yellow envelope in her hands, opened it carefully, brought the papers out, and started passing them one by one, watching his handwriting and the marks of his tears on most of the pages. Those marks of his tears on the paper touched her very much, and they reminded her of the real suffering and pain he had gone through for his first love, and she couldn't keep her tears too. She put the manuscript's papers on the table, approached and embraced him in tears.

"I love you, darling." That was all she could say at that moment, crying on his shoulders, while he fondled her hair and wiped her tears.

"You will be the first reader of my novel," he spoke after some minutes filled with tears and touching moments.

"Yes..., you are right. I'll read it with very great pleasure," Teuta answered.

She read the manuscript of his novel during three coming days, shedding tears on every page she passed through her hands. Even though she tried not to drop her tears on those papers, some of her tears fell on them, leaving their marks, adding and joining the ones of Alexander's tears. When she finished reading it, Teuta told Alexander:

"I finished reading your novel. It is wonderful. I think that you need to type it in a computer, and in this way, you can refine parts of it and make some necessary grammar corrections. After that, you will have the electronic copy ready for a possible publisher in the future," Teuta told him.

Alexander followed Teuta's advice and spent the spring months of 2004, typing the book on his computer. This typing process served as a reminder of all his love story, and he went through different psychological situations, from the astonishment of how he could have written such a beautiful book, to the profoundly moving moments and shedding tears for his lost love. After finishing typing, Alexander saved it in the only reading mode in a computer folder and two floppy discs. He printed a hard copy of the novel and gave it and two diskettes to Teuta. He showed her the folder where he had saved it among other computer folders because he didn't want their children to find and read it before becoming adults.

In this way, Alexander Papa had written the story of his first love. If published, it would be a real success for sure, but he didn't want to do that because his novel was based on actual events of his real life. He was afraid of humiliation because a lot of people in his city, his colleagues and students would easily understand that it was the actual history of his real life, and...:

"I don't want others to learn about my illness and the real reason behind this illness," he added while giving the hard copy of his book and the floppy disks to Teuta.

"I know in this book is your life and love, and you have described it wonderfully, but your health is the most important thing for me, too," Teuta told him, holding tight his hands.

"This book is only yours now. Keep it in a safe place for you. I'm not going to read it anymore. I don't want to think about her..., and I don't want to see her anymore. It is only you and our children I care for in my life," Alexander promised her.

"I know, my darling. It's not easy for you," she said and embraced him again.

Teuta, during the last two years, had become aware and worried about Alexander's mental health, seeing that he was going through a difficult situation. Ever since Margarita left the city and the country, leaving that moving farewell letter for him, Alexander was missing her very much, and he was wandering around the city streets time after time in a crazy, desperate search for Margarita. Every time that Alexander wasn't coming back home in time, Teuta knew the reason why and what he was doing in those moments, and she went out in search of him. She already knew very well where to find him—around Margarita's apartment building, around the evening high school building, or in the park, at "their bench" under the willow tree. These were the places where his sick mind always took him in remembrance of the lost first love. Teuta had always found him in one of these "sacred places" for him. After reaching him, she crossed her arm with his arm and returned home together in silence. Teuta's presence always made him feel better, safe, and secure and helped his mind return to reality. He obeyed her immediately, without any words or resistance and always telling her:

"You're my queen. It has been 'Teuta the First,' the Queen of the Illyrians, in the third century BC, and it is you, 'Teuta the Second,' my Queen," he told her, speaking and explaining the history about Teuta the Queen, with a lot of historical facts:

"Queen Teuta ruled the Ardiaean Kingdom, which included much of Illyria (a region in the western part of the Balkan Peninsula by the east side of the Adriatic Sea, inhabited by Illyrians, the ancient ancestors of Albanians). The Ardiaean Kingdom became a threat to Rome's trade routes that ran across the Adriatic Sea, going through this region of West Balkan," Alexander kept explaining to his wife, "Queen Teuta the Second," as he liked to call her very often.

"…"

"Queen Teuta ended her life by jumping off a cliff, instead of surrendering alive to Rome," Alexander repeated the story several times, breaking the silence on the way back home.

Teuta (his wife), was pleased with his passion for ancient history and liked to push him further in his endless monologues about the ancient and modern history of Balkans.

"If I am Queen Teuta of Illyria, you will be Alexander the Great of Macedonia." Teuta used to tease him.

And every time after that, Alexander brought and explained additional facts about the ancient history of Illyria, Epirus, and Macedonia—a determinant triangle in the Balkan Peninsula of that time that included territories inhabited nowadays by Albanians. He used to tell her:

"Macedonian king, Alexander the Great, was born to parents King Philip II and Queen Olympia in the fourth century BC, and he was tutored by the Greek philosopher Aristotle."

"…"

"Queen Olympia was the princess of Epirus, and that's why, when the royal family split apart after King Philip II married Cleopatra, Alexander took his mother, Queen Olympia, and fled the country going to Epirus. After the assassination of his father, King Philip II, in the spring of 336 BC, he returned to power as the King of Macedonia Alexander III."

"…"

"Alexander the Great reconquered Illyria because Illyrians rebelled against the Macedonian conquest after Philip's death. But all these events had happened one century before Queen Teuta's rule of the Ardiaean Kingdom, which included much of Illyria proper."

"…"

"Alexander the Great broke the power of Persia and overthrew the Persian King Darius III, stretching his empire from the Adriatic Sea in Illyrians' territories in Western Balkans, to the Indus River in India."

"Let me sum up," Teuta told him to engage him more in such a passionate explanation of history. "I am Queen Teuta of Illyria, and you are Alexander the Great of Macedonia, whose mother was Olympia, the princess of Epirus," she reminded him always the famous triangle—Illyria, Macedonia, and Epirus.

"Yes, you are right," he continued passionately. "Another fact about Epirus is the well-known phrase 'Pyrrhic victory,' named after King Pyrrhus of Epirus, one of the most vigorous opponents of early Rome in third century BC. Some of his battles, though successful, caused him heavy losses, from which the term 'Pyrrhic victory' was coined, meaning a 'hollow victory,' or gaining nothing by winning. After one such victory, Pyrrhus said: 'Another such victory, and I come back to Epirus alone.'"

After his precise explanations, Teuta urged him again by repeating to Alexander what she had already heard from him other times:

"I have heard that Miss Mary Edith Durham (a British artist, anthropologist, and writer who became famous for her anthropological accounts of life in Albania in the early 20th century) says that Albanians are the direct descendants of the ancient inhabitants of Illyria and Epirus."

"Yes, it is true, and you must know that the northern border of Epirus stretched from Vlorë to Lake Prespa, and sometimes Greeks want to bring it up to the Shkumbin River. That's the reason that some Greeks call the southern Albania as 'Vorio Epiri' meaning the 'Northern Epirus,' pretending that this territory—the southern half of modern Albania—belongs to Greece, and the Albanian people living in this area, are considered by them as Greek population. That was the pretext used by the Greek government during the First World War when Greece officially annexed 'Northern Epirus' in March 1916 but was forced to revoke by the Great Powers of that time."

"So, your family and relatives that live in Vlorë and my parents that have come from Korça are Greeks, according to them," Teuta told him.

"The good thing is that a lot of Albanian senior citizens from this area are taking good pensions from the Greek government, just because they supposedly are Greeks. Some relatives of my parents from Vlorë and relatives of your parents from Korça are taking this pension, but our parents are not taking it just because they don't like to be treated as Greeks, even though this money would be a good help for their living."

"It means that our parents are sincere people," Teuta teased him, and she already knew his answer.

"Yes, it means that our poor, but 'good, smart, and honest' parents, are nothing but very stupidly honest," Alexander always answered sarcastically.
" … "

"And another interesting issue nowadays is the name of the new state of Macedonia. The Greek government does not recognize it with this name, and that's why the international institutions and organizations recognize this country as the Former Yugoslavian Republic of Macedonia (FYROM).* Greeks say that ancient Macedonia and its population have been Greek, unlike the populace that lives in Macedonia today that is of Slavic origin that came to the Balkan Peninsula in the sixth century AD." Alexander continued endlessly with these historical and modern issues of Balkans, repeating things he had said before or recalling and bringing new facts time after time.

For several years, Alexander touched very rarely the guitar, still hanged on the wall of their bedroom. When his children asked him sometimes to play something for them, he fulfilled their desire by playing the guitar and singing for them a lot of real songs and funny stuff. After their children retreated to their places, he continued playing the guitar singing on his own. Sometimes he sang in Teuta's presence while she was staying to listen to him or doing something else or house chores. He never sang in Elsa's presence the songs he had composed for his first love, but he sang more often two especial songs that had become like anthems for him. The first one was the soft rock song "The Sound of Silence" of Simon & Garfunkel, with its famous opening verse, *"Hello darkness, my old friend."* The second song that he sang with the same spirit and passion was the Italian song "Parla piu Piano" of Gianni Morandi. This song is the Italian language version—with some different lyrics—of the English song "Speak Softly, Love," the theme song for the movie "The Godfather."

Teuta didn't understand all the lyrics of these two songs, but she was worried very much by the way Alexander articulated some of the mystical verses of the English song and some love verses of the Italian song. The melancholic immerse of him while he sang these two songs and the way he involved himself in those lyrics, made her understand that those verses were significant and meant a lot to him, to his conscience, to his emotional situation, to his silenced suffering and pain, and to the sickness of depression he was living with. It was clear for Teuta what Alexander was feeling and was going through when he was singing the lyrics of "The Sound of Silence." Some of its verses (such as; *"Hello darkness, my old friend, / I've come to talk with you again / Because a vision softly creeping, / Left its seeds while I was* *sleeping, / And the vision that was planted in my brain, / Still remains, / Within the sound of silence, / In restless dreams, I walked alone...,"*) became very especial lyrics for him. She knew that when he was singing the verses of the Italian love song (such as; *"Parla più piano e vieni più vicino a me, / Voglio sentire gli occhi miei dentro di te, / Nessuno sa la verità, / è un grande amore e mai più grande esisterà, / Insieme a te io restero, / Amore mio sempre cosi,"* (Speak softly and come closer to me, / I want to feel my eyes inside of you, / Nobody knows the truth, / It's a great love, and a greater love than this, can never exist, / Together with you I'll remain, / My darling, always like this,*) he had Margarita and her portrait in his mind, thinking and singing about her and their lost great love. The words of those lyrics and the way he sang those songs, disturbed Teuta very much, being concerned about his mental situation when she saw him singing these songs always with deep emotion and tears in his eyes.

That Friday afternoon (when Alexander met Margarita and was not returning home), Teuta worried about him, and she went in search of him as always in such cases. She looked for him in those usual places where she used to find him every time when he "forgot" to return home. First, she went to Margarita's apartment building and didn't see him there. Then, she went to the evening high school building, and he was not there. After that, she hurried towards the park (as the last place where she could find him), being sure that he would be there, sitting at the bench under the willow tree. When she arrived in the street in front of the park's main entrance, she saw from a distance Alexander holding hands tight with another woman, under the streetlamp at the park's entrance, hailing a taxi. Teuta stopped immediately. She continued watching them from a distance, being uncertain for what was happening with her husband. She stayed there watching them without being able to decide what to do in such a case. A taxi stopped in front of them, and they both got quickly on the cab holding hands like two happy children. Teuta understood what was going on when she recognized the woman—it was Margarita. Teuta turned back home, crying all the way. She told the children that their father had gone to Vlorë and wept all night lying alone in the matrimonial bed. It was the first time in entire their conjugal life for her to spend the night alone, and it looked like a terrifying situation, where the whole home and all the life looked empty to her, like the empty matrimonial bed without her husband by her side. "Sleeping alone in a matrimonial bed—the biggest spiritual emptiness," she thought and cried all that night.

Alexander felt better and looked very good after that last date with Margarita and during the following several months that he spent writing the book by hand and typing it on the computer. After he gave the typed manuscript to Teuta, with the decision and the promise not to think about Margarita and his first love anymore, his mental health condition worsened, with his mood changing time after time. For a long time since his sickness may have started (maybe since Margarita left the city in September 1997, or even before), Alexander had been successful in dealing with his inner demons in a way that doesn't make them visible for others. He had been suffering from such a concealed depression for a long time, weeping in his loneliness, without sharing his trouble with Teuta, and without being diagnosed with that dangerous illness. Depression is much more than just a visible mood because he had made all efforts to appear okay. He always tried to hide signs of depression, being afraid of humiliation and abandonment as it happens in such cases. He had read many medical articles about stress, anxiety, depression, schizophrenia, bipolarity, finding out that many of artists, musicians, writers, leaders, and genius people had suffered from such mental illnesses and they had had a serious depth of emotions, helping them express themselves in incredible ways, leading them to profound greatness. Alexander had always been tried to find a purpose in his life, even by just remembering, thinking, singing, speaking, and writing about his great first love, but during these last years, he couldn't find any other purpose. He wanted to keep his depression undisclosed because, in this way, he could protect himself, his mind, and his soul. At the same time, he wanted and tried to protect his wife, his children, and their dreams, because he knew that the world around us, our family and friends in general, encourages us to hide from others what is different, strange, dark, unusual, painful, and every such unpleasant thing for them. His depression that had started years before could not be concealed anymore because its symptoms became more serious, more visible, and more worrisome. He was showing low energy, depressed mood, sadness, melancholy, insomnia, and was breaking down and cried in Teuta's presence more often, complaining to her for the emptiness and worthlessness of his life. Teuta begged him to go together to a doctor, and he accepted. They went to a psychiatrist who prescribed the right medication for him. Teuta cared for him, giving the medicine every morning and evening, and while taking his medicines regularly, he felt and seemed very healthy.

They bought two mobile phones, and when he wasn't coming back home in time, she called him immediately, and he always answered, "Yes, my Queen. I'm coming, darling." Listening to her unique ringtone in his phone, was enough to bring him back to reality, and her loving, sweet voice was enough for him to return home, where she was always waiting anxiously, looking all the time in the window for him. After seeing him coming, she ran to the door and kept it open while he was climbing the stairs till his arrival. And she never forgot the welcome kiss full of love for him.

"You are my guardian angel. You are God's gift to me. You are my Queen. You are my medicine. I love you so much," he always told her, kissing her on both cheeks and her lips every time he returned home, and after taking his medicine in full obedience under her watch and splendid care.

But it wasn't enough for Alexander because the bad things didn't end here for him. Something terrible happened that summer of 2004. Alexander's sister and her two children were drowned in the Strait of Otranto of the Adriatic Sea while trying to reach Italy illegally together with other illegal migrants in an inflatable boat. They became part of the damned statistics of the ongoing tragedies of drowning people, boats, and ships in that forty-five-mile-long strait that connects (and separates) Albania with Italy. Only that year, more than one hundred people had been drowned in their attempt to reach Italy, starting with what is known as the "January 9, 2004, tragedy," where twenty-eight people died. This tragedy had the second-highest mortality rate for such events in the Strait of Otranto, after the "Otranto tragedy" of March 28, 1997, when an Albanian ship with clandestine emigrants was hit by the Italian warship "Sibilla," resulting in the death of eighty-four people. There are a lot of other tragic incidents with drowned people traveling on inflatable boats, Albanians, and foreigners, including women and children thrown by smugglers into the cold water of the sea at a long distance from the shore in their attempts to escape the Italian coastguard.

Alexander's sister and her innocent children were the last unfortunate victims of this ongoing tragedy in this part of the world. Her husband had gone illegally to Italy some years before, working there to keep his family and his old parents back home in Vlorë. His mother had the family originated from the rich, overthrown classes whose real estate property was taken by the communist regime after the Second World War. These legitimate owners are called now "ex-owners." The communist leader of the democratic party redistributed the state-owned land in 1992 reapplying the same communist motto of the agrarian reform of 1946; "The land belongs to those who work it," without thinking at all for the right of the "ex-owners," who were politically aligned behind him with a complete naiveté. During that democratic transition mess, another informal motto, "the land belongs to those who occupy it illegally," was used by people who occupied land forcefully and build illegally without any construction permit. Signs saying, "taken land," were placed on areas held by barbarians coming from every direction of the country, being encouraged by the silence of the state.

Monda's husband and his parents, like all "ex-owners," spent a lot of years in courtrooms trying to take back some of their family properties based on the laws passed by the democratic parliament but the corruption in the local and central government offices, in the justice system, in deeds registry offices, in state archives, and all respective state offices made the law implementation impossible. Other individuals and families used a lot of false documents earning the right of ownership on the plots of land that didn't belong to them at all. The falsity became a well-spread phenomenon during the "democratic transition," as another example of corruption in all levels of the Albanian society. After ten years of failure in the incriminated courtrooms, Monda's husband emigrated to Italy, where he was working hard to keep his family back in Albania. After so many years staying alone in Vlorë, Monda decided to go and join him in Italy, taking that damned trip that took the life of her and her children. The high unemployment rate, small salaries, severe living conditions, and corruption in their failed state and country, persuaded people to leave Albania by traveling illegally to other European countries or America and Canada. Demanding visa requirements produced great difficulties in obtaining travel or emigrating visas through foreign embassies. The lengthy, complicated, corrupt, and humiliating procedures, filled with a lot of illegal middlemen and corrupt officials of the respective embassies, trying to make a profit for themselves, were the main reasons leading to illegal emigration with the help of illegal human trafficking.

Alexander's parents, with their hearts in pieces for the death of their daughter and grandchildren, couldn't live longer, and they passed away one after another in two following years after that tragedy.

The loss of his sister and her children, followed by the death of his parents, were big blows for Alexander and his mental health. He became worst and worst, month after month and year after year, even by resisting

Teuta violently sometimes when she tried to convince him to take his medicine. Alexander spent all coming years situated in between the hard depression and Teuta's extraordinary love and tireless care for him. Only her presence and only being near her made him feel safer and better, and he never forgot to kiss and thank "Her Majesty, Queen Teuta" for her tremendous love and care.

---

* In June 2018, Macedonia and Greece resolved the conflict with an agreement that the country should rename itself the Republic of North Macedonia. This renaming came into effect in February 2019

34

In October 2007, their son, Erblin, became eighteen years old. That month, Alexander filed on-line three electronic applications for the American Diversity Immigrant Visa Program (known as the American Green Card Lottery)—one for himself plus family, one for Teuta plus family, and one for Erblin as a single. He filed the Erblin's application as a gift for his birthday. Erblin was lucky because he was among those selected for further procedures, declared by this lottery in May 2008. Erblin moved to the United States in the summer of 2009. He returned to Albania for vacations in summer 2010 together with an American friend of his, who fell in love with Mimosa. They returned to Albania again to celebrate New Year's Eve and made the official marriage, so that in summer 2011, Mimosa as well moved to the USA. After their two children moved to the USA, Alexander's illness was worsening even more, despite Teuta's great love and care for him.

"I'm very sorry, darling. I cannot cope with this damn illness anymore. Only your presence makes me feel alive. But I want you to be free of me, and you have to join and live with our children in America. Go and live there with them. I cannot join you, but please…, go there…, and kiss our children every morning and every evening for yourself and me as well, like we did every day when they were still little kids," Alexander told Teuta time after time.

After earning his doctorate in Italy, Alexander started teaching psychology and sociology at the Teachers College. It was a job that he liked to do, and a little bit easier for his health conditions. Students of this college were coming with bad grade point average from failed high schools of cities, towns, and villages. The education system in the country was collapsed, and most of the students were not capable of studying and learning at all.

Students attended public and private universities just for the sake of having a bachelor's degree. The level of universities went down, following the low level of the students that were attending them. Such a failure happened to all state universities and all private universities that grew like mushrooms after rain those years. All new private universities were authorized and licensed without any pedagogical criteria. State universities as well opened other colleges in a lot of small cities without any pedagogic standards. As a result, a new "business" had started and expanded year after year as well. Private universities were just selling with a high price, pieces of cardboard called "university diploma," doing such a thing even for some Italians that didn't speak any Albanian language at all. At the same time, a lot of professors of the state universities had started to sell grades of exams taking money from their students. These professors were making a lot of money in this way, and they were not ashamed and didn't try to hide it at all while buying new expensive houses and apartments, new cars for themselves and their spouses, costly clothes, watches, and other accessories, and going for vacations abroad.

What was happening in all the country, was like a frenetic race among state institutions and officials to win the first place in corruption, injustice, dysfunction, and failure in carrying their mission and duties. Officials of the central government, local government, justice system, state health service, state and private universities, police officers, customs service, financial service, tax offices, forestry police, all public, and private institutions and organizations were taking part in this crazy race. Everybody in its job position was trying to give their enormous contribution to the total destruction of the country and society. Alexander recalled what the American ambassador in Albania had said in a meeting with some students of Tirana State University some years earlier—"The corruption risks to become a culture and a way of living in Albania." Being said by a diplomat, it meant that it had already happened. He had said it many years ago, so that now, the corruption, lies, deception, injustice, had become a culture and a way of living for Albanians. Judges and prosecutors, tax and customs officers, doctors of state hospitals and clinics, university professors, police officers, parliament deputies and ministers of the government, prime ministers, local government officials, are active participants of this crazy race, causing the degeneration of the democratic system.

"That's the main reason why more than a third of Albanian population has already left the country in desperation, like fleeing from a war zone, because such emigration rate only happens when people are forcefully displaced or fleeing a war zone. That's why the 'democratic' Albania of corruption, injustice, unemployment, and poverty is worse than a war zone. It is a war zone created with the contribution of all of us, where we are killing each other as individuals and the society as a whole firing from our positions with weapons of wrongdoings, deceptions, manipulations, falsities, corruption, and injustice," Alexander used to tell Teuta, regarding the actual situation in Albania during the painful transition to democracy that had already taken more than twenty years of destroyed hopes and broken dreams.

Alexander had the same salary as his colleagues, but unlike them, he couldn't afford to buy such expensive things like them. He was still living in a one-bedroom apartment that he had purchased by the state in the process of house privatization in 1992. He knew that his colleagues were selling grades to their students, and he felt horrible about this disgusting act and for its long-term consequences. Alexander, for many years, had evaluated most of the students with the minimum grade "five," as a mercy for them to pass the school years. But these last three years he had decided not to do it anymore, not even for compassion, and about seventy-five percent of the students had failed in the exams of the subjects he taught; others had passed with only minimum grades that they deserved. In this way, Alexander became a big problem for students and other professors that raised the level of passing rate by taking money from their students.

As a result of his act, several times, when he entered the classroom to start his lecture, he had seen marks of some offending words on the chalkboard, that had been written by failed students and erased by somebody else. He had seen traces of wiped words such as; "psychopath, schizophrenia, bipolar, depression, idiot." He was facing these insults in silence and never said anything, just understanding and being aware of what was happening between him, as an honest man and professor, and the failed students. But one day, on Thursday, April 10, 2014, he found the word "psychopath," written on the chalkboard, but not erased. Perhaps the student with a good heart was absent that day or didn't have the time to wipe that word. Alexander took a piece of chalk of another color and drew a big heart leaving in the middle of it the small word "psychopath." After that, he walked toward his desk and stood next to it, watching outside the window. A deep, scary silence fell in the classroom. After spending some minutes there, staying and thinking in silence, he started walking in the aisle between student desks and began speaking loudly:

"Yes…, yes. You are right. I am a psychopath and a schizophrenic, and I've been like this entire my life. I am a schizophrenic because, before coming here, I was thinking how twenty-nine years ago today, I was having a marvelous time spending the afternoon, evening, and night making love by a small lake under the breathtaking beauty of the pristine nature. But the next morning, we learned that that night, the 'Great Leader,' the 'Dear Leader of the people of Albania,' was languishing on his death bed. He died, but he left behind a lot of other miscreants that still lead this country. But now, after I entered this classroom filled with the new generation of the people of Albania that has still the governance it deserves, I realized that I have been a psycho since I was young because, when I was your age, I had read over two hundred books and I had learned two foreign languages. I was a schizophrenic when, in your age, I played the guitar, played soccer and chess, and at the same time, I was the best student of the pedagogical institute, this institution that you today call 'university.' 'Lanet Universitet' (Malison University), our wise elders would say in the Turkish language. I was a psycho when I was assigned as a literature professor in the pedagogical institute after my graduation. I was schizophrenic when I studied and passed three post-graduate exams at Tirana University, in three consecutive years after my graduation. I was a psycho when they transferred me to the most remote village of the county, 'for signs of foreign bourgeois and revisionist ideology, and immoral behavior,' just because I dared to play the guitar and sing foreign songs in a dancing party, being in love and inspired by the most beautiful girl in the city. I was a psycho when I discovered that we were living under a tyrannical dictatorship and when I realized that the socialist realism was just a propaganda means, used by and serving the communist dictatorship and the dictator himself. I was schizophrenic when I told everybody that the most loyal communists and the state secret service agents took in their hands the flag of the democracy. I was a psycho when I understood how the crowd of the democratic revolution was eating all the baits and decoys of the cunning communist dictator. For one year and a half, he prepared everything for the so-called 'peaceful transition to democracy,' to protect his head and the communist elite by having still the political and economic power using his lackeys as new faces to take power as 'anti-communist' leaders. He dispatched abroad the most active youth that would become dangerous for him, by opening and allowing them to enter the foreign embassies, by opening the country's land borders with Greece, and by boarding all the ships and sailing toward Italy. The dictator started with the first bait by founding the new political parties of the new pluralist system, led by the most loyal communists and secret service agents. Then he continued with the second bait when his loyal pundits and surrogates disseminated his propaganda, giving him the merit of a peaceful transition toward the democracy without any bloodshed. His masquerade was finalized with his third bait when he threw to the hungry crowd a bone—the monument of the dead dictator—used by him as a decoy duck to lure, deceive, and deviate the foolish crowd who was eager to bring down the monument of the dead dictator, destroying and lugging it victoriously. The flock of sheep mangled the monument, but they forgot the alive dictator and the communist elite, the real victorious ones that stole and put under their control the democratic revolution, laughing and mocking the 'revolutionary crowd' that always went like sheep in the direction told by them. I was a psycho when I told everybody that the communist leader of the Democratic Party, didn't give the land back to ex-owners from whom it was taken forcefully by the communist regime, but he remade the communist agrarian reform in 1992 by delivering the state-owned land under the same motto used by his spiritual communist father in 1946, 'the land belongs to those who work it.' I was a schizophrenic in 1996 when I told people not to deposit their money in those fraudulent financial firms because I, and few 'psychos' like me, understood that they are just financial pyramids using the Ponzi scheme. I was a psychopath in 1997, when I told people armed with weapons and ammunition taken from the military barracks, not to kill each other, but to go and kill the communist president that intentionally caused this tragedy, aiming the civil war of north against the south in the country. I was a schizophrenic in 1998 when I told that people had to kill the leader of the armed coup d'état, which was the same communist leader of the Democratic Party, in opposition already. I was a psychopath in March 2008, when twenty-six people were killed, and the entire village of Gërdec was destroyed by the actions of a corrupt defense minister in cooperation with the son of the prime minister—the same criminal, the same communist leader of the Democratic Party that ignorant people like you, with their votes, returned him to power to cause more tragedies in Albania. I was a schizophrenic in January 2011, when the same criminal prime minister killed four innocent people in the middle of the boulevard just because they were demonstrating peacefully outside his office. I was a psychopath when I said that we, the people, are waiting in silence—like cows in a slaughterhouse yard—to be killed by the same slaughterer, the mobster in chief, the communist leader of the Democratic Party. He stole the democratic party and the democracy in 1990, being sent and helped by the communist dictator of that time. And he has always been in power for twenty-three years, even when he's been in opposition, just by taking turns with the communist leader of the socialist party and being helped by other renegades and henchmen of other smaller parties. I was a schizophrenic when I told my sister not to try to go to Italy with illegal inflatable boats because it was dangerous. She didn't listen to me and took with her, at the bottom of the sea, two innocent children, becoming part of the most tragic statistics of this country. I was a psycho when I taught the critique of socialist realism in an Italian university because I was not allowed to teach it here in my 'democratic' country. I was a psycho when I studied in a university in Rome, where I earned the master's degree, followed by a doctorate, after reading around one hundred books of Italian literature by cooperating with three Italian professors. I was schizophrenic when I used to give you the minimum passing grades just for mercy and didn't take money from you as most of my colleagues do. By the way, how much do you pay for a passing grade 'five'? I have heard you pay a minimum of fifty euros, depending on the shameless professors, and the man in the middle of this stinking trade. Fifty euros is the minimum price of prostitutes in the streets of European cities. So, your passing grade 'five,' costs as much as a sexual penetration to a prostitute. But let's find out who is the prostitute in this dirty trade that happens in all state universities of this country. Is it the professor..., or the student? Oh..., by comparison, the prostitute is who takes the money, and in this case, professors take money, so they are the prostitutes. But..., who are you? By continuing this reasoning and comparison, you are the buyers of this service, and for that, you pay money. What kind of service are you buying? You are not buying sexual penetration, but you are just buying with money, your grades, and your graduation diploma. In this way, you are screwing all prostitute professors, and you are fucking the entire higher education system, giving the last kick for the destruction of the present and the long-term future of this miserable country. And this entire great, ugly masquerade happens just because you are lazy and idiots, and you are not capable of reading and studying, and you find and choose the easiest way of cheating, falsification, injustice, and corruption as a solution. Who gives you this money to buy the grades of exams? Your honest, good parents! That means that they as well, support this immoral and ashamed solution. What do your parents do? They work in the local and central government offices. They might be doctors, nurses, judges, police officers, customs officers, prosecutors, directors of institutions, and they are all taking money from citizens in exchange for their state services. Or your parents might be entrepreneurs and small-business people, that try hard not to pay taxes and customs service, bribing the state officials and causing a big tax evasion. Some of you may have parents in a difficult financial situation, or you may come from low-income families, but you put them under pressure to find the money for you to pay professors to pass exams. You have already convinced your poor parents that paying professors is the only way to pass exams, and they feel this responsibility and borrow more money for every exam of yours. You and your parents have already forgotten about the first way to pass exams, the just, honest way, the hard way—reading and studying hard, spending several hours a day on books for every school subject and every exam. But you are not capable of doing that, and you, the new, lazy, ignorant generation, find other dishonest, easiest ways. In this way, we all are penetrating each other, and we are screwing the society and entire country, filling and covering ourselves in falsity, living, and suffering altogether in this mass craziness. I was neither schizophrenic nor psychopathic when I joined this collective falsity by giving you a passing grade 'five,' just for mercy. But I became schizophrenic and psychopathic after I decided to be honest with myself at first, and then with you and your parents, with this society and this impoverished country of ours. But you…, now…, after twenty-four years of democracy…, you…, the new generation…, the first generation born in this Albanian democracy…, you don't like and don't accept the honesty, justice, merits, capabilities, the truth, the meritocracy, and you have chosen the falsity, lies, deception, corruption, and injustice instead, and this is the end of democracy, the end of a decent human society, the end of entire Albanian society where each one in his position is contributing to this quick asphyxia of the society, transforming it into a society without any laws, without any ethical norms, without any principles, without any moral compass, and as a consequence, all of us together are suffering the lack of a true democracy, the lack of the justice, the bad economy, bad health service, bad education system, bad police forces, bad politics, bad governance, and bad everything else in this country. I become a schizophrenic again when I tell people that even now, in 2014, twenty-four years after the bloodless, peaceful, democratic revolution, the new prime minister is the son of the communist speaker of the People's Assembly of the dictatorship. His father co-signed the death punishment of a poet in the summer of 1988, by hanging him publicly in the central square of the city, using the same way the real criminals and killers were executed. I'm a psychopath again when I tell people that a lot of family names of the new leadership of the ruling Socialist Party remind me of the same family names of the old communist elite of the dictatorship. I see some of you recording me with your phones, and you are going to report to the dean of the college and the rector of the university about psychopathic stuff I'm saying, and they will expel me for this schizophrenic speech in front of you. They will bring another 'non-psychopathic' and 'non-schizophrenic' professor, a relative of them or a child of a politician of their political party, or a new activist and militant of their respective political parties—a son, a daughter, a niece, a nephew, a son in law, a daughter in law, a relative, even a neighbor or a paramour—and she or he, not being psychopathic or schizophrenic like me, will accept and take money you pay to pass your exams, and you will pass the school years one by one, you will graduate and become 'honored teachers,'—the ignorant teachers of the future generations, a 'guaranteed prosper future' for this poor, miserable country."

Alexander paused for a moment, standing in silence next to his desk, watching outside the window. Then, he sat down on his chair, always watching outside the window, and started speaking slowly, with a flat voice, like being immersed in deep meditation, like talking with himself:

"The great German writer and intellectual, Thomas Mann, the winner of Nobel Prize in literature in 1929, who fled the Nazis and went to America, has said: 'Democracy begins with one great truth—the infinite dignity of the individual man and woman. Unlike other animals, humans are morally responsible. Humans are the only creatures who can understand and seek justice, freedom, and truth.'"

In meanwhile, a female student approached the chalkboard, erased carefully the word "psychopath," written inside the big heart that Alexander had drawn, and she wrote there the word "sorry." But it was too late. After finishing Thomas Mann's citation, Alexander stood up again and walked toward the students, speaking loudly:

"But these moral and intellectual things are not for you, because knowledge and wisdom cannot be bought with money. You that buy university diplomas are not 'morally-responsible animals' anymore, so you are not humans. You are becoming like other animals. You have been transformed into empty-headed creatures, becoming just 'animals that talk' and, as such, you don't recognize the dignity, justice, freedom, and the truth. You don't accept a real democracy. You are representatives of your generation that the new communist leadership aimed to create during this long, democratic transition, with the wickedness to deceit and rule smoother and longer over these ignorant, poor people and this miserable country. And they, with your unlimited help, realized their final objective successfully. The old communist elite, the dead and alive ones, are watching us and are laughing loudly at me, at you, at these people, petting and praising the new leadership, their cubs, that have already accomplished the mission given to them. 'Congratulations! Mission accomplished!'" Alexander said the last words in English, using the phrase heard so often in American movies.

After that, he sat again to his desk, where he spent some more minutes in silence, watching outside the window. It seemed clear that he was not calm. His lower jaw was trembling, and his temples in both sides of the head were pulsating visibly. He stood up suddenly and started speaking with a nervous, louder voice.

"However, you are right. Yes…, yes. You are completely right. I agree with you. I'm a real psychopath and schizophrenic, simply for the fact that I am still staying here…, with you…, in this classroom, filled with parasites…, in this building, filled with lazy creatures, self-called students…, in this college, filled with crook professors…, in this university, invaded by political, corrupt leadership…, in this poor, miserable city.., in this country, infested with miscreants…, in this failed state…, a state without laws…, without justice…, without dignity…, without freedom…, without democracy…, in this damned state…, in this doomed country…, in this cursed society…, in this repellent world." Alexander said these last words with great rage, walking in front of the first desks, hitting with his fist on every desk after every word he said, making a distorted, frightening face. He arrived at the classroom door, opened it forcefully, and left the classroom slamming the door behind him, and still screaming through the hallway.

His long speech had been recorded by some students, who uploaded it on social media with the caption: "The Psychopathic Professor." This video became viral very fast and had a lot of clicks, likes, and comments and was aired on some TV channels too. All comments agreed that this "psychopathic professor" was very right in what he had said, and that's why he wasn't either psychopath or schizophrenic, but he was a brilliant and sincere man, who, with the unique style of his speech, tells us the naked, bitter truth that we all know. He makes the autopsy of the Albanian putridity in politics, economy, justice, society, education, health service, family, and everywhere. He showcases how lazy and ignorant are students in his classroom and all state and private universities of Albania, being degenerated into ignorance, injustice, and corruption, like all other institutions and like entire Albanian society.

His speech infuriated only corrupt professors and superiors of all Albanian universities and the leadership of the government and political parties—all miscreants and scoundrels of the time. The rector of the university decided to expel Alexander from the university. All rectors of state universities were active members of political parties and served as henchmen and lackeys of their political leaders. The university rector had been ordered by leaders of his party to cast out this "psychopathic professor" that speaks craziness to the students. The rector had switched positions with his deputy following the return in power of the respective political parties they belonged and served. They called Alexander at the office to communicate to him the expulsion with the reasoning: "The new democratic Albania and its reformed universities don't need such a negative professor that speaks irresponsibly to the students by blemishing the reality, the achievement, and successes of the democracy in Albania." This expulsion for the second time from the university reminded Alexander one of Karl Marx's most quoted statements: "History repeats itself, first as tragedy, second as farce." It happens when historical facts and personages appear (so to speak), twice. Alexander's mind went thirty years behind, reminding him the evening high school principal who (as a matter of fact), was clean as a crystal, compared with those two in front of him, who were merely bad hounds of their political parties in this deformed education system and in this failed and corrupt democracy. The principal of the evening high school (thirty years ago), was defending firmly the communist moral principles and the ruling ideology of that time. But these two senior education officials in this time of so-called democracy, like all officials in this time of nefarious people, don't represent and don't have any moral principles or ideology to protect. Their only moral compass is just the personal interest for power and money. Their membership in the political parties helps them to reach their goals by taking turns in leading positions in universities, or becoming city mayors, parliament deputies, ministers and deputy ministers of the corrupt governments, with the help of their party leaders and by helping the militants and activist of respective parties.

Alexander lost his job as a professor for the second time in his life. The first time he was a twenty-six-year-old lad and had coped very quickly with that situation happening in the dictatorship. While now, being a fifty-six-year-old man, and in democracy time, it was more difficult for him, and he felt awful, making him fall in a more profound depression. Teuta was always staying by his side and cared very much for him, telling him not to worry because, in one or two years, they would be going to join their children in America. But he didn't like it and never accepted such a thing.

"What will I do there? I don't want to be a burden for our children. I just wanted them to leave this dismal, hopeless country, and I'm happy that they did it," he told Teuta every time.

"Don't worry. We'll be together there, and everything will be okay. We'll support our children, and they will support us," Teuta told him time after time.

But her words could not convince him anymore because his sick mind was thinking and was taking him towards a dangerous direction.

35

It was the last weekend of August. That Saturday morning, August 30, 2014, about ten o'clock, Teuta left home to go to the food market and went to visit her parents after that, where, as always, she spent twenty to thirty minutes before coming back home.

When she entered home, she found Alexander lying on the bed, who was clearly moribund. He just whispered a few words in his last breath:

"Sorry…, my…, Queen…," and his life ended in her arms.

She screamed several times: "No…, no…, no…," keeping his head in her hands and shaking him: "Why did you do that…? Why did you do that to me…?" And she hurried to call the emergency, which, as always in such cases, arrived too late, when he was lifeless. The ambulance took the body to hospital for autopsy, and the police arrived later to check the apartment where they found a small bottle of phostoxin (a brand name for aluminum phosphide) and verified that he had bought it some days ago, in the nearest pesticide shop. Teuta remained home alone and later found his letter.

"My Queen,

I beg your pardon for what I'm doing and for all the troubles I have caused to you. I'm leaving this world to save you and myself from meaningless suffering. You were God's gift to me, and I'll die with my last pray for you: God bless you and our children.

Don't tell the children and anybody else tonight! I don't want any visits, funeral, and repast. I don't want anybody at my burial. It will be you and only you because you were everything to me: my friend, my lover, my wife, and my Queen. Don't dress in black for me. Join our children in America and look after them like you took care of me all my life. Take care of yourself too.

I'm writing in short because I don't want to change my mind like I did other times before.

Yours, Alex."

How could she hold herself while reading this terrifying letter? She read it several times, crying bitterly in her loneliness, spending all the afternoon and the night alone with his letter and a portrait of him in her hands, passing through her mind all the life she had spent with Alexander—already thirty years—and then she put that letter in the same box with the manuscript of his book.

On Sunday morning, she went to the morgue, where she stood some minutes crying next to his body until the arrival of the funeral service's car. Only she and the driver started his last journey going first through the city's main boulevard, where, as a tradition, all the funerals go—as the final walk of the dead person in the city's streets. When they arrived at the cemetery, the gravediggers took the coffin off the car, and she told the funeral car's driver to go back, because she would stay there longer, and would walk back home by herself.

"I don't know the person inside this casket," the driver said to her. "And such a thing has never happened to me, but I've heard about great people wanting such a simple funeral, and that's why I think he might be a great man. Let me help the gravediggers until they lay this great man to rest in his last shelter."

Teuta gave her approval saying "thank you" with a weak voice, in tears, and whispering:

"You are right. He was a great man, indeed."

Nor any funeral ceremony or final words were spoken, and the only witnesses were two gravediggers, the funeral service's car driver, and Teuta. The gravediggers finished their job, threw their handful of soil on the grave, and left in silence, leaving her alone there, next to the burial site. Teuta remained there, bringing in her mind all the memories of their marital life, counting thirty years they had spent together. September 1984 - August 2014. She was staying there and couldn't think of what to do next. She didn't know where to start and what actions to take after that. Till now, she had acted by his advice for a simple burial, without any funeral ceremony. But now, after fulfilling his last will, she couldn't think and decide what to do next.

After about two hours, the driver of the funeral car arrived there again. He had brought with him four big wreaths of fresh flowers and put them on both sides of the new grave.

"Sincere condolences from the funeral office's staff," he said, shaking her hands in the place where she was staying put. She wept harder at that moment, being touched by the action of these unknown, kind people, placing her forehead on the hands of this good man.

"Thank you... Thank you all. God bless you," she whispered, crying with her forehead always on his hands.

"Do you want to return home now?" the driver asked Teuta.

"No, thank you," she answered. "I want to stay longer here..., with him."

Later on, a woman worker of the cemetery, which had just finished the working time, approached there, and put some fresh flowers on the soil of the new grave.

"Sincere condolences from the cemetery workers," she told Teuta. "I'm going to stay here with you until you decide to go back home together with me," she added.

Teuta burst in tears even harder with her head on the chest of this nice woman. After some minutes, the woman pulled her lightly from her hand, like a request to leave, and Teuta didn't resist, accepting it in silence, and they moved away together toward her car. She took Teuta to her apartment building.

"You have to call your parents now," the woman told Teuta, before getting off the car. "Give me their number, and I'll call them for you," she added.

"No, thank you. I'll do it as soon as I enter the home," Teuta assured her. The advice of that woman made Teuta collect herself and find the answer to her question on what to do next. She called her parents immediately, which arrived quickly and very alarmed. Teuta showed them Alexander's letter, explaining to them why she had acted like that. Then she called her son in America, telling him what had happened and what she had done, reading to him the father's letter.

Alexander lived the last years of his life placed between the terrible illness of depression and Teuta's love and care until he surrendered himself to the killer depression. Teuta didn't follow his advice, and dressed in black for one year, to respect his loss by the Albanian tradition. She read and reread his manuscript several times during the first three months after his death, crying on those papers and next to a portrait of him on the table. She decided to publish his book for all the relatives and friends of Alexander, especially his children, to understand Alexander fully, in all his human and professional dimensions. After making some needed small corrections, she gave the electronic copy to an ex-student of Alexander that had a publishing house in Elbasan. They decided to publish the book before the sixth month's memorial ceremony of Alexander's death.

The book was a real success. In the situation where the book sale of the unknown Albanian authors was "zero"—as the publisher told Teuta—the novel "The First Love," was a surprise. The book was liked and bought by students of high schools and the universities in Elbasan and Tirana and became the best seller for the Albanian authors.

"He has taken the memory of his first love with him in his grave, but he left behind a wonderful book dedicated to the first love," Teuta thought.

While from the second love, he had left behind a wonderful wife and two marvelous children. Teuta felt happy about Alexander's legacy. She enjoyed touching and reading his book and seemed like it brought the author and all his memories nearer to her. Above all, she was happier with the beautiful children she had with him.

Their children, Erblin and Mimosa, were living in America. Erblin had just become a US citizen, and as such, he had started the visas procedure for his mother to join him in the USA. The two came in Elbasan for the sixth month's memorial service and the first anniversary of their father's death. After that, in September 2015, they returned to New York City, together with their mother. Her children read their father's book and wept together with their mother. Being encouraged by the book's success in Albania, they decided to translate and publish it in English. Teuta had to write some additional chapters to the Albanian language version, related to the period from where Alexander had left the book until his death, making the book more accurate and related to his real-life story. Teuta started doing that, and she was writing very fast by hand. She was surprised by all those thoughts and was wondering where this inspiration was coming from. She thought that it was her great love for Alexander. She was writing about the man she had loved so much, which was her first love. In this way, she understood Alexander's inspiration when he was writing about his first love and the girl he had loved so much. "Every person can write beautifully about his first love," she thought. "My first love—a tragic love," she wrote in a sheet of paper while thinking of her love, but she didn't like these words for her only love in her life and wrote a second line: "My first love—a great love," while remembering all the beautiful moments of their splendid love. "Alexander's first love had been a great and tragic one at the same time, and my first love was a great and tragic one as well," Teuta thought of these two loves.

"I came to live with you here in America, but I don't want to leave your father alone in two important dates," Teuta told her children. "I want to be next to him for his birthday and his last day in the life. I will go there with flowers, candies, and cookies for his birthday, and with flowers and candles for his commemoration day. I'll be pleased the day when you will lay me to rest next to him," she left her will to her children.

Teuta had found a lot of poems and other literary pieces and essays while searching through Alexander's stuff. Among them, she found two small poems that had been written some weeks before his death. The first one was titled *"Death does not forget."*

When I thought I was dying.
Death left, forgot about me.
When I thought I was living.
It came back and swallowed me.

The other one was titled *"Epitaph."*

I realized that I'm not well.
And it wasn't worth it anymore.
Living in this world of hell.

They looked like two possible epitaphs for himself. Teuta thought that Alexander had been trying to write his own epitaph, and that's why she told the marble workshop owner to print the verses of the poem titled *"Epitaph,"* on his marble tomb.

36

Erblin and Mimosa started to translate their father's novel. They kept asking each other whether this love story had happened for real to their father. Was it real, fiction, or maybe a realistic fiction? They wanted to ask their mother but were uncertain how to do that. One evening, in the first week of November 2015, while they were sitting in their living room, discussing the book's translation, Mimosa asked her mother:

"Mom, is this love story a real one or just a fiction?"

"It's real," Teuta answered, after some minutes of thinking in silence, having been prepared that this question would be asked by her children someday and being conscious of the other issue to come after the first one.

"Does the girl, called Eralda in father's novel, exists for real?" Mimosa asked after some minutes of silence.

"Yes…, she does," Teuta answered with a weak voice, already prepared for this question.

"And…, do you know her, mom?"

"Yes…, I do."

"Do you know her real name?" Mimosa continued with her next question.

"Sure," Teuta answered after some seconds of silence.

"And…, what's her name, mom?"

"Margarita L……" She told her children the name and surname of the woman she wanted to hate so much, but she couldn't.

Teuta wasn't clear on what to think about Margarita—the secret lover of her husband—and she was unsure how to treat her. That woman had been part of entire Alexander's life, and by respecting Alexander, she couldn't think bad and couldn't hate her. It was a kind of strange feeling mixed with hatred and respect, a peculiar mixture of these two senses without any specific name. It was just an unnamed feeling living inside Teuta's mind all the time. She had to hate her husband's mistress, but at the same time, she had to respect her husband's choice and actions because she loved him so much.

"Is she married?" Mimosa asked again after a few seconds.

"I don't know," Teuta answered.

"Is she still living in Elbasan?"

"No…, your father says in his book that she lives in Greece."

"What about the last date with her, the date father describes in a motel by the river Shkumbin?" Mimosa dared to ask for that mystified date that had given Alexander the so-much-needed muse and inspiration to help him find a beautiful ending for his book.

Mimosa and Erblin were waiting for an answer from their mother, but Teuta didn't speak for some minutes. She was looking at Alexander's portrait on the wall as if she wanted to ask him about the answer she had to give their adult children now. She was waiting in vain for help and for a response from his silent portrait hanging on the wall. Her children were waiting in vain for an answer from their silenced mother that kept staying mute and didn't answer their question. Some drops of tears dripped from her eyes, and those tears told everything.

"Sorry…, mom," said Mimosa, hugging her mother and wiping her tears.

"Let's search for her name on the internet. Maybe we'll find something," said Erblin, which had not spoken until that moment, listening to the dialog between Mimosa and her mother, understanding the problematic situation of Teuta. And he ran toward his computer in the bedroom.

Mimosa followed her brother, while Teuta remained alone on the sofa in the living room. Erblin wrote Margarita's name and surname on Google, where several accounts with her name appeared. A Facebook account looked more convincing to be of the woman they were searching for. Erblin opened his Facebook account and searched her name again. In her account appeared only her picture, her name, and address. By the photo of her young age, they recognized that was she, Margarita, based on the accurate description their father had done in his book. She was a gorgeous girl indeed, with a radiant, angelic face. Her address was in a city in Pennsylvania. They couldn't see anything else on her account because they weren't friends. Erblin sent a request for friendship, and both waited anxiously, staying for some minutes in front of the computer screen as if Margarita would be online to answer their request for friendship immediately. But it didn't happen. They went back to the living room, joining their mother on the sofa, staying silent, and thinking each one to himself.

"We found a Margarita L...... on Facebook, mom. In her profile was a beautiful photo of her young age," Mimosa broke the silence after some minutes, approaching Teuta, hugging her and sitting by her side.

"Mom, you as well have been a lovely and athletic girl, but daddy has had an even more beautiful girl before your relationship," Erblin said, approaching and hugging his mother from the other side.

"And she has a very romantic name..., 'Margarita'...," Mimosa added to their dialog.

"She was a charming girl, indeed. That's why your father used to call her 'the most beautiful girl in the city.' He loved her as much as he describes it in his novel, and even more than that, because you can never fully express a really great love in words."

"In his book, dad says that he has loved you very much as well, and he has described your intensive love very beautifully," Mimosa said to her mother.

"And I loved him even more because he was the first love for me. I miss him very much, even though he was very sick last years of his life, I have always loved and cared for him very much," and she wept in tears while Mimosa embraced her and wiped her tears with a tissue.

"Let me see if there is an answer," Erblin said, walking toward the bedroom where his computer was.

Margarita had accepted Erblin's friendship, and he called his mother and Mimosa to join him. He opened her full account where they could see a lot of other pictures. In most of the images, she was posing with a little boy that in his last photo might be ten to eleven years old. Then they found a photo album dedicated to the little boy. There were twenty-two photos taken on eleven birthdays of his. In eleven pictures, he was posing alone in front of the birthday cake with the respective number of his age on top of it, and in eleven other photos, it was he with Margarita, who looked clearly like being his mother. There were a lot of other people in other pictures of her account, but no one of them seemed to be her husband and the little boy's father. The images of the little boy and his actual age brought suspicion to Teuta's mind. With a quick counting of years in her mind, she calculated that Margarita was conceived in the year and month she and Alexander had spent the night and day in Elbasan in November 2003. At first, when Teuta realized that, it seemed to her like something terrible, surreal, and unimaginable. For that reason, Teuta had to cry and shout for what might have happened. But after a second thought, strangely enough, it didn't look as bad as she had just thought. Teuta was thinking about that in silence, and she started to think positively that a beautiful thing had happened to Margarita and Alexander. She decided at that moment to accept that boy as the brother of her children, and as a member of the family, acting like Alexander would want them to do if he were alive.

In a meanwhile, Erblin saw that Margarita was online and he started a chat with her.

"Hi, I'm Alexander's son," he wrote in the chatbox.

"Hi. I read your surname, and that's why I accepted your friendship as soon as I read it. Please accept my condolences for your father."

"Thank you. Mom is here with me. Would you like to continue chatting with her?"

"Yes. Sure. With great pleasure," Margarita responded very fast.

Teuta wasn't prepared for this delicate moment, and she felt unsure about this new situation and for this strange dialogue that they had just started and that she had to continue. She was undecided, and her hands started trembling.

"You have to continue this chat," Erblin told her. "At least just some courteous greetings. I'll be next to you and help you with it," he encouraged his mom.

Teuta was reluctant to do that, and some other minutes passed without writing anything until a message from Margarita arrived:

"Hi, Teuta."

"Hi, Rita," she answered, using the short name Alexander used to call her.

"Please accept my sincere condolences," was the next message from Margarita.

"Thank you."

"Alexander was a wonderful man, and you have been a lucky woman."

"I know, but it didn't have to finish like this," Teuta wrote slowly.

"A long life to you and your children. Let them become as good as their father and you," Margarita continued with the expression used by Albanians as part of condolences on such occasions.

Some more minutes passed in silence. Nobody was writing anything. It was Teuta's turn to write something, but she was not sure whether to start questioning about the little boy that might be Alexander's son.

"I see a little boy in a lot of your pictures," Teuta wrote slowly, thinking carefully about every letter and word she wrote.

No answer was coming from the other side of the line for some minutes that looked even longer than normal ones.

"And he is an adorable boy," Erblin interfered, writing this instead of his mother.

Silence, again. No answer from the other side of the communication. This long silence made everything clear for Teuta, understanding that he was Alexander's son. But now that she had started this dialogue, she wanted to get to the end of it.

"He looks very much like you," Teuta wrote, trying to encourage Margarita's participation in this dialogue.

Not any answers, again.

"He is as beautiful as you," Teuta wrote, persisting in making Margarita engage.

No answer from Margarita yet.

"Are you married?" Teuta wrote a little bit later, launching her "attack" from another side.

"No," a concise answer arrived from Margarita at last.

The critical moment had come. "The moment of truth," Teuta thought.

"Who is the boy's father?" Teuta dared to write the final question.

The moment of truth had arrived, but Margarita's answer was being delayed again for some more minutes. Teuta was choked up, and she felt the knot of tears in her throat.

"His father has passed away," the delayed answer from Margarita arrived at last.

After this answer was Teuta's turn to delay her part of chatting now, and she didn't know how to continue this dialogue that was going toward the target she had assumed.

"I have called him after his father," Margarita wrote a second message after a long pause.

"And he looks like his father," Margarita wrote again after another long pause without any answers from Teuta.

"And he is as intelligent and agile as his father," Margarita continued sending one by one her "coded messages" that Teuta could decode and understand very easily.

"He's been the best of his class and the entire school for five consecutive years," Margarita wrote another "coded message" for Teuta.

Teuta couldn't hold the knot in her throat anymore and broke down and cried. She rose from the chair and ran toward the living room. She lay down on the sofa and continued sobbing even more. Erblin and Mimosa had read all the chat between two women, and, from the way this dialog was taking place, they understood what might have happened. Teuta's breakdown and her actions made it clear to them, and they followed their mother into the living room, sitting on the floor by her side in silence. After some minutes, Teuta stopped crying, rose, opened her arms and hugged them, and in tears, with a facial expression like a mix of soreness and happiness, she told them:

"You have a little brother."

And after that, all of them couldn't keep their tears. Erblin, after some minutes, went to his computer in the bedroom.

"See you later," Erblin wrote in the chatbox, giving an end to their chat on Facebook.

"See you," Margarita's answer arrived immediately.

Erblin joined Teuta and Mimosa again on the sofa, staying all in silence for a while.

"Mom…, what do you think?" Mimosa asked with her eyes in tears after some minutes.

"I think that your father had the good feeling of a child of him. He never told me such a thing, but sometimes, when his mind was going through awkward moments, he mentioned his fear that a child and his mother were being maltreated and were in danger somewhere. 'The mother is suffering,' he said sometimes. 'They want to kill the child,' he told other times. I always thought that it was just his sick mind speaking like that, because of his horrific voices, visions, and hallucinations, and I never took those words seriously," Teuta explained to them, and paused for a long moment, thinking in silence for what else she should say to them, before restarting the speech:

"Now that your father is not among us, I'm missing him so much, and I don't feel bad about whatever he has done and whatever has happened because of his actions. I want to forgive him for everything he has done.

313

Now I'm feeling a kind of joy for that beautiful boy, for your little brother. It's a joy that comes from the idea that this child is the fruit of his magic first love. I have a good feeling that we must joyfully accept and enjoy your cute little brother because that's what your father would like us to do. I will accept and love your little brother with great pleasure and joy, the same way I loved and respected your father for all of my life and the same way I respected the first love that caused to him so much suffering and pain till his death," Teuta gave her conclusion and started weeping again.

37

Teuta, Erblin, and Mimosa discussed all the evening on what to do next. They wanted to start the relationship with their little brother and his mother as soon as possible. They decided to invite Margarita and their little brother to celebrate Thanksgiving Day together in New York City. On the morrow, Erblin connected again with Margarita on Facebook.

"We invite you and our little brother to come to New York City for Thanksgiving Day," Erblin wrote to her.

"Thank you very much for your invitation. Alexander will be thrilled when I tell him," Margarita wrote, accepting the invitation immediately.

"Macy's Thanksgiving Day Parade takes place in Manhattan, and it will be an excellent event to watch together with Alexander," Erblin told her about this beautiful annual activity for children and their parents.

On Thanksgiving Day, Thursday, November 26, 2015, was unusual, splendid weather. It was a warm sunny day, a perfect thing for thousands of spectators of Macy's Parade, and for a stroll in Manhattan and Central Park. Margarita and Alexander arrived in New York City on the morning of Thanksgiving Day. Teuta and her children waited for and met them in the central bus terminal in Manhattan, about nine o'clock. Erblin and Mimosa took their little brother, holding hands with him, and hurried toward Sixth Avenue to find a spot to attend the fantastic spectacle of Macy's Parade. Teuta and Margarita remained alone and started strolling toward Times Square, and then, via Broadway, they walked north toward Central Park. At first, it was a little tricky situation for both ladies to start a real conversation between them. They walked in silence most of the time, with only occasional words about the beauties of New York City, Manhattan, Time Square, Broadway, etc. They arrived in Columbus Circle from where they entered the Central Park, from its southwest corner. They walked through The Mall, visited the Cherry Hill, the Bethesda Terrace, and arrived at The Loeb Boathouse restaurant, where they found an empty table for two at the bar's outside area, with the lake and boats in front of them. There, while waiting for their coffee, Margarita started telling her story:

"A couple of weeks after I returned home in Greece, I understood that I was pregnant. From the very first moment, I called it God's gift for me. I told my mother about that, and she couldn't accept this pregnancy of an unmarried woman. In addition to the shame in other people's eyes, she brought as a good reason the danger of pregnancy and the risk of giving birth at my age of thirty-nine. She told me that I had to abort this child as soon as possible before the baby bump become noticeable to other people so that this fact would remain secret and nobody would know what had happened. She promised me that if I ended this pregnancy, she was not going to tell anybody, either to my father or my sister and brothers. I didn't want to abort this wonderful fruit of my only love in my life, and I refused my mother's request and promise. My mom threatened me that she was going to tell my father, who would be harsher with me. After one week of daily quarrels with my mother, she told my father. The situation in our family became unbearable when my father threatened and yelled at me every evening. The elder brother with his wife and my sister with her husband supported our parents, saying the same things, stressing that I had to abort because it was a shame and a dangerous pregnancy and labor at the same time. But God didn't leave me alone. The younger brother that was still single and lived with our parents and me, never said any words while listening to our strife every evening," Margarita smiled when she mentioned her younger brother, and made a pause.

"Is it the little brother that used to say, 'look what a good sister I have,' as Alexander writes in his novel?" Teuta asked Margarita, smiling at her.

"Yes, that's him. He is my little brother that I have raised with my hands, helping and supporting him in all steps of his life and for everything, and all my care and support for him paid off," Margarita answered with her beautiful smile on her lips, eyes, and cheeks. "My little brother only spoke once. One day, when only we two were home, he told me that he had a solution to this problem. 'Let's escape together and go to America,' he explained his surprise solution, and I didn't believe it at first. He used the word 'escape,' and I felt terrible because it was going to be seen as a real escape from my home, my family, and my parents. I thought about it, and I cried in my bed for three consecutive days, thinking about the difficult decision I had to take. On the fourth day, I told my brother, 'let's run away as soon as possible and let everybody be spared from these daily arguments.' I remembered an English language teacher of mine in high school who had gone to America immediately after the fall of communism. Her husband's relatives had come here in the USA after the Second World War to escape the communist regime installed in Albania, and they invited my teacher and her husband, who came and stayed here forever. I phoned a friend of mine in Elbasan, who asked some teacher's relatives for her telephone number, which she gave me. I called my teacher from Greece, and I told her that my brother and I were going to visit the USA, and she gave me her full address. She is a woman with a great heart. She is the best woman in the world for me. She was an excellent teacher, but she was punished with a transfer to a remote village school just because she wanted to protect me from the trouble I had at that time."

"Is she the teacher who Alexander has written about in his book?" Teuta interfered again because she already knew the book by heart.

"Yes, that's her. And look at how God helps good people like her. She and her family were among the first people to leave Albania and move to America, after the dictatorship's fall."

"My brother and I came to the USA illegally going through some Central America countries," Margarita continued telling her story. "Only the child in my tummy kept me alive, made me strong enough, and gave me the courage to face all difficulties of that terrible and dangerous trip. In that time, there was a very well-organized illegal human traffic from Bulgaria to the USA. My brother found somebody in Tirana, whom he paid as a facilitator to this traffic. We spent all our life savings on this trip. First, we went via Macedonia to Bulgaria, where they gave us false Bulgarian passports, with which we flew to Spain, and from there, to a Central America's country. There we joined other people, and we spent two weeks, using trains, buses, vans, and walking through mountains, forests, and rivers to pass through some international borders before arriving in Mexico, in a town near the border with Texas. We stayed one more week there, from where we tried twice to pass the border, but we returned because of the unsafe pass. Only the third time, at night, and with bad weather, with wind and rain, we finally passed the border, and a van took us to San Antonio. A school friend of my brother lived there. He had been an army officer in Albania and had come to San Antonio to attend an English language course in a military base near the city. At the end of the course, he didn't return to

Albania, but he stayed there, marring a Hispanic American woman. My brother had his address and his telephone number, and we found his house, where we stayed for four days. From there, I called my teacher, telling her that we had arrived there illegally and that I was pregnant. She took the airplane the next day and came and found us in San Antonio. Then we traveled for two days, changing three buses to arrive in her city, because we didn't have any valid identification, and couldn't fly by airplanes. During that long travel, I told her about my love story, my pregnancy, and my family. She wept together with me for all I had suffered, embracing me in her arms, and telling me that my child would be like her grandchild, promising me all her help and support. She took me to her church from the first Sunday after my arrival and introduced me to all church members, telling them my story. They together prayed for me, for my child in my belly, for my parents and family. Members of that church are against abortion, and they were very active in the pro-life movement in their state. My story and I became a symbol of their action at that time, and they helped me with everything. One of them was a lawyer who helped me build a strong legal case and a robust defense with the immigration office saying that if I returned home in Albania, my family members and relatives would force me to undergo the abortion of my child. And if I didn't obey them, my life and my child's life would be in danger by them because they would feel ashamed of the pregnancy of an unmarried woman in their family. So, I won the right to the residency year after year, until I took my green card. All church members raised money all the time to help me with all spending on medical visits and hospitals until I gave birth to Alexander. Being born in the USA, he became an American citizen automatically. After the first sonography, when I learned that my child was a boy, I told them about my decision to call him after his father, Alexander. They liked the name very much, and I, together with Alexander still in my belly, became their heroes, and they prayed continuously for us. They used to ask me every time, 'how are you, how is Alexander,' telling me not to worry about anything, because all of them would be there for us. Americans are magnificent people. God blesses this land and these people because they believe in God, they pray to God, and they thank God every day of their life. They paid for me to attend English language courses, always telling me, 'we look after you, and you look after our little Alexander,' considering Alexander as their child. I have stayed all the time in my teacher's house, and I'm still staying there without paying anything. Some months after birth, they paid for me to attend a course to become a medical assistant, and after that, they found me a job in the hospital, where I'm still working. My brother married an American woman, and he is an American citizen now."

"What about your parents?" Teuta asked her.

"They are still in Greece, suffering a little bit from the economic crisis there. We are helping them from here now. After my arrival here in America, I used to call my sister once a month, talking only with her because my parents were still angry at us leaving home in that way. After I had given birth to Alexander, my mother started going to my sister's home from where I started talking with her as well, because she didn't want my father to learn that she was talking with me. After some telephone calls, my mother found the courage to say 'sorry' for their persistence to abort the child, but she still justified that attitude with the fear of the dangerous pregnancy and labor in my age. Now my life is only Alexander because only he gives a meaning to my life, and he is the reason I'm still alive. I only live for him. He is not only the beautiful fruit of our great love, but for me, he is now the last will, the legacy, and the testament of his father," and here, both women wept, leaving their tears to drop freely from their eyes pouring down to their cheeks.

They wept in silence for some moments, just watching the picturesque view of the small lake and boats in front of them outside the Boathouse restaurant. Margarita wiped her tears and started speaking again.

"Ever since I stepped in this blessed country, with all the support given by these blessed people, I have been thrilled, and I have only cried by happiness. Since I brought Alexander in life, I have been blissful. But, starting from today, when I saw Alexander meet and join his sister and brother, I'm feeling on top of the world. And for that, I want to thank you, Teuta. Thank you very much, with all of my soul and from the bottom of my heart. Thank you! Thank you! Thank you! Hundred times, thank you! May God bless you and your children," and they reached each other's hand in the middle of the table, holding them tight and weeping again.

"Sometimes, I'm afraid of great happiness, but it comes and finds us without asking for our permission. But I'm sure that God is watching on us and is helping us and, as they say, everything in our life happens for a reason. Thank you again, Teuta, for accepting my little Alexander and me in your life," Margarita ended her speech.

Teuta understood that it was her turn to say something about this new friendship and their families' union.

"I think that you, Rita, have deserved Alexander's love, and I forgave him after the mistake and his cheating on me that night and day he spent with you. I've always respected his feelings, suffering, and pain for his first love. Based on such respect, I've come together with him to meet you at your store and in the hospital the day you were injured after they assaulted you in your store. I didn't know you before I started my relationship with Alexander. He talked a lot about you, your beauty, and your cleverness, without thinking that I, like every other girl in this world, might be offended by that. He always called you 'the most beautiful girl in the city,' as he writes in his book, which he dedicated to you using the same expression. From the first days when I offered him my love, and during all the life I spent with him, I found out that you were forever on his mind, like a second life for him, as his spiritual life, and I never attempted to stop and deny this thing to him. Even though this affaire was against me, as his wife, and against the good marital relations, sometimes it seemed to me like a fantastic thing, like a great first love of a great man like him might be," Teuta told Margarita.

After a short pause, Teuta continued:

"That afternoon, when you two met and spent the night together, I was waiting for him to come back home as always. When he didn't return on time, I left home in search of him in places where I used to find him in such cases; around your apartment building, around the evening high school building, or in the park, at "your bench," as he called it. When I arrived at the street in front of the park's main entrance, I saw both of you waiting for a taxi until you took one. I returned home exhausted, and I cried all night long without sleeping at all. Time after time, I watched from the window, hoping for his arrival. The morrow afternoon, when I heard his steps climbing the stairs behind the apartment door when he opened the door and entered the living room, I felt happy that he returned home, and I didn't feel so bad about whatever he might have done that night. And then, when he told me with his mouth that he had spent the night with you, I felt a kind of relief instead of anger, and I didn't say anything to him. I loved him so much. I respected him so much. I cared for him so much. And that's why, every time I saw his suffering and pain for his first love, I felt an obligation to respect this feeling of his as well, just because it was his feeling, his personal spiritual life, and I had to accept these things the same way as I took him into my life. On the day after your last date, he made a firm promise that I had never asked for. He promised me that from that moment and on, he would forget about his first love and you, saying that the only real passion for him was our children and me. This was such a great promise that would make happy every wife in this world, but I didn't feel satisfied at all. I felt sorry for him forcing himself to make this promise, almost like a commitment, a pledge, or a solemn oath in front of me. He just wanted to show his love and respect for me, but I didn't want him to impinge on his spiritual life that might bring more meaning, enjoyment, and fulfillment to his life. And it was not a coincidence that he became sicker after that, falling into a more profound depression. I would rather accept his return to you for him to feel better and have some relief and recovery from that dangerous sickness that took his life in the end."

"I'm very sorry for what my actions have caused to you," Margarita said, reaching and holding Teuta's hands. "I left Elbasan that day with a mixture of feelings. I felt happier than ever and sadder than ever at the same time. I felt satisfied and fulfilled as a woman at last, after spending twenty-four hours with the only man I had loved my entire life and doing what I had yearned so much for twenty years. In those moments that we spent together, it wasn't us, but the magic of us. It wasn't us to control our actions, but we had been kidnaped by the subconscious that helped us satisfy our intense longing, giving ourselves only pleasure and tears. For me, those twenty-four hours equal the rest of my life. I hadn't come to Elbasan intending to remain pregnant. I only thought about it during the twelve-hour-long bus travel back to Greece. When I thought about the probability of a pregnancy (even though it might be almost zero percent), I felt a kind of joy, pleasure, happiness, and even pride, because, in this way, I would have him…, the fruit of my first love…, already gestated inside my body, feeding him with my blood and care. When I started to feel the common early signs and symptoms of pregnancy, I was delighted, and when I learned that I had remained pregnant for real, I had been prepared for that day, and I had already taken my decision. Except for the pressure from my family, as I told you before, everything else that happened after that, up to this day that we are here, talking together, has been God's will and blessing that rewarded my great first love. The baby in my belly healed my loneliness and the pain caused by the loss of my first love, giving a new meaning to my life. After moving to America, I disconnected from my close friend in Elbasan, to avoid her knowledge about my pregnancy with Alexander, because he used to go to her store, always asking if she knew anything about me. When I spoke with my sister in Greece, we made our plans that she and my family to spread the word of my marriage with an American, to take the American green card. Later on, she would say that I had given birth to a boy after my marriage with that man. After some years, when I opened my Facebook account, we spread the word that I was divorced. So, when our relatives and friends watched my pictures with little Alexander on Facebook, everything was clear, and without any suspicion or misunderstanding by them," Margarita ended her explanation.

"We, in Elbasan, didn't have the internet at home," Teuta said. "When Erblin left for America in 2009, for two years, we spoke with him once a week via Skype from an internet café. After Mimosa moved to America in 2011, we installed the internet at home. Alexander used the internet for his readings and studies, but he never opened a Facebook account. Perhaps he was afraid of searching and finding you, and in this way, he would break the promise he had given to me. I as well didn't open any Facebook account for the same reason, because I would have searched your name just for curiosity. You saw how fast Erblin found you. Alexander, in his bad moments of raving talking, mentioned time after time a child and his mother being maltreated somewhere. When I heard him saying those words, I thought that it was just his hallucinations, but when I think about it now, I realize that he has thought about your potential pregnancy. Or maybe, he was sure about that from the first day after that event. Perhaps he made it consciously, as a good thing for you to have a child from him since you remained single all your life just because of him. Being pleased and sure for what he had done, he told the truth as soon as he entered home that day. And that's why he promised me that he was going to forget about you, accompanied by a hidden joy inside him given by the pleasure that he, at last, would have a child from the first love that he never forgot."

Teuta and Margarita left the Boathouse restaurant and walked through the Central Park, toward the subway station to take a train back home. They walked for some minutes in silence. Both needed to meditate about their separate lives brought together by the same man whom they had loved so much. They were two grieving ladies that had remained widows by the death of the same man. They were two beautiful ladies in their early fifties, a blond and a brunette, walking together and adding their charm to Central Park's natural beauty. Their love for the same man, his great love for both of them, and his death has united them and has brought them and their love stories from Elbasan, in Albania, to Central Park in New York City.

"What do you think about Alexander's book?" Teuta asked Margarita after a long silence, with another apparent reason in her mind.

"I liked it very much. It is a fascinating book. I wept all the time when I read it, and I think that all readers feel the same," Margarita answered.

"Do you think Alexander has told everything in his book, or maybe he has forgotten something?" Teuta asked the second question, trying to bring the discussion in the direction she wanted, to clarify a suspicion of hers whether Alexander had made love with Margarita after he started the relationship with Teuta and married her.

Margarita wanted to be sincere and tell her that Alexander has not revealed everything in his book. In this way, she had to tell Teuta about some dates that she and Alexander had spent together making love in her store since he returned as a professor in the pedagogical institute (January 1989), until the time when her store was destroyed (December 1990). She had to tell her for some other dates as well, when they had made love after her store was destroyed until she left Albania in September 1997. Margarita stayed silent for some minutes, and her silence in that crucial moment made those minutes look even longer. She could tell Teuta that Alexander had been to her store many more times than he explained in his book, but she couldn't tell her the fact that they had made love in the small private room behind the vitrines of her store. Margarita understood the reason behind Teuta's question, and she was thinking so long about her answer because she couldn't decide what to say to her. Margarita wasn't sure whether Teuta asked just based on suspicion of hers (as a natural tendency that all married women have in their instincts and intuition, indicating the presence of a real sixth sense at them), or maybe Alexander, unlike what he had written in his book, might have been that naive and frank to tell his wife the dangerous truth about his uninterrupted love affair with her. Margarita realized that her long silence and her answer's delay would cause more suspicion to Teuta, and she thought about her answer like being a double-edged sword. "Do I have to tell her the truth—bringing in this way new troubles for both of us and for Alexander's remembrance—or not tell the truth, keeping it as a big secret of mine, bringing more good for the present and future of the relationship that our families have just started."

"I think he has told it all," she answered short and very carefully to avoid any suspicions, and while giving this torturous answer, she let her tears shed from her eyes, saving her from this challenging situation of telling a lie.

"Alexander has described very well everything regarding your situation, your thoughts, and feelings, your troubles and difficulties, and it seems like you have told him about all those things," Teuta continued, insisting on her aimed target. "Is everything he describes in his book the same as it has happened to you and between you two?" she added with the same persistence.

"Yes," Margarita answered very fast this time, attempting not to cause any further suspicion to Teuta. But this quick answer brought the other quick question from Teuta.

"How did he learn about all your thoughts, feelings, difficulties, and other problems in your life?"

"We had discussed those things a couple of times when he came to my store and the day we met by accident in front of the Court House, in Elbasan. The rest might be just his imagination," Margarita explained her version about the accuracy of Alexander's descriptions.

"And..., that's all?" Teuta asked again.

"Yes..., I think so," Margarita answered short, quickly, and decisively, understanding what Teuta meant with her question. She had already decided not to say anything about other dates and her torrid love affair with Alexander because it would be unnecessary to reveal such things now. She liked the idea to keep this secret only for herself for all her life as loyalty to Alexander—if he had not told Teuta about that.

After these answers given by Margarita, Teuta didn't ask any more questions. They continued walking in silence while Teuta was thinking: "If I believe more in her long silence than in her words, something more has happened between them, something untold in Alexander's book. But..., it might be better like this. Let it remain like an untold story, like Margarita's secret, because such a thing does not serve anybody anymore."

They entered the subway station near Central Park and took the train back home to prepare the Thanksgiving Dinner. They stayed silent during the entire travel, without exchanging any words. Both widowed ladies were thinking about their love relationship with the same man and potential undisclosed facts of Alexander's life and love in his book.

Margarita recalled Alexander's numerous visits to her store, telling her: "I returned to the city, I returned to the pedagogical institute, and I would like to return to my first love as well. I want to return to you. Please, do this favor to me." After his continuous begging, Margarita had surrendered, and they had spent several lunch breaks together in her store, making love in the small private room behind vitrines, during a two-year-long period. She couldn't resist very long to his constant begging her for love every time he went to her store. Margarita finally surrendered, telling him that she was doing that just as a favor to him. But, she as well, had been feeling the sexual need for a long time, and thus, she fulfilled her great desire harvesting the great pleasure of lovemaking with the man she had loved so much. For Margarita, it was not a big problem as long as she didn't see Alexander entering her store, but as soon as he appeared in the store door, the trouble started for her. She couldn't resist his requests and her desire to make love with him, a passion that burst on fire in those moments that only called for love and led to making love. At first, Margarita just wanted to respect the love relationship they had had, and that's why she allowed him her friendship. But later, she understood that she was feeling and wanting more from him, but she never thought to cause the separation from his wife and to destroy his family, even though he had mentioned such a thing several times. It seemed like Alexander never thought that what he was doing was just infidelity, cheating on his wife, and adultery. While Margarita—every time after ending those crazy minutes filled with vigor, lust, and great sexual pleasure of making love with him—always felt deeply guilty for what she was doing. When Margarita thought about men's infidelity and adultery in general, she concluded that it seemed like only girls and women have the responsibility to guard the morality and the honor of society. That's like this because men are always ready to go with every girl and woman that could accept them. "Men enter every door that opens for them," an old Greek lady had told her years ago when she was living and working in Greece.

Margarita was thinking that keeping the secret of her love affair till her death, made her feel like being still connected with Alexander, and this thing gave her a special feeling and pleasure. It was a secret that only they two knew, while now that Alexander had passed away, it was only she that knew this fact, and she liked to keep that only for herself. It was like a guilty pleasure given by the secret that only you know and nobody else. This thing was giving Margarita a special joy, something like a hidden superiority feeling and the final victory of the challenge over Teuta.

It reminded Margarita of another reason why she had accepted to make love with Alexander at that time. She was being affected by a strange feeling that was like a need for silent revenge against the other girl that was enjoying the love with the wonderful man that she had lost because she had not been capable of having him for herself. It sounded clearly like an urge for a direct retaliation against the other girl, but in reality it was just a rebellion against herself that had been so incapable when that man belonged to her.

The most sublime feeling that inspired Margarita was the great admiration for Alexander and her pleasure to fulfill his desire for love. She was in awe of him, and she felt more excited while watching the great joy he gained and expressed while making love to her. Margarita recalled the fact that since the very first moment of her surrender and acceptance of making love with him, it seemed like even her skin and every part of her body had recognized him and had been waiting full of longing and passion the return of the magical touch of his hands, his grasps, his lips, and his body's skin, till the climax and the mystical pleasure of making love. Margarita never forgot to justify herself every time at the end of every sexual act by telling him that she was doing that only to fulfill his desire. At the same time, she was realizing her hidden passion as well, because she was enjoying everything, satisfying her lust and her libido. In this way, she was making the dream of making love with Alexander come true.

38

When their children arrived home, dinner was ready. The little Alexander was delighted, and as soon as they entered the room, he went to his mother, telling her with enthusiasm about what he had seen in Macy's Parade.

"Mom, it was a wonderful parade. I saw all the giant balloons of movie characters I've seen on TV. They were huge, mom. There were a lot of floats, big balloons on cars and trucks, marching bands, dancers, cheerleaders, performers, clowns, and a huge crowd of spectators, children, and parents on both sides of the street and in windows and balconies of all surrounding buildings. This parade takes place every year, mom, and we'll come again next year. Mimosa says that I will come here for Christmas Holidays too, and then for Easter and summer holidays as well," Alexander said all these words in one breath, speaking very fast.

"Tell your mother about all the famous characters we saw in the parade today," Mimosa told Alexander, approaching him and his mother.

"I've seen Santa Claus, Finn and Jake, Angry Birds, Diary of a Wimpy Kid, Dino, Elf on the Shelf, Hello Kitty, Dragon's Toothless, Ice Age's Scrat, Paddington, Pikachu, Pillsbury Doughboy, Red Mighty Morphin Power Ranger, Ronald McDonald waving from a red car, Skylanders Eruptor, Snoopy and Woodstock, SpongeBob SquarePants, Thomas the Tank Engine, Harold the Policeman, Santa Claus with Mrs. Claus, the Aflac Duck, Kool-Aid Man, Sesame Street, Mount Rushmore's American Pride, Teenage Mutant Ninja Turtles, Treasure Hunt, Santaland Express, Santa's Sleigh, Tom Turkey, Planters Nutmobile, etc., etc.," Alexander mentioned one by one all the characters he had seen in the Parade.

Then they sat down around the dinner table prepared by Teuta and Margarita. Erblin, acting as the host of Thanksgiving gratitude ritual, said:

"Now is the moment that all of us, one by one, to express our thanks on what we are grateful for, and I would like that you, mom, to be the first one," he sent a smile toward his mother.

"Today, I want to express my gratitude and say 'thank you' to your father. I want to thank him for the great love he gave me, for the joyful and happy life we spent together, and for the marvelous children we raised together," Teuta opened the Thanksgiving dinner with tears of gratitude in her eyes. "He has given a lot of love and care to all of us, but unfortunately, we haven't shown all deserved gratitude to him, and he hasn't been properly thanked for all of that while he was still alive," Teuta concluded her Thanksgiving declarations of gratitude for her late husband.

"Now is my turn," Erblin said. "I'm grateful to my parents for everything they've done for me. They've made a lot of sacrifices in their life to bring us up. Thank you, Dad, for your great love and care you gave us. Thank you for your tireless help in our school studies, and especially for the English and Italian languages that you taught us. When I look at his portrait today, I feel this tremendous gratitude for what he has done for me," Erblin concluded by standing up, touching his father's portrait on the wall, and hugging his mother that was still shedding tears.

"Thank you, my dad, for everything you have done for us," Mimosa started her thanks. "Now that we are going through hard grieving times, looking back into my life, I think that I am what I am today just because of you. Thank you for your wonderful book, and I promise you that we are going to make a perfect English translation to it. On this occasion, I want to offer my deep gratitude to my mom as well, for all teachings she has given to me," Mimosa concluded her statement of gratitude.

It was Margarita's turn who already had her eyes in tears.

"I am shedding tears of joy and gratitude for the welcoming and love you gave to us, to Alexander and me. I offer my gratitude and appreciation to all of you that accepted us as part of your family." She paused few seconds looking at Alexander's portrait on the wall and added: "Thank you, Alexander..., for your great love..., and for the little Alexander," she concluded, letting her tears drop down her cheeks.

Up to this point, they all had spoken in the Albanian language, and Alexander had not understood everything.

"Now is your turn," Erblin told him in English.

"Who's that man in the picture on the wall?" Alexander asked, pointing to the portrait on the wall.

"He is your father, my little soul," Mimosa answered to him.

"Mom says my father is in Albania," Alexander continued with his childish innocence.

"Yes, he is in Albania," Mimosa answered again with tears in her eyes.

"Mom says my father is called Alexander," the little Alexander added.

"Yes, my little heart..., your father's name is Alexander," Teuta answered to him this time, without trying to stop her tears in her eyes.

"Mom says that my father is Alexander senior, and I am Alexander junior."

"Yes, you are right, my little brother," Erblin answered, seeing that all three women were crying in silence being touched by Alexander's words.

"Mom says my father is a university professor, and I look like my father," the little boy continued.

"Yes, it's true. You do look like your father," Erblin answered again, seeing that everybody else was shedding tears in silence, being unable to speak.

"Mom says that my father is sick now, and he cannot come to see us. I've seen mom crying a lot during the last year," Alexander spoke with a sad face and voice this time, with his head down, making everybody break down and sob after those last words said by the little boy.

"Why are you guys crying?" Alexander asked this innocent childish question after a few minutes when he saw everybody crying in silence, and he touched his mother's wet cheeks and chin, trying to raise her head.

"Because we all miss your father very much, my little heart," Margarita answered, wiping her tears.

"I too miss him very much," little Alexander finished, with a childish melancholy, retreating deeper in his chair.

For some minutes that looked longer than ever, nobody was finding the needed courage to speak, until the little Alexander restarted his questions, bringing another atmosphere into the room.

"You're my sister?" he asked Mimosa, pointing his finger at her.

"Yes..., my sweetheart. I'm your sister," Mimosa answered full of joy, embracing and squeezing him in her arms.

"You are my brother?" he asked Erblin, pointing at him now.

"Yes..., yes, my little brother," Erblin answered full of joy, embracing Alexander. He took the little brother in his arms, moving from the dining table to the area between the TV table and sofa in the middle of the living room, where he started dancing and singing, holding hands with Alexander and Mimosa that followed and joined the two.

Erblin started singing with his deep baritone voice:

"I have e little brother,
His name is Alexander,"

Mimosa repeated those two verses after Erblin, with her sweet soprano voice:

"I have e little brother,
His name is Alexander,"

Both Erblin and Mimosa, sang in two voices, repeating these two verses several times while dancing around a small table, holding hands with their little brother:

"I have e little brother,
His name is Alexander,"

After some rounds of singing these verses, Alexander interfered, interrupting their dance and song:

"Stop…, stop, please. It's my turn now," he told them, and he started dancing and singing by changing verses sung by Erblin and Mimosa.

"My name is Alexander,
I have an elder sister,
I have an elder brother."

All three of them repeated these verses several times, and in the end, with a burst of big loud laughter, applause, joy, and happiness, they embraced each other in the middle of the living room.

Margarita and Teuta were still sitting on the table, weeping in silence, holding each other's hands, and whispering together:

"Thank you, Alexander. Thank you, Alexander. Thank you, Alexander."

"I wish you were here…, Alexander," Teuta whispered several times in tears.

"He is here, though," Margarita answered with her sweet voice.

"You are right. He's still here…, together with us…, among us…, in us," Teuta spoke softly and continued to think in silence:

"His heart is here…, with us. His blood is here…, in us. His soul is here…, among us. His love is here…, at us. His life is here…, in all of us. His big family is here…, all of us together. He will always be with us…, in our bitterness and our joy. He is watching us from above, and he is happy for all of us. He left us indeed, passing over to the other side, but out of the deep desperation and killer depression, he left behind his deserved legacy— these beautiful children, and the novel of his life," Teuta concluded her meditation, looking at his portrait on the wall at first, and then at three happy siblings that were enjoying their union in the presence of their two mothers, whose bitterness tears were mixed with enjoyment tears while watching their children singing and dancing together as a big happy family.

Teuta turned her eyes once more toward Alexander's portrait on the wall, looking at him for some minutes, like asking him whether he was pleased with her acts.

It seemed like he smiled to her for a moment, winking his eye as an approval sign, and she heard the echo of his grateful words in her head:

"Yes…, my Queen. Thank you…, my Queen."

And Teuta was filled with great joy and happiness.

The End

Arben Nestur Prifti

New York City, 2015 - 2020